美国亚裔文学研究丛书

总主编　郭英剑

An Anthology of South Asian American Literature

美国南亚裔文学作品选

主编　郭英剑　何乃婷　刘向辉

本研究受中国人民大学科学研究基金资助，系 2017 年度重大规划项目"美国亚裔文学研究"（编号：17XNLG10）阶段性成果。

中国人民大学出版社
·北京·

图书在版编目（CIP）数据

美国南亚裔文学作品选：英文 / 郭英剑，何乃婷，刘向辉主编. -- 北京：中国人民大学出版社，2022.10
（美国亚裔文学研究丛书 / 郭英剑总主编）
ISBN 978-7-300-31091-6

Ⅰ.①美… Ⅱ.①郭… ②何… ③刘… Ⅲ.①文学—作品综合集—美国—英文 Ⅳ.①I712.11

中国版本图书馆 CIP 数据核字（2022）第 184119 号

美国亚裔文学研究丛书
美国南亚裔文学作品选
总主编　郭英剑
主　编　郭英剑　何乃婷　刘向辉
Meiguo Nanyayi Wenxue Zuopinxuan

出版发行	中国人民大学出版社	
社　　址	北京中关村大街 31 号	邮政编码　100080
电　　话	010-62511242（总编室）	010-62511770（质管部）
	010-82501766（邮购部）	010-62514148（门市部）
	010-62515195（发行公司）	010-62515275（盗版举报）
网　　址	http://www.crup.com.cn	
经　　销	新华书店	
印　　刷	唐山玺诚印务有限公司	
规　　格	170 mm×240 mm　16 开本	版　次　2022 年 10 月第 1 版
印　　张	16.5	印　次　2022 年 10 月第 1 次印刷
字　　数	310 000	定　价　68.00 元

版权所有　　侵权必究　　印装差错　　负责调换

总 序

美国亚裔文学的历史、现状与未来

郭英剑

一、何谓"美国亚裔文学"？

"美国亚裔文学"（Asian American Literature），简言之，是指由美国社会中的亚裔群体作家所创作的文学。也有人称之为"亚裔美国文学"。

然而，"美国亚裔文学"这个由两个核心词汇——"美国亚裔"和"文学"——所组成的术语，远没有它看上去那么简单。说它极其复杂，一点也不为过。因此，要想对"美国亚裔文学"有基本的了解，就需要从其中的两个关键词入手。

首先，"美国亚裔"中的"亚裔"，是指具有亚裔血统的美国人，但其所指并非一个单一的族裔，其组成包括美国来自亚洲各国（或者与亚洲各国有关联）的人员群体及其后裔，比如美国华裔（Chinese Americans）、日裔（Japanese Americans）、菲律宾裔（Filipino Americans）、韩裔（Korean Americans）、越南裔（Vietnamese Americans）、印度裔（Indian Americans）、泰国裔（Thai Americans）等等。

根据联合国的统计，亚洲总计有48个国家。因此，所谓"美国亚裔"自然包括在美国的所有这48个亚洲国家的后裔，或者有其血统的人员。由此所涉及的各国（以及地区）迥异的语言、不同的文化、独特的人生体验，以及群体交叉所产生的多样性，包括亚洲各国由于战争交恶所带给后裔及其有关人员的深刻影响，就构成了"美国亚裔"这一群体具有的极端复杂性。在美国统计局的定义中，美国亚裔是细分为"东亚"（East Asia）、"东南亚"（Southeast Asia）和南亚（South Asia）。[1] 当然，也正由于其复杂性，到现在有些亚洲国家在美国的后裔或者移民，尚未形成一个相对固定的族裔群体。

---

[1] 参见：Humes, Karen R, Jones, Nicholas A, Ramirez, Roberto R (March 2011). "Overview of Race and Hispanic Origin: 2010" (PDF). United States Census Bureau. U.S. Department of Commerce.

其次，文学主要由作家创作而成，由于"美国亚裔"群体的复杂性，自然导致"美国亚裔"的"作家"群体同样处于极其复杂的状态，但也因此使这一群体的概念具有相当大的包容性。凡是身在美国的亚裔后裔、具有亚洲血统或者后来移民美国的亚裔作家，都可以称之为"美国亚裔作家"。

由于亚裔群体的语言众多，加上一些移民作家的母语并非英语，因此，"美国亚裔文学"一般指的是美国亚裔作家使用英语所创作的文学作品。但由于历史的原因，学术界也把最早进入美国时，亚裔用本国语言所创作的文学作品，无论是口头作品还是文字作品——比如19世纪中期，华人进入美国时遭到拘禁时所创作的诗句，也都纳入"美国亚裔文学"的范畴之内。同时，随着全球化时代的到来，各国之间的文学与文化交流日益加强，加之移民日渐增加，因此，也将部分发表时为亚洲各国语言，但后来被翻译成英语的文学作品，同样纳入"美国亚裔文学"的范畴。

最后，"美国亚裔"的划分，除了语言、历史、文化之外，还有一个地理的因素需要考虑。随着时间的推移与学术界研究，特别是离散研究（Diaspora Studies）的进一步深化，"美国亚裔"中的"美国"（America），也不单单指"the United States"了。我们知道，由于全球化时代所带来的人口流动性的极度增加，国与国之间的界限有时候变得模糊起来，人们的身份也变得日益具有多样性和流动性。比如，由于经济全球化的原因，美国已不单单是一个地理概念上的美国。经济与文化的构成，造就了可口可乐、麦当劳等商业品牌，它们都已经变成了流动的美国的概念。这样的美国不断在"侵入"其他国家，并对其他国家产生了巨大的影响。当然，一个作家的流动性，也无形中扩大了"美国"的概念。比如，一个亚洲作家可能移民到美国，但一个美国亚裔作家也可能移民到其他国家。这样的流动性拓展了"美国亚裔"的定义与范畴。

为此，"美国亚裔文学"这一概念，有时候也包括一些身在美洲地区，但与美国有关联的作家，他们用英语进行创作；或者被翻译成英语的文学作品，也会被纳入这一范畴之内。

应该指出的是，由于"亚裔"群体进入美国的时间早晚不同，加上"亚裔"群体的复杂性，那么，每一个"亚裔"群体，都有其独有的美国族裔特征，比如华裔与日裔有所不同，印度裔与日裔也有所不同。如此一来，正如一些学者所认为那样，各个族裔的特征最好应该分开来叙述和加以研究。[1]

---

[1] 参见: Chin, Frank, et al. 1991. "Preface" to *Aiiieeeee! An Anthology of Asian American Writers*. Edited by Frank China, Jeffery Paul Chan, Lawson Fusao Inada, and Shawn Wong. A Mentor Book. p.xi.

二、为何要研究"美国亚裔文学"？

虽然上文中提出，"美国亚裔"是个复杂而多元的群体，"美国亚裔文学"包含了极具多样化的亚裔群体作家，但是我们还是要把"美国亚裔文学"当作一个整体来进行研究。理由有三：

首先，"美国亚裔文学"与"美国亚裔作家"（Asian American Writers）最早出现时，即是作为一个统一的概念而提出的。1974年，赵健秀（Frank Chin）等学者出版了《哎咿！美国亚裔作家选集》。[1] 作为首部划时代的"美国亚裔作家"的文学作品选集，该书通过发现和挖掘此前50年中被遗忘的华裔、日裔与菲律宾裔中的重要作家，选取其代表性作品，进而提出要建立作为独立的研究领域的"美国亚裔文学"（Asian American Literature）。[2]

其次，在亚裔崛起的过程中，无论是亚裔的无心之为，还是美国主流社会与其他族裔的有意为之，亚裔都是作为一个整体被安置在一起的。因此，亚裔文学也是作为一个整体而存在的。近年来，我国的"美国华裔文学"研究成为美国文学研究学界的一个热点。但在美国，虽然有"美国华裔文学"（Chinese American Literature）的说法，但真正作为学科存在的，则是"美国亚裔文学"（Asian American Literature），甚至更多的则是"美国亚裔研究"（Asian American Studies）。

再次，1970年代之后，"美国亚裔文学"的发展在美国学术界逐渐成为研究的热点，引发了研究者的广泛关注，为此，包括耶鲁大学、哥伦比亚大学、布朗大学、宾夕法尼亚大学等常青藤盟校以及斯坦福大学、加州大学系统的伯克利分校、洛杉矶分校等美国众多高校，都设置了"美国亚裔研究"（Asian American Studies）专业，也设置了"美国亚裔学系"（Department of Asian American Studies）或者"亚裔研究中心"，开设了丰富多彩的亚裔文学与亚裔研究方面的课程。包括哈佛大学在内的众多高校也都陆续开设了众多的美国亚裔研究以及美国亚裔文学的课程，学术研究成果丰富多彩。

那么，我们需要提出的一个问题是，在中国语境下，研究"美国亚裔文学"的意义与价值究竟何在？我的看法如下：

第一，"美国亚裔文学"是"美国文学"的重要组成部分。不研究亚裔文学或者忽视甚至贬低亚裔文学，学术界对于美国文学的研究就是不完整的。如上文所说，亚裔文学的真正兴起是在20世纪六七十年代。美国六七十年代特殊的时

---

[1] Chin, Frank, Chan, Jeffery Paul, Inada, Lawson Fusao, et al. 1974. *Aiiieeeee! An Anthology of Asian-American Writers*. Howard University Press.

[2] 参见：Chin, Frank, et al. 1991. "Preface" to *Aiiieeeee! An Anthology of Asian American Writers*. Edited by Frank China, Jeffery Paul Chan, Lawson Fusao Inada, and Shawn Wong. A Mentor Book. pp.xi–xxii.

代背景极大促进了亚裔文学发展，自此，亚裔文学作品层出不穷，包括小说、戏剧、传记、短篇小说、诗歌等各种文学形式。在当下的美国，亚裔文学及其研究与亚裔的整体生存状态息息相关；种族、历史、人口以及政治诉求等因素促使被总称为"亚裔"的各个少数族裔联合发声，以期在美国政治领域和主流社会达到最大的影响力与辐射度。对此，学术界不能视而不见。

第二，我国现有的"美国华裔文学"研究，无法替代更不能取代"美国亚裔文学"研究。自从1980年代开始译介美国亚裔文学以来，我国国内的研究就主要集中在华裔文学领域，研究对象也仅为少数知名华裔作家及长篇小说创作领域。相较于当代国外亚裔文学研究的全面与广博，国内对于亚裔的其他族裔作家的作品关注太少。即使是那些亚裔文学的经典之作，如菲律宾裔作家卡罗斯·布鲁桑（Carlos Bulosan）的《美国在我心中》（*America Is in the Heart*，1946），日裔女作家山本久惠（Hisaye Yamamoto）的《第十七个音节及其他故事》（*Seventeen Syllables and Other Stories*，1949）、日裔约翰·冈田（John Okada）的《不－不仔》（*NO-NO Boy*，1959），以及如今在美国文学界如日中天的青年印度裔作家裘帕·拉希莉（Jhumpa Lahiri）的作品，专题研究均十分少见。即便是像华裔作家任璧莲（Gish Jen）这样已经受到学者很大关注和研究的作家，其长篇小说之外体裁的作品同样没有得到足够的重视，更遑论国内学术界对亚裔文学在诗歌、戏剧方面的研究了。换句话说，我国学术界对于整个"美国亚裔文学"的研究来说还很匮乏，属于亟待开发的领域。实际上，在我看来，不研究"美国亚裔文学"，也无法真正理解"美国华裔文学"。

第三，在中国"一带一路"倡议与中国文化走出去的今天，作为美国文学研究的新型增长点，大力开展"美国亚裔文学"研究，特别是研究中国的亚洲周边国家如韩国、日本、印度等国在美国移民状况的文学表现，以及与华裔在美国的文学再现，使之与美国和世界其他国家的"美国亚裔文学"保持同步发展，具有较大的理论意义与学术价值。

三、"美国亚裔文学"及其研究：历史与现状

历史上看，来自亚洲国家的移民进入美国，可以追溯到18世纪。但真正开始较大规模的移民则是到了19世纪中后期。然而，亚裔从进入美国一开始，就遭遇到来自美国社会与官方的阻力与法律限制。从1880年代到1940年代这半个多世纪的岁月中，为了保护美国本土而出台的一系列移民法，都将亚洲各国人民排除在外，禁止他们当中的大部分人进入美国大陆地区。直到20世纪40至60年代移民法有所改革时，这种状况才有所改观。其中的改革措施之一就是取消了

国家配额。如此一来，亚洲移民人数才开始大规模上升。2010年的美国国家统计局分析显示，亚裔是美国社会移民人数增长最快的少数族裔。[1]

"美国亚裔"实际是个新兴词汇。这个词汇的创立与诞生实际上已经到了1960年代后期。在此之前，亚洲人或者具有亚洲血统者通常被称为"Oriental"（东方人）、"Asiatic"（亚洲人）和"Mongoloid"（蒙古人、黄种人）。[2]美国历史学家市冈裕次（Yuji Ichioka）在1960年代末期，开创性地开始使用Asian American这个术语，[3]从此，这一词汇开始被人普遍接受和广泛使用。

与此时间同步，"美国亚裔文学"在随后的1970年代作为一个文学类别开始出现并逐步产生影响。1974年，有两部著作几乎同时出版，都以美国亚裔命名。一部是《美国亚裔传统：散文与诗歌选集》，[4]另外一部则是前面提到过的《哎咿！美国亚裔作家选集》。[5]这两部著作，将过去长期被人遗忘的亚裔文学带到了聚光灯下，让人们仿佛看到了一种新的文学形式。其后，新的亚裔作家不断涌现，文学作品层出不穷。

最初亚裔文学的主要主题与主要内容为种族（race）、身份（identity）、亚洲文化传统、亚洲与美国或者西方国家之间的文化冲突，当然也少不了性别（sexuality）、社会性别（gender）、性别歧视、社会歧视等。后来，随着移民作家的大规模出现，离散文学的兴起，亚裔文学也开始关注移民、语言、家国、想象、全球化、劳工、战争、帝国主义、殖民主义等问题。

如果说，上述1974年的两部著作代表着亚裔文学进入美国文学的世界版图之中，那么，1982年著名美国亚裔研究专家金惠经（Elaine Kim）的《美国亚裔文学的创作及其社会语境》的出版，作为第一部学术著作，则代表着美国亚裔文学研究正式登上美国学术界的舞台。自此以后，不仅亚裔文学创作兴盛起来，而且亚裔文学研究也逐渐成为热点，成果不断推陈出新。

同时，人们对于如何界定"美国亚裔文学"等众多问题进行了深入的探讨，

---

1 参见：Wikipedia依据"U.S. Census Show Asians Are Fastest Growing Racial Group"（NPR.org）所得出的数据统计。https://en.wikipedia.org/wiki/Asian_Americans。
2 Mio, Jeffrey Scott, ed. 1999. *Key Words in Multicultural Interventions: A Dictionary*. ABC-Clio ebook. Greenwood Publishing Group, p.20.
3 K. Connie Kang, "Yuji Ichioka, 66; Led Way in Studying Lives of Asian Americans," *Los Angeles Times*, September 7, 2002. Reproduced at ucla.edu by the Asian American Studies Center.
4 Wand, David Hsin-fu, ed. 1974. *Asian American Heritage: An Anthology of Prose and Poetry*. New York: Pocket Books.
5 Chin, Frank, Chan, Jeffery Paul, Inada, Lawson Fusao, et al. 1974. *Aiiieeeee! An Anthology of Asian-American Writers*. Howard University Press.
6 Kim, Elaine. 1982. *Asian American Literature: An Introduction to the Writings and Their Social Context*. Philadelphia: Temple University Press.

进一步推动了这一学科向前发展。相关问题包括：究竟谁可以说自己是美国亚裔（an Asian America）？这里的 America 是不是就是单指"美国"（the United States）？是否可以包括"美洲"（Americas）？如果亚裔作家所写的内容与亚裔无关，能否算是"亚裔文学"？如果不是亚裔作家，但所写内容与亚裔有关，能否算在"亚裔文学"之内？

总体上看，早期的亚裔文学研究专注于美国身份的建构，即界定亚裔文学的范畴，以及争取其在美国文化与美国文学中应得的席位，是 20 世纪七八十年代亚裔民权运动的前沿阵地。早期学者如赵健秀、徐忠雄（Shawn Wong）等为领军人物。随后出现的金惠经、张敬珏（King-Kok Cheung）、骆里山（Lisa Lowe）等人均成为了亚裔文学研究领域的权威学者，他/她们的著作影响并造就了第二代美国亚裔文学研究者。20 世纪 90 年代之后的亚裔文学研究逐渐淡化了早期研究中对于意识形态的侧重，开始向传统的学科分支、研究方法以及研究理论靠拢，研究视角多集中在学术马克思主义（academic Marxism）、后结构主义、后殖民、女权主义以及心理分析等。

进入 21 世纪以来，"美国亚裔文学"研究开始向多元化、全球化与跨学科方向发展。随着亚裔文学作品爆炸式的增长，来自阿富汗、印度、巴基斯坦、越南等族裔作家的作品开始受到关注，极大丰富与拓展了亚裔文学研究的领域。当代"美国亚裔文学"研究的视角与方法也不断创新，战争研究、帝国研究、跨国研究、视觉文化理论、空间理论、身体研究、环境理论等层出不穷。新的理论与常规性研究交叉进行，不但开创了新的研究领域，对于经典问题（例如身份建构）的研究也提供了新的解读方式与方法。

四、作为课题的"美国亚裔文学"研究及其丛书

"美国亚裔文学"研究，是由我担任课题负责人的 2017 年度中国人民大学科学研究基金重大规划项目。"美国亚裔文学研究丛书"，即是该项课题的结题成果。作为"美国亚裔文学"方面的系列丛书，将由文学史、文学作品选、文学评论集、学术论著等组成，由我担任该丛书的总主编。

"美国亚裔文学"研究在 2017 年 4 月立项。随后，该丛书的论证计划，得到了国内外专家的一致认可。2017 年 5 月 27 日，中国人民大学科学研究基金重大规划项目"美国亚裔文学研究"开题报告会暨"美国亚裔文学研究高端论坛"在中国人民大学隆重召开。参加此次会议的专家学者全部为美国亚裔文学研究领域中的顶尖学者，包括美国加州大学洛杉矶分校的张敬珏教授、南京大学海外教育学院前院长程爱民教授、南京大学海外教育学院院长赵文书教授、北京语言大学

应用外语学院院长陆薇教授、北京外国语大学潘志明教授、解放军外国语学院石平萍教授等。在此次会议上，我向与会专家介绍了该项目的基本情况、未来研究方向与预计出版成果。与会专家对该项目的设立给予高度评价，强调在当今时代加强"美国亚裔文学"研究的必要性，针对该项目的预计研究及其成果，也提出了一些很好的建议。

根据最初的计划，这套丛书将包括文学史2部：《美国亚裔文学史》和《美国华裔文学史》；文学选集2部：《美国亚裔文学作品选》和《美国华裔文学作品选》；批评文选2部：《美国亚裔文学评论集》和《美国华裔文学评论集》；访谈录1部：《美国亚裔作家访谈录》；学术论著3部，包括美国学者张敬珏教授的《静默留声》和《文心无界》。总计10部著作。

根据我的基本设想，《美国亚裔文学史》和《美国华裔文学史》的撰写，将力图体现研究者对美国亚裔文学的研究进入到了较为深入的阶段。由于文学史是建立在研究者对该研究领域发展变化的总体认识上，涉及文学流派、创作方式、文学与社会变化的关系、作家间的关联等各方面的问题，我们试图通过对亚裔文学发展进行总结和评价，旨在为当前亚裔文学和华裔文学的研究和推广做出一定贡献。

《美国亚裔文学作品选》和《美国华裔文学作品选》，除了记录、介绍等基本功能，还将在一定程度上发挥形成民族认同、促进意识形态整合等功能。作品选编是民族共同体想象性构建的重要途径，也是作为文学经典得以确立和修正的最基本方式之一。因此，这样的作品选编，也要对美国亚裔文学的研究起到重要的促进作用。

《美国亚裔文学评论集》和《美国华裔文学评论集》，将主要选编美国、中国以及世界上最有学术价值的学术论文，虽然有些可能因为版权问题而不得不舍弃，但我们努力使之成为中国学术界研究"美国亚裔文学"和"美国华裔文学"的重要参考书目。

《美国亚裔作家访谈录》、美国学者的著作汉译、中国学者的美国亚裔文学学术专著等，将力图促使中美两国学者之间的学术对话，特别是希望中国的"美国亚裔文学"研究，既在中国的美国文学研究界，也要在美国和世界上的美国文学研究界发出中国学者的声音。"一带一路"倡议的实施，使得文学研究的关注发生了转变，从过分关注西方话语，到逐步转向关注中国（亚洲）话语，我们的美国亚裔（华裔）文学研究，正是从全球化视角切入，思考美国亚裔（华裔）文学的世界性。

2018年，我们按照原计划出版了《美国亚裔文学作品选》《美国华裔文学作品选》《美国亚裔文学评论集》《美国华裔文学评论集》。2022年上半年，我们出版了学术专著《文心无界——不拘性别、文类与形式的华美文学》。2022年下半年，还将出版《美国日裔文学作品选》《美国韩裔文学作品选》《美国越南裔文学作品选》《美国西亚裔文学作品选》《美国南亚裔文学作品选》等5部文学选集。

需要说明的是，这5部选集是在原有计划之外的产物。之所以在《美国亚裔文学作品选》之外又专门将其中最主要的国家与区域的文学作品结集出版，是因为在研究过程中我发现，现有的《美国亚裔文学作品选》已经无法涵盖丰富多彩的亚裔文学。更重要的是，无论是在国内还是在美国，像这样将美国亚裔按照国别与区域划分后的文学作品选全部是空白，国内外学术界对这些国别与区域的文学创作的整体关注也较少，可以说它们都属于亟待开垦的新研究领域。通过这5部选集，可以让国内对于美国亚裔文学有更为完整的了解。我也希望借此填补国内外在这个领域的空白。

等到丛书全部完成出版，将会成为一套由15部著作所组成的系列丛书。2018年的时候，我曾经把这套丛书界定为"国内第一套较为完整的美国亚裔文学方面的系列丛书"。现在，时隔4年之后，特别是在有了这新出版的5部选集之后，我可以说这套丛书将是"国内外第一套最为完整的美国亚裔文学方面的系列丛书"。

那么，我们为什么要对"美国亚裔文学"进行深入研究，并要编辑、撰写和翻译这套丛书呢？

首先，虽然"美国亚裔文学"在国外已有较大的影响，学术界也对此具有相当规模的研究，但在国内学术界，出于对"美国华裔文学"的偏爱与关注，"美国亚裔文学"相对还是一个较为陌生的领域。因此，本课题首次以"亚裔"集体的形式标示亚裔文学的存在，旨在介绍"美国亚裔文学"，推介具有族裔特色和代表性的作家作品。

其次，选择"美国亚裔文学"为研究对象，其中也有对"美国华裔文学"的研究，希望能够体现我们对全球化视野中华裔文学的关注，也体现试图融合亚裔、深入亚裔文学研究的学术自觉。同时，在多元化多种族的美国社会语境中，我们力主打破国内长久以来专注"美国华裔文学"研究的固有模式，转而关注包括华裔作家在内的亚裔作家所具有的世界性眼光。

最后，顺应美国亚裔文学发展的趋势，对美国亚裔文学的研究不仅是文学研究界的关注热点，还是我国外语与文学教育的关注焦点。我们希望为高校未来"美国亚裔文学"的课程教学，提供一套高水平的参考丛书。

五、"美国亚裔文学"及其研究的未来

如前所述,"美国亚裔文学"在20世纪70年代逐渐崛起后,使得亚裔文学从沉默走向了发声。到21世纪,亚裔文学呈现出多元化的发展特征,更重要的是,许多新生代作家开始崭露头角。单就这些新的亚裔作家群体,就有许多值得我们关注的话题。

2018年6月23日,"2018美国亚裔文学高端论坛——跨界:21世纪的美国亚裔文学"在中国人民大学隆重召开。参加会议的专家学者将近150人。

在此次会议上,我提出来:今天,为什么要研究美国亚裔文学?我们要研究什么?

正如我们在会议通知上所说,美国亚裔文学在一百多年的风雨沧桑中历经"沉默""觉醒",走向"发声",见证了美国亚裔族群的沉浮兴衰。21世纪以来,美国亚裔文学在全球冷战思维升温和战火硝烟不断的时空背景下,不囿于狭隘的种族主义藩篱,以"众声合奏"与"兼容并蓄"之势构筑出一道跨洋、跨国、跨种族、跨语言、跨文化、跨媒介、跨学科的文学景观,呈现出鲜明的世界主义意识。为此,我们拟定了一些主要议题。包括:1. 美国亚裔文学中的跨洋书写;2. 美国亚裔文学中的跨国书写;3. 美国亚裔文学中的跨种族书写;4. 美国亚裔文学中的跨语言书写;5. 美国亚裔文学中的跨文化书写;6. 美国亚裔文学的翻译跨界研究;7. 美国亚裔文学的跨媒介研究;8. 美国亚裔文学的跨学科研究等。

2019年6月22日,"2019美国亚裔文学高端论坛"在中国人民大学举行,会议的主题是"战争与和平:美国亚裔文学研究中的生命书写"。那次会议,依旧有来自中国的近80所高校的150余位教师和硕博研究生参加我们的论坛。

2020年年初,全球疫情大暴发,我们的"2020美国亚裔文学高端论坛"一直往后推迟,直到2020年12月5日在延边大学举行,会议的主题是"疫情之思:变局中的美国亚裔文学"。因为疫情原因,我们劝阻了很多愿意来参会的学者,但即便如此,也有近百位来自各地的专家学者与研究生前来参会。

2021年6月26—27日,"相遇与融合:2021首届华文/华裔文学研讨会"在西北师范大学举行。这次会议是由我在延边大学的会议上提出倡议,得到了中国社会科学院文学所赵稀方教授的积极响应,由他和我一起联合发起并主办,由西北师范大学外国语学院承办。我们知道,长期以来,华裔文学和华文文学分属不同的学科和研究领域,其研究对象、传统和范式都有所不同,但血脉相承的天然联系终究会让两者相遇、走向融合。从时下的研究看,虽然两者的研究范式自成体系、独树一帜,但都面临着华裔作家用中文创作和华人作家用外文创作的新趋势,这给双方的学科发展与研究领域都带来了新的挑战,也带来了新的学科发

展机遇。我们都相信，在学科交叉融合已成为实现创新发展必然趋势的当下语境中，华裔/华文文学走到了相遇与融合的最佳时机。为此，我们倡议并搭建平台，希望两个领域的学者同台进行学术交流与对话，探讨文学研究的新发展，以求实现华裔文学和华文文学的跨界融通。

事实上，21世纪以来，亚裔群体、亚裔所面临的问题、亚裔研究都发生了巨大的变化。从过去较为单纯的亚裔走向了跨越太平洋（transpacific）；从过去的彰显美国身份（claiming America）到今天的批评美国身份（critiquing America）；过去单一的America，现在变成了复数的Americas，这些变化都值得引起我们的高度重视。由此所引发的诸多问题，也需要我们去认真对待。比如：如何在"21世纪"这个特殊的时间区间内去理解"美国亚裔文学"这一概念？有关"美国亚裔文学"的概念构建，是否本身就存在着作家的身份焦虑与书写的界限划分？如何把握"美国亚裔文学"的整体性与区域性？"亚裔"身份是否是作家在表达过程中去主动拥抱的归属之地？等等。

2021年年底，国家社会科学基金重大招标课题揭晓，我申请的"美国族裔文学中的文化共同体思想研究"喜获中标。这将进一步推动我目前所从事的美国亚裔文学研究，并在未来由现在的美国亚裔文学研究走向美国的整个族裔文学研究。

展望未来，"美国亚裔文学"呈现出更加生机勃勃的生命力，"美国亚裔文学"的研究也将迎来更加光明的前途。

2018年8月28日定稿于哈佛大学
2022年8月28日修改于北京

前　言

"美国亚裔文学"研究，是由中国人民大学"杰出学者"特聘教授郭英剑先生担任课题负责人的2017年度中国人民大学科学研究基金重大规划项目。"美国亚裔文学研究丛书"，是该项课题的结题成果。由郭英剑教授担任该套丛书的总主编。这是国内第一套最为完整的"美国亚裔文学"方面的系列丛书，由文学史、文学作品选、文学评论集、学术论著等所组成。

所谓"美国南亚裔文学"，是指具有南亚血统的美国人（即南亚裔）用英语创作的文学作品。这里的南亚裔包括来自印度、巴基斯坦、尼泊尔、孟加拉国、斯里兰卡、马尔代夫、不丹等七个国家（或与这些国家有关联）的人员群体及其后裔。"美国南亚裔文学"的题材不仅局限于反映南亚裔在美国的经历，还可以是关于南亚乃至世界的故事。

"美国南亚裔文学"无疑是"美国亚裔文学"版图中不可或缺的一部分，它在短时间内取得了引人注目的成绩，成为美国少数族裔文学中的佼佼者。现在，"美国南亚裔文学"已经成为观察美国社会历史与现在的一个重要平台，有助于人们了解这个国家在短暂的历史中所发生的许多重大变化，同时作为观照，也促使我们进行自我文化反思。

南亚人移居美国的历史可以追溯到19世纪。这一时期南亚移民中的知识分子开创了早期的南亚裔文学，代表作家有丹·戈帕尔·慕克吉、达利普·辛格·桑德和拉贾·劳等。丹·戈帕尔·慕克吉是美国历史上第一位成功的南亚裔作家，他在1927年出版的《花颈鸽，一只信鸽的传奇》是早期南亚裔文学的代表作。

"美国南亚裔文学"在第二次世界大战之后得到了长足的发展，呈现百家争鸣的繁荣景象，代表作家有巴普西·西德瓦、巴拉蒂·慕克吉、米娜·亚历山大、奇塔·蒂娃卡鲁尼、阿兰达蒂·洛伊和裘帕·拉希莉等。进入21世纪以来，"美国南亚裔文学"保持蓬勃发展的态势，老一代作家笔耕不辍，新一代作家佳作频现。这个时期的代表人物包括阿亚德·阿赫塔尔、基兰·德赛、卡米拉·夏姆斯和纳克维等。

鉴于越来越多的南亚裔作家涌上文坛及其愈加显著的影响力，我们认为需要将"南亚裔文学"单独列出来，编写这部《美国南亚裔文学作品选》，便于让人们领略更多南亚裔作家的风采。

《美国南亚裔文学作品选》以历史为发展脉络，精选了 38 位美国南亚裔作家的作品，并以作家的出生年代为顺序进行编目排列。

作品选力图反映"美国南亚裔文学"一百多年间的发展历程和变化，深刻反映抗争、身份认同与文化冲突所构成的南亚裔文学传统的重要议题。作品选努力求新，体现更大的兼容性。我们选取了多位新生代作家/后起之秀（如 60 后阿兰达蒂·罗伊、斯瑞迪·乌姆里加、裘帕·拉希莉，70 后阿亚德·阿赫塔尔、基兰·德赛、卡米拉·夏姆斯以及 80 后 V. V. 加内桑坦等），以彰显南亚裔文学最近几十年的发展与繁荣，同时也表明南亚裔文学生机勃勃，后继有人。同时，对于老一代作家，不仅选其经典之作，也特意选取他们晚近的"新"作品，反映他们老骥伏枥、笔耕不辍的精神，这种精神成为南亚裔文学向前发展的动力。

《美国南亚裔文学作品选》力图体现南亚裔文学的新发展、新现象。为此，我们扩展了所选南亚裔文学作品的体裁范围。虽然选集仍然以长篇小说、短篇小说、诗歌、戏剧几大体裁为主，但就小说而言，我们还选取了自传体小说、科幻传奇小说、儿童文学等门类，以反映南亚裔文学发展的整体概貌。

当然，令人遗憾的是，任何一部选集都会因为篇幅问题而难以做到面面俱到，《美国南亚裔文学作品选》也是如此，因为各种历史与现实的原因，一些作家的作品未能收录其中，但通过这些入选作品，大家可以进入更大的美国南亚裔文学的海洋之中。

无论如何，我们都希望《美国南亚裔文学作品选》能够成为中国学术界研究"美国亚裔文学"，特别是"美国南亚裔文学"的重要参考书目。

编　者
2022 年 8 月 28 日

目　录

1. 丹·戈帕尔·慕克吉 (Dhan Gopal Mukerji, 1890—1936) ········· 1
   Gay Neck, the Story of a Pigeon ········· 2

2. 达利普·辛格·桑德 (Dalip Singh Saund, 1899—1973) ········· 6
   Congressman from India ········· 7

3. 拉贾·劳 (Raja Rao, 1908—2006) ········· 11
   The Serpent and the Rope ········· 12

4. 戈温达斯·维什努达斯·德萨尼 (Govindas Vishnudas Desani, 1909—2000) ···· 16
   All about H. Hatterr ········· 17

5. 维德·梅塔 (Ved Mehta, 1934—2021) ········· 21
   Sound-Shadows of the New World ········· 22

6. G. S. 沙拉特·钱德拉 (G. S. Sharat Chandra, 1935—2000) ········· 25
   Brother ········· 26
   After the Earthquake in India ········· 28

7. 巴普西·西德瓦 (Bapsi Sidhwa, 1938—) ········· 29
   Cracking India ········· 30
   An American Brat ········· 34

8. 巴拉蒂·慕克吉 (Bharati Mukherjee, 1940—2017) ········· 38
   The Tenant ········· 39
   Desirable Daughters ········· 43

9. 比娜·谢里夫 (Bina Sharif, 1940—) ········· 49
   My Ancestor's House ········· 50

10. 塔拉特·阿巴西 (Talat Abbasi, 1942—) ········· 55
    Mirage ········· 56

11. 吉塔·梅塔 (Gita Mehta, 1943—) ··· 60
　　Raj ··· 61

12. 塔希拉·纳克维 (Tahira Naqvi, 1945—) ··································· 65
　　A Fair Exchange ·· 66

13. 阿加·沙希德·阿里 (Agha Shahid Ali, 1949—2001) ················ 71
　　In Lenox Hill ·· 72
　　I See Chile in My Rearview Mirror ·· 74

14. 米娜·亚历山大 (Meena Alexander, 1951—2018) ······················ 77
　　Fault Lines ··· 78
　　Illiterate Heart ·· 80

15. 萨拉·苏莱里·古德伊尔 (Sara Suleri Goodyear, 1953—2022) ···· 86
　　Excellent Things in Women ·· 87

16. 维贾伊·瑟哈德里 (Vijay Seshadri, 1954—) ······························· 91
　　New Media ·· 92
　　Nursing Home ·· 93

17. 亚伯拉罕·韦尔盖塞 (Abraham Verghese, 1955—) ···················· 95
　　Cutting for Stone ·· 96

18. 奇塔·班纳吉·蒂娃卡鲁尼 (Chitra Banerjee Divakaruni, 1956—) ···· 100
　　Cutting the Sun ·· 101
　　Sister of My Heart ·· 102

19. 基琳·娜拉杨 (Kirin Narayan, 1959—) ······································ 106
　　Love, Stars and All That ··· 107

20. 因德尼·阿米拉纳亚加姆 (Indran Amirthanayagam, 1960—) ······· 111
　　The City, with Elephants ·· 112
　　The Migrant's Reply ··· 114

21. 英迪拉·加内桑 (Indira Ganesan, 1960—) ·································· 116
　　Inheritance ··· 117
　　As Sweet as Honey ··· 122

22. 阿兰达蒂·罗伊 (Arundhati Roy, 1961—) ·································· 126
　　The God of Small Things ·· 127

23. 斯瑞迪·乌姆里加 (Thrity Umrigar, 1961—) ········· 132
　　The Space Between Us ········· 133
　　Everybody's Son ········· 135

24. 瑞蒂卡·瓦齐拉尼 (Reetika Vazirani, 1962—2003) ········· 140
　　It's a Young Country ········· 141
　　Friday Mixer ········· 142

25. 戴尼亚尔·穆伊努丁 (Daniyal Mueenuddin, 1963—) ········· 143
　　Nawabdin Electrician—The Life of a Wily Pakistani Electrician ········· 144
　　Our Lady of Paris ········· 147

26. 裘帕·拉希莉 (Jhumpa Lahiri, 1967—) ········· 153
　　Interpreter of Maladies ········· 154
　　The Lowland ········· 158

27. 玛雅·科斯拉 (Maya Khosla, 1970—) ········· 162
　　Dispersal ········· 163
　　Offerings ········· 163

28. 悉达多·穆克吉 (Siddhartha Mukherjee, 1970—) ········· 165
　　The Emperor of All Maladies: A Biography of Cancer ········· 166

29. 阿亚德·阿赫塔尔 (Ayad Akhtar, 1970—) ········· 170
　　Disgraced ········· 171
　　Homeland Elegies ········· 176

30. 基兰·德赛 (Kiran Desai, 1971—) ········· 181
　　Hullabaloo in the Guava Orchard ········· 182
　　The Inheritance of Loss ········· 185

31. 阿基尔·夏尔马 (Akhil Sharma, 1971—) ········· 190
　　An Obedient Father ········· 191
　　Family Life ········· 195

32. 沙巴里·佐赫拉·艾哈迈德 (Sharbari Zohra Ahmed, 1971—) ········· 198
　　Raisins Not Virgins ········· 199

33. 凡达娜·卡娜 (Vandana Khanna, 1972—) ········· 203
　　Train to Agra ········· 204
　　Mantra for a New Bride ········· 206

34. 卡米拉·夏姆斯 (Kamila Shamsie, 1973—) ···················· 207
    In the City by the Sea ···················· 208
    Home Fire ···················· 212

35. 艾梅·内茨库马塔尔 (Aimee Nezhukumatathil, 1974—) ···················· 217
    One Bite ···················· 218
    A Globe Is Just an Asterick and Every Home Should Have an Asterick ······ 219

36. 纳克维 (H. M. Naqvi, 1974—) ···················· 220
    Home Boy ···················· 221
    The Selected Works of Abdullah the Cossack ···················· 226

37. 阿米特·马吉穆达尔 (Amit Majmudar, 1979—) ···················· 231
    Partitions ···················· 232
    Dothead ···················· 237

38. V. V. 加内桑坦 (V. V. Ganeshananthan, 1980—) ···················· 239
    Love Marriage ···················· 240

1

(Dhan Gopal Mukerji, 1890—1936)
丹·戈帕尔·慕克吉

作者简介

丹·戈帕尔·慕克吉（Dhan Gopal Mukerji, 1890—1936），美国印度裔诗人、剧作家、小说家，出生在印度加尔各答（Calcutta）的一个婆罗门种姓家庭。1908年，慕克吉在印度加尔各答大学杜夫学院（Duff College within the University of Calcutta）学习，随后移居日本，1909年考入日本东京大学（University of Tokyo）。1910年移居美国后，在加州大学伯克利分校（UC Berkeley）学习，之后继续深造获得斯坦福大学（Stanford University）硕士学位，毕业之后留校任教，担任比较文学讲师。

慕克吉是美国历史上第一位成功的印裔作家。他著作颇丰，出版了戏剧、诗集、儿童读物和自传等。戏剧作品包括他与玛丽·卡洛琳·戴维斯（Mary Carolyn Davies）共同创作的《钦塔米尼：象征戏剧》（Chintamini: A Symbolic Drama, 1914）及《印度的审判》（The Judgment of India, 1922）。诗集包括《拉贾尼：夜之歌》（Rajani: Songs of the Night, 1916）和《桑德亚：黄昏之歌》（Sandhya: Songs of Twilight, 1917）。儿童读物包括《花颈鸽，一只信鸽的传奇》（Gay Neck: the Story of a Pigeon, 1927）、《印度儿童寓言》（Hindu Fables for Little Children, 1929）、《牧群首领》（The Chief of the Herd, 1929）、《猴王》（The Master Monkey, 1932）、《凶脸：老虎的故事》（Fierce-Face: The Story of a Tiger, 1936）等。除此之外，他还著有一部自传《种姓与驱逐》（Caste and Outcast, 1923）。其中《花颈鸽，一只信鸽的传奇》获得1928年美国图书馆学会颁发的纽伯瑞奖（Newbery Medal），慕克吉成为获得这一奖项的首位美国亚裔作家。

慕克吉擅长寓言和民间故事写作，其笔下的主人公一般都是小动物，文字质朴优美，充满细腻、迷人的印度风情。《花颈鸽，一只信鸽的传奇》讲述了一只鸽子的传奇故事。它不仅要和大自然进行殊死搏斗，还要在世界战场上为盟军传递情报。选段部分出自第二章，描写了花颈鸽如何被训练学习飞行的故事，情节生动，富含哲理。

作品选读

Gay Neck, the Story of a Pigeon

Chapter Two

By Dhan Gopal Mukerji

  There are two sweet sights in the bird world: one when the mother breaks open her egg in order to bring to light her child, and the other when she broods and feeds him. Gay-Neck was brooded most affectionately by both his parents. This brooding did for him what cuddling does for human children. It gives the helpless ones warmth and happiness. It is as necessary to them as food. This is the time when a pigeon-hole should not be stuffed with too much cotton or flannel, which should be put there more and more sparingly so that the temperature of the nest does not get too hot. Ignorant pigeon fanciers do not realize that as the baby grows larger he puts forth more and more heat from his own body. And I think it is wise not to clean the nest frequently during this time. Everything that the parents allow to remain in the nest contributes to making their baby comfortable and happy.

  I remember distinctly how, from the second day of his birth, little Gay-Neck automatically opened his beak and expanded his carnation-coloured body like a bellows every time one of his parents flew back to their nest. The father or the mother put their beaks into his wide-open maw and poured into it the milk made in their own organs from millet seeds that they had eaten. I noticed this; the food that was poured into his mouth was very soft. No pigeon ever gives any seeds to its baby even when it is nearly a month old without first keeping them in its throat for some time, which softens the food before it enters the delicate stomach of the baby.

Our Gay-Neck was a tremendous eater. He kept one of his parents busy getting food while the other brooded or stayed with him. I think the father bird brooded and worked for him no less hard than the mother. No wonder his body grew very fat. His carnation colour changed into a yellowish-white—the first sign of feathers coming on. Then that gave way to prickly white feathers, round and somewhat stiff, like a porcupine needle. The yellow things that hung about his mouth and eyes fell away. Slowly the beak emerged, firm, sharp and long. What a powerful jaw! When he was about three weeks old, an ant was crawling past him into the pigeon-hole at whose entrance he was sitting. Without any instruction from anybody he struck it with his beak. Where there had been a whole ant now lay its two halves. He brought his nose down to the dead ant and examined what he had done. There was no doubt that he had taken that black ant for a seed, and killed an innocent passer-by who was friendly to his race. Let us hope he was ashamed of it. Anyway, he never killed another ant the rest of his life.

By the time he was five weeks old he could hop out of his birth-nest and take a drink from the pan of water left near the pigeon-holes. Even now he had to be fed by his parents, though every day he tried to get food on his own account. He would sit on my wrist and dig up a seed at a time from the palm of my hand. He juggled it two or three times in his throat like a juggler throwing up balls in the air, and swallowed it. Every time Gay-Neck did that, he turned his head and looked into my eyes as much as to say: "Am I not doing it well? You must tell my parents how clever I am when they come down from sunning themselves on the roof." All the same, he was the slowest of my pigeons in developing his powers.

Just at this time I made a discovery. I never knew before how pigeons could fly in a dust-storm without going blind. But as I watched the ever-growing Gay-Neck, I noticed one day that a film was drawn over his eyes. I thought he was losing his sight. In my consternation I put forth my hand to draw him nearer to my face in order to examine him closely. No sooner had I made the gesture than he opened his golden eyes and receded into the rear of the hole. But just the same I caught him and took him up on the roof, and in the burning sunlight of May I scrutinized his eyelids. Yes, there it was: he had, attached to his eyelid, another thin lid as delicate as tissue-paper, and every time I put his face toward the sun he drew that film over the two orbits of gold. And so I learned that it was a protective film for the eye that enabled the bird to fly in a duststorm or straight toward the sun.

In another fortnight Gay-Neck was taught how to fly. It was not at all easy, bird though he was by birth. A human child may love the water, yet he has to make mistakes and swallow water while learning the art of swimming. Similarly with my pigeon. He had a mild distrust of opening his wings, and for hours he sat on our roof, where the winds of the sky blew without quickening him to flight. In order to make the situation clear, let me describe our roof to you. It was railed with a solid concrete wall as high as a boy of fourteen. That prevented even a sleep-walker from slipping off the height of four stories on summer nights, when most of us slept on the roof.

Gay-Neck I put on that concrete wall every day. There he sat for hours at a time, facing the wind, but that was all. One day I put some peanuts on the roof and called him to hop down and get them. He looked at me with an inquiring eye for a few moments. Turning from me, he looked down again at the peanuts. He repeated this process several times. When at last he was convinced that I was not going to bring these delicious morsels up for him to eat, he began to walk up and down the railing, craning his neck occasionally towards the peanuts about three feet below. At last, after fifteen minutes of heart-breaking hesitancy, he hopped down. Just as his feet struck the floor, his wings, hitherto unopened, suddenly spread themselves out full sail as he balanced himself over the nuts. What a triumph!

About this time I noticed the change of colours on his feathers. Instead of a nondescript grey-blue, a glossy aquamarine glowed all over him. And suddenly one morning in the sunlight his throat glistened like iridescent beads.

Now came the supreme question of flight. I waited for his parents to teach him the first lessons, though I helped the only way I could. Every day for a few minutes I made him perch on my wrist; then I would swing my arm up and down many times, and in order to balance himself on such a difficult perch he had to shut and open his wings frequently. That was good for him, but there ended my part of the teaching. You may ask me the reason of my hurrying matters so. He was already behind in his flying lessons, and in June the rains begin to fall in India; and with the approach of the rainy season any long flight becomes impossible. I wished to train him in learning his directions as soon as I could.

However, one day long before the end of May, his father undertook the task. This particular day a brisk north wind, which had been sweeping about and cooling the atmosphere of the city, had just died down. The sky was as clear as a limpid sapphire. The spaces were so clear that you could see the house-tops of our town, then the fields and arbours of the country in the farthest distance. About three o'clock in the afternoon, Gay-Neck was sunning himself on the concrete wall of the roof. His father, who had been flying about in the air, came down and perched next to him. He looked at his son with a queer glance, as much as to say: "Here, lazy-bones, you are nearly three months old, yet you do not dare to fly. Are you a pigeon or an earthworm?" But Gay-Neck, the soul of dignity, made no answer. That exasperated his father, who began to coo and boom at him in pigeon-language. In order to get away from that volubility, Gay-Neck moved; but his father followed, cooing, booming and banging his wings. Gay-Neck went on removing himself farther and farther; and the old fellow, instead of relenting, redoubled his talk, and pursued. At last the father pushed him so close to the edge that Gay-Neck had only one alternative, that is, to slip off the roof. Suddenly his father thrust upon his young body all the weight of his old frame. Gay-Neck slipped. Hardly had he fallen half a foot when he opened his wings, and flew. Oh, what an exhilarating moment for all concerned! His mother, who was downstairs dipping herself in the water, and performing her afternoon toilet, came up through the staircase and flew to keep her son company. They circled above the roof for at least ten minutes before they came down to perch. When they reached the roof the mother folded her wings as a matter of course, and sat still. Not so the son: he was in a panic, like a boy walking into cold and deep water. His whole body shook, and his feet trod the roof gingerly as he alighted, skating over it furiously and flapping his wings in order to balance himself. At last he stopped, as his chest struck the side of the wall, and he folded his wings as swiftly as we shut a fan. Gay-Neck was panting with excitement, while his mother rubbed him and placed her chest against him as if he were a mere baby who badly needed brooding. Seeing that his task had been done successfully, Gay-Neck's father went down to take his bath.

2

(Dalip Singh Saund, 1899—1973)
达利普·辛格·桑德

作者简介

达利普·辛格·桑德（Dalip Singh Saund, 1899—1973），美国印度裔小说家、政治家，出生于印度旁遮普邦（Punjab），家境富足。桑德于1919年在旁遮普大学（University of the Punjab）获得数学学士学位。22岁那年，桑德前往美国加州大学伯克利分校求学，并于1924年获得数学博士学位。他在1956年被选为美国众议院议员，成为首位被选为众议员的亚裔美国人。

桑德的创作主要包括专论《甘地：他和他的信息》(*Gandhi: The Man and His Message*, 1924)，散文集《我的母亲印度》(*My Mother India*, 1930) 以及回忆录《来自印度的国会议员》(*Congressman from India*, 1960) 等。这部回忆录讲述了桑德如何成为美国国会议员的故事，其中悲伤与欢乐、失败与痛苦并存。节选部分出自回忆录《来自印度的国会议员》第二章，讲述了桑德初到美国之后的各种经历和遭遇。

作品选读

Congressman from India

Chapter II

(excerpt)

By Dalip Singh Saund

At long last I was finally able to secure passage to the United States on the S. S. Philadelphia leaving Southampton. The only space available was in steerage. When I boarded the ship I found the accommodations were a far cry from the first-class luxury I had experienced from Bombay to Plymouth. We crossed the English Channel during the night and stopped at Cherbourg where the ship took on hundreds of passengers from Europe.

The week's trip across the Atlantic was not very pleasant for me principally because the food was so poor. All I could bring myself to eat was milk and fruit. I was amazed that my fellow passengers were able to eat some of the food that was served until I realized that most of them were people from Europe, many of whom had actually experienced hunger and starvation during wartime. Even though I had come from a very poor country, I had never known what it was like to be hungry.

Among the passengers aboard the S. S. Philadelphia was an attractive and charming young blonde lady who was returning to New York to join her husband. She was interested in India and we talked together quite often. She had an eleven-year-old daughter with her and we all became very good friends. New York was their destination while I was bound for San Francisco. Eight years later we were to meet in Los Angeles again under very strange and providential circumstances.

When we reached New York Harbor we were delayed by heavy fog for two days. Then at last the fog lifted a little and I could see the faint outlines of the Statue of Liberty. It was an exhilarating experience. I had finally arrived in the United States of America.

During the stay at Ellis Island, while waiting to be cleared for entry, I felt lonesome for the first time since I left India. Here I was at Ellis Island. I had come to the United States but I was not yet free to go into the country. Then while I was standing in a long line to have my passport examined a kindly inspector who obviously knew India took me out of the line and had my papers stamped. Finally, warmly shaking my hand, he said to me, "You are now a free man in a free country." Then he whispered into my ear, "You do not have to Worry about the C.I.D. either." (C.I.D. stood for the Criminal Investigation Department in India—the dread and hated secret police.)

I looked around and said to myself, "Yes, at long last you are a free man in a free country. You may go where you wish and say what you please." That certainly proved true, for as long as I have been in the United States, particularly in the early years, while I was cruelly discriminated against many a time because of the place of my birth, not once has my right to say what I pleased been questioned by any man. To me, coming as I did from India, freedom of speech and liberty to go wherever I wished without having any fears of secret police hounding me were of profound and lasting significance.

I set out from New York for San Francisco, California, where I intended to enroll as a student at the University of California to study food preservation and canning. It was a long train trip and I had not as yet become accustomed to American food. So all the way across the country I lived on milk and bread.

At the Ferry Building in San Francisco the attendant at the Traveler's Aid Society booth directed me to a Hindu temple. There I was told that I should stay in San Francisco that night and take a ferry the next morning across the bay to Berkeley. I was further advised that if I went to Mission Street I would be able to find a hotel room in which to spend the night. It was the most uncomfortable night I have ever spent in my life. I had heard about bedbugs, but this was the first time I had actually encountered a bed infested with them. The bed was impossible, and my only refuge was the floor, but that yielded scant comfort.

The next morning I rushed to the Ferry Building and took the ferry to Berkeley, the seat of the University of California. I went straight to 1731 Allston Way, where I found the clubhouse established and maintained by the Sikh Temple in Stockton, California. The temple had bought this two-story house for the use and benefit of students from India who could live there rent free. The only requirement was that residents of the club be enrolled at a high school or the university. It was run by the resident members on a cooperative basis—students paid for their gas and electricity and we took turns at cooking Hindu-style meals. When my turn came around, I always prepared my specialty—chicken curry.

For the next two years I was a resident member of the club. The resultant saving was a great help to me as it was to other students, because in those days no students from India received any government scholarships since the British Government of India was not interested in educating Indians in the United States. We had all come over on our own and we were all short of funds.

One of the senior members of the club was studying agriculture and he very kindly helped me enter the university as a graduate student, a further help, since no tuition fees were required of graduate students. In the course of my studies I took part in several experiments which were being carried on at the university at that time in the line of food preservation. I worked very diligently in the laboratory and had the opportunity to experiment with the canning and dehydration of fruits and vegetables. It was at this time that a number of tragic deaths were reported as a result of ptomaine poisoning contracted after eating canned olives. It was in the food preservation laboratories of the University of California that a safe formula for canning olives was finally perfected.

Contact with Americans was limited to associations made in my university classes; my other contacts were almost exclusively with my fellow citizens from India of whom there were some eighty at the university. The only times that students of different nationalities ever got together were at meetings of the Cosmopolitan Club, sponsored by the YMCA in Berkeley, under the leadership of the YMCA secretary, Dr. Day.

The student group from India was very well organized and we all belonged to the Hindustan Association of America, which had chapters throughout the United States in different university centers. After I had been at Berkeley two years I was elected national president of the association, which gave me many opportunities to make speeches on India and meet with other groups as a representative of the Indian students at the university. All of us were ardent Nationalists and we never passed up an opportunity to expound on India's rights to self-government. I took part in several debates and spoke before many groups and organizations.

It was my habit at the time to write my speeches out very carefully in advance. Sometimes I would take two or more weeks to write a speech and then memorize it. I used the best possible language and tried to follow the style of old English orators who believed in melodious phrases couched in flawless grammar. But I soon found this special preparation could get me into trouble. It allowed for no spontaneity, and when I had to have a comeback or an answer to a question on controversial subjects such as Indian independence I was often very slow.

On one occasion when I was president of the Hindustan Association of America, the annual convention was scheduled to be held at the university. I had previously gone to Palo Alto and made arrangements with the president of Stanford University, Dr. David Starr Jordan, to be our principal speaker. A few days before the convention, however, Dr. Jordan had to go East and could not be present. We had difficulty in finding a substitute, but finally a professor of political science at the university agreed to pinch-hit.

I delivered a half-hour talk on the right of India to independence and the inequities of British rule. Then our main speaker rose and proceeded to tear me apart. He floored me with questions I couldn't promptly answer. "How about the primitive agriculture in India?" he asked. "How about the caste system? How about the disunity between the Hindus and the Mohammedans?"

He easily got the better of me and I felt very sick and sad that the meeting ended by creating an unfavorable impression for the cause of India.

A leadership position among my group was not always an enviable one. Once I was chairman of the annual faculty dinner to which students invited instructors as guests. I worked for two weeks preparing my speeches and introductions of honored guests, and I recall my feelings quite vividly. While sitting at the head table next to the dean of the Agricultural College who was to be our principal speaker, I worried as I tried to remember the big words and resounding passages in my forthcoming speech of welcome. Meanwhile, I could see my fellow students having a wonderful time, chatting and talking with their girl friends and faculty guests. Most of the extra work was my own fault. I now know it was not necessary for me to worry and work so hard on my speeches, but I was a perfectionist, and there was no helping it.

3

(Raja Rao, 1908—2006)
拉贾·劳

作者简介

拉贾·劳（Raja Rao, 1908—2006），美国印度裔小说家，出生于印度南部的哈桑市（Hassan）。拉贾·劳曾在海得拉巴（Hyderabad）的尼扎姆学院（Nizam College）学习英语，随后在马德拉斯大学（University of Madras）学习，并于1929年获得学士学位。后来，他离开印度前往法国，在蒙彼利埃大学（University of Montpellier）学习文学和历史。1931年，在法国期间，他与卡米尔·穆莉（Camille Mouly）结婚。他早年曾参加印度的民族解放运动，印度独立后移民美国。1966年，他任职于得克萨斯大学奥斯汀分校（University of Texas at Austin），1980年退休后被任命为荣誉教授。

拉贾·劳斩获颇多荣誉和奖项，包括1969年印度政府颁发的莲花装勋章（Padma Bhushan）、1997年印度国家文学院奖（Sahitya Akademi Award）以及2007年追授的帕德玛·维布山奖（Padma Vibhushan Award）等。

拉贾·劳是一位较早在美国文坛确立自己地位的印度裔作家，成果丰硕。主要有小说《根特浦尔》（*Kanthapura*, 1938）、《蛇与绳》（*The Serpent and the Rope*, 1960）与《象棋大师和他的出招》（*The Chessmaster and His Moves*, 1988）；短篇小说集《街垒上的牛，及其他故事》（*The Cow of the Barricades, and Other Stories*, 1947）、《警察与玫瑰》（*The Policeman and the Rose*, 1978）；寓言故事《猫和莎士比亚：印度故事》（*The Cat and Shakespeare: A Tale of India*, 1965）等。他创作的非小说类作品包括《印度的意义》（*The Meaning of India*, 1996），以及《伟大的印度方式》（*The Great Indian Way*, 1998）等。其中小说《蛇与绳》荣获1988年

纽斯塔国际文学奖（Neustadt International Prize for Literature），记述了他在印度、欧洲和美国探寻真理的心路历程。这部作品集传记、游记、哲学玄思等文类特征于一体，是一部兼具故事性与思想性的不可多得的文学佳作。

选段出自小说《蛇与绳》的结尾部分，讲述了主人公拉马斯瓦米（Ramaswamy）在经历婚姻失败后而生发的感悟：纯粹的爱的价值，可以通过真正的婚姻来实现。

作品选读

The Serpent and the Rope
(excerpt)
By Raja Rao

Yes, I say to myself: "I must leave this world, I must leave, leave this world." But, Lord, where shall I go, where? How can one go anywhere? How can one go from oneself?

I walk up and down this mansard, and say: "There must be something that exalts and explains why we are here, what is it we seek." And suddenly, as though I've forgotten where I am, I begin to sing out aloud, "Shivoham, Shivoham," as if I were in Benares, on the banks of the Ganges, sitting on Harishchandra Ghat and singing away. In Benares, it may still sound true—but here against the dull sky of Paris, this yellow wallpaper, with its curved and curling clematis, going back and forth, and all about my room ... I say, "Clematis is the truth, must be in the truth." I count, one, two, three, simply like that, and count 177 clematis in my room. "If I add a zero," I say to myself, "it will make 1,770 and they would cover ten mansard rooms." I look out and count the number of windows in the Lycée St Louis. It has eighteen windows: one, two, three, five, eleven, eighteen windows. And I say, "If they had clematis on their walls, how many would there be? Each room there is about three times the width of my room." My arithmetic goes all wrong, for I must subtract one wall out of every three, and that's too complicated. I roll back into my bed. "Hara-Hara, Shiva-Shiva," I say to myself, as if I were in Benares again, then "Chidananda rupah, Shivoham, Shivoham."

I began to clap hands and sing. The Romanian lady next door again knocks to remind me I am in Paris. I go out, with my overcoat on, wander round and round the Luxembourg Gardens by the Rue d' Assas, feeling that three times round anything you love must give you meaning, must give you peace. Buses still go on the streets, and students are still there chez shining, mirrored Dupont. I wish I could drink: "It must be wonderful to drink," I say to myself. The students get drunk and are so gay. That Dutch boy, the other day, was quite drunk; he sat in the hotel lounge, with his mouth on one side, and started singing songs. If you don't feel too warm at heart, you can always warm yourself in the Quartier Latin. You never saw more generous girls in the world. Existentialism has cleared the libido out of the knots of hair. Wherever you go, girls have rich bosoms, fiery red lips. They don't need cards—not because the gendarme does not ask for them, but because girls have grown too pure. Purity is not in the act but in the meaning of the act. Had I been less of a Brahmin, I might have known more of "love."

I go down the Boulevard St Michel, stand before the lit fountain and come back. I am sure I am much better. I go round the "100, 000 Chemises" shop, who know their arithmetic. I see that a cravat costs 1,990 francs, the good ones—shoes cost twice as much; the best one four times in the next shop. There is a brawl on the corner of my street, and I look at everyone, thinking as if I am not looking at them, but I am counting them. "One, two, three, four, five," I say, and one threatens to beat four and four threatens to beat me. Fear is such a spontaneous experience—I slink away, I run and run till I reach my hotel. I think it was a political battle of some sort. A group of Moroccan and Indo-Chinese students were having a brawl with some elderly Frenchman. Then I understood. They thought—the fat, threatening Frenchman thought—that I must be a Tunisian. You must fight for something. You cannot flow like the Rhone, dividing Avignon into the Avignon of the Popes and Petit Avignon.

I get my key from the concierge and come up to my room. I feel the room to be so spacious, so kind; I could touch the sky with my fingers. You can have 177 clematis in your room and yet touch the sky of Paris. A Brahmin can touch anything, he is so high—the higher the freer. I look at the carefully arranged manuscript of my thesis. It has 278 pages. It has been finished for over a week. Dr Robin-Bessaignac said it is very interesting, very very interesting indeed, but blue-pencilled several passages. One in particular, in my preface, made him laugh. "History is not a straight line, it is not even a curved line," I had written. "History is a straight line turned into a round circle. It has no beginning, it has no end—it is movement without itself moving. History is an act to deny fact. History, truly speaking, is seminal."

"You don't know our professors," Dr Robin said. "They would hide behind their notes if they saw a girl with too much rouge on her lips. Besides, my friend, there is an ancient tradition in this country: Beware of too much truth. We French live on heresies. If only poor Abelard had ended with a question mark and not with a 'Scito Teipsum,' he might have walked Paris un-castrate, and be canonized a saint by now. You must go to the end of philosophy, go near enough to truth—but you must end with a question mark. The question mark is, I repeat, the sign of French intelligence; it is the tradition of Descartes, that great successor of Abelard. And as for anything imaginative... There's a famous story about Sylvain Lévi, the orientalist, you know. He had said, and that was seventy good years ago, something about Kalidasa's plays. His books ended, as all good literature ended in those days, with a noble sentence, rounded like one of Mallarmé's. Would you believe it, the thesis was refused: he had to write it again. I do not want to see your thesis refused. I knew what they will say. This is supposed to be a thesis on the philosophical origins, mainly oriental, primarily Hindu, of the Cathar philosophy. But it is too poetic. It lacks historical discipline! Get someone—preferably a professor—to help you to remove everything that does not end in a question.

"Can you find one?" he asked me. Of course I know one. Who could be more helpful to me than good Georges? I often discuss my thesis with him, and I have read him bits of it. He does not say whether it would be suitable or not as a thesis: he is happy at my defence of Catholicism, and finds my logic inescapable. Here and there, however, he has suggested a few corrections. And then, somebody has to translate the whole text into French. I wonder whether Georges would do. Good Georges, of course, agrees. I must give it to him tomorrow.

I roll and roll in my bed. Not that I am ill; no, I am not so ill. In fact the doctors are very satisfied with the state of my lungs; hardly any complications with my ribs or my chest, they say. I could, in fact, stay in Europe if I cared. But why should I? What is there to do? I think of Saroja. She is not happy, but she is settled. I think of Little Mother going and dipping in the Ganges every morning. And now, this year, with the Kumbha Méla and the sun in Capricorn, she must be very happy. Could I give Little Mother such joy if I were back? What can a poor Professor in Hyderabad do? At best I could take her on a pilgrimage once in two years. There is nobody to go to now: no home, no temple, no city, no climate, no age.

Kashwam koham kutha āyatha ka mē janani ko mē tātah? Who are you and whose; whence have you come?

Wheresoever I am is my country, and I weep into my bed. I am ashamed to say

I weep a lot these days. I go to bed reading something, and some thought comes, I know not what—thoughts have no names—or have they?—and I lie on my bed and sob. Sometimes singing some chant of Sankara, I burst into sobs. Grandfather Kittanna used to say that sometimes the longing for ... becomes so great, so acute, you weep and that weeping has no name. Do I long for ...? ... is an object and I cannot long for him. I cannot long for a round, red thing, that one calls ..., and he becomes .... It would be like that statue down the road. I asked someone there, "What is this statue, Monsieur?" He was surprised and said, "Why, it's St Michel!" Since then I have known why this road here is called St Michel and that St Michel kills a dragon. Being a Brahmin I know about Indra and Prajapathi, but not about St Michel or St Denis. I will have to look into the Encyclopédie des religions. And that's not too helpful either. ..., in this Encyclopédie, has sixty-two pages, and they do not illuminate my need.

No, not a ... but a guru is what I need. "Oh Lord, my guru, my Lord," I cried, in the middle of this dreadful winter night. It was last night; the winds of April had arisen, the trees of the Luxembourg were crying till you could hear them like the triple oceans of the ... at Cape Comorin. "Lord, Lord, my guru, come to me, tell me; give me thy touch, vouch-safe," I cried, "the vision of Truth. Lord, my Lord."

I do not know where I went, but I was happy there, for it was free and broad like a sunny day and like a single broad white river it was. I had reached Benares—Benares. I had risen from the Ganges, and saw the luminous world, my home. I saw the silvery boat, and the boatman had a face I knew.

I knew His face, as one knows one's face in deep sleep. He called me, and said: "It is so long, so long my son. I have awaited you. Come, we go." I went, and man, I tell you, my brother, my friend, I will not return. I have gone whence there is no returning. To return you must not be. For if you are, where can you return? Do you, my brother, my friend, need a candle to show the light of the sun? Such a Sun I have seen, it is more splendid than a million suns. It sits on a river bank, it sits as the formless form of Truth; it walks without walking, speaks without talking, moves without gesticulating, shows without naming, reveals what is Known. To such a Truth was I taken, and I became its servant, I kissed the perfume of its Holy Feet, and called myself a disciple.

4

(Govindas Vishnudas Desani, 1909—2000)
戈温达斯·维什努达斯·德萨尼

作者简介

戈温达斯·维什努达斯·德萨尼（Govindas Vishnudas Desani, 1909—2000），美国印度裔剧作家、小说家，出生在肯尼亚的内罗毕（Nairobi, Kenya），父亲和母亲均是商人，从小接受私立教育。德萨尼于1926年前往英国，在那里开始了长达30年的记者生涯，之后又回到了印度。他于1934年成为《印度时报》（*Times of India*）的记者，1936年成为英国广播公司的广播员。1970年移居美国，先后任教于波士顿大学（Boston University）和得克萨斯大学奥斯汀分校。

1948年，德萨尼出版了他最重要的作品——小说《关于哈特尔的一切》（*All about H. Hatterr*），两年后又出版了戏剧《哈里》（*Hali*, 1950）。1952—1966年，德萨尼主要研究印度和缅甸的佛教与印度教文化。德萨尼在1960—1968年，曾为《印度画刊周报》（*Illustrated Weekly of India*）和《印度时报》撰稿。虽然德萨尼只写了一部小说、一部戏剧和少量的短篇小说，但他与同时代的多产作家如穆尔克·拉吉·阿南德（Mulk Raj Anand）、R. K. 纳拉扬（R. K. Narayan）和拉贾·劳（Raja Rao）等人地位相当。

《关于哈特尔的一切》被誉为一部喜剧杰作，是当年最畅销的书籍之一，讲述了一个年轻人在印度寻找真理的冒险故事。德萨尼将英语改造为一种语言混合体，凸显了一个重要的主题：不可能通过一个主叙述将各式各样的生活归结为一体，因为生活从根本上是荒谬的。德萨尼在表面的机智和幻想、语言的裂变和疯狂的冒险中，暗示了复杂的问题。选段出自小说《关于哈特尔的一切》第一部分，描述了哈特尔因欠下酒钱，被俱乐部开除后，再次决定接受东方传统的故事。

作品选读

All about H. Hatterr

I

(excerpt)

By Govindas Vishnudas Desani

She banged the door in my face.

She *refused* to take the money due to her!

The next step the parly took was downright singular!

She went to my club.

Damme, to a feller's club!

The Secretary tried to disperse her: and failed.

She remained on the premises, squatting on the green lawn, and wept loudly!

Facing the sundry sahibs and memsahibs, poised at'em at an alternating angle of forty-five degrees, a living metronome, the woman swang, pulled her hair, tore up her clothes, and wailed, "O my mothers and fathers! I am a poor woman! I am starving! My children are starving! H. Hatterr sahib owes me money! He owes me money!"

Damme, damme, damme!

Wham!

Fellers out East do away with themselves following such exhibitions against themselves!

The sahibs, who had reluctantly heard her poignant sorrow, were dumbfounded!

Right through the curry-courses, not a feller could cough up a single word, except such sundry expressions of pain as, "The fellah is a cad, sir!" "Gad, the man wants a birching!"

While commenting in this derogatory vein was going on behind my back, the Club Secretary, Harcourt Pankhurst-Sykes, summoned an extraordinary meeting.

And the agenda alleged that I, H. Hatterr, fellow-member of the Club, was letting down my brother-sahibs!

As a member of the Club, I owed on drinks, same as any other feller.

Black on white, and I was bound to honour the chits.

Yet, the Secretary held that too against me!

In the light of the exhibition made by the *dhobin*, extreme loss of confidence in my integrity prevailed in the Club.

At the extraordinary meeting, thank ..., ideals came to my rescue.

I avoided all mention of the *dhobin*.

I never gave away a woman, not even a *dhobin*!

And I spoke at the meeting concisely.

"If you censure me," I said to the fellers, "I won't disguise the fact that it would be a blow to my prestige. If the Club is so dam' keen on members' financial status quo, the Club should advance me a loan. I am forthwith applying to you for same. Otherwise, damme, Harcourt Pankhurst-Sykes, you can't touch me! Hands off, I say! Can't nail me to the barn-door for *nothing*! Otherwise, damme, I shall see the whole bunch of you in hell first! You can't hold lucre same as honour! Mark my words, damme, all of you!"

After being kept waiting for nearly four hours—during which time the extraordinary meeting were dealing with the liquor contractor, the scavenger's wage-increase application, every blasted thing but my matter—I was unanimously declared a defaulter, blackballed, and *struck off!*

Hell, did you ever!

I hadn't for a moment imagined that they would do that to me, swine fever to 'em! and all because of a *dhobin*!

When I heard the committee-decision, the earth beneath my feet felt like being pulled away by a supernatural sub-agent!

Till this happened, I don't mind admitting that I had regarded life as a bed of roses: and thorns absent.

I ate the finest chilly-hot curries in the land, did a good square job of it, remained a sahib, and life on the whole had been fine.

I walked from the Club, alone, and when in the digs, wept without restraint.

Banerrji called in soon after.

I told the feller I didn't wish to breathe no more. I meant to do the Dutch act to myself that very evening.

"Mr H. Hatterr," said my brother, upset to his foundations, "I have already heard that you have been mercilessly kicked out. I came to appeal, please, do not contemplate the drastic action! Life is sacred. No man may destroy same. Excuse me, but my heart bleeds for you! May I, therefore, make a present to you of this parcel of an all-in-one pantie-vest? It has just come from Bond Street of dear England. It is delightfully snug, made in Huddersfield, forming no wrinkles. Its colour is a charming peach, with a stylish elastic round the waist and the knees. Also, it has got gay little le-dandy motifs in lazy-daisy stitch, and will make a perfect foundation garment for you in the coming severe winter. Originally, I had ordered the parcel for my own use. Please accept it with my kindest regards."

This spontaneous gesture from a true friend, the gift of a valuable garment, and made out of pure love, braced me up instantly.

"Banerrji," I said, accepting the pantie, my eyes still red from the previous orgy of grief, "don't worry, old feller. I won't take the drastic step. To hell with the sahibs! Not an anna-piece for the drink chits! Not a ruddy chip! Damme, I will go Indian! Live like you fellers, your neighbourhood, and no dam' fears! Go to flannel dances! No fancy rags! The sahibs have kicked me. But for that kick, mark me, I will return ten, till the seats of their pants wear out!"

And, by all the pits of the Punjab country-side, I tried to do so, *and* live up to it!

I went completely Indian, and kicked out of the house the only sahib who came to condole!

The chap was the hearty sort, respected no institutions, and had made me wink off my real origin. He had got me into the Club under false pretences, as an India-born, pure Cento-per- Cento Anglo-Saxon breed. Consequence, used to flirt with the wife as his natural due.

To celebrate the bust-up with the feller, and, to spite the Club, I gave Banerrji the exclusive news-item for his uncle's fortnightly journal: "*Ex-member of the Sahib Club kicks a member out of the house! Mr Haakon K. Olsen, prominent Norwegian grid-bias battery manufacnurer, defies Thou shalt not covet thy neighbour's wife commandment! Involved in the eternal triangle! Alleged found making love 10 the ex-mem-ber's wife!*"

Thereupon, a social highlight by the name of A. Arnot-Smith, O.B.E., came to see me.

Said A-Smith, "It is the climate, old chap. Fellows can't help loving other fellows' wives. Gad, no need to kick up a row! Think of the Club, man! You are running down a fellow-European by allowing trash like this to be published in vernacular rags. Jerry Olsen's a scout. We don't wish to take notice, but if you want to prosecute the paper, the Club would render financial aid. It will all be confidential, of course. Sir Cyril and I strongly advise legal action."

I threw A. Arnot-Smith out of the house, and wished his ancestors, and Sir Cyril's, to a hotting up in Flames.

I told Banerrji of the facts.

"Do not let Mr Albion Arnot-Smith, O.B.E, persecute you," said my brother. "You may regard yourself as merely human. It is rightly said, *Sie vos non vobis*."

"What does it mean?"

"It is Latin. Nevertheless, I am saying, now that you have openly turned Indian, you don't have to depend on any O.B.E. of the sahib community for kind regards. You are going to be independent. As my best friend, you shall have a job too. I have arranged for an appointment for you. You meet tomorrow Mr Chari-Charier, the Indian extreme-wing gentleman. He will give you a journalistic job on his daily without question. He is a great friend of the underdog. Mr Chari-Charier himself was struck off from All Souls' College, Oxford. He has a very high regard for struck-off gentlemen."

5

(Ved Mehta, 1934—2021)
维德·梅塔

作者简介

维德·梅塔（Ved Mehta, 1934—2021），美国印度裔作家，生于英属印度时期的拉合尔（Lahore）（今巴基斯坦旁遮普省）的一个印度教家庭。他在三岁时因患脑膜炎不幸失明，五岁时被送到达德盲校（Dadar School for the Blind）学习盲文和英语。十四岁时来到美国，进入阿肯色州的盲人学校（Arkansas School for the Blind）接受正规教育。1956年梅塔在加州波莫纳学院（Pomona College）获得文学学士学位，1959年在牛津大学贝利奥尔学院（Balloil College, Oxford University）获得学士学位（现代历史专业），1961年获得哈佛大学（Harvard University）文学硕士学位。梅塔自学生时代起就为《纽约客》（New Yorker）撰稿，成为其长期特约作家，并在许多机构兼职客座教授。

梅塔著作颇丰，包括自传、小说、报告文学及散文等。第一本自传《面对面》（Face to Face, 1957）出版后，梅塔于1972—2004年陆续发表纪念性自传集《流亡大陆》（Continents of Exile）。该系列包括《父亲》（Daddyji, 1972）、《母亲》（Mamaji, 1979）、《新世界的声音阴影》（Sound-Shadows of the New World, 1984）以及《红色字母：我父亲的魔法时期》（Red Letters: My Father's Enchanted Period, 2004）等11本自传。1966年出版小说《少年恰恰》（Delinquent Chacha）。此外，他还出版了二十多本关于印度的报告文学、散文，其中包括《印度街头漫步》（Walking the Indian Streets, 1960）、《印度肖像》（Portrait of India, 1970）和《圣雄甘地和他的使徒》（Mahatma Gandhi and His Apostles, 1977）以及其他一些关于探索印度哲学、神学和语言学的作品。

梅塔是自传体文学的大师，也是印度英语文学的先驱，他荣获许多重要奖项，包括 1971 年的古根海姆奖（Guggenheim Fellowships）、1982 年的麦克阿瑟基金会（MacArthur Foundation）"天才奖"（Genius Grants）。他于 2009 年当选为英国皇家文学学会（Royal Society of Literature）的成员。梅塔被誉为"20 世纪以来，向美国读者介绍印度的最重要的作家"。他的作品以直率、清爽的文风，既有对印度社会的敏锐洞察，又有弥合东西方鸿沟的努力，揭示了美国和印度社会的复杂性及其不为人知的黑暗面。

《新世界的声音阴影》是梅塔具有代表性的自传作品之一，被收录在《生活在美国：美国南亚裔作家的诗歌和小说》（*Living in America: Poetry and Fiction by South Asian American Writers*, 1995）、《隔壁的世界：美国南亚裔文学》（*The World Next Door: South Asian American Literature*, 2004）等文学选集中。梅塔在书中讲述了他在美国阿肯色州盲人学校的前三年的经历。选段讲述了梅塔初入美国，在机场被美国移民官员质询的场景。

作品选读

Sound-Shadows of the New World
(excerpt)
By Ved Mehta

At the airport, I was questioned by an immigration official. "You're blind—totally blind—and they gave you a visa? You say it's for your studies, but studies where?"

"At the Arkansas School for the Blind. It is in Little Rock, in Arkansas."

He shuffled through the pages of a book. Sleep was in my eyes. Drops of sweat were running down my back. My shirt and trousers felt dirty.

"Arkansas School is not on our list of approved schools for foreign students."

"I know," I said. "That is why the immigration officials in Delhi gave me only a visitor's visa. They said that when I got to the school I should tell the authorities to apply to be on your list of approved schools, so that I could get a student visa." I showed him a big manila envelope I was carrying. It contained my chest X-rays, medical reports, and fingerprint charts, which were necessary for a student visa, and which I'd had prepared in advance.

"Why didn't you apply to an approved school in the first place and come here on a proper student visa?" he asked, looking through the material.

My knowledge of English was limited. With difficulty, I explained to him that I had applied to some thirty schools but that, because I had been able to get little formal education in India, the Arkansas School was the only one that would accept me; that I had needed a letter of acceptance from an American school to get dollars sanctioned by the Reserve Bank of India; and that now that I was in America I was sure I could change schools if the Arkansas School was not suitable or did not get the necessary approval.

Muttering to himself, the immigration official looked up at me, down at his book, and up at me again. He finally announced, "I think you'll have to go to Washington and apply to get your visa changed to a student visa before you can go to any school."

I recalled things that Daddyji used to say as we were growing up: "In life, there is only fight or flight. You must always fight," and "America is ...'s own country. People there are the most hospitable and generous people in the world." I told myself I had nothing to worry about. Then I remembered that Daddyji had mentioned a Mr. and Mrs. Dickens in Washington—they were friends of friends of his—and told me that I could get in touch with them in case of emergency.

"I will do whatever is necessary," I now said to the immigration official. "I will go to Washington."

He hesitated, as if he were thinking something, and then stamped my passport and returned it to me. "We Mehtas carry our luck with us," Daddyji used to say. He is right, I thought.

The immigration official suddenly became helpful, as if he were a friend. "You shouldn't have any trouble with the immigration people in Washington," he said, and asked, "Is anybody meeting you here?"

"Mr. and Mrs. di Francesco," I said.

Mrs. di Francesco was a niece of Manmath Nath Chatterjee, whom Daddyji had known when he himself was a student, in London, in 1920. Daddyji had asked Mr. Chatterjee, who had a Scottish-American wife and was now settled in Yellow Springs, Ohio, if he could suggest anyone with whom I might stay in New York, so that I could get acclimatized to America before proceeding to the Arkansas School, which was not due to open until the eleventh of September. Mr. Chatterjee had written back that, as it happened, his wife's niece was married to John di Francesco, a singer who was totally blind, and that Mr. and Mrs. di Francesco lived in New York, and would be delighted to meet me at the airport and keep me as a paying guest at fifteen dollars a week.

"How greedy of them to ask for money!" I had cried when I learned of the arrangement. "People come and stay with us for months and we never ask for an anna."

Daddyji had said, "In the West, people do not, as a rule, stay with relatives and friends but put up in hotels, or in houses as paying guests. That is the custom there. Mr. and Mrs. di Francesco are probably a young, struggling couple who could do with a little extra money."

The immigration official now came from behind the counter, led me to an open area, and shouted, with increasing volume, "Francisco!... Franchesca!... De Franco!" I wasn't sure what the correct pronunciation was, but his shouting sounded really disrespectful. I asked him to call for Mr. and Mrs. di Francesco softly. He bellowed, "Di Fransesco!"

No one came. My mouth went dry. Mr. and Mrs. di Francesco had sent me such a warm invitation. I couldn't imagine why they would have let me down or what I should do next.

Then I heard the footsteps of someone running toward us. "Here I am. You must be Ved. I'm Muriel di Francesco. I'm sorry John couldn't come." I noted that the name was pronounced the way it was spelled, and that hers was a Yankee voice—the kind I had heard when I first encountered Americans at home, during the war—but it had the sweetness of the voices of my sisters.

We shook hands; she had a nice firm grip. I had an impulse to call her Auntie Muriel—at home, an older person was always called by an honorific, like "Auntie" or "Uncle"—but I greeted her as Daddyji had told me that Westerners liked to be greeted: "Mrs. di Francesco, I'm delighted to make your acquaintance."

6

(G. S. Sharat Chandra, 1935—2000)
G. S. 沙拉特·钱德拉

作者简介

G. S. 沙拉特·钱德拉（G. S. Sharat Chandra, 1935—2000），美国印度裔诗人、小说家，出生于印度迈索尔（Mysore）。1962年前往加拿大学习法律，然后移民到美国，获得艾奥瓦作家工作室（Iowa Writers Workshop）创意写作硕士学位（M.F.A）。在他职业生涯的大部分时间里，钱德拉在密苏里-堪萨斯城大学（University of Missouri-Kansas City）担任创意写作和英语教授（1983—2000年）。

钱德拉因其诗歌和小说获得了国际认可。他的作品发表在许多期刊上，包括《美国诗歌评论》（*American Poetry Review*）、《伦敦杂志》（*London Magazine*）、《国家》（*The Nation*）和《党派评论》（*Partisan Review*）等。他曾担任富布赖特研究员（Fulbright Fellow），并获得NEA创意写作奖学金（NEA Fellowship in Creative Writing）等奖项。

钱德拉共出版了九本诗集，包括《婆罗多·纳蒂亚姆舞者和其他诗歌》（*Bharata Natyam Dancer and Other Poems*, 1968）、《这会是森林吗》（*Will This Forest*, 1968）、《留下来的理由》（*Reasons for Staying*, 1970）、《南瞻部洲的四月》（*April in Nanjangud*, 1971）、《一两次》（*Once or Twice*, 1974）、《意义的幽灵》（*The Ghost of Meaning*, 1978）、《传家宝》（*Heirloom*, 1982）、《镜子之家》（*Family of Mirrors*, 1993）和《失落的移民》（*Immigrants of Loss*, 1993）。此外，他还著有一部短篇小说集《神的纱丽》（*Sari of the Gods*, 1998）。诗集《镜子之家》获得1993年普利策奖诗歌奖提名。《失落的移民》获得1993年英联邦诗歌奖（Commonwealth Poetry Prize）和T. S. 艾略特诗歌奖（T. S. Eliot Poetry Prize）。

钱德拉的诗歌语言凝练而形象性强，具有鲜明的节奏、和谐的音韵和新鲜的音调，极具跳跃性和感染力。

　　诗歌《兄弟》("Brother")、《地震后的印度》("After the Earthquake in India")选自诗集《镜子之家》。《兄弟》表达了诗人在生活经历变迁之后对亲人的思念之情。在《地震后的印度》中，诗人运用拟人等手法描述地震后的印度惨状，刻画出萦绕在他心中的无力与悲伤情绪。

作品选读

Brother

By G. S. Sharat Chandra

Last night I arrived
a few minutes
before the storm,
on the lake the waves slow,
a gray froth cresting.
Again and again the computer voice said
you were disconnected
while the wind rattled
the motel sign outside my room
to gather
its nightlong arctic howl,
like an orphan moaning in sleep
for words in the ceaseless
pelting of sleet,

the night falling
to hold a truce with the dark

In the Botticellian stillness
of a clear dawn I drove

by the backroads to your house,
autumn leaves like a school of yellow tails
hitting the windshield
in a ceremony of bloodletting.

Your doorbell rang hollow,
I peered through the glass door,
for a moment I thought
my reflection was you
on the otherside,
staring back,
holding hands to my face.

It was only the blurred hold of memory
escaping through a field of glass.

Under the juniper bush
you planted when your wife died,
I found the discarded sale sign,

and looked for a window
where you'd prove me wrong
signaling to say
it was all a bad joke.

As I head back, I see the new
owners, pale behind car windows
driving to your house,
You're gone who knows where,
sliced into small portions
in the aisles of dust and memory.

After the Earthquake in India

By G. S. Sharat Chandra

It's a habit by now
head bent
at four a.m., the birds wake
to complain

they do this cackling in
forgotten dialects of the poor

yesterday's count was thirty-one-thousand
as if longing for more

the morning news will bring
more bodies to the surface

counting is one way
of thinning the eye
to a diet of faith

someone says if there's divine justice
it favors solid foundations

mud & rock slip through ...'s fingers

we can discuss this at length

but if prayers are shouts
pain is the lost argument

7

(Bapsi Sidhwa, 1938—)
巴普西·西德瓦

作者简介

巴普西·西德瓦（Bapsi Sidhwa, 1938— ），美国巴基斯坦裔小说家，出生于卡拉奇（Karachi）。因为从小患有小儿麻痹症，所以她在15岁之前都在家里接受教育，在拉合尔的金纳德女子学院（Kinnaird College for Women）获得文学学士学位。她19岁结婚后，从事社会工作，代表巴基斯坦参加了1974年的亚洲妇女大会（Asian Women's Congress）。在1975—1977年任拉合尔国际妇女俱乐部（International Women's Club of Lahore）主席。西德瓦曾于1994—1996年担任总理妇女发展咨询委员会委员（Advisory Committee to Prime Minister on Women's Development）。1984年移民美国后，在莱斯大学（Rice University）创办小说写作讲习班。她曾任休斯顿大学（University of Houston）创意写作助理教授，也曾任教于美国哥伦比亚大学（Columbia University）、布兰代斯大学（Brandeis University）及南安普顿大学（University of Southampton）。现居住在休斯敦。

她的主要作品包括小说《食乌鸦者》（*The Crow Eaters*, 1978）、《新娘》（*The Bride*, 1983）、《冰糖果人》（*Ice Candy Man*, 1988）、《一个美国小孩》（*An American Brat*, 1993）和《水》（*Water*, 2006）。《冰糖果人》这部小说在1991年的美国版中更名为《分裂的印度》（*Cracking India*），1998年被加拿大导演迪帕·梅塔（Deepa Mehta）翻拍成了电影《大地》（*Earth*）。这部影片曾获当年奥斯卡最佳外语电影奖提名。2008年，《一个美国小孩》以舞台剧形式在休斯敦上演。此外，西德瓦还编辑了一本选集《罪恶与辉煌之城：拉合尔著述》（*City of Sin and Splendor: Writings on Lahore*, 2006）。西德瓦的创作主题包括种族和宗教差异、后殖民和散居的遗产，以及想象中的国家和跨国关系。

西德瓦的作品已被翻译成多种语言，包括意大利语、法语和俄语，并且荣获了许多奖项，包括1987年国家艺术基金奖（National Endowment for the Arts Grant）、1991年巴基斯坦艺术最高奖项（Sitara-I-Imtiaz）、1993年美国莱拉·华莱士－读者文摘奖（Lila Wallace-Reader's Digest Award）、德国文学奖（Liberaturpreis in Germany）、英联邦作家奖（Commonwealth Writers' Prize）、意大利蒙德罗奖（Italian Mondello Award）以及2008年索尼亚洲电视南亚优秀文学奖（Sony Asia TV's South Asian Excellence Award for Literature）等各类奖项。西德瓦是第一个被列入琐罗亚斯德教女性名人堂（Hall of Fame for Women of the Zoroastrian）的作家。

《分裂的印度》是西德瓦最著名的一部小说，是由女性发表的关于印度独立和分割的最早文本之一。小说从儿童莱尼（Lenny）的叙述角度出发，通过塑造其印度教保姆阿雅（Ayah）的角色，表现了女性身体在国家冲突中易受虐待的脆弱性。选段部分出自《分裂的印度》第二十三章，讲述了一群暴徒来到莱尼家后将保姆阿雅带走的过程。

《一个美国小孩》是西德瓦另外一部颇具影响力的作品。讲述了在巴基斯坦日益高涨的宗教激进主义浪潮下，16岁的费洛莎·金瓦拉（Feroza Ginwalla）被家人送往美国的冒险经历。节选部分讲述了费洛莎·金瓦拉初到美国时，在面对机场移民官员的各种检查和盘问之下，终于与叔叔相见。西德瓦让我们从新移民的角度来看待美国人，同时温和地阐明宗教激进主义对一种文化和个人的潜在破坏性影响。

作品选读

Cracking India

Chapter 23

(excerpt)

By Bapsi Sidhwa

Ayah is not on the veranda. She has disappeared.

"Where's Ayah?" I ask. I'm hushed by a hiss of whispers. Mother communicates a quick, secret warning that is reflected on all faces. Ayah is Hindu. The situation with all its implications is clear. She must hide. We all have a part to play. My intelligence and complicity are taken for granted.

Then they are roaring and charging up our drive, wheels creaking, hooves clattering as the whipped horses stretch their scabby necks and knotted hocks to haul the load for the short gallop. Up the drive come the charioteers, feet planted firmly in shallow carts, in singlets and clinging linen lungis, shoulders gleaming in the bright sun. Calculating men, whose ideals and passions have cooled to ice.

They pour into our drive in an endless cavalry and the looters jump off in front of the kitchen as the carts make room for more carts and the portico and drive are filled with men and horses; some of the horses' noses already in the feed bags around their necks. The men in front are quiet—tike merchants going about their business—but those stalled in the choked drive and on the road chant perfunctorily.

The men's eyes, lined with black antimony, rake us. Note the doors behind us and assess the well-tended premises with its surfeit of pots holding ferns and palm fronds. A hesitancy sparks in their brash eyes when they look at our mother. Flanked by her cubs, her hands resting on our heads, she is the noble embodiment of theatrical motherhood. Undaunted. Endearing. Her cut-crystal lips set in a defiant pucker beneath her tinted glasses and her cropped, waved hair.

Men gather round Yousaf and Hari asking questions, peering here and there. Papoo and I, holding hands, step down into the porch. Mother doesn't stop us.

Still beating eggs, aluminum bowl in hand, Imam Din suddenly fills the open kitchen doorway. He bellows: "What d'you *haramzadas* think you're up to?" There is a lull in the processionists' clamor. Even the men on the road hear him and suspend their desultory chanting. The door snaps shut and Imam Din stands on the kitchen steps looking bomb-bellied and magnificently *goondaish*—the grandfather of all the *goondas* milling about us—with his shaven head, hennaed beard and grimy lungi.

"Where are the Hindus?" a man shouts.

"There are no Hindus here! ... There are no Hindus here!"

"There are Hindu nameplates on the gates ... Shankar and Sethi!"

"The Shankars took off long ago... They were Hindu. The Sethis are Parsee. I serve them. Sethi is a Parsee name too, you ignorant bastards!"

The men look disappointed and shedding a little of their surety and arrogance look at Imam Din as at an elder. Imam Din's manner changes. He descends among them, bowl and fork in hand, a Mussulman among Muslims. Imam Din's voice is low, conversational. He goes into the kitchen and brings out a large pan of water with ice cubes floating in it. He and Yousaf hand out the water in frosted aluminum glasses.

"Where's Hari, the gardener?" someone from the back shouts.

"Hari-the-gardener has become Himat Ali!" says Imam Din, roaring genially and glancing at the gardener.

Himat Ali's resigned, dusky face begins to twitch nervously as some men move towards him.

"Let's make sure," a man says, hitching up his lungi, his swaggering gait bent on mischief. "Undo your shalwar, Himat Ali. Let's see if you're a proper Muslim." He is young and very handsome.

"He's Ramzana-the-butcher's brother," says Papoo, nudging me excitedly.

I notice the resemblance to the butcher. And then the men are no longer just fragmented parts of a procession: they become individual personalities whose faces I study, seeking friends.

......

The men let it pass.

"Where is the sweeper? Where's Moti?" shouts a hoarse Punjabi voice. It sounds familiar but I can't place it.

"He's here," says Yousaf, putting an arm round Moti. "He's become a believer... A Christian. Behold... Mister David Masih!"

The men smile and joke: "O ho! He's become a black-faced gen-tle-man! Mister sweeper David Masih! Next he'll be sailing off to Eng-a-land and marrying a memsahib!"

And then someone asks, "Where's the Hindu woman? The ayah!"

There is a split second's silence before Imam Din's reassuring voice calmly says: "She's gone."

"She's gone nowhere! Where is she?"

"I told you. She left Lahore."

"When?"

"Yesterday."

"He's lying," says the familiar voice again. "Oye, Imam Din, why are you lying?" I recognize the voice. It is Butcher.

"*Oye, Baray Mian!* Don't disgrace your venerable beard!"

"For shame, old man! And you so close to meeting your Maker!"

"Lying does not become your years, you old goat."

The raucous voices are turning ugly.

......

I study the men's faces in the silence that follows. Some of them still don't believe him. Some turn away, or look at the ground. It is an oath a Muslim will not take lightly.

Something strange happened then. The whole disorderly melee dissolved and consolidated into a single face. The face, amber-eyed, spread before me: hypnotic, reassuring, blotting out the ugly frightening crowd. Ice-candy-man's versatile face transformed into a savior's in our hour of need.

Ice-candy-man is crouched before me. "Don't be scared, Lenny baby," he says. "I'm here." And putting his arms around me he whispers, so that only I can hear: "I'll protect Ayah with my life! You know I will... I know she's here. Where is she?"

And dredging from some foul truthful depth in me a fragment of overheard conversation that I had not registered at the time, I say: "On the roof—or in one of the godowns... "

Ice-candy-man's face undergoes a subtle change before my eyes, and as he slowly uncoils his lank frame into an upright position, I know I have betrayed Ayah.

The news is swiftly transmitted. In a daze I see Mother approach, her face stricken. Adi and Papoo look at me out of stunned faces. There is no judgment in their eyes—no reproach—only stone-faced incredulity.

Imam Din and Yousaf are taking small steps back, their arms spread, as three men try to push past. "Where're you going? You can't go to the back! Our women are there, they observe purdah!" says Imam Din, again futilely lying. The men are not aggressive, their game is at hand. It is only a matter of minutes. And while the three men insouciantly confront Imam Din and Yousaf, other men, eyes averted, slip past them.

I cannot see Butcher. Ice-candy-man too has disappeared.

"No!" I scream. "She's gone to Amritsar!"

I try to run after them but Mother holds me. I butt my head into her, bouncing it off her stomach, and every time I throw my head back, I see Adi and Papoo's stunned faces.

The three men shove past Imam Din and something about their insolent and determined movements affects the proprieties that have restrained the mob so far.

They move forward from all points. They swarm into our bedrooms, search the servants' quarters, climb to the roofs, break locks and enter our godowns and the small storerooms near the bathrooms.

They drag Ayah out. They drag her by her arms stretched taut, and her bare feet—that want to move backwards—are forced forward instead. Her lips are drawn away from her teeth, and the resisting curve of her throat opens her mouth like the dead child's screamless mouth. Her violet sari slips off her shoulder, and her breasts strain at her sari-blouse stretching the cloth so that the white stitching at the seams shows. A sleeve tears under her arm.

An American Brat
(excerpt)
By Bapsi Sidhwa

Her wide-open eyes soaking in the new impressions as she pushed the cart, a strange awareness seeped into Feroza: She knew no one, and no one knew her! It was a heady feeling to be suddenly so free—for the moment, at least—of the thousand constraints that governed her life.

The two panels of a heavy exit door at the far end opened to allow a stack of crates to pass, and, suddenly, Feroza saw Manek leaning against the demarcation railing just outside the exit. One ankle comfortably crossed over the other, arms patiently folded, Manek had peered into the abruptly revealed interior also.

After an initial start, and without the slightest change in his laid-back posture, he at once contorted his features to display a gamut of scatty emotions—surprise, confusion, helplessness—to reflect Feroza's presumed condition. At the same time, he raised a languid forearm from the elbow and waved his hand from side to side like a mechanical paw.

Feroza squealed and waved her whole arm and, with a huge grin on her face, steered the cart towards him. She was so excited, and also relieved, to see him. Even from the distance, his skin looked lighter, his face fuller. He had grown a mustache. Knowing him as she did, his deliberate insouciance and the regal wave of the mechanical paw filled her with delight. He hadn't changed as much as her mother had imagined. He was the same old Manek, except he was really glad to see her. Three years of separation have a mellowing effect, make remembered ways dearer. Feroza's heart filled with affection for her former tormentor. Having no brothers, she hadn't realized how much she missed him.

A woman in a blue uniform, stationed at a counter to the left of Feroza's path, checked her. "Hey! You can't leave the terminal. Your passport, please." She held out her hand.

The woman read the white slip inserted in the passport. She looked sternly at Feroza. "You must go for secondary inspection." Again the cryptic instruction.

The woman said something to a man in a white shirt and navy pants standing by her. She showed him the slip and gave him Feroza's passport.

Feroza noticed the "Immigration" badge pinned to the man's shirt. He motioned to her.

As she followed him, Feroza quickly glanced back at the exit to see if Manek was still there, but the heavy metal panels were closed. An inset door in one of the panels opened just enough to let the passengers and their carts through, one at a time.

Feroza followed the immigration officer past the row of ribbonlike wooden counters. A few open suitcases lay on them at uneven distances. These were being searched by absorbed customs inspectors who acted as if they had all the time in the world at their disposal. The weary passengers standing before their disarrayed possessions looked subdued and, as happens when law-abiding citizens are accosted with unwarranted suspicion, unaccountably guilty.

The man led her to the very last counter and told her to place her bags on it.

Applying leverage with her legs, struggling with the stiff leather straps that bound the suitcases, Feroza hoisted the bags, one by one, to the counter.

"Are you a student?" he asked.

"What?" The officer leaned forward in response to Feroza's nervous mumbling and cupped his ear. He had slightly bulging, watery blue eyes and a moist, pale face that called to Feroza's mind images of soft-boiled eggs.

"What're you speaking—English? Do you want an interpreter?"

"No." Feroza shook her head and, managing a somewhat louder pitch, breathlessly repeated, "I'm a tourist."

"I'm an officer of the United States Immigration and Naturalization Service, authorized by law to take testimony."

The man spoke gravely, and it took Feroza a while to realize he was reciting something he must have parroted hundreds of times.

"I desire to take your sworn statement regarding your application for entering the United States. Are you willing to answer my questions at this time?"

"Y-es," Feroza stammered, her voice a doubtful quaver.

Why was she being asked to give sworn statements? Was it normal procedure?

"Do you swear that all the statements you are about to make will be the truth, the whole truth, and nothing but the truth, so help you ...?"

Feroza looked at the man, speechless, then numbly nodded. "Yes."

"If you give false testimony in this proceeding, you may be prosecuted for perjury. If you are convicted of perjury, you can be fined two thousand dollars or imprisoned for not more than five years, or both. Do you understand?"

"Y-yes." By now Feroza's pulse was throbbing.

"Please speak up. What is your complete and correct name?"

"Feroza Cyrus Ginwalla."

"Are you known by any other name?"

"No."

"What is your date of birth?"

"November 19, 1961."

He asked her where she was born, what her nationality was, her Pakistan address, her parents' address. Had her parents ever applied for U. S. citizenship? Was she single or married? Did she have any relatives in the United States? Anyone else besides her uncle?

"How long do you wish to stay in the United States?"

"Two or three months."

"What'll it be? Two months or three months? Don't you know?"

"Probably three months."

"Probably?"

The officer had placed a trim, booted foot on the counter; her green passport was open on his knee. His soft-boiled, lashless eyes were looking at Feroza with such humiliating mistrust that Feroza's posture instinctively assumed the stolid sheath of dignity that had served her so well since childhood.

"Where will you reside in the United States?" The officer appeared edgy, provoked by her haughty air.

An olive-skinned Hispanic customs inspector in a pale gray uniform sauntered up to them. He had rebellious, straight black hair that fell over his narrow, close-set eyes.

"With my uncle," Feroza said.

"*Where will you* stay... What is the *address*?"

The officer spoke with exaggerated patience, as if asking the question for the tenth time of an idiot.

"I don't know," Feroza answered, her offended expression concealing how stupid she felt, how intimidated.

"You don't know?" The man appeared to be suddenly in a rage. "You should know!"

But why was he so angry?

The Hispanic customs inspector with the unruly hair indicated a suitcase with a thrust of his chin. "Open it." He sounded crude and discomfitingly foreign to Feroza.

Rummaging in her handbag, Feroza withdrew a tiny key and tried clumsily to fit it into the lock.

"What is your uncle's occupation?" her interrogator asked. "Can he support you?"

"He's a student. But he also works at two other jobs to make extra money."

She had stepped into the trap. Didn't she know it was a crime for foreign students to work, he asked. Her uncle would be hauled before an immigration judge and, most likely, deported. She would have to go back on the next available flight. He knew she was a liar. She had no uncle in America. Her so-called "uncle" was in fact her fiancé. He wished to point out that she was making false statements; would she now speak the truth?

Feroza could not credit what her ears heard. Her eyes were smarting. The fear that had lain dormant during the fight, manifesting itself only in an unnoticed flutter of her heart, now sprang into her consciousness like a wild beast and made her heart pound. "I'm telling you the truth," she said shakily.

Sensing that some people were staring at them, Feroza cast her eyes down and took a small step, backing away from the luggage, wishing to disassociate herself from the intolerable scene the man was creating. The key dangled in the tiny lock.

"Open your bags," the customs inspector said, intent on his duty. He sounded hostile.

Feroza fumbled with the lock again. She unbuckled the leather straps, pressed open the snaps, and lifted the lid. She opened the other suitcase.

8

(Bharati Mukherjee, 1940—2017)
巴拉蒂·慕克吉

作者简介

巴拉蒂·慕克吉（Bharati Mukherjee, 1940—2017），美国印度裔小说家和社会评论家，出生于印度加尔各答，自幼接受英国传统式教育。慕克吉1959年从加尔各答大学毕业，1961年获得英语和印度古代文化硕士学位，同年进入艾奥瓦大学作家工作室学习，1969年获得艾奥瓦大学比较文学博士学位。慕克吉本打算返回印度，但她在艾奥瓦与加拿大/美国作家克拉克·布莱斯（Clark Blaise）相识，随后两人决定成婚。慕克吉获得博士学位后，在加拿大麦克吉尔大学（McGill University）等高校执教十余年后返回美国定居。她曾在纽约城市大学（City University of New York）和加州大学伯克利分校任教。

慕克吉著有小说和散文。她的主要作品有长篇小说《老虎的女儿》（*The Tiger's Daughter*, 1971）、《妻子》（*Wife*, 1975）、《茉莉花》（*Jasmine*, 1989）、《坐拥世界》（*The Holder of the World*, 1993）、《称心的女儿》（*Desirable Daughters*, 2002）和短篇小说集《黑暗》（*Darkness*, 1983）、《中介》（*The Middleman and Other Stories*, 1988）。慕克吉与克拉克·布莱斯合著回忆录《加尔各答的日日夜夜》（*Days and Nights in Calcutta*, 1986）和《悲情与恐怖：印度航空公司惨案遗事》（*The Sorrow and the Terror: The Haunting Legacy of the Air India Tragedy*, 1987）。慕克吉曾凭借短篇小说集《中介》获1988年美国国家图书评论界奖（National Book Critics Circle Award）。慕克吉坚持小说创作，笔耕不辍。慕克吉认为自己是一名美国作家，而非印度移民作家。她的作品描写印度移民在美国的生活，不仅表现了作者对保持印度传统的自豪感，还反映了她融入美国的喜悦之情。

《房客》("The Tenant")选自短篇小说集《中介》，获评1987年美国最佳短篇小说(The Best Amerian Short Stories 1987)。小说女主人公马娅(Maya Sanyal)在美国大学教授世界文学，自认为是美国人，可是却受到印度传统文化的束缚。小说塑造了一个"解放的"印度女性形象，反映印度移民在两种文化中的孤独感和漂泊感。节选部分讲述经历婚姻失败、倍感孤独的马娅在异国他乡联系征婚人的故事。小说《称心的女儿》具有自传色彩，讲述出生于印度上层社会的三姐妹从古老印度到现代美国的不同的人生旅程。小说情节扣人心弦，可读性强。选读部分出自《称心的女儿》第一章，介绍三姐妹中最小的妹妹塔拉(Tara)的包办婚姻。

作品选读

The Tenant

(excerpt)

By Bharati Mukherjee

The next day, Monday, instead of getting a ride home with Fran—Fran says she likes to give rides, she needs the chance to talk, and she won't share gas expenses, absolutely not—Maya goes to the periodicals room of the library. There are newspapers from everywhere, even from Madagascar and New Caledonia. She thinks of the periodicals room as an asylum for homesick aliens. There are two aliens already in the room, both Orientals, both absorbed in the politics and gossip of their far off homes.

She goes straight to the newspapers from India. She bunches her raincoat like a bolster to make herself more comfortable. There's so much to catch up on. A village headman, a known Congress-Indira party worker, has been shot at by scooter-riding snipers. An Indian pugilist has won an international medal—in Nepal. A child drawing well water—the reporter calls the child "a neo-Buddhist, a convert from the now-outlawed untouchable caste"—has been stoned. An editorial explains that the story about stoning is not a story about caste but about failed idealism; a story about promises of green fields and clean, potable water broken, a story about bribes paid and wells not dug. But no, thinks Maya, it's about caste.

Out here, in the heartland of the new world, the India of serious newspapers unsettles. Maya longs again to feel what she had felt in the Chatterjis' living room: virtues made physical. It is a familiar feeling, a longing. Had a suitable man presented himself in the reading room at that instant, she would have seduced him. She goes on to the stack of *India Abroads*, reads through matrimonial columns, and steals an issue to take home.

Indian men want Indian brides. Married Indian men want Indian mistresses. All over America, "handsome, tall, fair" engineers, doctors, data processors—the new pioneers—cry their eerie love calls.

Maya runs a finger down the first column; her finger tip, dark with newsprint, stops at random.

Hello! Hi! Yes, you *are* the one I'm looking for. You are the new emancipated Indo-American woman. You have a zest for life. You are at ease in USA and yet your ethics are rooted in Indian tradition. The man of your dreams has come. Yours truly is handsome, ear-nose-throat specialist, well-settled in Connecticut. Age is 41 but never married, physically fit, sportsmanly, and strong. I adore idealism, poetry, beauty. I abhor smugness, passivity, caste system. Write with recent photo. Better still, call!!!

Maya calls. Hullo, hullo, hullo! She hears immigrant lovers cry in crowded shopping malls. Yes, you who are at ease in both worlds, you are the one. She feels she has a fair chance.

A man answers. "Ashoke Mehta speaking."

She speaks quickly into the bright-red mouthpiece of her telephone. He will be in Chicago, in transit, passing through O'Hare. United counter, Saturday, two p.m. As easy as that.

"Good," Ashoke Mehta says. "For these encounters I, too, prefer a neutral zone."

On Saturday at exactly two o'clock the man of Maya's dreams floats toward her as lovers used to in shampoo commercials. The United counter is a loud, harassed place but passengers and piled-up luggage fall away from him. Full-cheeked and fleshy-lipped, he is handsome. He hasn't lied. He is serene, assured, a Hindu ... touching down in Illinois.

She can't move. She feels ugly and unworthy. Her adult life no longer seems miraculously rebellious; it is grim, it is perverse. She has accomplished nothing. She has changed her citizenship but she hasn't broken through into the light, the vigor, the *hustle* of the New World. She is stuck in dead space.

"Hullo, hullo!" Their fingers touch.

Oh, the excitement! Ashoke Mehta's palm feels so right in the small of her back. Hullo, hullo, hullo. He pushes her out of the reach of anti-Khomeini Iranians, Hare Krishnas, American Fascists, men with fierce wants, and guides her to an empty gate. They have less than an hour.

"What would you like, Maya?"

She knows he can read her mind, she knows her thoughts are open to him. *You,* she's almost giddy with the thought, with simple desire. "From the snack bar," he says, as though to clarify. "I'm afraid I'm starved."

Below them, where the light is strong and hurtful, a Boeing is being serviced. "Nothing," she says.

He leans forward. She can feel the nap of his scarf—she recognizes the Cambridge colors—she can smell the wool of his Icelandic sweater. She runs her hand along the scarf, then against the flesh of his neck. "Only the impulsive ones call," he says.

The immigrant courtship proceeds. It's easy, he's good with facts. He knows how to come across to a stranger who may end up a lover, a spouse. He makes over a hundred thousand. He owns a house in Hartford, and two income properties in Newark. He plays the market but he's cautious. He's good at badminton but plays handball to keep in shape. He watches all the sports on television. Last August he visited Copenhagen, Helsinki and Leningrad. Once upon a time he collected stamps but now he doesn't have hobbies, except for reading. He counts himself an intellectual, he spends too much on books. Ludlum, Forsyth, MacInnes; other names she doesn't catch. She suppresses a smile, she's told him only she's a graduate student. He's not without his vices. He's a spender, not a saver. He's a sensualist: good food—all foods, but easy on the Indian—good wine. Some temptations he doesn't try to resist.

And I, she wants to ask, do I tempt?

"Now tell me about yourself, Maya." He makes it easy for her. "Have you ever been in love?"

"No."

"But many have loved you, I can see that." He says it not unkindly. It is the fate of women like her, and men like him. Their karmic duty, to be loved. It is expected, not judged. She feels he can see them all, the sad parade of need and demand. This isn't the time to reveal all.

And so the courtship enters a second phase.

When she gets back to Cedar Falls, Ted Suminski is standing on the front porch.

It's late at night, chilly. He is wearing a down vest. She's never seen him on the porch. In fact there's no chair to sit on. He looks chilled through. He's waited around a while.

"Hi." She has her keys ready. This isn't the night to offer the sixpack in the fridge. He looks expectant, ready to pounce.

"Hi." He looks like a man who might have aimed the dart at her. What has he done to his wife, his kids? Why isn't there at least a dog? "Say, I left a note upstairs."

The note is written in Magic Marker and thumb-tacked to her apartment door. DUE TO PERSONAL REASONS, NAMELY REMARRIAGE, I REQUEST THAT YOU VACATE MY PLACE AT THE END OF THE SEMESTER.

Maya takes the note down and retacks it to the kitchen wall. The whole wall is like a bulletin board, made of some new, crumbly building-material. Her kitchen, Ted Suminski had told her, was once a child's bedroom. Suminski in love: the idea stuns her. She has misread her landlord. The dart at her window speaks of no twisted fantasy. The landlord wants the tenant out.

She gets a glass out of the kitchen cabinet, gets out a tray of ice, pours herself a shot of Fran's bourbon. She is happy for Ted Suminski. She is. She wants to tell someone how moved she'd been by Mrs. Chatterji's singing. How she'd felt in O'Hare, even about Dr. Rab Chatterji in the car. But Fran is not the person. No one she's ever met is the person. She can't talk about the dead space she lives in. She wishes Ashoke Mehta would call. Right now.

Weeks pass. Then two months. She finds a new room, signs another lease. Her new landlord calls himself Fred. He has no arms, but he helps her move her things. He drives between Ted Suminski's place and his twice in his station wagon. He uses his toes the way Maya uses her fingers. He likes to do things. He pushes garbage sacks full of Maya's clothes up the stairs.

"It's all right to stare," Fred says. "Hell, I would."

That first afternoon in Fred's rooming house, they share a Chianti. Fred wants to cook her pork chops but he's a little shy about Indians and meat. Is it beef, or pork? Or any meat? She says it's okay, any meat, but not tonight. He has an ex-wife in Des Moines, two kids in Portland, Oregon. The kids are both normal; he's the only freak in the family. But he's self-reliant. He shops in the supermarket like anyone else, he carries out the garbage, shovels the snow off the sidewalk. He needs Maya's help with one thing. Just one thing. The box of Tide is a bit too heavy to manage. Could she get him the giant size every so often and leave it in the basement?

The dead space need not suffocate. Over the months, Fred and she will settle into companionship. She has never slept with a man without arms. Two wounded people, he will joke during their nightly contortions. It will shock her, this assumed equivalence with a man so strikingly deficient. She knows she is strange, and lonely, but being Indian is not the same, she would have thought, as being a freak.

One night in spring, Fred's phone rings. "Ashoke Mehta speaking." None of this "do you remember me?" nonsense. The ... has tracked her down. He hasn't forgotten. "Hullo," he says, in their special way. And because she doesn't answer back, "Hullo, hullo, hullo." She is aware of Fred in the back of the room. He is lighting a cigarette with his toes.

"Yes," she says, "I remember."

"I had to take care of a problem," Ashoke Mehta says. "You know that I have my vices. That time at O'Hare I was honest with you."

She is breathless.

"Who is it, May?" asks Fred.

"You also have a problem," says the voice. His laugh echoes. "You will come to Hartford, I know."

When she moves out, she tells herself, it will not be the end of Fred's world.

Desirable Daughters

Chapter One

(excerpt)

By Bharati Mukherjee

In the mind's eye, a one-way procession of flickering oil lamps sways along the muddy shanko between rice paddies and flooded ponds, and finally disappears into a distant wall of impenetrable jungle. Banks of fog rise from warmer waters, mingle with smoke from the cooking fires, and press in a dense sooty collar, a permeable gray wall that parts, then seals, igniting a winter chorus of retching coughs and loud spitting. Tuberculosis is everywhere. The air, the water, the soil are septic. Thirty-five years is a long life. Smog obscures the moon and dims the man-made light to faintness deeper than the stars'. In such darkness perspective disappears. It is a two-dimensional world impossible to penetrate. But for the intimacy of shared discomfort, it is difficult even to estimate the space separating each traveler.

The narrow, raised trail stretches ten miles from Mishtigunj town to the jungle's edge. In a palanquin borne by four servants sit a rich man's three daughters, the youngest dressed in her bridal sari, her little hands painted with red lac dye, her hair oiled and set. Her arms are heavy with dowry gold; bangles ring tiny arms from wrist to shoulder. Childish voices chant a song, hands clap, gold bracelets tinkle. I cannot imagine the loneliness of this child. A Bengali girl's happiest night is about to become her lifetime imprisonment. It seems all the sorrow of history, all that is unjust in society and cruel in religion has settled on her. Even constructing it from the merest scraps of family memory fills me with rage and bitterness.

The bride-to-be whispers the "Tush Tusli Brata," a hymn to the sacredness of marriage, a petition for a kind and generous husband:

> *What do I hope for in worshipping you? That my father's wisdom be endless. My mother's kindness bottomless. May my husband be as powerful as a king of .... May my future son-in-law light up the royal court. Bestow on me a brother who is learned and intellectual, A son as handsome as the best-looking courtier. And a daughter who is beauteous. Let my hair-part glow red with vermilion powder, as a wife's should. On my wrists and arms, let bangles glitter and jangle. Load down my clothes-rack with the finest saris. Fill my kitchen with scoured-shiny utensils. Reward my wifely virtue with a rice-filled granary. These are the boons that this young virgin begs of thee.*

In a second, larger palki borne by four men sit the family priest and the father of the bride. Younger uncles and cousins follow in a vigilant file. Two more guards, sharp-bladed daos drawn, bring up the rear. Two servants walk ahead of the eight litter-bearers, holding naphtha lamps. No one has seen such brilliant European light, too strong to stare into, purer white than the moon. It is a town light, a rich man's light, a light that knows English invention. If bandits are crouching in the gullies they will know to strike this reckless Hindu who announces his wealth with light and by arming his servants. What treasures lie inside, how much gold and jewels, what target ripe for kidnapping? The nearest town, where such a wealthy man must have come from, lies behind him. Only the jungle lies ahead. Even the woodcutters desert it at night, relinquishing it to goondahs and marauders, snakes and tigers.

The bride is named Tara Lata, a name we almost share. The name of the father is Jai Krishna Gangooly. Tara Lata is five years old and headed deep into the forest to marry a tree.

I have had the time, the motivation, and even the passion to undertake this history. When my friends, my child, or my sisters ask me why, I say I am exploring the making of a consciousness. Your consciousness? they tease, and I tell them, No. Yours.

On this night, flesh-and-blood emerges from the unretrievable past. I have Jai Krishna's photo, I know the name of Jai Krishna's father, but they have always been ghosts. But Tara Lata is not, nor will her father be, after the events of this special day. And so my history begins with a family wedding on the coldest, darkest night in the Bengali month of Paush—December/January—in a district of the Bengal Presidency that lies east of Calcutta—now Kolkata—and south of Dacca—now Dhaka—as the English year of 1879 is about to shed its final two digits, although the Hindu year of 1285 still has four months to run and the Muslim year of 1297 has barely begun.

(......)

And so, the story of the three great-granddaughters of Jai Krishna Gangooly starts on the day of a wedding, a few hours before the palki ride where fates have already been decided, in the decorated ancestral house of the Gangoolys on the river in Mishtigunj town. The decorations signify a biye-bari, a wedding house. Beggars have already camped in the alleys adjacent to the canopy under which giant copper vats of milk, stirred by professional cooks, have been boiling and thickening for sweet-meats, and where other vats, woks, and cauldrons receive the chunks of giant hilsa fish netted fresh from the river and hold the rice pilao, lamb curry, spiced lentils, and deep-fried and saucesteeped vegetables, a feast for a thousand invited guests and the small city of self-invited men, women, and children camped outside the gates.

The astrologers have spoken; the horoscopes have been compared. The match between Jai Krishna's youngest daughter and a thirteen-year-old youth, another Kuhn Brahmin from an upright and pious family from a nearby village, has been blessed. The prewedding religious rites have been meticulously performed, and the prewedding stree-achar, married women's rituals, boisterously observed. To protect the husband-to-be from poisonous snakebite, married women relatives and Brahmin women neighbors have propitiated ... Manasha with prescribed offerings.

All of this has been undertaken at a moment in the evolution of Jai Krishna from student of Darwin and Bentham and Comte and practitioner of icy logic, to reader of the Upanishads and believer in Vedic wisdom. He had become a seeker of truth, not a synthesizer of cultures. He found himself starting arguments with pleaders and barristers, those who actually favored morning toast with marmalade, English suits, and leather shoes. Now nearing forty, he was in full flight from his younger self joining a debate that was to split bhadra lok society between progressives and traditionalists for over a century.

A Dacca barrister, Keshub Miner, teased him for behaving more like a once-rich Muslim nawab wedded to a fanciful past and visions of lost glory than an educated, middle-class Hindu lawyer. Everyone knew that the Indian past was a rubbish heap of shameful superstition. Keshub Miner's insult would have been unforgivable if it hadn't been delivered deftly, with a smile and a Bengali lawyer's wit and charm. My dear Gangooly, English is but a stepping-stone to the deeper refinement of German and French. Where does our Bangla language lead you? A big frog in a small, stagnant pond. Let us leave the sweet euphony of Bangla to our poets, and the salvation-enhancement of Sanskrit to our priests. Packet boats delivered Berlin and Paris papers to the Dacca High Court, along with the venerated *Times*.

The cases Jai Krishna pleaded in court often cast him as the apostle of enlightenment and upholder of law against outmoded custom, or the adjudicator of outrages undefined and unimaginable under British law. The majesty of law was in conflict with Jai Krishna's search for an uncorrupted, un-British, un-Muslim, fully Hindu consciousness. He removed his wife and children from cosmopolitan Dacca and installed them in Mishtigunj. He sought a purer life for himself, English pleader by day, Sanskrit scholar by night. He regretted the lack of a rigorous Brahminical upbringing, the years spent in Calcutta learning the superior ways of arrogant Englishmen and English laws, ingesting English contempt for his background and ridicule for babus like him. He had grown up in a secularized home with frequent Muslim visitors and the occasional wayward Englishman. In consideration of nonHindu guests, his father had made certain that his mother's brass deities and stone lingams stayed confined in the closed-off worship-room.

On the morning of Tara Lata's wedding, female relatives waited along the riverbank for the arrival of the groom and his all-male wedding party. The groom was Satindranath Lahiri, fifth son of Surendranath Lahiri, of the landowning Lahiri family; in his own right, a healthy youth, whose astrological signs pointed to continued wealth and many sons. Back in Dacca, Jai Krishna had defended the ancient Hindu practices, the caste consciousness, the star charts, the observance of auspicious days, the giving of a dowry, the intact integrity of his community's rituals. His colleague, Keshub Miner, to be known two decades later as Sir Keshub, and his physician, Dr. Ashim Lai Roy, both prominent members of the most progressive, most Westernized segment of Bengali society, the Brahmo Samaj, had attempted to dissuade him. The two men had cited example after example of astrologically arranged marriages, full of astral promise, turning disastrous. The only worthwhile dowry, they'd proclaimed, is an educated bride. Child-marriage is barbarous. How could horoscopes influence lives, especially obscure lives, in dusty villages like Mishtigunj? Jai Krishna knew these men to be eaters of beef and drinkers of gin.

"I consider myself a student of modern science," Jai Krishna had explained, "and because I am a student of modern science, I cannot reject any theory until I test it." And so far, the tests had all turned out positive. His two older daughters, seven and nine, were successfully married and would soon be moving to their husbands' houses and living as wives, then as mothers. They were placid and obedient daughters who would make loving and obedient wives. Tara Lata, his favorite, would be no exception.

In the wintry bright hour just before twilight blackens Mishtigunj, the decorated bajra from the Lahiri family finally sailed into view. The bride's female relatives stood at the stone bathing-steps leading from the steep bank down to the river as servants prepared to help the groom's party of two hundred disembark. Women began the oo-loo ululation, the almost instrumental, pitched-voice welcome. Two of Jai Krishna's younger brothers supervised the unrolling of mats on the swampy path that connected the private dock and Jai Krishna's two-storied brick house.

The bajra anchored, but none on board rushed to the deck railings to be ceremoniously greeted by the welcoming party of the bride's relatives. The bridegroom's father and uncles had a servant deliver a cruel message in an insulting tone to the bride's father. They would not disembark on Jai Krishna's property for Jai Krishna and his entire clan were carriers of a curse, and that curse, thanks to Jai Krishna's home-destroying, misfortune-showering daughter, had been visited on their sinless son instead of on Jai Krishna's flesh-and-blood. They demanded that Jai Krishna meet them in the sheltered cabin of the bajra.

Jai Krishna ordered the wedding musicians to stop their shenai playing and dhol beating. His women relatives, shocked at the tone in which the servant repeated his master's message to Jai Krishna babu, the renowned Dacca lawyer, had given up their conch shell blowing and their ululating on their own. For several minutes, Jai Krishna stood still on the bathing-steps, trying to conceal at first his bewilderment, then his fury, that the man who was to have full patriarchal authority over his beloved daughter had called her names. Then he heard a bullying voice from inside the cabin yell instructions to the boatmen to pull up anchor.

"They're bargaining for more dowry," muttered one of Jai Krishna's brothers.

"No beggar is as greedy as that Lahiri bastard!" spat another brother.

Two boatmen played at reeling in ropes and readying the bajra to sail back.

9

(Bina Sharif, 1940—)
比娜·谢里夫

作者简介

比娜·谢里夫（Bina Sharif, 1940—），美国巴基斯坦裔作家、诗人、导演，出生于巴基斯坦的利亚尔普尔（Lyallpur）（现为费萨拉巴德，Faisalabad）。在巴基斯坦拉合尔的法蒂玛·真纳医科大学（Fatima Jinnah Medical University）获得医学学士学位。在美国约翰·霍普金斯大学（Johns Hopkins University）获得了公共卫生硕士学位，但随后结束了她的医学生涯，转向对写作和戏剧的强烈追求。

谢里夫有24部戏剧在美国、欧洲各国和巴基斯坦演出。"9·11"事件之后，她创作的剧作涉及恐怖主义和战争等主题，包括《伊斯兰教的民主》（*Democracy in Islam*）、《穆斯林的闪光》（*Muslim Glitter*）、《伊克拉共和国》（*Republic of Iqra*）、《为什么》（*Why?*）和《变化来了》（*Here Comes the Change*）等，这些剧作都曾在纽约新城剧院（Theatre for the New City in New York）上演。谢里夫不仅写作，而且还是演员、导演。她曾在多部电影中担任角色，如詹姆斯·艾弗里导演的《侧街》（*Side Streets*）和威廉·弗里德金导演的《吉普赛人之王》（*King of the Gypsies*）等。

谢里夫因其作品获得了众多奖项和资助，包括芝加哥古德曼剧院（Chicago's Goodman Theatre）的约瑟夫·杰斐逊奖（Joseph Jefferson Award）提名、爱丁堡戏剧节艺穗节奖（Pick of the Fringe Award of the Edinburgh Theater Festival）以及纽约州委员会（New York State Council）艺术项目、富兰克林基金会新兴剧作家（Franklin Foundation Emerging Playwright）及杰罗姆基金会（Jerome Foundation）的资助。

《我的祖先的房子》(*My Ancestor's House*, 1996) 是一部两幕家庭剧，收录在《有色人种女性的当代戏剧：一部选集》(*Contemporary Plays by Women of Color: An Anthology*, 1996) 中。2000 年 11 月在美国亚裔作家工作坊 (Asian American Writers' Workshop) 上演。这部剧讲述了一个解体的巴基斯坦家庭的故事。围绕移民女儿因母亲的重病而"回家"展开。选段部分出自《我的祖先的房子》的第一幕。宾迪雅 (Bindia) 因为母亲生病住院从美国回到了巴基斯坦，但家庭的对抗和指责让她觉得无所适从。归属感的缺失让宾迪雅觉得她没有权利在任何地方占有任何空间。

作品选读

My Ancestor's House

Act I

(excerpt)

By Bina Sharif

NAZO I am sorry. I don't want her to feel bad. We are all feeling bad. It is quite unfortunate what has happened to this family. We haven't recovered from our father's death yet. I am not against her living in America. Or in any other country. All I am trying to say is why live some place feeling alienated... with remorse and guilt while you can live as a perfectly decent human being in your own country? I am your older sister, I am at your mother's place now. I love you. I love you all. I worry about you. She doesn't seem very happy in New York. I just want the best for her. She is an educated woman. She doesn't have to feel this bewildered. Mother always wanted her to come back and live with her. She could get a job here tomorrow. If she had come back, mother would not have felt so left out and Bindia would have been more comfortable. Does she seem happy to you? (Asks ROONA; Does she? (ROONA *doesn't answer*.) People who graduated with her have their own private practice, they have houses, gardens, plots, property, cars, jewelry. They live in their own country, visit their parents once in a while like normal people. What is wrong with that? People go abroad to achieve something. What did she achieve? Abandoned a highly respectable profession, left her home, a loving home, made herself isolated for no reason.

BINDIA You are doing a great job... making me feel guilty... you people have done a great job... for the last ten years blaming me for deserting mother and father, for abandoning the family, for not taking care of them in their old age. For not being a practicing doctor in this country, for not practicing medicine in America, for not buying all of you bungalows, and cars, for not sending your children gifts, for not bringing VCRs and diamond rings, for not living here as a spinster... as a good, obedient daughter, a Muslim spinster...

ROONA Victims of traditions like Deedi, our forgotten sister... who is never a part of this loving family anymore. It is a sin to love ourselves in our beloved society but when one destroys oneself by its demands and taboos—they are the first ones to blame you for your own self-destruction—like they have been blaming her for so long that she finally let the exhaustion set in—the willingness to let anything be done to her.

BINDIA I was stronger than Deedi. I... left... but wasn't strong enough to survive in another jungle. In a massive jungle of loneliness, of poverty, of disillusionment, with the shame... with the shame of leaving my own... with the shame of not— returning, with the shame of abandonment, with the shame of being abandoned... with the shame of being dark... I was not strong enough.

ROONA Our religion, our parents, our Qur'an, our men, had weakened our soul.

BINDIA Even before I left I felt weak. But I left... from one billiant country to another... from one brilliant job to another... from one brilliant nervous breakdown to another... I crossed the ocen... I wanted to cut the cord... the cord... stretched, and stretched across the Atlantic like a strong nylon that never breaks... distance was so long... it stretched... and stretched... soon it will get tangled... soon it will suffocate me.

ROONA Soon it will suffocate Deedi... soon the uncut cord will choke us... suffocation is creeping all over us... over our brains... over our eyes.

BINDIA Over my face, over my chest, in my heart. My heart is being torn... You are killing me, mother's approaching death is killing me, Deedi's disintegration is killing me... I want to ignore my history altogether.

But even if I do... where do I go from there? Everything I do takes me right back into the womb, my womb, my mother's womb... I am on an exiled land.

ROONA I feel like I have always been on an exiled land.

BINDIA I feel as if I have no right to take any space anywhere... (*Sobs*) (*Everyone is shook up. Nobody moves. Complete silence.* NAZO *gets up, comes slowly to* BINDIA, *holds her.*)

NAZO I am sorry. I did not mean... I did not mean to hurt you. I am terribly sorry. You are exhausted. It is wrong of me to talk about things which... are so sensitive to you... I was only trying to help... believe me... I will run a cool bath for you... you should rest for a while. (*Exits*)

(ROONA *and* BINDIA *sit very quietly*—BINDIA *lights a cigarette. Lights fade on them. And lights up on* DEEDI—*she sings a plaintive lament. After her song,* BINDIA *starts to speak.*)

BINDIA How come Deedi is not here?

ROONA They don't want her here.

BINDIA Who?

ROONA Sahid...

BINDIA But it is not his house.

ROONA Nazo and Sahid are very tight these days. She will do anything to please him, and you know he never cared for Deedi.

BINDIA But this is entirely different, mother being so ill. They managed to get me here from the United States. Did they never tell her about mother?

ROONA They casually mentioned it a few days ago over the phone that mother is not feeling well.

BINDIA You mean Deedi doesn't know mother is in the hospital?

ROONA NO.

BINDIA This is awful.

ROONA They are afraid she will come with her husband and they hate his guts.

BINDIA I hate his guts, too. He has ruined Deedi's life... if this kind of situation happened in America... to an American woman, man she would kick his ass in one minute. Deedi should have left him a long time ago. That devil skunk of a husband. What does he do for a living?

ROONA Nothing... he has no job.

BINDIA He hasn't worked for a long time, has he?

ROONA As long as I can remember.

BINDIA How does he feed the kids?

ROONA Sells Deedi's gold.

BINDIA Oh, what a mess we have been in all our lives.

ROONA I hate the sight of that man but believe it or not Nazo's husband is more dangerous and manipulative than any man I have ever known. They have exploited mother against everyone—you, me, Deedi. You know, right after father's death, I became pregnant. Throughout my pregnancy I had rough times. Ashoo was still very young I was working. It was hard for me to drive twelve hours to go visit mother. My husband had a pretty bad relationship with his boss. He could never get leave for an extended period of time, and Nazo... who claims to be such a loving, compassionate elder sister never sat down with me and asked me, if... I needed something... She made mother her exclusive property... you know why? They wanted her house. They know two of the brothers live in foreign countries, you live away... Deedi... doesn't know what's going on. She, poor thing, is so completely lost and she is sick a lot... I worry about her... I worry about her children... I worry about you... Nazo and Sahid are more worried about mother's house than her illness... I am only very close to you and Deedi... and... you left, and Deedi... she is here... but her mind is so shattered... I wish I could do something for her.

BINDIA I wish I could do something too. I miss Deedi a lot. And I missed you in America, I miss all the children, I pass in front of a toy store in New York, one of the big ones on Fifth Avenue, and I never go in... It breaks my heart... I would love to send so many toys and gifts to them. They are so fond of me, and I am so fond of them... they imagine me as their wonderful Aunt living in America. I am so totally unhappy there... Roona, I am not a doctor. I never could pass that exam. Those medical books I can't go through them anymore. They remind me of Deedi's enlarged heart, which flickers a million beats per minute. They remind me of the ultimate impotence of doctors in the face of death. Death has frightened me from such an early age that I cannot deal with sick people. I cannot face death. Every time I saw a person dying it reminded me of the uselessness of life, the absurdity of life... and the truth of being no more. I know the unbearable story of watching people's last breath stuck in their throats. I know the story of watching that last breath vanishing forever. I became too old and too sad when I was too young. I could not go back to the medical books. Sometimes I even forced myself but I thought I would lose my sanity. But I never established myself in America. And all the pressure from back home... the pull... "come home"... "come back." The more I suffered there, the less I wanted to come back... I felt exactly like Deedi, My dilemma was exactly like Deedi's... the difference was only the obvious distance. I left, she didn't. I had no one to turn to in a foreign country. I have been so frightened. I felt like a lost child—looking for other lost children. I ran in circles... hoped... maybe one day... something will happen... something good will happen... I will be able to get Deedi in America... Away from that husband of hers. Maybe one day I will be able to get everybody in America and we will all be together like the old days. The good days. Remember our jasmine-filled courtyard... father with his hookah pipe... the tea... us laughing all night... father getting upset at us... "Turn off those lights, the electricity costs too much." But we would just giggle and giggle and talk all night and tell each other stories.

ROONA Remember we used to sit by the fire and tell each other about our princes. I would say to you, who are you going to marry? And you would say...

BINDIA Who are you going to marry?

ROONA And I would say, my prince will be taller than your prince.

BINDIA And my prince will be as tall as father. We had hopes and dreams, we had no sorrow, we had no pain, we had no... shame... and then father died without me ever being able to take him there, to New York, to the Plaza Hotel... the afternoon tea... I always fantasized... father... with me and you and all of us. We taking him to this elegant hotel, him being dressed in his white, starched native clothes... with his turban. Everyone... everyone will look at him... so tall, and so handsome, and then we will all have tea. And then the bill will come and of course I will pay and father will ask me, "How much?" and I will smile and say, "Not much." And he will say, "How much?" And I will say, "This much!" And he will say, "That much, for tea only?" But that was just a fantasy, and the desire to get Deedi to America and have her go through heart surgery, another fantasy... If I were only a practicing doctor in America. Just for Deedi's sake.

10

(Talat Abbasi, 1942—)
塔拉特·阿巴西

作者简介

塔拉特·阿巴西（Talat Abbasi, 1942—），美国巴基斯坦裔小说家，生于勒克瑙（Lucknow），在卡拉奇（Karachi）长大。她曾在卡拉奇的圣约瑟夫学院（St. Joseph's College）、拉合尔的金纳德学院（Kinnaird College），以及英国的伦敦经济学院（London School of Economics）学习，在卡拉奇的国家公共管理学院（National Institute of Public Administration）担任过研究员。1978年，她带着两个孩子搬到了纽约。从那时起，她就在联合国人口基金会（United Nations Population Fund）工作，专门研究人口和性别问题。她定期访问巴基斯坦，特别是她的家乡卡拉奇。

阿巴西的短篇小说在美国、法国和印度的许多文学期刊上发表，也被列入一些文学选集和美国大学生的教科书中。阿巴西已出版了短篇小说集《苦瓜及其他故事》（*Bitter Gourd and Other Stories*, 2001）。这是一部由17个短篇小说组成的作品集，探索了卡拉奇及其周边地区的巴基斯坦人以及纽约的巴基斯坦人的世界。

《海市蜃楼》（"Mirage"）出自《苦瓜及其他故事》。这篇故事获得2000年英国广播公司国际频道（BBC World Service）短篇小说奖。在这个故事中，阿巴西讲述了一位母亲为照顾严重残疾的孩子所作的英勇斗争。节选部分描述了母亲选择将孩子留在福利院的复杂情绪。

作品选读

Mirage
(excerpt)
By Talat Abbasi

There's something very practiced about the way she says it. Perhaps they all falter at this point, the last thing after all on the last form they'll sign. Scores of parents over the years have come through the front door of Hope House to hand their children over to Sister Agnes because they're mentally retarded, schizophrenic, autistic, epileptic, or have cerebral palsy. Hardly the complete list of reasons, just a sample. Young parents on the whole, many still in their thirties, because Hope House is only for ten-year-olds and under. Many coming alone, on their own, as I have with Omar.

Mind you, I'm not faltering, not me. Not one bit. If I'm behaving like a puppet it's because I'm drained, exhausted. I was exhausted at least mentally even before we left home today. I'm always tense, in quite a state when I have to take him out in public and, of course, today I was worse than usual. He sensed it and acted up. I must've flung a bag of candies into his mouth by the time the diaper was done. A dozen pieces of candy at a time every time he bared his teeth to shred it. Understandable, of course, his reaction to a diaper at his age. It isn't always needed, but I have to, just in case. It's candy corn, the sticky kind he can't just swallow, is forced to chew, gives me time.

"Candy corn's bad for his teeth."

The pediatrician says that every time I take him to get the prescription refilled for his tranquilizer. But not very seriously. He doesn't expect me to give up on the candy corn. Then I zipped him into his jeans, fastened his belt which he doesn't have the skill to undo. That's why it's jeans, not pull-on pants. And then to keep his hands as well as his mouth really busy for what he hates most of all—his harness—I gave him half a bag of potato chips, his greatest weakness, the salted kind with lots of MSG. It hasn't occurred to the doctor to tell me that MSG is also bad for him.

Then all of a sudden I threw myself on top of him, pinning down both his arms with my elbows, taking him by surprise. Rammed the spoon between his teeth and held it there to keep his mouth open until he'd swallowed every drop of his tranquilizer, until it had all gone down. I realized that I had gritted my teeth so hard, I'd bitten my own tongue! I cried a bit so there was no time left to cut his nails. The taxi driver was buzzing me from downstairs. He was parked across the street two blocks away from the apartment building. That's another reason I'm exhausted. Just the thought of traffic lights and having to cross the street with him before they turn green!

He hates his harness. And that, too, is understandable. A full-grown energetic ten-year-old in a toddler's harness. Imagine being allowed to walk but in leg irons! Still, I have to use that harness when I take him out just in case he decides to stage a sit-in in the middle of traffic. He did that only once before I thought of a harness and believe me, it wasn't easy, dragging him by the collar of his shirt, inch by inch, like a dead weight across the road. And on top of it—

"Pair of loonies!" yelled the driver who had to brake suddenly.

"Who let you out?"

He meant both of us. And who could blame him? Who could blame them all for staring? Unexpected, let's face it, even for New York.

Still he was wrong about me. Not a loony, not me. But always at my wits' end, it's true, no matter what. Cooped up with a hyperactive frustrated boy in the bare two-room apartment. I lined the floor with mattresses, quilts and foam after receiving warnings from the landlord about the neighbors complaining of "a herd, at least, of thumping, marauding elephants up there." They too were wrong, of course. No threatening elephants. Just a small exquisite bird trapped in the room, flying in panic from wall to wall, hurling itself against them, hurting only itself, incapable of harming others. Watched in silence by the mother.

I thanked ... it was at least a corner apartment, no neighbors on the bedroom side. Imagine having to line the walls too with mattresses, I thought, as I watched in empathy. Then as the weeks grew into months, even a year and more, and the frightened bird still found no peace—neither smashed itself against the walls nor found a way to fly out—I watched in rage and self-pity.

And becoming melodramatic at the end, likened myself bitterly to a Pharaoh's slave buried alive with him. Nothing happened this time though, thank goodness. The taxi's brought us without incident to Hope House, Omar's home.

But "Omar's home" sounds wrong. How can he have a home apart from me?

Am I faltering now?

Maybe I am.

Only ten and strikingly pretty. His black hair, which I am stroking to soothe him, keep him quiet on my lap, is amazingly still baby soft though the curls are showing signs of straightening out. His fine features are in perfect proportion, chiseled on a small delicate face. Strangers have always been drawn to him, impulsively reaching out to pet him, complimenting me. In fact only last month I took him to the pediatrician. He had had his tranquilizer and so he was sitting quietly by my side. I didn't notice this woman, being in quite a state myself as I usually am when I have to bring him out in public—there I go, repeating myself—especially to small enclosed places like the doctor's office. Yes, there can be trouble even with a tranquilizer! But suddenly she's there before me, chapped red lips parted in a smile, hands reaching out to fondle his curls.

"What a beauti..."

That's usually how far they get! Then they all stop, awkward, embarrassed, because close up they all see something. It's the eyes, of course, under those fantastic long eyelashes they were all set to coo over. They're not blind eyes, seeing nothing. They're seeing as well as you and I, but what they're seeing is nothing you and I can understand. That much they tell you as they confront you in one long, unblinking stare before they go back to darting constantly, nervously, from left to right and back again, never at rest.

And then they notice other little things about him which can be quite off-putting. The perfectly shaped lips—which I can tell you have rarely parted in a smile—are twitching uncontrollably, quite unprettily. And the ceaseless whimpering sound can be quite unnerving. It's very soft, barely audible, a call which seems to come from miles below.

And I understand the disappointment of strangers at being thus tricked. I, too, have been taken in by a mirage.

But as I said, there can be trouble even with a tranquilizer! So now, in a flash, the pen which I am passing back to Sister Agnes is knocked out of my hand and I am looking up at Omar from the floor where somehow I have landed. He's lunging toward the forms to tear them up with his teeth. But Sister Agnes is quicker. Scores of children, after all, who have a taste for paper!

There's nothing left but my face and to this he turns. I wince as he rakes my cheek, and grab his hands. He bares his teeth but I'm holding him as far from myself as I can. There's absolute hatred in his eyes. He cannot speak of it, he can speak only two words. One is *pani*, the Urdu word for water, which he learned late as a toddler in Karachi, where he was born. The other is na, which can mean both no and yes. He's saying neither now and suddenly he's neither scratching nor biting. His nails though are biting into my arms as he clings to me, face hidden against my chest. He's shaking, his eyes will now be filled with terror.

"I meant to cut his nails, Sister. I'm so sorry, Sister."

In fact I'm so sorry about his nails that I am close to tears. She must see that because she comes over, presses my shoulder. Another practiced gesture! The touch is sympathetic but brief. Scores of parents, after all! Perhaps those others too all remember something that makes them feel as guilty as I do about his nails. I never do hand him over to her. She simply lifts him off my lap, stands him up on the floor. He doesn't resist. Puppets, both of us, now.

"He won't need this anymore," she says gently, removing his harness and handing it to me.

The harness goes into the garbage chute as soon as I get home.

Also the foam and plastic which line the floor. Then the mattresses and quilts are disposed of. The freshly vacuumed Bokhara at last flaunts its buried jewel colors in the sunlight as the blinds are raised for the first time since I moved into the apartment. And a curious neighbor runs to her window to see at last, then turns back in embarrassment and disappointment, both. An apartment, then, just like any other.

An apartment, moreover, where knives, kitchen shears, scissors, nail cutters have found their rightful places. They've emerged from an old battered attaché case hidden under the kitchen sink. It makes me smile now, that battered attaché case, as I think of that wretched burglar caught red-handed by the super with it, holding razor blades as he stood dazed by his catch—what a treasure! He took too long over it, it looked so promising, a locked case hidden under the kitchen sink. I didn't see the funny side of it then but I'm beginning to now. I have a mad urge to write and commiserate with him. Dear Mr. Burglar, I want to say, what you must think of me, hiding knives, scissors, razor blades in a locked attaché case like a treasure!

Mad for sure, you must think, eccentric at best. And who can blame you?

I go to bed early and sleep right through the night because the lights don't suddenly go on, off, on again at one a.m., the taps don't run and flood the bath at three, and I have absolutely no fear that the stove will turn itself on. So in the morning I wake up, rested and at peace, and yet in pain as you might expect of someone who has had an arm amputated to save the rest.

11

(Gita Mehta, 1943—)
吉塔·梅塔

作者简介

吉塔·梅塔（Gita Mehta, 1943—），美国印度裔小说家、散文家、纪录片导演、记者，出生在德里（Delhi）。父亲比朱·帕特奈克（Biju Patnaik）曾因印度独立抗争与民主改革数度入狱。梅塔三岁的时候，被送往寄宿学校。成年后她远赴英国剑桥大学（University of Cambridge）深造。她的丈夫阿贾·辛格·梅塔（Ajai Singh Mehta）是克诺夫出版社（Alfred A. Knopf）的总裁。由于他在纽约出版界的显赫地位，这对夫妇成了纽约文学出版界的核心人物。

梅塔的主要作品包括散文集、小说。其中，散文集有《可乐经：营销神秘东方》（*Karma Cola: Marketing the Mystic East*, 1979）和《蛇与梯子：现代印度一瞥》（*Snakes and Ladders: Glimpses of Modern India*, 1997）；长篇小说《统治》（*Raj*, 1989）和《河经》（*A River Sutra*, 1993）以及非虚构类作品《永恒的甘尼萨：从出生到重生》（*Eternal Ganesha: From Birth to Rebirth*, 2006）等。梅塔的作品已经被翻译成13种语言，在27个国家出版。除了写作，梅塔还作为一名纪录片导演为英国广播公司（BBC）和美国广播公司（NBC）执导过十几部电视纪录片。

梅塔的第一部小说《统治》畅销欧美和印度等国家，是一部全面而丰富多彩的历史小说，故事背景设定为印度追求自由解放的20世纪40—90年代，描写了在英国统治下，一个出生在印度贵族家庭的年轻女子贾雅·辛格（Jaya Singh）的人生旅程。小说以非常现实的方式描绘了印度女性问题，揭示了在父权社会中，无论女性是农民还是公主，她们的苦难和经历都是一样的。

选段出自《统治》第三部分。尽管普拉塔剥夺了贾雅作为一个妻子、一个妈妈的尊严，但是在这段没有任何感情的婚姻中，贾雅始终保持忠实妻子的身份，跟随丈夫的脚步，因为她对丈夫的这种尊重在她一生的祈祷和仪式中已经根深蒂固。

作品选读

Raj

Book Three (42)

(excerpt)

By Gita Mehta

  With the departure of the Viceroy of India, Jaya found herself once again vulnerable to Maharajah Pratap, violated by the very act that should have been proof of love. Every morning she dutifully recited prayers for her husband's long life, and tried to rid herself of the uncleansing memory of his embrace.

  When he had finally taken her in his arms in the wooden hut with its curtain of flowers, the moment had carved away the memory of his other women as the long knives of the tribals sliced the skin from an animal, and she had hoped her empty life would overflow with the abundance for which all wives prayed. But night after night she watched him blow out the scented candles as though he could not bear to touch her until he could no longer see her, as if the night soiled him as it did her, and her humiliations hardened into a rage that mirrored her husband's.

  She remembered the long years she had waited for him to consummate their marriage. Now only the necessity of an heir forced her to admit the ruler to her rooms, and when the palace doctors confirmed at last that she was with child, she moved into the Purdah Palace, eager to be away from the ruler.

  The excitement of the purdah ladies in her confinement erased the indignities of Maharajah Pratap's conjugal visits. At dusk Jaya sat on the balcony listening to the purdah ladies sing of her unborn child's heroic ancestors, soothed by their serene voices, until the memory of her husband receded like a garish picture. When Sir Akbar sent news that Maharajah Pratap had left for Europe in the company of the dancer from Calcutta, Esme Moore, Jaya was almost relieved.

The Dowager Maharani opened the storerooms where the traditional playthings for an heir to the throne were kept. "Choose toys for a son. So much kicking can only mean a boy."

Cradles, frames for the unborn child's horoscope, small puja objects with which he would perform his first prayers, brocades for his first tunic coat, and aigrettes for his first turban were piled high in the chambers.

Jaya took out a globe made of ivory and gold, enamelled with scenes of tiger hunts and war. The Dowager rattled the globe in Jaya's ear. "See, this one still has earth in it. He must learn about earth, water, light, air—the four elements that make up the world. What is a ruler who does not understand the fundamentals of nature?"

Jaya rolled the smooth object in her hand, rounded so an infant would not cut himself.

"And this is to teach him about the heavens." The Dowager Maharani held up a necklace of cabuchon gems so the sunlight caught its colours. "The nine gems that represent the planets, which govern the moods and changes of our lives, as the tides govern the sea."

As the child grew in her womb Jaya spent hours in the storerooms, choosing little—but dreaming, in the afternoon sun, of the baby.

In April, a son was born to Maharani Jaya Devi. Holding the squalling infant in her arms while the Dowager Maharani's stiff fingers swept the long hair matted with sweat from her face, Jaya felt she belonged to Sirpur at last. She had kept the Sirpur line intact, and the knowledge filled her with unfamiliar security.

While Maharajah Pratap travelled back from Europe, the overjoyed Dowager Maharani celebrated the birth with appropriate ceremony. At dawn and at dusk, firing cannons drowned the clanging of temple bells, announcing the birth of the kingdom's heir. Prisoners were released. New clothes were distributed to the people of the kingdom. Twice a day the poor were fed under vast tents put up in the main courtyard of the City Palace.

When the wives of the Sirpur nobles circled her son's head with coins to deflect the evil eye, Jaya felt the celebrations were as much a recognition of herself as of her child.

On her husband's return, Jaya drove to the City Palace, staring proudly into the bright eyes of the baby held close to her breast. Enveloped in her own world, she was only amused by Maharajah Pratap's charming apologies at not being present for the birth of his son.

But when he bent forward, Jaya turned her head so that his lips only brushed her cheek. She smiled at the crying baby as she pulled down her sari to feed him.

"Stop that!"

Jaya looked up in surprise from the infant suckling at her breast.

"The Maharanis of Sirpur employ wet nurses. I will not have my wife feeding a baby like a peasant woman."

"Hukam." The blood rose to Jaya's face. Maharajah Pratap had already robbed her of the dignity of being a wife. Now he was stealing the rights of maternity. She lowered her eyes so he would not see the silent anger breaking in waves against the respect for a husband which had been ingrained so deeply by the prayers and ceremonies that had marked her whole life.

With an iciness she had not known she possessed she sat at his side in the Durbar Hall while the wet nurse fed the baby in her apartments, listening to the list of guests prepared by Sir Akbar for the child's name ceremony.

Her fury at her husband's crude display of power briefly evaporated when Tiny Dungra reached Sirpur.

"Your mother is thrilled at the news of her grandson." Dungra circled the baby's head with a crimson purse filled with gold coins and handed the purse to Chandni. "When my father was dying, he asked for your mother's blessing, and now that I am ruler of Dungra, her presence in the kingdom is a great comfort to me." He settled his large frame into an armchair. "But I don't think the British were comforted to see Pratap playing in London when their own people are starving."

"Is there famine in England, hukam?"

"A famine of jobs, Bai-sa. Men who survived the war cannot feed their children because they cannot find work. Last month, in despair, they marched on London, only to be met by bullets. There is even talk of revolution in England if the situation does not improve. He reached across and took the baby's small hand in his own. In your private moments, persuade Pratap to cultivate the nationalists. If England collapses, our future lies with them."

"At this moment my husband seems interested only in pleasure, hukam. Even his son takes second place."

Irritation exploded from the large frame. "Pratap is a charming man, but like the other Sirpur rulers, he cannot endure reality. And the reality is this, Bai-sa. Last month, the People's Councils formed a Reformist organization in Bombay to push for revolution in the Indian kingdoms."

Jaya hugged the baby, knowing the Sirpur family's strength came from its close links with the British Empire, carefully cultivated over four generations.

The shouts of a Household Guard signalled the Maharajah's approach. Dungra rose to congratulate Maharajah Pratap. "We rejoice in the birth of your son, Pratap."

"And my Resident tells me he wants to go home next year, Tiny. A second reason for rejoicing."

"This is no time for making jokes, Pratap. The new Reformist movement is a real threat to our futures. And now the British Empire is sending Indian officials in place of Englishmen to our kingdoms. Some of these Indians hate us more than the British ever did. At least Sir Henry is someone you know. His successor may prove much worse."

"Don't get excited, Tiny. The ever-efficient Sir Akbar has a list of successors, stolen from the British Residency by our spies. He'll manage to find someone sympathetic to Sirpur. Come on, I want to show you the two new aeroplanes that have just arrived from England. They are being unpacked in the hangars right now."

In October, the name ceremony took place in the courtyard where Maharajah Pratap had been invested with his ruling powers by the Viceroy. Once again eager citizens sat on the high walls, watching the priests perform the pujas for the heir to the Sirpur throne.

The Raj Guru carried the child to the sacred fire. Grains of rice were placed in the small hands. The crowds shouted with pleasure when the infant's hands opened at just the right moment to allow the grains to fall into the fire. Ganges water was sprinkled on the baby's body; sindoor was rubbed over his forehead. Raising his voice, the Raj Guru announced that the new prince of the Sirpur family would be called Arjun.

Pleased that the baby had not cried once through the long prayers but had stared with his big eyes at the flames leaping up whenever the priests ladled butterfat into the fire, Jaya thought it fitting that her son should be named after the great king whose chariot had been driven by the ... Krishna.

12

(Tahira Naqvi, 1945—)
塔希拉·纳克维

作者简介

塔希拉·纳克维（Tahira Naqvi, 1945—），美国巴基斯坦裔小说家，翻译家，出生在伊朗，从小在巴基斯坦的拉合尔长大。从耶稣和玛丽修道院（Convent of Jesus and Mary）毕业后，纳克维在拉合尔学院（Lahore College）获得了英语文学学士学位，在拉合尔的政府学院（Government College）获得心理学硕士学位。1972年随丈夫移居美国，继而在西康涅狄格州立大学（Western Connecticut State University）深造，获得硕士学位。她曾在西康涅狄格州立大学（Western Connecticut State University）和纽约州韦斯切斯特社区学院（Westchester Community College）教授英语，曾在哥伦比亚大学（Columbia University）和纽约大学（New York University）教授乌尔都语（Urdu）。

纳克维主要创作短篇故事集，包括《玫瑰油和巴基斯坦的其他故事》（*Attar of Roses and Other Stories of Pakistan*, 1997）和《死在陌生的国度》（*Dying in a Strange Country*, 2001）。她的作品被收录在许多文学杂志和文学选集中，如《马萨诸塞州评论》（*The Massachusetts Review*）、《南亚文学杂志》（*The Journal for South Asian Literature*）、《想象美国：来自应许之地的故事》（*Imagining America: Stories from the Promised Land*, 1991）、《穿越黑暗水域：美国南亚裔文学选集》（*Crossing the Dark Waters: An Anthology of South Asian-American Literature*, 1995）及《世界已改变：巴基斯坦女性书写的当代故事》（*And the World Changed: Contemporary Stories by Pakistani Women*, 2008）等。

纳克维因翻译印度著名作家伊斯马特·楚泰（Ismat Chughtai）的作品而

深受好评,包括《弯曲的线》(*The Crooked Line*, 1995)、《陌生人》(*A Strange Man*, 2007)等。此外,她还翻译了巴基斯坦女作家卡迪亚·马斯图尔(Khadija Mastur)的乌尔都语小说。

《玫瑰油和巴基斯坦的其他故事》包含13个故事。纳克维将失落、怀旧和记忆的情绪置于文本之中,将人物的个人经历和见解与历史、政治事件和社会困境等交织在一起。在短篇小说《公平交易》("A Fair Exchange")中,作者细致入微地探索了人物复杂的心理。这些心理导致一位出身传统家庭、受过良好教育的女性误解自己的梦境,并诉诸迷信,用暗示表达压抑、不明、混乱的情感。选段讲述了女主人公玛丽亚姆(Mariam)选择将仆人吉娜(Jeena)嫁给自己丈夫的挣扎与困惑等一系列心理活动。

作品选读

A Fair Exchange
(excerpt)
By Tahira Naqvi

In the last week of October, just when summer was edging its way out, four months after Mariam had made her vow and begun her spell of unfettered, carefree sleep, her husband returned from the front. The war had ended. The danger had passed.

On the day of his return, Mariam made several attempts to bring up the subject of her vow. It wasn't easy. The children were eager to talk to their father, there was all that mail that had accumulated, and also a steady stream of visitors to inquire about the doctor's well-being and congratulate him on his safe return—husband and wife were afforded little chance to be alone for any length of time.

When he came to her bed at night she knew this was no time to talk of serious matters. But later she wished she had broached the subject then. Unable to help herself, she placed her arms on his back as he lay on top of her, felt the tautness between his shoulder blades, and a feeling stirred inside her that she had never known before. His warm skin responded to her touch. Shame engulfed her and reticence tangled her in a web, but her blood raced as if it were a torrent. Her heart beat violently, wildly. She forgot what it was to be shy. Her skin tingled, her arms tightened around her husband's body. The warmth between her legs filled her with strange pleasure and her mouth opened in a moan. She forgot she did not like to be visited in the night by her husband, that she had always allowed it only because it was something that he seemed to need and want.

All those feelings of revulsion that she struggled with when he touched her in the dark vanished. Tonight the world was shut out, and everything else with it. A few days of waiting would cause no harm, she told herself the next morning.

The second night and the one after that, Mariam lay in her husband's arms and banished the vow from her mind. On the third night, some time after she had fallen into a deep and tranquil sleep, the dreams returned. They unfolded simultaneously, all of them mixed up this time, as if some essential component that had kept them in sequence were missing. At the end came a new dream in which her mother-in-law was pulling Mariam's ring from her finger, and the two women tugged and pushed until the ring came off and disappeared into the voluminous folds of Mariam's dark red bridal dupatta. There was more, much more, but on waking this was all Mariam could remember. Her heart sank. What had she done?

"I made a mannat when you were away," Mariam began tremulously the next morning. "I was so afraid something... something terrible might happen." Mariam addressed her husband while he was tying his shoelaces and she couldn't see his face. There wasn't much time. He would be leaving for the hospital soon.

"Oh? What was it? Why didn't you take care of it already? You know one shouldn't delay these things." He straightened and looked at her.

Mariam hesitated. Would he think less of her when she told him?

"There was no other choice, there were such bad dreams," she murmured, turning away from his stare to smooth the wrinkles in the bedsheet.

"You're always paying too much attention to dreams. Anyway, what is it?" He stood up and adjusted his tie.

"I'm to give you Jeena." The words fell out. Like saliva that's been kept in the mouth too long.

Mariam's husband stopped what he was doing. His face darkened. A frown gathered on his forehead.

"Are you mad, Mariam?" He glared at her as if she had surprised him with disobedience.

Her chest constricted. Her ears vibrated with echoes that sounded like jumbled screams. "The dreams wouldn't give me any peace, the danger was lurking in the shadows, it had to be something that was difficult to surrender, what's a sacrifice that doesn't hurt?" Mariam blurted out the sentences hurriedly. She was on the other side of the bed, a pillow held tightly against her chest. "Islam allows more than one marriage, doesn't it? I'll give my permission." Her voice cracked.

"I don't want your permission," her husband thundered. "You are not seriously suggesting that I marry... this girl." He sat down, the muscles on his face quivering in anger.

"You are definitely mad. I go away for a few months and this is how you conduct yourself!"

"You cannot say no, it's a mannat, it's a question of your life. I don't mind, I really don't mind, and Jeena... well, she's like a younger sister and she's pretty and I'll be here as well, I'm not going anywhere..." She edged forward like a beggar, her hands extended, her tone pleading.

"Be quiet, Mariam, be quiet this minute! I don't want to hear another word. I'm late for work, and when I return I don't want to hear any more of this nonsense." He raised a finger in warning, scolding her as if she were a child.

What she could do, she had done. Was it her fault that her husband would not relent? In the days that followed Mariam did not talk of Jeena or her mannat and was relieved that her husband did not either, although he seemed somewhat pensive, somewhat quieter than usual. He is just recuperating from the experience at the front, Mariam told herself. It takes time to forget the horrors of war.

She noticed that sometimes when Jeena removed the dishes from the table or was helping Razia or Ahmer with their clothes in the morning, her husband glanced at the girl as if seeing her for the first time. As if she were a stranger in their house. Mariam caught a look in his eyes that she couldn't understand. She blamed herself. She had made her husband uncomfortable by mentioning the mannat to him. He was only looking at the young woman to see what his wife had been thinking, and why. Perhaps he wished to understand Mariam's motives.

Once, when Jeena bent down to tie Ahmer's shoelaces and her dupatta slipped from her shoulders, the fullness at her shirtfront was revealed and, just then, Mariam became aware that her husband had seen it too. Quickly, he looked away and Jeena straightened up and adjusted her dupatta, all in the matter of a few moments, but Mariam realized she had to redeem her pledge, the mannat. The dreams were gone, at least for now, but Mariam was not so foolish as to let the mannat go unheeded. Without offering specific details, stressing that due to unforeseen circumstances the vow could not be executed as pledged, she consulted the maulvi sahib who came to instruct the children in the reading of the Quran. Stroking his beard thoughtfully, his eyes lowered in deference to a woman's presence, he listened patiently as Mariam outlined the details of her dilemma.

"Such vows should not be undertaken lightly," he admonished gently, "but Allah understands."

He put Mariam's mind at ease. Give money to a needy person or perform another act of charity, making sure it is a fair exchange, he explained. Mariam already knew that was what she should have done, but receiving the maulvi sahib's approval made her feel better. And she also knew what that act of charity was to be.

"We should think of Jeena's marriage," she informed her husband one night, a week after her conversation with the maulvi sahib. He had just eaten dinner and was getting ready to say his nighttime prayers.

At first he looked up in alarm, perhaps suspecting that she was planning to bring up the mannat again.

"She's old enough and too much of a responsibility," Mariam continued, ignoring the expression of disquiet on her husband's face.

"Hmm," he mumbled.

"Ghulam Din's son has a job as a clerk in the telephone department. He's educated and I've seen him, he's not at all bad to look at. I know our old caretaker will be happy that we're approaching him for his son. He knows we'll give Jeena a good dowry." Mariam spoke with authority, as if Jeena were indeed her younger sister and hence her responsibility.

Mariam's husband had no objections. Why should he? Her spirits lifted, Mariam began making arrangements soon thereafter. She had already spoken to the old caretaker, he had humbly and joyfully expressed his gratitude. True, his son was an educated boy, a clerk in an office, yet he would never have found a girl like Jeena who, even though she was a servant in this household, was nevertheless treated as a member of the family. No doubt this connection with a family of such high status would continue even after she was married. And she was young and beautiful. He brought the groom-to-be to meet Mariam's husband, who seemed satisfied after his interview with the young man. What was most important was that the young man had a government job and would also receive living accommodation once he was married. A wedding date was immediately agreed upon.

In addition to the five suits that Mariam specially had embroidered in gold thread and sequins for Jeena, she rummaged through her own things and brought out a dark red brocade suit that was too heavily ornamented with gilded trimmings and sequined designs for her own use, and added that to the young woman's dowry. The bridal dupatta that went with it was heavy with shimmering gold-and-silver-tasseled edging on all four sides. That, she decided, would be Jeena's wedding suit. She bought her a gold necklace and ear rings, a lightweight set, but one that gave the impression of being heavy because of the way the design had been wrought. Jeena helped with embroidering tablecloths, bedsheets, and pillowcases, and stitched all of her own clothes herself on Mariam's sewing machine with Mariam's guidance at every step. There was no skimping on Mariam's part. She was no fool. Pledges made to Allah could not be taken lightly.

A week after Jeena's wedding, on a night that Mariam had slept in her husband's arms longer than any other night she could remember, the dreams, each one clearer and more disturbing than the one before it, returned.

13

(Agha Shahid Ali, 1949—2001)
阿加·沙希德·阿里

作者简介

阿加·沙希德·阿里（Agha Shahid Ali, 1949—2001），美国印度裔诗人，出生于印度新德里（New Delhi），在克什米尔（Kashmir）长大，后来移民美国。在移居美国之前，曾在克什米尔大学（University of Kashmir）和新德里大学（University of New Delhi）接受教育。1984年，他在宾夕法尼亚州立大学（Pennsylvania State University）获得博士学位，1985年在亚利桑那大学（University of Arizona）获得诗歌艺术硕士学位。阿里曾任教于纽约的汉密尔顿学院（Hamilton College），曾任马萨诸塞大学（University of Massachusetts）创意写作项目主任，也曾任教于犹他大学（University of Utah）和沃伦威尔逊学院（Warren Wilson College）。他曾荣获古根海姆创意艺术奖学金（Guggenheim Fellowship for Creative Arts）和英格拉姆·美林奖学金（Ingram-Merrill Fellowship）等奖项。

阿里的作品主要有诗集《骨雕》（*Bone Sculpture*, 1972）、《纪念贝古姆·阿赫塔尔和其他诗歌》（*In Memory of Begum Akhtar and Other Poems*, 1979）、《半英寸的喜马拉雅》（*The Half-Inch Himalayas*, 1987）、《走过黄页》（*A Walk Through the Yellow Pages*, 1987）、《怀旧者的美国地图》（*A Nostalgist's Map of America*, 1991）、《心爱的见证人：诗集》（*The Beloved Witness: Selected Poems*, 1992）、《没有邮局的国家》（*The Country Without a Post Office*, 1997）、《永不完成的房间》（*Rooms Are Never Finished*, 2001）等。

《永不完成的房间》入围2001年美国国家图书奖（National Book Award）。在这本令人惊叹的、富有创造性的诗集中，阿里挖掘了他童年的家园克什米尔所遭受的破坏，并揭示了更多个人所遭受的破坏：他母亲的死亡和带着她的尸体返回克什米尔的旅程。诗歌《在莱诺克斯山》("In Lenox Hill")出自这一诗集，表达了诗人对即将失去母亲的悲伤之情，这是他对祖国克什米尔状况的绝望的缩影。

《怀旧者的美国地图》讲述了穿梭在美国居住地和克什米尔的一系列旅行故事。诗人通过想象链接过去和现在、美国和印度，表达抒情和幻想。在诗歌《后视镜里的智利》("I See Chile in My Rearview Mirror")中，诗人反观"1973年智利政变"等历史事件，表达了对新殖民主义和美帝国主义的批判，带给读者震撼和对恐怖的想象。

作品选读

In Lenox Hill

By Agha Shahid Ali

(In Lenox Hill Hospital, after surgery, my
mother said the sirens sounded like the
elephants of Mihiragula when his men drove
them off cliffs in the Pir Panjal Range.)
The Hun so loved the cry, one falling elephant's,
he wished to hear it again. At dawn, my mother
heard, in her hospital-dream of elephants,
sirens wail through Manhattan like elephants
forced off Pir Panjal's rock cliffs in Kashmir:
the soldiers, so ruled, had rushed the elephant,
The greatest of all footprints is the elephant's,
said the Buddha. But not lifted from the universe,
those prints vanished forever into the universe,
though nomads still break news of those elephants
as if it were just yesterday the air spread the dye
("War's annals will fade into night / Ere their story die"),
the punishing khaki whereby the world sees us die

out, mourning you, O massacred elephants!
Months later, in Amherst, she dreamt: She was, with diamonds, being stoned to death. I prayed: If she must die,
let it only be some dream. But there were times, Mother,
while you slept, that I prayed, "Saints, let her die."
Not, I swear by you, that I wished you to die
but to save you as you were, young, in song in Kashmir,
and I, one festival, crowned Krishna by you, Kashmir
listening to my flute. You never let ... die.
Thus I swear, here and now, not to forgive the universe
that would let me get used to a universe
without you. She, she alone, was the universe
as she earned, like a galaxy, her right not to die,
defying the Merciful of the Universe,
Master of Disease, "in the circle of her traverse"
of drug-bound time. And where was the ... of elephants,
plump with Fate, when tusk to tusk, the universe,
dyed green, became ivory? Then let the universe,
like Paradise, be considered a tomb. Mother,
they asked me, So how's the writing? I answered My mother
is my poem. What did they expect? For no verse
sufficed except the promise, fading, of Kashmir
and the cries that reached you from the cliffs of Kashmir
(across fifteen centuries) in the hospital. Kashmir,
she's dying! How her breathing drowns out the universe
as she sleeps in Amherst. Windows open on Kashmir:
There, the fragile wood-shrines—so far away—of Kashmir!
O Destroyer, let her return there, if just to die.
Save the right she gave its earth to cover her, Kashmir
has no rights. When the windows close on Kashmir,
I see the blizzard-fall of ghost-elephants.
I hold back—she couldn't bear it—one elephant's
story: his return (in a country far from Kashmir)
to the jungle where each year, on the day his mother
died, he touches with his trunk the bones of his mother.

"As you sit here by me, you're just like my mother,"
she tells me. I imagine her: a bride in Kashmir,
she's watching, at the Regal, her first film with Father.
If only I could gather you in my arms, Mother,
I'd save you—now my daughter—from .... The universe
opens its ledger. I write: How helpless was ...'s mother!
Each page is turned to enter grief's accounts. Mother,

I See Chile in My Rearview Mirror

By Agha Shahid Ali

By dark the world is once again intact,
Or so the mirrors, wiped clean, try to reason...
                              —*James Merrill*

This dream of water—what does it harbor?
I see Argentina and Paraguay
under a curfew of glass, their colors
breaking, like oil. The night in Uruguay

is black salt. I'm driving toward Utah,
keeping the entire hemisphere in view—
Colombia vermilion, Brazil blue tar,
some countries wiped clean of color: Peru

is titanium white. And always oceans
that hide in mirrors: when beveled edges
arrest tides or this world's destinations
forsake ships. There's Sedona, Nogales

far behind. Once I went through a mirror—
from there too the world, so intact, resembled

only itself. When I returned I tore
the skin off the glass. The sea was unsealed

by dark, and I saw ships sink off the coast
of a wounded republic. Now from a blur
of tanks in Santiago, a white horse
gallops, riderless, chased by drunk soldiers

in a jeep; they're firing into the moon.
And as I keep driving in the desert,
someone is running to catch the last bus, men
hanging on to its sides. And he's missed it.

He is running again; crescents of steel
fall from the sky. And here the rocks
are under fog, the cedars a temple,
Sedona carved by the wind into ...—

each shadow their worshiper. The siren
empties Santiago; he watches
—from a hush of windows—blindfolded men
blurred in gleaming vans. The horse vanishes

into a dream. I'm passing skeletal
figures carved in 700 B.C.
Whoever deciphers these canyon walls
remains forsaken, alone with history,

no harbor for his dream. And what else will
this mirror now reason, filled with water?
I see Peru without rain, Brazil
without forests—and here in Utah a dagger

of sunlight: it's splitting—it's the summer
solstice—the quartz center of a spiral.
Did the Anasazi know the darker
answer also—given now in crystal

by the mirrored continent? The solstice,
but of winter? A beam stabs the window,

diamonds him, a funeral in his eyes.
In the lit stadium of Santiago,

this is the shortest day. He's taken there.
Those about to die are looking at him,
his eyes the ledger of the disappeared.
What will the mirror try now? I'm driving,

still north, always followed by that country,
its floors ice, its citizens so lovesick
that the ground—sheer glass—of every city
is torn up. They demand the republic

give back, jeweled, their every reflection.
They dig till dawn but find only corpses.
He has returned to this dream for his bones.
The waters darken. The continent vanishes.

14

(Meena Alexander, 1951—2018)
米娜·亚历山大

作者简介

米娜·亚历山大（Meena Alexander, 1951—2018），美国印度裔诗人小说家，出生于印度中北部城市阿拉哈巴德（Allahabad），在克拉拉邦（Kerala）和苏丹（Sudan）度过童年。她在喀土穆大学（Khartoum University）获得学士学位，18岁留学英国，获诺丁汉大学（Nottingham University）博士学位。1979年移居美国。米娜曾先后执教于苏丹的喀土穆大学、印度的新德里大学（University of New Delhi）和海德拉巴大学（University of Hyderabad）等数所高等学府，曾任印度高级研究所（Indian Institute for Advanced Study）国家研究员，是纽约城市大学（City University of New York）研究生院杰出教授。

米娜才华横溢，在多个领域皆有建树，著述丰厚，包括诗集、小说、自传、论文集等。诗集主要有《不识字的心》（*Illiterate Heart*, 2002）、《生丝》（*Raw Silk*, 2004）、《急变之河》（*Quickly Changing River*, 2008）、《掩埋之石的出生地》（*Birthplace with Buried Stones*, 2013）、《大气渲染》（*Atmospheric Embroidery*, 2018）等。小说包括《南帕利之路》（*Nampally Road*, 1991）和《曼哈顿音乐》（*Manhattan Music*, 1997）；论文集《抵达的冲击：对后殖民经验的反思》（*The Shock of Arrival: Reflections on Postcolonial Experience*, 1996）、《错位诗学》（*Poetics of Dislocation*, 2009）及个人传记《错误的诗行》（*Fault Lines*, 1993）等其他作品。米娜荣获多个奖项，包括南亚文学协会杰出成就奖（South Asian Literary Association's Distinguished Achievement Award）、英邦吉·耶西兹韦国际诗歌奖（Imbongi Yesizwe International Poetry Award），以及纽约艺术基金会奖金（New York Foundation for the Arts）等。

《错误的诗行》（*Fault Lines*, 1993）被美国《出版商周刊》（*Publishers Weekly*）封为"年度最佳图书"，并于 2003 年修订发行。米娜在这部作品中追溯了她作为孩子、妻子、母亲和作家跨越国界和多种文化的成长历程，让世界听到女性移民的声音。选段部分出自《错误的诗行》第一章，表达了作者面对身份破裂的困境之后的反思。

《不识字的心》一经出版便获 2002 年度笔会开卷图书奖（PEN Open Book Award）。在诗歌《不识字的心》中，诗人在英语与马拉雅拉姆语和法语的语言交织中传达了断裂和错位感以及艺术的选择，语言富有音乐节奏，融入了米娜对殖民教育问题的反思。

作品选读

Fault Lines

Chapter 1
By Meena Alexander

1. Dark Mirror

What would it mean for one such as I to pick up a mirror and try to see her face in it?

Night after night, I asked myself that question. What might it mean to look at myself straight, see myself? How many different gazes would that need? And what to do with the crookedness of flesh, thrown back at the eyes? The more I thought about it, the less sense any of it seemed to make. My voice splintered in my ears into a cacophony: whispering cadences, shouts, moans, the quick delight of bodily pleasure, all rising up as if the condition of being fractured had freed the selves jammed into my skin, multiple beings locked into the journeys of one body.

And what of all the cities and small towns and villages I have lived in since birth: Allahabad, Tiruvella, Kozencheri, Pune, Delhi, Hyderabad, all within the boundaries of India; Khartoum in the Sudan; Nottingham in Britain; and now this island of Manhattan? How should I spell out these fragments of a broken geography?

And what of all the languages compacted in my brain: Malayalam, my mother tongue, the language of first speech; Hindi, which I learnt as a child; Arabic from my years in the Sudan—odd shards survive; French; English? How would I map all this in a book of days? After all, my life did not fall into the narratives I had been taught to honor, tales that closed back on themselves, as a snake might, swallowing its own ending: birth, an appropriate education—not too much, not too little—an arranged marriage to a man of suitable birth and background, somewhere within the boundaries of India.

Sometimes in my fantasies, the kind that hit you in broad daylight, riding the subway, I have imagined being a dutiful wife, my life perfect as a bud opening in the cool monsoon winds, then blossoming on its stalk on the gulmohar tree, petals dark red, falling onto rich soil outside my mother's house in Tiruvella. In the inner life coiled within me, I have sometimes longed to be a bud on a tree, blooming in due season, the tree trunk well rooted in a sweet, perpetual place. But everything I think of is filled with ghosts, even this longing. This imagined past—what never was—is a choke hold.

I sit here writing, for I know that time does not come fluid and whole into my trembling hands. All that is here comes piecemeal, though sometimes the joints have fallen into place miraculously, as if the heavens had opened and mango trees fruited in the rough asphalt of upper Broadway.

But questions persist: Where did I come from? How did I become what I am? How shall I start to write myself, configure my "I" as Other, image this life I lead, here, now, in America? What could I ever be but a mass of faults, a fault mass?

I looked it up in the *Oxford English Dictionary*. It went like this:

> Fault: Deficiency, lack, want of something... Default, failing, neglect. A defect, imperfection, blameable quality or feature: a. in moral character, b. in physical or intellectual constitution, appearance, structure or workmanship. From geology or mining: a dislocation or break in the strata or vein. Examples: "Every coal field is... split asunder, and broken into tiny fragments by faults." (Anstead, *Ancient World*, 1847) "There are several kinds of fault e.g., faults of Dislocation; of Denudation; of Upheaval; etc." (Greasley, *Glossary of Terms in Coal Mining*, 1883) "Fragments of the adjoining rocks mashed and jumbled together, in some cases bound into a solid mass called fault-stuff or faultrock." (Green, Physical *Geography*, 1877)

That's it, I thought. That's all I am, a woman cracked by multiple migrations. Uprooted so many times she can connect nothing with nothing. Her words are all askew. And so I tormented myself on summer nights, and in the chill wind of autumn, tossing back and forth, worrying myself sick. Till my mind slipped back to my mother—amma—she who gave birth to me, and to amma's amma, my veliammechi, grandmother Kunju, drawing me back into the darkness of the Tiruvella house with its cool bedrooms and coiled verandas: the shelter of memory.

But the house of memory is fragile; made up in the mind's space. Even what I remember best, I am forced to admit, is what has flashed up for me in the face of present danger, at the tail end of the century, where everything is to be elaborated, spelt out, precariously reconstructed. And there is little sanctity, even in remembrance.

What I have forgotten is what I have written: a rag of words wrapped around a shard of recollection. A book with torn ends visible. Writing in search of a homeland.

"What are you writing about?" Roshni asked me just the other day. We were speaking on the phone as we so often do, sharing bits of our lives.

"About being born into a female body; about the difficulty of living in space."

"Space?" she asked quizzically.

"Really: living without fixed ground rules, moving about so much; giving birth, all that stuff," I replied shamelessly and laughed into the telephone. I could hear her breathing on the other end, all the way from Sonoma County, California; dear Roshni who has lived in Bombay, Karachi, Beirut, Oaxaca, and Boston. And then her gentle laughter.

Illiterate Heart

By Meena Alexander

I.

One summer holiday I returned
to the house where I was raised.
Nineteen years old, I crouched
on the damp door where grandfather's
library used to be, thumbed through

Conrad's *Heart of Darkness*
thinking why should they imagine no one else
has such rivers in their lives?

I was Marlowe and Kurtz and still more
a black woman just visible at the shore.
I thought it's all happened, all happened before.

So it was I began, unsure of the words
I was to use still waiting for a ghost
to stop me crying out:
You think you write poetry! Hey you —

as he sidestepped me dressed neatly
in his kurta and dhoti,
a mahakavi from the temples of
right thought.

Or one in white flannels
unerringly English, lured from Dove Cottage,
transfixed by carousels of blood,
Danton's daring, stumbling over stones
never noticing his outstretched
hand passed through me.

II.

How did I come to this script?
Amma taught me from the Reading Made Easy
books, Steps 1 & 2 pointed out Tom and Bess
little English children
sweet vowels of flesh they mouthed to perfection:
aa ee ii oo uu a(apple) b(bat) c(cat) d(dat)
Dat? I could not get, so keen the rhymes made me,
sense overthrown.

Those children wore starched knicker
bockers or sailor suits and caps,

waved Union Jacks,
tilted at sugar beets.

O white as milk
their winding sheets!

I imagined them dead all winter
packed into icicles,
tiny and red, frail homunculus each one
sucking on alphabets.

Amma took great care with the books,
wrapped them in newsprint lest something
should spill, set them on the rosewood sill.
When wild doves perched they shook
droplets from quicksilver wings
onto fading covers.

The books sat between Gandhi's Experiments
with Truth and a minute crown of thorns
a visiting bishop had brought.

He told us that the people of Jerusalem
spoke many tongues including Arabic, Persian
Syriac as in our liturgy, Aramaic too.

Donkeys dragged weights through tiny streets.
Like our buffaloes, he laughed.
I had to perform my *Jana Gana Mana* for him
and Wordsworth's daffodil poem—

the latter I turned into a rural terror
my version of the chartered streets.

III.

What beats in my heart? Who can tell?
I cannot tease my writing hand around
that burnt hole of sense, figure out the
quickstep of syllables.

On pages where I read the words of Gandhi
and Marx, saw the light of the Gospels,
the script started to quiver and flick.

Letters grew fins and tails.
Swords sprang from the hips of consonants,
vowels grew ribbed and sharp.
Pages bound into leather
turned the color of ink.

My body flew apart:
wrist, throat, elbow, thigh,
knee where a mole rose,
bony scapula, blunt cut hair,

then utter stillness as a white sheet
dropped on nostrils and neck.

Black milk of childhood drunk
and drunk again!

I longed to be like Tom and Bess
dead flat on paper.

IV.

At noon I burrowed through
Malayalam sounds,
slashes of sense, a floating trail.

Nights I raced into the garden.

Smoke on my tongue, wet earth
from twisted roots of banyan
and fiscus Indica.

What burnt in the mirror
of the great house
became a fierce condiment.
A metier almost:

aa i ii u uu au um aha ka kh
ga gha nga cha chha ja ja nja
njana (my sole self), njaman (knowledge)
nunni (gratitude) ammechi, appechan,
veliappechan (grandfather).

Uproar of sense, harsh tutelage:
aana (elephant) amma (tortoise)
ambjuan (lotus).

A child mouthing words
to flee family.

I will never enter that house I swore,
I'll never be locked in a cage of script.

And the lotus rose, quietly, quietly,
I committed that to memory,
later added: *ce lieu me plaît*
dominé de flambeaux.

V.

In dreams I was a child babbling
at the gate splitting into two,
three to make herself safe.

Grown women combing black hair
in moonlight by the railroad track,
stuck forever at the accidental edge.

O the body in parts,
bruised buttress of heaven!
she cries,

a child in a village church
clambering into embroidered vestements
to sing at midnight a high sweet tune.

Or older now
musing in sunlight

combing a few white strands of hair.

To be able to fail.
To set oneself up
so that failure is also possible.

Yes,
that too
however it is grasped.

The movement towards self definition.
A woman walking the streets,
a woman combing her hair.

Can this make music in your head?
Can you whistle hot tunes
to educate the barbarians?

These lines took decades to etch free,
the heart's illiterate,
the map is torn.

Someone I learn to recognise,
cries out at Kurtz, thrusts skulls aside,
lets the floodwaters pour.

15

(Sara Suleri Goodyear, 1953—2022)
萨拉·苏莱里·古德伊尔

作者简介

萨拉·苏莱里·古德伊尔（Sara Suleri Goodyear，1953—2022），美国巴基斯坦裔作家、评论家，在拉合尔长大。在金纳德学院和旁遮普大学相继获得学位后继续深造，获得美国印第安纳大学（Indiana University）博士学位。

古德伊尔是耶鲁大学（Yale University）的英语教授，她的研究和教学领域包括浪漫主义和维多利亚时期的诗歌。她特别关注的问题包括后殖民主义文学和理论、当代文化批评、文学和法律。她是《耶鲁批评杂志》（*Yale Journal of Criticism*）的创始编辑，也是《耶鲁评论》（*The Yale Review*）编辑委员会成员。

她的主要作品有评论性著作《印度英语的修辞》（*The Rhetoric of English India*，1992），两本备受赞誉的回忆录《无肉的日子》（*Meatless Days*，1989）和《男孩会是男孩》（*Boys Will Be Boys*，2003），以及一本译著和散文等。她与朋友阿兹拉·拉扎（Azra Raza）合作，将伟大的乌尔都语诗人米尔扎·阿萨杜拉·汗·加利布（Mirza Asadullah Khan Ghalib）的加扎尔诗集《优雅的认识论》（*Epistomologies of Elegance*）翻译成英文。

古德伊尔也发表了一系列散文，其中《女性的美好事物》（"Excellent Things in Women"）备受赞誉，曾获得1987年手推车奖（Pushcart Prize）。这部作品为读者提供了关于后殖民时代巴基斯坦生活的精巧回忆。她将巴基斯坦独立的暴力历史与自己的亲身经历交织在一起。选段出自《女性的美好事物》，讲述了她的祖母达迪（Dadi）以及她母亲的部分回忆。

作品选读

Excellent Things in Women

(excerpt)

By Sara Suleri Goodyear

Leaving Pakistan was, of course, tantamount to giving up the company of women. I can tell this only to someone like Anita, in all the faith that she will understand, as we go perambulating through the grimness of New Haven and feed on the pleasures of our conversational way. Dale, who lives in Boston, would also understand. She will one day write a book about the stern and secretive life of breastfeeding and is partial to fantasies that culminate in an abundance of resolution. And Fawzi, with a grimace of recognition, knows because she knows the impulse to forget.

To a stranger or an acquaintance, however, some vesitigial remoteness obliges me to explain that my reference is to a place where the concept of woman was not really part of an available vocabulary: We were too busy for that, just living, and conducting precise negotiations with what it meant to be a sister or a child or a wife or a mother or a servant. By this point admittedly I am damned by my own discourse, and doubly damned when I add, yes, once in a while, we naturally thought of ourselves as women, but only in some perfunctory biological way that we happened on perchance. Or else it was a hugely practical joke, we thought, hidden somewhere among our clothes. But formulating that definition is about as impossible as attempting to locate the luminous qualities of an Islamic landscape, which can on occasion generate such aesthetically pleasing moments of life. My audience is lost, and angry to be lost, and both of us must find some token of exchange for this failed conversation. I try to lay the subject down and change its clothes, but before I know it, it has sprinted off evilly in the direction of ocular evidence. It goads me into saying, with the defiance of a plea, "You did not deal with Dadi."

Dadi, my father's mother, was born in Meerut toward the end of the last century. She was married at sixteen and widowed in her thirties, and by her latter decades could never exactly recall how many children she had borne. When India was partitioned, in August of 1947, she moved her thin pure Urdu into the Punjab of Pakistan and waited for the return of her eldest son, my father. He had gone careening off to a place called Inglestan, or England, fired by one of the several enthusiasms made available by the proliferating talk of independence. Dadi was peeved. She had long since dispensed with any loyalties larger than the pitiless give-and-take of people who are forced to live together in the same place, and she resented independence for the distances it made. She was not among those who, on the fourteenth of August, unfurled flags and festivities against the backdrop of people running and cities burning. About that era she would only say, looking up sour and cryptic over the edge of her Quran, "And I was also burned." She was, but that came years later.

By the time I knew her, Dadi with her flair for drama had allowed life to sit so heavily upon her back that her spine wilted and froze into a perfect curve, and so it was in the posture of a shrimp that she went scuttling through the day. She either scuttled or did not: It all depended on the nature of her fight with the Devil. There were days when she so hated him that all she could do was stretch herself out straight and tiny on her bed, uttering most awful imprecation. Sometimes, to my mother's great distress, Dadi could berate Satan in full eloquence only after she had clambered on top of the dining-room table and lain there like a little molding centerpiece. Satan was to blame: He had after all made her older son linger long enough in Inglestan to give up his rightful wife, a cousin, and take up instead with a white-legged woman. Satan had stolen away her only daughter Ayesha when Ayesha lay in childbirth. And he'd sent her youngest son to Swaziland, or Switzerland; her thin hand waved away such sophistries of name.

... she loved, and she understood him better than anyone. Her favorite days were those when she could circumnavigate both the gardener and my father, all in the solemn service of her .... With a pilfered knife, she'd wheedle her way to the nearest sapling in the garden, some sprightly poplar or a newly planted eucalyptus. She'd squat, she'd hack it down, and then she'd peel its bark away until she had a walking stick, all white and virgin and her own. It drove my father into tears of rage. He must have bought her a dozen walking sticks, one for each of our trips to the mountains, but it was like assembling a row of briar pipes for one who will not smoke: Dadi had different aims. Armed with implements of her own creation, she would creep down the driveway unperceived to stop cars and people on the street and give them all the gossip that she had on ....

Food, too, could move her to intensities. Her eyesight always took a sharp turn for the worse over meals—she could point hazily at a perfectly ordinary potato and murmur with Adamic reverence "What is it, what is it called?" With some shortness of manner one of us would describe and catalog the items on the table. "*Alu ka bhartha,*" Dadi repeated with wonderment and joy; "Yes, Saira Begum, you can put some here." "Not too much," she'd add pleadingly. For ritual had it that the more she demurred, the more she expected her plate to be piled with an amplitude her own politeness would never allow. The ritual happened three times a day.

We pondered it but never quite determined whether food or ... constituted her most profound delight. Obvious problems, however, occurred whenever the two converged. One such occasion was the Muslim festival called Eid—not the one that ends the month of fasting, but the second Eid, which celebrates the seductions of the Abraham story in a remarkably literal way. In Pakistan, at least, people buy sheeps or goats beforehand and fatten them up for weeks with delectables. Then, on the appointed day, the animals are chopped, in place of sons, and neighbors graciously exchange silver trays heaped with raw and quivering meat. Following Eid prayers the men come home, and the animal is killed, and shortly thereafter rush out of the kitchen steaming plates of grilled lung and liver, of a freshness quite superlative.

It was a freshness to which my Welsh mother did not immediately take. She observed the custom but discerned in it a conundrum that allowed no ready solution. Liberal to an extravagant degree on thoughts abstract, she found herself to be remarkably squeamish about particular things. Chopping up animals for ... was one. She could not locate the metaphor and was uneasy when obeisance played such a truant to the metaphoric realm. My father the writer quite agreed: He was so civilized in those days.

Dadi didn't agree. She pined for choppable things. Once she made the mistake of buying a baby goat and bringing him home months in advance of Eid. She wanted to guarantee the texture of his festive flesh by a daily feeding of tender peas and clarified butter. Ifat, Shahid, and I greeted a goat into the family with boisterous rapture, and, soon after, he ravished us completely when we found him at the washingline nonchalantly eating Shahid's pajamas. Of course there was no argument: The little goat was our delight, and even Dadi knew there was no killing him. He became my brother's and my sister's and my first pet, and he grew huge, a big and grinning thing.

Years after, Dadi had her will. We were old enough, she must have thought, to set the house sprawling, abstracted, into a multitude of secrets. This was true, but still we all noticed one another's secretive ways. When, the day before Eid, our Dadi disappeared, my brothers and sisters and I just shook our heads. We hid the fact from my father, who at this time of life had begun to equate petulance with extreme vociferation. So we went about our jobs and tried to be Islamic for a day. We waited to sight moons on the wrong occasion, and watched the food come into lavishment. Dried dates change shape when they are soaked in milk, and carrots rich and strange turn magically sweet when deftly covered with green nutty shavings and smatterings of silver. Dusk was sweet as we sat out, the day's work done, in an evening garden. Lahore spread like peace around us. My father spoke, and when Papa talked, it was of Pakistan. But we were glad, then, at being audience to that familiar conversation, till his voice looked up, and failed. There was Dadi making her return, and she was prodigal. Like a question mark interested only in its own conclusions, her body crawled through the gates. Our guests were spellbound, then they looked away. Dadi, moving in her eerie crab formations, ignored the hangman's rope she firmly held as behind her in the gloaming minced, hugely affable, a goat.

That goat was still smiling the following day when Dadi's victory brought the butcher, who came and went just as he should on Eid. The goat was killed and cooked: A scrawny beast that required much cooking and never melted into succulence, he winked and glistened on our plates as we sat eating him on Eid. Dadi ate, that is: Papa had taken his mortification to some distant corner of the house; Ifat refused to chew on hemp; Tillat and Irfan gulped their baby sobs over such a slaughter. "Honestly," said Mamma, "honestly." For Dadi had successfully cut through tissues of festivity just as the butcher slit the goat, but there was something else that she was eating with that meat. I saw it in her concentration; I know that she was making ... talk to her as to Abraham and was showing him what she could do—for him—to sons. ... didn't dare, and she ate on alone.

16

(Vijay Seshadri, 1954—)
维贾伊·瑟哈德里

作者简介

维贾伊·瑟哈德里（Vijay Seshadri, 1954— ），美国印度裔诗人、散文家、批评家，出生于印度班加罗尔（Bangalore），5岁时来到美国。他曾修读哥伦比亚大学（Columbia University）中东语言和文学博士，拥有欧柏林学院（Oberlin College）学士学位和哥伦比亚大学艺术硕士学位。他曾在《纽约客》担任编辑，并在萨拉·劳伦斯学院（Sarah Lawrence College）教授诗歌和散文写作。瑟哈德里荣获纽约艺术基金会（New York Foundation for the Arts）、国家教育协会（NEA）和古根海姆基金会（Guggenheim Foundation）等各类奖学金。

瑟哈德里的作品主要包括诗集《野生动物王国》(*Wild Kingdom*, 1996)、《长草地》(*Long Meadow*, 2003)和《三部分》(*3 Sections*, 2013)。他的第一部诗集《野生动物王国》一经出版便引起美国文坛的广泛关注，被认为是美国诗歌史上又一大胆的新声。第二部诗集《长草地》荣获美国诗人学院（Academy of American Poets）颁发的詹姆斯·劳克林奖（James Laughlin Award）。第三部诗集《三部分》荣获2014年普利策诗歌奖（Pulitzer Prize for Poetry），他是第一个获得该奖的亚洲裔诗人。从押韵的抒情诗到哲学冥想的散文，评委会认为他"用诙谐而庄重、怜悯亦无情的语言检验了人类从出生到生命退化过程中的人性意识"。

《三部分》这部诗集中包括诗歌和散文，形式新颖，体现了作者对历史及未来的一种超越时间的思考。诗歌《新媒体》("New Media")、《疗养院》("Nursing Home")均选自诗集《三部分》。在《新媒体》这首诗中，诗人阐述了"分离的自我"的经历。在《疗养院》中诗人描述了我们在考虑退化性精神疾病时如何依赖于语言。这首诗探索了人类对失去处理世界的能力的焦虑和讲故事的需要。

作品节选

New Media

By Vijay Seshadri

Why I wanted to escape experience is nobody's business but my own,
but I always believed I could if I could
put experience into words.
Now I know better.
Now I know words are experience.
"But ah thought kills me that I am not thought"
"2 People Searched for You"
"In the beginning was the..."
"re: Miss Exotic World"
"I Want Us To Executed Transaction"
It's not the thing,
there is no thing,
there's no thing in itself,
there's nothing but what's said about the thing,
there are no things but words
about the things
said over and over,
perching, grooming their wings,
on the subject lines.

Nursing Home

By Vijay Seshadri

1.

She had dreams fifty years ago
she remembers on this day.
She dreamed about Bombay.
It looked like Rio.
She dreamed about Rio,
which looked like itself, though
Rio was a city she'd never seen—
not on TV, not in a magazine.
Brain scans done on her show
her perisylvian pathways and declivities
choked by cities,
microscopic mercurial cities
made from her memories,
good and bad,
from the things she saw but didn't see,
from the remembered pressure
of every lover she ever had.

2.

Unexpected useful combinations between cognitive psychology and neuroscience have fostered new observational protocols not only for eldely patients in the Lewy body pathologic subgroup but those discovered across a wide spectrum of dementias and dementia-induced phenomena, including but not limited to Normal Pressure Hydrocephalus (NPH), classical Alzheimer's disease (AD), and the deformations in mental recognition and function (Dear, eat the soup with the spoon, not the fork), the coruscating visions (Who is that laid out in my bed?), the spontaneous motor features of Parkinsonism. Synaptic patterns embodied in sparks, showers, electrical cascades, waterfalls, and shooting stars are increasingly revealing an etiology proximately to be fully established and suggestive links between processes strictly biochemical and ideational and linguistic explosions for which documentation has been massive while analysis has, so far, been scant. While an adequate conceptual apparatus still remains out of reach, progress across a broad frontier of research has been sufficiently dramatic to suggest possible developments that will lead both to therapeutic remedies for distressed elderly patients and to a synthesis among various disciplines that have heretofore seemed not just incompatible but in direct conflict with one another. Certain coherencies have been unearthed that have truly startled our consensus…

3.

—She doesn't know any better than to act the fool.
—Is she dead? No, she's not dead.
—Is she dead?
—No, I'm not dead, and I don't want anybody to think I'm dead.
—Do you think it's funny?
—Wonder why she acts like that?
—Is she dead? No, she's not dead, and I'm not dead, neither.
—Is she really dead? No, she's not dead, but she's acting the fool.
—Are you really dead? No, I'm not really dead. I'm just acting the fool.
—I'll show you how I can act the fool.
—No, I don't think I look nice. I think I look purty.
—No, I'm not dead. I just act like I'm dead.
—What makes you want to act like she's dead?
—Do you think she's dead?
—Do you think she's dead, or is she just acting the fool?

17

(Abraham Verghese, 1955—)
亚伯拉罕·韦尔盖塞

作者简介

亚伯拉罕·韦尔盖塞（Abraham Verghese, 1955—），美国印度裔小说家、医生，出生于埃塞俄比亚（Ethiopia），父母来自印度克拉拉邦。1980年来到美国之前，他曾在埃塞俄比亚和印度学习和生活。从马德拉斯医学院（Madras Medical College）毕业后，他离开印度到美国做住院医生，担任斯坦福大学医学院医学理论与实践教授，内科高级副主任（Senior Associate Chair of the Department of Internal Medicine）。2011年，他被推选为医学研究所（Institute of Medicine）成员。2015年，他获得了美国总统奥巴马颁发的"国家人文奖章"（National Humanities Medal）。

冰冷和缺乏想象力的科学语言无法捕捉到病人和家属的经历，也无法表达他目睹他们的旅程时的感受，于是韦尔盖塞对写作产生了极大的兴趣。他在艾奥瓦作家工作室学习深造，并于1991年获得了创意写作硕士学位。从那以后，他的作品出现在《纽约客》《得克萨斯月刊》（Texas Monthly）、《纽约时报》（The New York Times）、《纽约时报杂志》（The New York Times Magazine）、《福布斯》（Forbes）、《华尔街日报》（The Wall Street Journal）等各类报纸和杂志上。

韦尔盖塞的作品主要包括两部回忆录和一部小说。回忆录《我的祖国：一个医生的故事》（My Own Country: A Doctor's Story, 1994）讲述了他在田纳西州的约翰斯顿小镇治疗艾滋病的经历。这部作品被《时代》（Time）杂志评为"年度最佳书籍"之一，后来被拍摄成电影《我自己的国家》，由米拉·奈尔（Mira Nair）导演，纳文·安德鲁斯（Naveen Andrews）主演。回忆录《网球伙伴：友谊和失去的故事》(*The Tennis Partner: A Story of Friendship and Loss*, 1997) 描述了韦尔盖塞在经历婚姻危机期间遇到了一位实习医生，并与其成为网球伙伴的经历。这本书被《纽约时报》评为"年度最佳书籍"。

小说《割裂斯通》(*Cutting for Stone*, 2009) 是一部关于爱与背叛、宽恕与自我牺牲、生命与死亡不可分割的故事。韦尔盖塞对医学世界的洞察力，以及关于医生如何工作的大量精确细节的描写，在美国小说中是无与伦比的。这部小说被《出版人周刊》评为2009年度"最佳图书"之一。选段部分出自《割裂斯通》第五十五章，讲述了叙述者马里恩（Marion）在发现母亲留给自己的那封信之后，自我、兄弟、父亲终于达成和解。

作品选读

Cutting for Stone

Chapter 55

By Abraham Verghese

CHAPTER 55

The Afterbird September 19 Dear Thomas, Last night, ... told me I must confess to you what I have never confessed, even to .... Years ago, in Aden, I turned from ... as He turned from me. Something happened to me there that should not happen to any woman. I could not forgive the man who harmed me. I could not forgive .... Death would have been better than what I endured. But I came here, to Missing. I came in the dress of a nun to hide my bitterness and shame from the world. In Jeremiah 17 it is written, "The heart is deceitful above all things and beyond cure, and who can understand it?" I came to Ethiopia in deceit. But our work changed me. I would have been your assistant till my last breath. Now, things have changed again. A few months ago, you were like a man possessed, and I tried to comfort you. Now I am with child. Do not blame yourself. It was difficult to hide my body from Matron and the others. Many times I thought of telling you. I could never find a way. But now I am frightened. My time is short. Last night the movements *became strong. It made me think, What if Thomas wishes me to stay? I should not leave in the way I came to Missing and to you, hiding and in deceit. That is why I write. I must flee Missing to spare it my shame just as I once fled to it to hide my shame. If you come to me when you get this letter, I will know that you wish me to be with you. But whatever you do, my love will always be the same. Mary*

It took such concentration to finish my last surgical case—a routine vagotomy and gastrojejunostomy for a duodenal ulcer—and not let my mind wander. At last, with that letter in hand, I walked back to my quarters, feeling as if I had never come up this path before.

She loved him. She loved him so much she ran to him from Aden. The bloodstains with which she came to Missing told me what she could not. She made her way to the doctor—the man—she had met on that ship out of India. And then, years later, she loved him so much she was ready to leave him. At the eleventh hour she decided to write and tell him. Then she waited for him to come, or not.

But Thomas Stone did come. Surely she would have registered his arrival. As he picked her up, carried her, ran with her, every tear that fell from his eyes onto her face she would have interpreted as affirmations of his love. He came not because of the letter: he never got it. He came because some part of him knew what he had done, and what he had to do: some part of him knew what he felt.

I pictured Ghosh visiting Thomas Stone's quarters after my mother's death, searching for him. He would have seen on Stone's desk the new textbook and bookmark, and on top of them, conspicuously perhaps, this letter. Thomas Stone never saw the book or the letter because he spent the previous night sleeping in the lounge chair in his Missing office, as he often did, and then after my mother's death he never returned to his quarters. Why hadn't Ghosh simply mailed the letter directly to Thomas Stone? Thomas never wrote or communicated; Ghosh had no address at first. But as the years went by, Ghosh could probably have found Stone's whereabouts. After all, Eli Harris had always known them. But perhaps by then Ghosh was hurt by Stone's silence and his willingness to forget his old friend and leave him caring for his children as he ran from his past. As more years went by, Ghosh might have pondered the effect of the letter on Stone—perhaps it would in fact be a disservice to send it to him. It might have precipitated another meltdown, or, as Hema had always feared, Stone might have returned to claim the children. And perhaps Stone wouldn't understand—or believe—anything the letter said.

Then, as death approached, it must have worked on Ghosh's conscience to be the keeper of this letter. What if the contents could save Stone, put his heart at ease? What if it made Stone do, even belatedly, the right thing by his sons? By this time all Ghosh's resentment for Stone, if he ever had any, had vanished.

So ultimately Ghosh gave the textbook and bookmark to Shiva, and the letter to me, but hidden from me. I marveled at the foresight of a dying man who would entomb a letter within a framed picture. He would leave it to fate—how like Ghosh this was! When would I find Thomas Stone? When would I find the letter? If and when I found it, would I give the letter to its intended recipient? Ghosh trusted me to do whatever it is I would choose to do. That, too, is love. Had been dead more than a quarter century and he was still teaching me about the trust that comes only from true love.

"Shiva," I said, looking up at the sky where the stars were warming up for their nightly show while I recalled the night I fled Missing in haste, and how Shiva had thrust at me my father's book—*A Short Practice*, that bookmark inside. The few words on the bookmark penned by my mother were the only way any of us knew a letter even existed. Years ago, over the telephone, I had asked him, "Shiva, what made you give me the book?" He didn't know. "I wanted you to have it" was all he could say. The world turns on our every action, and our every omission, whether we know it or not.

WHEN I REACHED MY QUARTERS, I sat down and spread the letter on my lap, and with shaky hands I dialed Thomas Stone's number. My father was well past eighty now, an emeritus professor. Deepak said the old man's eyes were fading, but his touch was so good he could have operated in the dark. Still, he rarely operated anymore, though he would often assist. Thomas Stone was once known for *The Expedient Operator: A Short Practice of Tropical Surgery*. Now he was famous for pioneering a breakthrough transplant procedure. I was proof that the operation worked, but Shiva's death was proof of the attendant risks. Surgeons around the world had learned to do the operation, and many infants born without a working bile-drainage system had been saved by a parent's gift of a part of his or her liver.

IN MY EARPIECE I heard the hush of the void that hangs over the earth, and then out of that ether, the sound of the phone ringing far away, its high-pitched summons so brisk and efficient, so different from the lackadaisical analog clicks and the coarse ring when I dialed an Addis Ababa number. I pictured the phone trill and echo in the apartment that I had visited once, and which I had left open like a sardine can so that Thomas Stone would know that his son had arrived in his world.

I thought of my mother writing this letter, her whole life compressed on one side of this parchment. She had probably delivered it (and the book with bookmark) in the late afternoon when the pains hit her. She had worsened in the night, slowly slipping into shock, and then the next day she died. But not before Thomas Stone came to her. It was the sign she had waited for. He did the right thing, and yet for the last half century, he was unaware that he had done so.

Thomas Stone answered after the first ring. It made me wonder if he were wide awake even though it was the middle of the night in Boston.

"Yes?" My father's voice was crisp and alert, as if he expected this intrusion, as if he were ready for the story of trauma or massive brain bleed that made an organ available, or ready to hear of a child, one in ten thousand, born with biliary atresia who would die without a liver transplant. The voice I heard was that of someone who would bring all the skill and experience he carried in his nine fingers to the rescue of a fellow human being, and who would pass on that legacy to another generation of interns and residents—it was what he was born to do; he knew nothing else. "Stone here," he said, his voice sounding so very dose, as if he were there with me, as if nothing at all separated our two worlds.

18

(Chitra Banerjee Divakaruni, 1956—)
奇塔·班纳吉·蒂娃卡鲁尼

作者简介

奇塔·班纳吉·蒂娃卡鲁尼（Chitra Banerjee Divakaruni, 1956—），著名美籍印度裔诗人、小说家，出生于印度加尔各答。蒂娃卡鲁尼获得印度加尔各答大学学士学位、美国莱特州立大学（Wright State University）硕士学位、加州大学伯克利分校博士学位。蒂娃卡鲁尼现居得克萨斯州（Texas），在休斯敦大学（University of Houston）教授创意写作课程。

蒂娃卡鲁尼著作颇丰，主要有诗歌和小说。诗集有《旱金莲的原因》(*The Reason for Nasturtiums*, 1990)、《黑色蜡烛》(*Black Candle*, 1991)、《离开尤巴城》(*Leaving Yuba City*, 1997)等。小说主要有《香料情妇》(*The Mistress of Spices*, 1997)、《我心姐妹》(*Sister of My Heart*, 1999)、《欲望的藤蔓》(*Vine of Desire*, 2002)、《美梦女王》(*Queen of Dreams*, 2004)、《一件美事》(*One Amazing Thing*, 2010)、《幻影宫殿》(*The Palace of Illusions*, 2008)、《夹竹桃女孩》(*Oleander Girl*, 2013)、《在我们拜访女神之前》(*Before We Visit the Goddess*, 2016)和《最后的女王》(*The Last Queen*, 2022)。短篇小说集《媒妁婚姻》(*Arranged Marriage*, 1995)。青少年小说有《海螺护卫》(*The Conch Bearer*, 2003)、《火与梦之镜》(*The Mirror of Fire and Dreaming*, 2005)和《影子土地》(*Shadowland*, 2009)。

蒂娃卡鲁尼荣获各类奖项，包括美国图书奖（American Book Award）、印度之光奖（Light of India Award）、SALA 奖、手推车奖、艾伦·金斯伯格奖（Allen Ginsberg Award）、芭芭拉·戴明纪念奖（Barbara Deming Memorial Award）和休斯敦文学奖（Houston Literary Award）以及国际职业妇女协会（The International

Association of Working Women)最佳图书奖(Best Book Award)。

印度和美国的双重文化身份使得她的作品总是聚焦于印度经历和当代美国社会。她的作品情节精巧,感情细腻动人,她的文字糅合东西方传统,兼具印度的乡愁、英诗的优美等特点,富含诗韵。诗歌《切割太阳》("Cutting the Sun")选自诗集《离开尤巴城》,描绘了移民的心理与处境。小说《我心姐妹》讲述一对来自印度上层社会的表姐妹在经历世事变故后仍然互相关爱、互相支持的故事。选段部分出自《我心姐妹》第一章,介绍两个命运相连的表姐妹安珠(Anju)和苏哈(Sudha)的基本信息。

作品选读

Cutting the Sun

By Chitra Banerjee Divakaruni

After Francesco Clemente's *Indian Miniature* #16
The sun-face looms over me, gigantic-hot, smelling
of iron. Its rays striated,
rasp-red and muscled as the tongues
of iguanas. They are trying to lick away
my name. But I
am not afraid. I hold in my hands
(where did I get them)
enormous blue scissors that are
just the color of sky. I bring
the blades together, like
a song. The rays fall around me
curling a bit, like dried carrot peel. A far sound
in the air—fire
or rain? And when I've cut
all the way to the center of the sun
I see
flowers, flowers, flowers.

Sister of My Heart

Chapter One Sudha

(excerpt)

By Chitra Banerjee Divakaruni

THEY say in the old tales that the first night after a child is born, the Bidhata Purush comes down to earth himself to decide what its fortune is to be. That is why they bathe babies in sandalwood water and wrap them in soft red malmal, color of luck. That is why they leave sweetmeats by the cradle. Silver-leafed sandesh, dark pantuas floating in golden syrup, jilipis orange as the heart of a fire, glazed with honey-sugar. If the child is especially lucky, in the morning it will all be gone.

"That's because the servants sneak in during the night and eat them," says Anju, giving her head an impatient shake as Abha Pishi oils her hair. This is how she is, my cousin, always scoffing, refusing to believe. But she knows, as I do, that no servant in all of Calcutta would dare eat sweets meant for a ....

The old tales say this also: In the wake of the Bidhata Purush come the demons, for that is the world's nature, good and evil mingled. That is why they leave an oil lamp burning. That is why they place the sacred tulsi leaf under the baby's pillow for protection. In richer households, like the one my mother grew up in, she has told us, they hire a brahmin to sit in the corridor and recite auspicious prayers all night.

"What nonsense," Anju says. "There are no demons."

I am not so sure. Perhaps they do not have the huge teeth, the curved blood-dripping claws and bulging red eyes of our Children's Ramayan Picture Book, but I have a feeling they exist. Haven't I sensed their breath, like slime-black fingers brushing my spine? Later, when we are alone, I will tell Anju this.

But in front of others I am always loyal to her. So I say, bravely, "That's right. Those are just old stories."

It is early evening on our terrace, its bricks overgrown with moss. A time when the sun hangs low on the horizon, half hidden by the pipal trees which line our compound walls all the way down the long driveway to the bolted wrought-iron gates. Our great-grandfather had them planted one hundred years ago to keep the women of his house safe from the gaze of strangers. Abha Pishi, one of our three mothers, has told us this.

Yes, we have three mothers—perhaps to make up for the fact that we have no fathers.

There's Pishi, our widow aunt who threw herself heart-first into her younger brother's household when she lost her husband at the age of eighteen. Dressed in austere white, her graying hair cut close to her scalp in the orthodox style so that the bristly ends tickle my palms when I run my hands over them, she's the one who makes sure we are suitably dressed for school in the one-inch-below-the-knee uniforms the nuns insist on. She finds for us, miraculously, stray pens and inkpots and missing pages of homework. She makes us our favorite dishes: luchis rolled out and fried a puffy golden-brown, potato and cauliflower curry cooked without chilies, thick sweet payesh made from the milk of Budhi-cow, whose owner brings her to our house each morning to be milked under Pishi's stern, miss-nothing stare. On holidays she plaits jasmine into our hair. But most of all Pishi is our fount of information, the one who tells us the stories our mothers will not, the secret, delicious, forbidden tales of our past.

There's Anju's mother, whom I call Gouri Ma, her fine cheekbones and regal forehead hinting at generations of breeding, for she comes from a family as old and respected as that of the Chatterjees, which she married into. Her face is not beautiful in the traditional sense—even I, young as I am, know this. Lines of hardship are etched around her mouth and on her forehead, for she was the one who shouldered the burden of keeping the family safe on that thunderclap day eight years ago when she received news of our fathers' deaths. But her eyes, dark and endless-deep—they make me think of Kalodighi, the enormous lake behind the country mansion our family used to own before Anju and I were born. When Gouri Ma smiles at me with her eyes, I stand up straighter. I want to be noble and brave, just like her.

Lastly (I use this word with some guilt), there's my own mother, Nalini. Her skin is still golden, for though she's a widow my mother is careful to apply turmeric paste to her face each day. Her perfect-shaped lips glisten red from paan, which she loves to chew—mostly for the color it leaves on her mouth, I think. She laughs often, my mother, especially when her friends come for tea and talk. It is a glittery, tinkling sound, like jeweled ankle bells, people say, though I myself feel it is more like a thin glass struck with a spoon. Her cheek feels as soft as the lotus flower she's named after on those rare occasions when she presses her face to mine. But more often when she looks at me a frown ridges her forehead between eyebrows beautiful as wings. Is it from worry or displeasure? I can never tell. Then she remembers that frowns cause age lines and smoothes it away with a finger.

Now Pishi stops oiling Anju's hair to give us a wicked smile. Her voice grows low and shivery, the way it does when she's telling ghost stories. "They're listening, you know. The demons. And they don't like little eight-year-old girls talking like this. Just wait till tonight..."

Because I am scared I interrupt her with the first thought that comes into my head. "Pishi Ma, tell no, did the sweets disappear for us?"

Sorrow moves like smoke-shadow over Pishi's face. I can see that she would like to make up another of those outrageous tales that we so love her to tell, full of magic glimmer and hoping. But finally she says, her voice flat, "No, Sudha. You weren't so lucky."

I know this already. Anju and I have heard the whispers. Still, I must ask one more time.

"Did you see anything that night?" I ask. Because she was the one who stayed with us the night of our birth while our mothers lay in bed, still in shock from the terrible telegram which had sent them both into early labor that morning. Our mothers, lying in beds they would never again share with their husbands. My mother weeping, her beautiful hair tangling about her swollen face, punching at a pillow until it burst, spilling cotton stuffing white as grief. Gouri Ma, still and silent, staring up into a darkness which pressed upon her like the responsibilities she knew no one else in the family could take on.

To push them from my mind I ask urgently, "Did you at least hear something?"

Pishi shakes her head in regret. "Maybe the Bidhata Purush doesn't come for girl-babies." In her kindness she leaves the rest unspoken, but I've heard the whispers often enough to complete it in my head. For girl-babies who are so much bad luck that they cause their fathers to die even before they are born.

Anju scowls, and I know that as always she can see into my thoughts with the X-ray vision of her fiercely loving eyes. "Maybe there's no Bidhata Purush either," she states and yanks her hair from Pishi's hands though it is only half-braided. She ignores Pishi's scolding shouts and stalks to her room, where she will slam the door.

But I sit very still while Pishi's fingers rub the hibiscus oil into my scalp, while she combs away knots with the long, soothing rhythm I have known since the beginning of memory. The sun is a deep, sad red, and I can smell, faint on the evening air, wood smoke. The pavement dwellers are lighting their cooking fires. I've seen them many times when Singhji, our chauffeur, drives us to school: the mother in a worn green sari bent over a spice-grinding stone, the daughter watching the baby, keeping him from falling into the gutter. The father is never there. Maybe he is running up a platform in Howrah station in his red turban, his shoulders knotted from carrying years of trunks and bedding rolls, crying out, "Coolie chahiye, want a coolie, memsaab?" Or maybe, like my father, he too is dead.

Whenever I thought this my eyes would sting with sympathy, and if by chance Ramur Ma, the vinegary old servant woman who chaperones us everywhere, was not in the car, I'd beg Singhji to stop so I could hand the girl a sweet out of my lunch box. And he always did.

19

(Kirin Narayan, 1959—)
基琳·娜拉杨

作者简介

基琳·娜拉杨（Kirin Narayan, 1959—），美国印度裔作家、人类学家、民俗学家，出生于印度孟买（Mumbai），1976年移民美国。她在加利福尼亚大学伯克利分校学习文化人类学和民俗学，并获得博士学位。她是澳大利亚国立大学（Australian National University）的人类学教授。

娜拉杨的创作得到了国家人文科学基金会（National Endowment for the Humanities）、美国印度研究所（American Institute of Indian Studies）、美国研究学院（School of American Research）、约翰·西蒙·古根海姆纪念基金会（John Simon Guggenheim Memorial Foundation）、社会科学研究委员会（Social Science Research Council）的大力支持。她于2011年获得了威斯康星大学的"校长杰出教学奖"（Chancellor's Distinguished Teaching Award），成为约翰·西蒙·古根海姆纪念基金会评选委员会的成员。

娜拉杨的创作主要包括民族志及小说。民族志作品包括《讲故事的人、圣人和恶棍：印度教宗教教学中的民间叙事》（*Storytellers, Saints and Scoundrels: Folk Narrative in Hindu Religious Teaching*, 1989）、与乌尔米拉·德维·苏德（Urmila Devi Sood）合作完成的《月黑风高之夜的星期一：喜马拉雅山麓的民间故事》（*Mondays on the Dark Night of the Moon: Himalayan Foothill Folktales*, 1997）、《我的家庭和其他圣徒》（*My Family and Other Saints*, 2007）、《生活在写作中：在契诃夫的陪伴下创作民族志》（*Alive in the Writing: Crafting Ethnography in the Company of Chekhov*, 2012）、《日常创意：喜马拉雅山麓的歌唱女神》（*Everyday Creativity:*

Singing Goddesses of the Himalayan Foothills, 2016）。小说《爱、星星和所有》（*Love, Stars and All That*, 1994）。《讲故事的人、圣人和恶棍：印度教宗教教学中的民间叙事》荣获美国人类学协会（American Anthropological Association）颁发的首届维克多·特纳民族学写作奖（Victor Turner Prize for Ethnographic Writing）以及美国民俗学会（American Folklore Society）颁发的埃尔西·克莱斯民俗学奖（Elsie Clews Prize for Folklore）。

小说《爱、星星和所有》融合了她对性别政治、印度上层阶级的日常生活以及当代美国学术界的探索，在美国和印度广受好评。选段部分出自《爱、星星和所有》第一部分，介绍了主人公吉塔（Gita）与两位男性相遇的故事。

作品选读

Love, Stars and All That
(excerpt)
By Kirin Narayan

***Love, Stars, and All That* (Selection One)**

"Holy cow! Not Timothy Stilling." Bet squinted one eye open. She was soaking in the afternoon sun on the deck in case she was called back for an audition.

"Who is he?" Gita asked, so excited that the name was recognized that she forgot to wonder if Bet was making fun of her. She was never sure whether people in California only said "Holy cow" to Indians. She was also trying to ignore the expanse of nude flesh before her. Thank goodness, Bet was lying on her stomach; it would have been quite diffcult the other way.

"Well, he's sure a Bay Area celebrity. I don't know how well he's known elsewhere. One of those postmodern Susan Sontag kind of men. He's in the *Chronicle* sometimes. I read an interview about him once; I think he writes essays and poetry. You'd better get your little ass right over to the Telegraph Avenue bookstores to check out his writing. Well! It looks like that astrologer of yours has something going for him."

"Nothing," said Gita, smiling broadly. She stopped, listening to her voice. She hadn't used the word that way in months, maybe years. It was the way girls at the convent had said "Shut up" or "Nonsense." Nothing—it seemed to fling away the other person's position even if you suspected it was right.

"Before you go, remember to pick up, will you? I already told you I might have some folks stopping by."

"Sure," said Gita. That was the arrangement: if either of them had a visitor they had to issue advance warning. She put her books in her room, closed the door, and sped off through streets festive with pink blossoms.

There were two slim volumes of poetry by Timothy Stilling in stock. The back covers were filled with praise but no picture, alas. Gita turned a few pages and soon she felt that she was visiting an old, dear friend. The bookstore bustle disappeared. He was holding up a mirror for her to see herself. He understood the nuances of what she had never been able to express. He spoke about places inside her she would like to discover. She felt herself hugging, hugged by his words, felt herself expanding to incorporate his mind.

If the books hadn't been hardbacks she would have bought them both even though they weren't assigned for a class. Instead she checked them out of the library, reading and rereading them with someone else's marginal notes (yes, he was worthy of a paper, maybe even a dissertation!). She calculated that there was a fourteen-year age difference between them, the right amount of time for someone to grow wise. She stopped dressing up and forcing herself into cafes. It was clear now, she was to be devoted to this man. But being shy, she did not let on to anyone, though it was all she thought about most of the time. Shani Maharaj, with all his weight and presence, and seven gyrating moons, was slowly lumbering ahead.

He was not handsome. Hardly the dark-haired, broad-shouldered prince Gita had always expected. Timothy Stilling was very skinny and quite bald, and the hair hanging low around his scalp was a nondescript brown. His eyes were small under the jutting forehead. His shoulders sloped. If she took him home to Delhi surely everyone would laugh. "Couldn't you have done better, dear?" Kookoo would say in an undertone, leaning forward as she handed back the salad spoons to the uniformed servant standing behind her chair. Dilip would bring out imported whisky and invite Timothy to have a few pegs, then remark later that it was a pity the old chap wasn't much of a drinker, and a terrible shame about cricket and those Yanks. Riding with Timothy on the train to Bombay would be a disaster too; she could already feel the heat of the stares from other passengers. How he would be received by the Shahs wasn't clear yet: after all, they must have liked him if they had forwarded him onward.

As soon as he started introducing his poems, her opinions began to shift. His voice was filled with golden light. His eyes shimmered, blue, wise. His hands were long fingered and eloquent when he spread them out to make a point. Even the teeth, set so tight and crooked in his mouth, were charming. Yes, Saroj Aunty had picked the right kind of man. Sitting in the back row, Gita became conscious of her breath pumping into her stomach, playing intoxicatingly out over her upper lip. She had felt this way only a few fleeting times before in her life. She remembered the thrill of algorithms taught by the sole male teacher who was not in robes, a nervous young man whom every girl in the convent school longed for but who disappointed them all by getting married over an Easter vacation. She thought of the neighbor's son in Delhi with his short shorts and hairy legs, off with a tennis racket in the early mornings, and how when the parents got together for dinner she had once spent an entire evening in his room wondering what to say as he sucked, scowling, on a cigarette. Before she had pricked up her ears at college for the kinds of things one might talk about with a boy, he had gone off to England on a Rhodes scholarship. It was sad but true that though Gita was so accomplished in other spheres of life, when it came to romance she felt like an ignoramus. Even if Bet was sometimes so awfully condescending, it might not be a bad idea to open up to her in search of advice.

Gita had dressed in Indian clothes for the poetry reading. Before March she had mostly tried to disappear into crowds by wearing jeans and running shoes, hair severely braided down her back. But this day she had loosely anchored her hair in a bamboo hair clip and spent the time before the reading ironing a red-and-black tie-dyed *kurta* to wear over tight-fitting black *churidars*. Saroj Aunty had chosen this outfit from a boutique in Bombay run by two elderly sisters pledged to natural fabrics and vegetable dyes. It bore luck. As Gita waited for the crowds to clear away from Timothy Stilling when he finished his reading, she felt pretty and unique.

Women were fluttering around him, men were shaking his hand, books were thrust before him for a signature. A short Indian (Pakistani? Bangladeshi? Sri Lankan?) girl with a halo of hair around a self-possessed, smiling face went up and extended a hand, accentuating Gita's awkwardness to herself. He was taller than most people, Gita observed. That bald head would be like a white beacon in any crowd, in any situation of the shared story that was rising up with such certainty before them. Finally he was left with just one man.

"I am Gita," she presented herself, conscious of her voice being different, a "charming lilt."

"Gita? Oh yes—" He was puzzled but smiling down at her with all those wonderful crooked teeth.

"Gita!" the other man said. He was short, tanned, with wiry black hair and glasses. "I've seen you around Feeler Hall, haven't I? Aren't you a new graduate student?"

"Yes." It seemed to Gita that she could do nothing but smile as though her cheeks would split.

"Oh no. The present," Timothy Stilling said. "I knew I forgot something. I'm so sorry you had to come all this way. This is terrible. I've been doing this kind of thing lately—there's just too much going on with, you know, the British editions coming out and proofreading for the new book and all the traveling."

"At least you made it here on the right day, Tim," the other man said. "Right month, right time. That's something."

"Oh, cut it out, Norvin," said Timothy. "This is Norvin Weinstein, Gita. He's kidding around because I, umm, wrote down a reading in Cambridge wrong in my calendar. I got there a month early."

Gita was wishing she could disappear. She recognized the name Norvin Weinstein. He was a famous professor, someone her adviser had suggested she take a course with sometime. There was no reason to feel publicly shamed at what wasn't even an obvious assignation, but she did. The professor would surely know that she could have been decoding Foucault's *The History of Sexuality* this evening instead of looking for her March Man. "And then?" she asked, her smile suddenly awkward in its fit.

20

(Indran Amirthanayagam, 1960—)
因德尼·阿米拉纳亚加姆

作者简介

因德尼·阿米拉纳亚加姆（Indran Amirthanayagam, 1960— ），美国斯里兰卡裔诗人、散文家和翻译家，出生于锡兰（Ceylon）（现在的斯里兰卡）的科伦坡（Colombo），14 岁时随家人搬到夏威夷，现居住在马里兰州（Maryland）。他在哈弗福德学院（Haverford College）学习英国文学，并在哥伦比亚大学获得新闻学硕士学位。他用英语、西班牙语、法语、葡萄牙语和海地克里奥尔语（Haitian Creole）进行写作、翻译活动，是 DC-ALT（文学翻译协会）的董事会成员，同时也是美国外交部门的一名荣誉外交官，获得国务院颁发的高级荣誉奖（Superior Honor Award）和有功荣誉奖（Meritorious Honor Award）。

阿米拉纳亚加姆是一位多产的作家，创作了很多优秀的作品。主要作品有诗集《清算的大象》（*The Elephants of Reckoning*, 1993）、《锡兰，R. I. P.》（*Ceylon, R. I. P.*, 2001）、《分裂的脸》（*The Splintered Face*, 2008）、《野蛮战争》（*Uncivil War*, 2013）、《火星上的椰子》（*Coconuts on Mars*, 2019）和《移民国家》（*The Migrant States*, 2020）等。

他的作品发表在《纽约时报》、《新英格兰评论》（*New England Review*）、《西普》（*Siempre*）等报纸和杂志上，同时还被收录在许多选集中，包括《美国诗歌》（*The United States of Poetry*）、《新世纪的语言：来自中东、亚洲及其他国家的当代诗歌》（*Language for a New Century: Contemporary Poetry from the Middle East, Asia, and Beyond*）。阿米拉纳亚加姆荣获纽约艺术基金会（New York Foundation for the Arts）、美国–墨西哥文化基金（U.S.-Mexico Fund for Culture）和麦克道

威尔·科勒尼（MacDowell Colony）的奖学金以及 2020 年美国当代艺术基金会（Foundation for the Contemporary Arts）的诗歌授予奖。他的作品探讨了人类痛苦和复原力的普遍主题，试图用语言来消除不同文化、种族和具有不同社会经济地位的人们之间的障碍。

诗歌《城市，大象》（"The City, with Elephants"）选自诗集《大象的清算》，这部诗集曾荣获 1994 年美国帕特森诗歌奖（Paterson Poetry Prize）。诗人通过描述斯里兰卡的大象的生存状态引发人们对人与动物、人与人之间的关系的思考。诗歌《移民的回应》（"The Migrant's Reply"）节选自最新一部诗集《移民国家》，诗句冗长曲折，旋律独特，表达了对难民群体生存困境的同情，蕴含了诗人对人类不顾政治制度的障碍，为追求更好的生活而进行斗争的深切赞赏。

作品选读

The City, with Elephants

By Indran Amirthanayagam

The elephants of reckoning
are bunches of scruff
men and women picking up
thrown out antennae
from the rubbish
bins of the city

to fix on their tubular
bells and horn about
by oil can fires
in the freezing midnight
of the old new year

We ride by their music
every hour in cabs on trains
hearing the pit pat

of our grown-wise pulse
shut in shut out

from the animals
of the dry season
the losers and boozers,
we must not admit our eyes
into the courtyard

the whimsy of chance
and our other excuses—
dollars in pocket—
to write beautiful songs
is all I ask, ...

to do right with friends
and love a woman
and live to eighty
have people listen
to the story of my trip to America

The elephants of reckoning
are beaten and hungry
and walk their solitary horrors
out every sunrise slurping
coffee bought with change

while in some houses
freedom-bound lovers
embrace late and read Tagore
about the people working
underneath the falling of empires.

The Migrant's Reply

By Indran Amirthanayagam

We have been running for so long. We are tired. We want to rest.
 We don't want
to wake up tomorrow and pack our bags. We have gone 10,000 miles.
 We have

boarded a row boat, tug boat, bus, freight train. We have a cell phone
 and some bread.
Our eyes are dry. Our breath needs washing. What next? You are
 putting up
a wall on your Southern flank? What an irony. The country that
 accepts refugees
does not want us. We qualify. We have scars and our host
 governments hunted

at least some of us. The rest fled in fear. Gangs do not spare
 even the children.
White vans took away our uncles, our cousins. Do you think they
 have been made
into plowshares? Ay, what are you saying? Too easy. Too easy to
 wear our hearts

in these words, in slings, on our faces, furrowed, perplexed.
 What happened
in kindness to strangers? Why do we have to be herded like prisoners, held
in a holding camp? We are human beings and, like you, in safer countries,

we have the same obligation to save ourselves and our children.
 Oh, the children.

Look at them. Give them food and school and a new set of
clothes.
       Give them
a chance. Whether you are red or blue the eye of the hurricane
does not

discriminate. We are your tumbling weeds, hurling cars,
       flooding banks. And
we are diggers of the dikes. We can teach you so many languages
       and visions.
You would learn so much: you would never ever say lock us up.

21

(Indira Ganesan, 1960—)
英迪拉·加内桑

作者简介

英迪拉·加内桑（Indira Ganesan, 1960—），美国印度裔小说家、散文家，出生于印度南部的斯里兰加姆（Srirangam）。五岁时，她跟随父亲来到美国。1982年在纽约瓦萨学院（Vassar College）获得英语学位，1984年在艾奥瓦大学作家工作室获得创意写作硕士学位。加内桑在纽约长岛大学南安普顿学院（Southampton College of Long Island University）和莱斯利大学（Lesley University）教授写作和文学课程，除此之外还担任《多山移动：当代不同声音的文学杂志》（*Many Mountains Moving: A Literary Journal of Diverse Contemporary Voices*）的小说编辑，以及普罗温斯敦的 WOMR-FM 社区电台全球音乐节目主持人。

加内桑荣获拉德克利夫学院玛丽·英格拉姆·邦汀奖学金（Mary Ingraham Bunting Fellowship of Radcliffe College）、W. K. 罗斯奖学金（W. K. Rose Fellowship）、艺术工作中心（The Fine Arts Work Center）等各类奖学金。1995 年被评选为"格兰塔 20 位最佳美国青年小说家"（Granta Twenty Best Young American Novelists），1998 年入选"巴恩斯 & 诺布尔发掘新作家"（Barnes & Noble Discover New Writers）名单，还曾担任 2014 年笔会/海明威处女作小说奖评委（Pen/Hemingway Award for Debut Fiction）。她的作品被选为"巴恩斯和诺布尔著名书籍"（Barnes and Noble Notable Book），并被列入知名小说名单。

加内桑的作品主要包括三部小说，《旅程》（*The Journey*, 1990）、《继承》（*Inheritance*, 1998）以及《甜如蜜糖》（*As Sweet as Honey*, 2013）。《继承》是一部成长小说，以印度小岛为背景，讲述了一个 15 岁的女孩索妮尔（Sonil）从慢性病中康复,并开始了对自己和父母的探索之旅。选段部分出自《继承》第七章,讲述了索尼尔的表妹詹妮(Jani)来祖母家拜访,祖母试图为詹妮与 C. P. 先生之间安排一桩婚事,但詹妮对祖母的这一努力仍持消极态度。

《甜如蜜糖》是一部关于爱情和家庭的多种组合的小说,表达了探索文化认同与融合的主题,呈现出(一点)魔幻现实主义的味道。尽管有一些轻微的情节扭曲,但人物的真正魅力和故事中女孩般的、诙谐的能量是不可抗拒的。选段部分出自小说的第一部分,描述了米特林(Meterling)的婚礼以及她如何从新娘戏剧性地变成了寡妇。

作品选读

Inheritance

Chapter Seven

By Indira Ganesan

The next two days it rained. Everything was drenched. There had been no news of Jani's suitor.

"Do you think you're in love with C. P.?" I asked, unable to stand Jani's silence any longer.

"Love? No, I don't think so," answered Jani.

"But could you grow to love him?"

"I don't know."

We were in our room, in bed, but not talking. Usually, Jani would tell me straightaway what was in her heart, but now she was on guard. She was afraid of something, and I dearly wished I could make it all right for her.

"Are you going to marry C. P.?"

"I suppose I have to—unless—"

"Unless what?" But she just laughed.

"Unless one of your heroes arrives and rescues me, In guess."

"Why can't C. P. rescue you?"

I wanted to rescue her. I was ready to be Jani's knight, to wear her favor upon my sleeve and fight for her.

"There's so much you don't know," she told me.

I guess it was true. One by one, Jani refused to meet any other suitors selected for her. At first she complained that she didn't like this one's nose, this one's hair, when she was presented with their photographs, but then she started to say nothing, becoming glum and silent. Grandmother became exasperated, sometimes trying to coax her nicely to give one a try—here, this one is a genius, and he is loved by his three sisters—but Jani would have none of it. Then Grandmother would lose her temper, stamp her foot, appeal to the .... Jani would close her ears and retire with a devotional.

I became distracted by the rain. It pounded on the roof and gushed across the windows; the trees would sway back under its assault. I caught a little cold and had to stay in bed. Jani brought me trays of orange juice and toast. The entire household was a firm believer in bed rest and vitamin C. I was agonizingly bored.

"Come, now, it's not so bad," said Jani, but she didn't like to sit at the window while it poured and listen to the singing of the wind. She didn't like to lie under the awning of the balcony where the water dripped into saucepans and watch the villagers make their way through the puddles, protecting their heads with plantain leaves. Not for her the vibrant pounding that made you want to dance in imitation of the raindrops, plunk, plunk your feet up and down, and then thunk, thunk, thunk for thunder. Rain was something to avoid for Jani, something to come out from.

Surprisingly, my mother came once or twice to check up on me. She looked at me through the doorway, but if I attempted a smile, she didn't respond. Once she did smile at me, but it was my turn to pout and stew. All right for her to stand and smile, while I was bedridden. Where was she when I was well and able? I scowled quite fiercely.

When the days were bright again, I soon went back to the market. I brought along a book of zoology to a cafe I had lately discovered. It was a well-lit place full of scuffed tables and patrons who nursed their drinks for hours. I had a rose milk, which I took to a corner table by a window that poured in sunlight.

I liked what zoology offered me. In the study of animals, I saw how environment affects a certain species and what bearing it has on its life. I thought about Jani's upbringing, how she had no parents, how she seemed docile and able to adapt to any given environment. Her stubbornness in refusing even to be nice to C. P. must be the result of all that former adaptability. If Jani were an animal, her species would die out in her refusal to mate and create offspring. All Grandmother was trying to do was to continue the species.

I looked at my book of animal classifications. There were nineteen categories of animal life before even getting to the class of mammal and man. If all the protozoa and the mollusks and segmented worms reproduced regularly, why couldn't Jani? Even my mother followed the biological urges that maintained mankind, although she should certainly retire her wares by now. I expected to marry and have children. Maybe I'd settle on Pi, in a nice house with a garden, and work at the wildlife preserve in Cootij. It was a place with lots of protected land and full of options for a zoologist. I could come back from Radcliffe, get married, and go to work immediately. Idly, I began to wonder who would be at my wedding. My sisters, of course, but what of my mother? I was interrupted in my musings by a tap on the shoulder.

"Hello, my friend," said an American voice. Turning around, I looked up to see the American from the mango stand. Wonderingly, my face grew warm.

"Hi," I said finally.

"I'm happy to say no one else has been trying to swindle me," he said.

"That's good."

"Anyway, it's not like I'm wealthy or anything," he said.

"But you're American—that's enough," I said. It was true, America and money went hand in hand.

"What are you reading?"

I showed him my book, feeling a bit foolish. But together we looked at the insides of a great blue whale.

"I once went on a whale watch and saw a whale breaching. It was magnificent; it leapt into the air, and it kept on emerging. It didn't look like anything I'd seen before," he said.

"Wow," I said.

It was the only response I could think of. I could say I'd seen a jellyfish, lots of seaweed, an eel or two, and once, a shark's carcass, but what were those next to whales?

"It was enormous. It's hard to imagine something so enormous," he said.

"Yes," I said.

"Are you studying for school?" he asked.

"No, I'm on holiday. I just like to read."

Seeing that my rose milk was almost empty, he asked if I wanted another one and soon joined me at the table.

"I was never any good in science. I liked music, though. I played violin for years.

My mother wanted me to be the next great violinist; she was deaf to the sounds I produced. Treat it like an instrument, Richard, not like a device for torture, my teacher would say."

"My aunts used to make me take classical dance, until I finally convinced them it was a lost cause. I like music, too," I said. "I also like rose milk. Do you?"

"No. I like lassi, and buttermilk."

"I like curds and rice with cucumber and mustard."

"What I love are the bhajis, anything fried. It's not at all good for you, though."

"My grandmother is a stickler for healthy type foods. We never have bhajis."

"Well, maybe we should order some now."

I agreed, thinking it only a slight indiscretion.

Munching on the fried onions and potatoes, we talked some more. I liked the way he looked and the quiet shy smile. He didn't smile often, which made me smile all the more. He wasn't handsome in the way of a model or film star, but handsome in that his features were composed, his expression calm. I felt I could learn from him, although I didn't know what I wanted to learn. He was sexy, too. Sitting next to him, I found my attention wandering from what he was saying to the nice color of his shirt, his darkish whitish skin, the depth of his unfathomable eyes. Then I snapped myself out of this spell. He was just an American talking to a kid, me.

"What do you do, Richard?" I asked, testing out his name.

"I give English lessons to schoolboys. Not girls, of course, they're too shy. I came to India to study ayurvedic medicine, and I take classes here on the island."

"Do you have a lot of money?" I asked, not shy.

"No." He laughed. "The classes I take are free. Do you know Guru Gowmathi?"

I shook my head.

"He teaches all of us—there are six of us—for free, with the idea we will spread his knowledge."

I had heard of foreigners coming to study Indian arts but had never met one.

"Are you full Indian?" he asked me.

I told him my father had been white.

"Your features are just slightly different from most of the Indians and islanders."

I became self-conscious then and told him I had to go.

We parted when it began to grow dark. Thinking my grandmother would be annoyed that I'd stayed out so long, I hurried. As I walked along, I realized how starved I had been for a real conversation, that the person I knew most was myself. Talking with Richard made my heart light, and even the flowers around me seemed more potent. I was heady with excitement at the time I'd just had. He had seen a whale!

Fully expecting to be reprimanded at home, I was surprised at my grandmother's abstracted greeting. She yelled just a little, and then she urged me to see my cousin. I followed her to our room, where I discovered Jani weeping on the bed.

"She has been like this all afternoon," said my grandmother, wringing her hands.

She left me with Jani, and I approached the bed.

"What's wrong, Jani? Tell me what's the matter," I said softly, putting out my hand to stroke her back. But my words only made her weep harder, so I sat quietly.

"It's no use—I can't pretend," she finally said between sobs.

I stroked her long black hair, untangling the knots. She said I was too young to understand, that I couldn't comprehend. But I begged her to try, and slowly, she told me. She spoke of her friends, of Nalani and Rohini, both of them recently married, and how they told her that it hurt to give birth to a baby. How could they do this to her, Grandmother Kamala and our relatives, marry her off and subject her to such pain? I said, no, no, it's not like that, there doesn't have to be pain. I had read a lot more books than she, I told her, and I knew it didn't have to be so. I said, think of all the others, think of the drugs, think of most of the world, think of *The Good Earth* and how babies just dropped in the fields while the mothers worked. But Jani said that there were always some exceptions, that some girls never feel the monthly pain and some scream for hours, and what would I know anyway? I know, I know, I said, I know the thing between men and women, and how they fight for each other, how they brave fire and exile to sleep with one another, how they adore their babies. Jani, because she felt she had already told me so much and there was no reason to hold back, said she was really afraid of killing her baby. What can I do? she wailed. I won't be able to give birth! And if I do, the baby will die! You can't know that, I said, you can't possibly know. But Jani said there were some things you just knew about your body, and she was absolutely, positively sure.

I tried to calm her and soothe her, but she kept crying.

"I cannot marry C. P.," she said.

"You need to fall in love with someone," I offered.

"No one will ever love me, no one that gentle," she said.

"Maybe you don't have to sleep with your husband," I said, but even as I said that, I knew it was preposterous. Children were always the object of marriage; everyone knew that.

"There is only one thing I can do, and I need to do it soon," she said.

I became alarmed, and thought she meant to take her life, but she merely clasped a blue prayer book to her heart and closed her eyes.

"What will you do, Jani?" I asked finally, scared.

"I am going into the convent."

"Convent!"

"I'm devoting myself to ...."

As Sweet as Honey

Part One: Marriage
(excerpt)

By Indira Ganesan

Our aunt Meterling stood over six feet tall, a giantess, a tree. From her limbs came large hands, which always held a shower of snacks for us children. We could place two of our feet in one of her sandals, and her green shawl made for a roof to cover our play forts. We loved Meterling, because she was so devotedly freakish, because she rained everyone with affection, and because we felt that anyone that tall had to be supernaturally gifted. No one actually said she was a ghost, or a saint, or a witch, but we watched for signs nevertheless. She knew we suspected her of tricks, for she often smiled at us and displayed sleight of hand, pulling coins and shells out of thin air. But that, said Rasi, didn't prove anything; Rasi had read *The Puffin Book of Magic Tricks* and pretty much knew them all, and was not so easily impressed.

What was interesting, and never expected, was that Aunt Meterling married the littlest man she knew. He was four feet seven, dapper, and jolly. The grown-ups were embarrassed and affronted, for like Auntie Sita said, it was bad enough having a freakishly tall woman in the family. Yet, they were all relieved that Aunt Meterling found Uncle Archer and he, her.

The wedding was a small enough affair as weddings go, but the bridegroom did ride to town in a white baby Aston Martin decked with garlands of roses and basil. The first marriage rites took place at dawn.

Someone said how sad it was that Meterling's parents could not be at the wedding, but neither could Archer's. I wondered what Meterling's father had been like. He had named her, after all. Who had he been? A man smitten with the German language, it seemed, for her name sounded German, and smitten, too, with his family. A man who died, with his beloved wife, in a car accident, all those years ago. A man who loved his daughter enough to name her something special. A man who must be still alive in Meterling's heart, I thought.

And her mother? A small, sweet woman who must have loved her daughter, even as she might have seen something in her that marked her for a fragile future. Also absent, also loved, also missing the wedding. I could comprehend Meterling's longing for her family, because my own father and mother were in America, land of dreams and snow. But lose a mother and a father—no, that was impossible! I could only imagine so far.

I rubbed the sleep out of my eyes, straining to see if my aunt would change somehow after the fire ceremony, the part where she walked seven steps hand in hand with Uncle Archer, but she kept her eyes downcast, as became a modest bride, while the priests chanted all around her. She wore a reddish-pinkish gold sari from Kanchi, with twelve inches of gold *jhari* on its border and thirty-six on the paloo; she had *mendhi* on her hands and feet, a glow from a bath of turmeric and sandal. In her hair was jasmine, rose, and tulsi. She wore an engagement ring, and during the ceremony she'd get a gold ring on her third finger, left hand, and a ring on her toe. Uncle Archer would get a ring as well. He wore a white pajama suit of heavy material all the way from Bombay, a pink tie, a boutonnière, and sandals. That he was wearing a suit instead of a formal dhoti was radical enough, whispered the aunts, but to hold hands before the ceremony was too much. We knew something was afoot but were not quite sure what the problem was. He's being intimate, giggled Sanjay, stamping his feet while Rasi and I pretended not to know him. We just shook our heads as our aunts did—we were smart enough to know that rules were being broken left and right, and didn't need Sanjay to tell us, even if it appeared that he did know more than us. Afterwards, Auntie Pa (her real name was Auntie Parvati, but Sanjay started saying Pa when he was two and could not roll his r's, and the name stuck) said that she had had a funny feeling in her heart that something was not right, but at that moment, when they were simply standing at the ceremony and later at the reception, everything was fine and there was plenty to eat and drink and toast the couple's happiness. He was now our uncle. Auntie Pa smiled and playfully tugged Sanjay's hair.

But no one could have predicted what happened next. One minute Uncle Archer was laughing and dancing with the littlest cousins, and then he took Aunt Meterling out to the dance floor. She had gone to Western dance classes, whispered an aunt, just for this moment. No one doubted Uncle could dance; he was born to wear a suit and tails—in fact, he bore more than a striking resemblance to the Monopoly man, with a full white mustache and a round tummy. A Western waltz was struck up, and everyone left the dance floor. Some of the elders among the guests frowned and turned away, because touch dancing was severely looked down upon, even though we lived in town. As my grandmother would say, this was not Delhi, not Bombay, but Madhupur, a town on the island of Pi in the Bay of Bengal: a place as sweet as honey, where people lived decent lives. Touching was meant for procreation, nothing else. Once, we had looked up "procreation" in the Animal Encyclopedia, but didn't learn much except about the mating habits of the stickleback fish. But there she was, Aunt Meterling, swathed in gold tissue silk, and there was he, monocled and marvelous, and the music from the hired band began. One turn, two, three, and he was down. Uncle Archer was on the ground. A flurry of activity, then a scream, and we children were pushed aside. The youngest of us didn't understand but started to cry anyway. Rasi, Sanjay, and I didn't really understand, either. When it was all over, no one had any appetite for the plates of round halvah and sugared grapes.

We were stunned into silence. We had not been paying attention. We never would have believed it if someone told us. We grew still with shock. We were eleven, nine, and ten. Plus all of our other cousins. All of us kids. It was the worst thing we had seen, or nearly seen. He had died in an instant.

There was not even a chance to see where exactly he measured up, someone said, in a half-giggle or cry, whether to her knee ("That's silly," said Rasi), her elbow, her chin. In truth, most of the guests hardly knew him, had only seen him once or twice, and mostly from afar. And it was hard for us to see much during all of the ceremony, because Sanjay started chasing Mani, who had swiped his spin top, and Rasi joined in to help Mani, and she dragged me with her. Mary Angel from two doors down called to us to share her caramels. We forgot about Mani and Sanjay as we ate the caramels. Rasi said we had to avoid her schoolteacher. She did not look so menacing to me when I saw her, a perfectly nice woman with her husband, who smiled broadly, making me think Rasi hadn't done some schoolwork, or had skipped out on a class. All in all, we hardly saw them wed.

But their love was palpable, like a color that was visible, almost heard. Their arms reached for each other with the sweetest sigh. Fingertips touching, swish of gold, monocle flash. One step, two step, three, gone.

Meterling sobbed in a corner. She sat right down, three feet of her against the wall, another three and more stretched on the floor. Her crying was fraught and unabashed, and no one seemed to know what to do. No one had ever seen her cry, because her height made her seem protected from whatever ill might befall ordinary women. Grandmother, no slouch, sharply spoke to anyone who said "It's too bad," and gave them work to do. The other aunties crowded around; some, you know, were waiting for a moment like this, because Meterling, that awkward fish, had landed a man before they did. But others, like Nalani, just burst into tears for the loss and grief.

The marriage hall quickly cleared, and they took Uncle Archer's body away. Uncle Darshan and Uncle Thakur ushered Aunt Meterling out. I looked back at the decorated hall, the garlands of pink, white, and orange flowers trailing from the ceiling, and those crushed on the floor. A funny feeling filled my stomach as I stared at the trampled blooms. A handful of cooks and cleaners began to clear up the food and sweep up, while a priest continued to pray, and there was a loud murmur of voices all at once as we exited. Outside, the musicians bowed their hands to our grandmother, offering condolences.

We gathered on the veranda that evening, not sure what to do. In an instant, our house had gone from celebration to mourning. The family doctor had been a guest, and now she was in charge of the body. Was it a heart attack? An attack on the brain? All we heard was the muffled crying of Meterling, which made Auntie Pa want to have us stay with neighbors, but my grandmother decided we should stay home and not cause trouble.

22

(Arundhati Roy, 1961—)
阿兰达蒂·罗伊

作者简介

阿兰达蒂·罗伊（Arundhati Roy, 1961—），美国印度裔作家、政治家，出生在印度东北部梅加拉亚邦（Meghalaya）的西隆（Shillong）。父亲是孟加拉族的印度教徒，从事茶园工作。母亲来自印度南部克拉拉邦的叙利亚基督教（Keralite Syrian Christian）家族，是一位著名的女权运动家。16岁时，罗伊就读于新德里著名的规划与建筑学院（School of Planning and Architecture），毕业后从事编辑、记者、剧本编写等职业。

罗伊著有小说、随笔和散文集。小说主要有《微物之神》（*The God of Small Things*, 1997）、《极乐之邦》（*The Ministry of Utmost Happiness*, 2017）。随笔和论文集包括《生存的代价》（*The Cost of Living*, 1999）、《强权政治》（*Power Politics*, 2002）和《谈战争》（*War Talk*, 2003）等。罗伊凭借《微物之神》获得全美国图书奖、英国文学大奖布克奖，震惊世界文坛。《极乐之邦》获得布克奖提名，被美国国家公共电台（NPR）、亚马逊（Amazon）、柯克斯（Kirkus）、《华盛顿邮报》（*The Washington Post*）等评为2017年最佳书籍。此外，罗伊凭借其公共影响力大力倡导人权，2002年获得"兰南文化自由奖"（Lannan Cultural Freedom Award），2004年获得"悉尼和平奖"（Sydney Peace Prize）。无论是小说还是政论集，罗伊的创作聚焦权力问题。

《微物之神》通过家族故事表达根深蒂固的种姓制度对人性的摧残以及后殖民时期印度社会的面貌。作者采用多角度的叙事手法，通过讲述印度南部小村庄中一对孪生兄妹瑞海尔和艾斯沙曲折的童年经历，揭开他们的母亲阿慕与木匠维鲁沙的爱情秘密。选段部分出自小说第二十一章"生命的代价"("The Cost of Living"),讲述了阿慕和维鲁沙因爱而聚但最终付出生命代价的故事,表达了对印度种姓制度的控诉,呼吁人们关注社会中微物的生存状态。

作品选读

The God of Small Things

Chapter 21
The Cost of Living
By Arundhati Roy

When the old house had closed its bleary eyes and settled into sleep, Ammu, wearing one of Chacko's old shirts over a long white petticoat, walked out onto the front verandah. She paced up and down for awhile. Restless. Feral. Then she sat on the wicker chair below the moldy, button-eyed bison head and the portraits of the Little Blessed One and Aleyooty Ammachi that hung on either side of it. Her twins were sleeping the way they did when they were exhausted—with their eyes half open, two small monsters. They got that from their father.

Ammu switched on her tangerine transistor. A man's voice crackled through it. An English song she hadn't heard before.

She sat there in the dark. A lonely, lambent woman looking out at her embittered aunt's ornamental garden, listening to a tangerine. To a voice from far away. Wafting through the night. Sailing over lakes and rivers. Over dense heads of trees. Past the yellow church. Past the school. Bumping up the dirt road. Up the steps of the verandah. To her.

Barely listening to the music, she watched the frenzy of insects flitting around the light, vying to kill themselves.

The words of the song exploded in her head.

There's no time to lose
I heard her say

Cash your dreams before
They slip away
Dying all the time
Lose your dreams and you
Will lose your mind.

Ammu drew her knees up and hugged them. She couldn't believe it. The cheap coincidence of those words. She stared fiercely out at the garden. Ousa the Bar Nowl flew past on a silent nocturnal patrol. The fleshy anthuriums gleamed like gunmetal.

She remained sitting for awhile. Long after the song had ended. Then suddenly she rose from her chair and walked out of her world like a witch. To a better, happier place.

She moved quickly through the darkness, like an insect following a chemical trail. She knew the path to the river as well as her children did and could have found her way there blindfolded. She didn't know what it was that made her hurry through the undergrowth. That turned her walk into a run. That made her arrive on the banks of the Meenachal breathless. Sobbing. As though she was late for something. As though her life depended on getting there in time. As though she knew he would be there. Waiting. As though he knew she would come.

He did.

Know.

That knowledge had slid into him that afternoon. Cleanly. Like the sharp edge of a knife. When history had slipped up. While he had held her little daughter in his arms. When her eyes had told him he was not the only giver of gifts. That she had gifts to give him too, that in return for his boats, his boxes, his small windmills, she would trade her deep dimples when she smiled. Her smooth brown skin. Her shining shoulders. Her eyes that were always somewhere else.

He wasn't there.

Ammu sat on the stone steps that led to the water. She buried her head in her arms, feeling foolish for having been so sure. So certain.

Farther downstream in the middle of the river, Velutha floated on his back, looking up at the stars. His paralyzed brother and his one-eyed father had eaten the dinner he had cooked them and were asleep. So he was free to lie in the river and drift slowly with the current. A log. A serene crocodile. Coconut trees bent into the river and watched him float by. Yellow bamboo wept Small fish took coquettish liberties with him. Pecked him.

He flipped over and began to swim. Upstream. Against the current. He turned towards the bank for one last look, treading water, feeling foolish for having been so sure. So certain.

When he saw her the detonation almost drowned him. It took all his strength to stay afloat. He trod water, standing in the middle of a dark river.

She didn't see the knob of his head bobbing over the dark river. He could have been anything. A floating coconut. In any case she wasn't looking. Her head was buried in her arms.

He watched her. He took his time.

Had he known that he was about to enter a tunnel whose only egress was his own annihilation, would he have turned away?

Perhaps.

Perhaps not.

Who can tell?

He began to swim towards her. Quietly. Cutting through the water with no fuss. He had almost reached the bank when she looked up and saw him. His feet touched the muddy riverbed. As he rose from the dark river and walked up the stone steps, she saw that the world they stood in was his. That he belonged to it. That it belonged to him. The water. The mud. The trees. The fish. The stars. He moved so easily through it. As she watched him she understood the quality of his beauty. How his labor had shaped him. How the wood he fashioned had fashioned him. Each plank he planed, each nail he drove, each thing he made had molded him. Had left its stamp on him. Had given him his strength, his supple grace.

He wore a thin white cloth around his loins, looped between his dark legs. He shook the water from his hair. She could see his smile in the dark. His white, sudden smile that he had carried with him from boyhood into manhood. His only luggage.

They looked at each other. They weren't thinking anymore. The time for that had come and gone. Smashed smiles lay ahead of them. But that would be later.

Lay Ter.

He stood before her with the river dripping from him. She stayed sitting on the steps, watching him. Her face pale in the moonlight. A sudden chill crept over him. His heart hammered. It was all a terrible mistake. He had misunderstood her. The whole thing was a figment of his imagination. This was a trap. There were people in the bushes. Watching. She was the delectable bait. How could it be otherwise? They had seen him in the march. He tried to make his voice casual. Normal. It came out in a croak.

"Ammukutty… what is it—" She went to him and laid the length of her body against his. He just stood there. He didn't touch her. He was shivering. Partly with cold. Partly terror. Partly aching desire. Despite his fear his body was prepared to take the bait. It wanted her. Urgently. His wetness wet her. She put her arms around him.

He tried to be rational. What's the worst thing that can happen?

I could lose everything. My job. My family. My livelihood. Everything.

She could hear the wild hammering of his heart.

She held him till it calmed down. Somewhat.

She unbuttoned her shirt. They stood there. Skin to skin. Her brownness against his blackness. Her softness against his hardness. Her nut-brown breasts (that wouldn't support a toothbrush) against his smooth ebony chest. She smelled the river on him. His Particular Paravan smell that so disgusted Baby Kochamma. Ammu put out her tongue and tasted it, in the hollow of his throat. On the lobe of his ear. She pulled his head down toward her and kissed his mouth. A cloudy kiss. A kiss that demanded a kiss back. He kissed her back. First cautiously. Then urgently. Slowly his arms came up behind her. He stroked her back. Very gently. She could feel the skin on his palms. Rough. Callused. Sandpaper. He was careful not to hurt her. She could feel how soft she felt to him. She could feel herself through him. Her skin. The way her body existed only where he touched her. The rest of her was smoke. She felt him shudder against her. His hands were on her haunches (that could support a whole array of toothbrushes), pulling her hips against his, to let her know how much he wanted her.

Biology designed the dance. Terror timed it. Dictated the rhythm with which their bodies answered each other. As though they knew already that for each tremor of pleasure they would pay with an equal measure of pain. As though they knew that how far they went would be measured against how far they would be taken. So they held back. Tormented each other. Gave of each other slowly. But that only made it worse. It only raised the stakes. It only cost them more. Because it smoothed the wrinkles, the fumble and rush of unfamiliar love and roused them to fever pitch.

Behind them the river pulsed through the darkness, shimmering like wild silk. Yellow bamboo wept.

……

They knew that things could change in a day. They were right about that.

They were wrong about Chappu Thamburan, though. He outlived Velutha. He fathered future generations.

He died of natural causes.

That first night, on the day that Sophie Mol came, Velutha watched his lover dress. When she was ready she squatted facing him. She touched him lightly with her fingers and left a trail of goosebumps on his skin. Like flat chalk on a blackboard. Like breeze in a paddyfield. Like jet-streaks in a blue church sky. He took her face in his hands and drew it towards his. He closed his eyes and smelled her skin. Ammu laughed.

Yes, Margaret, she thought. *We do it to each other too.*

She kissed his closed eyes and stood up. Velutha with his back against the mangosteen tree watched her walk away.

She had a dry rose in her hair.

She turned to say it once again: "*Naaley.*"

Tomorrow.

23

(Thrity Umrigar, 1961—)
斯瑞迪·乌姆里加

作者简介

斯瑞迪·乌姆里加（Thrity Umrigar, 1961— ），美国印度裔小说家、评论家、记者，出生于印度孟买（Mumbai），21岁时移民美国。乌姆里加获得孟买大学（Bombay University）学士学位、俄亥俄州立大学（Ohio State University）硕士学位和肯特州立大学（Kent State University）英语博士学位。目前在凯斯西储大学（Case Western Reserve University）任教，同时也为《华盛顿邮报》、《赫芬顿邮报》（The Huffington Post）和《波士顿环球报》（The Boston Globe）等报纸撰写文章。

乌姆里加著有小说《孟买时间》（Bombay Time, 2001）、《我们之间的空间》（The Space Between Us, 2006）、《如果今天是甜蜜的》（If Today Be Sweet, 2007）、《天堂的重量》（The Weight of Heaven, 2009）、《我们发现的世界》（The World We Found, 2012）、《故事时刻》（The Story Hour, 2014）、《每个人的儿子》（Everybody's Son, 2017）、《荣耀》（Honor, 2022）与回忆录《清晨的宠儿：印度童年回忆录》（First Darling of the Morning: Selected Memories of an Indian Childhood, 2004）。她的小说出版后颇受好评，被翻译成多种语言，在超过15个国家出版。《我们之间的空间》入围笔会/超越边界奖（PEN/Beyond Margins Award）。回忆录《清晨的宠儿：印度童年回忆录》进入米兰达作家协会奖决选名单。

乌姆里加获得多项荣誉，包括克利夫兰艺术奖（Cleveland Arts Prize）、朗姆达文学奖（Lambda Literary Award）和赛斯·罗森伯格奖（Seth Rosenberg Prize）。她的作品以印度和美国为背景，既探讨家庭、爱、死亡等主题，也探讨种族、性别、阶级等话题，文字流畅生动，人物刻画栩栩如生。

小说《我们之间的空间》以印度孟买为背景,阶级和性别的影响、传统与现代的碰撞在小说中上演,故事情节跌宕起伏,引人入胜。此处选自小说《我们之间的空间》第一章,刻画年逾花甲的印度女佣皮马面对未婚先孕的外孙女马娅(Maya)的复杂心理活动。《每个人的儿子》讲述了一个关于欲望、宽恕和父母与子女之间的超凡纽带的紧张、精致的动人故事。选段出自小说第十一章,讲述了戴维与妻子德洛丽丝(Delores)就安东的终身监护权问题产生分歧,夫妻关系也出现裂隙的故事。

作品选读

The Space Between Us

Chapter One
(excerpt)
By Thrity Umrigar

Although it is dawn, inside Bhima's heart it is dusk.

Rolling onto her left side on the thin cotton mattress on the floor, she sits up abruptly, as she does every morning. She lifts one bony hand over her head in a yawn and a stretch, and a strong, mildewy smell wafts from her armpit and assails her nostrils. For an idle moment she sits at the edge of the mattress with her callused feet flat on the mud floor, her knees bent, and her head resting on her folded arms. In that time she is almost at rest, her mind thankfully blank and empty of the trials that await her today and the next day and the next... To prolong this state of mindless grace, she reaches absently for the tin of chewing tobacco that she keeps by her bedside. She pushes a wad into her mouth, so that it protrudes out of her fleshless face like a cricket ball.

Bhima's idyll is short-lived. In the faint, delicate light of a new day, she makes out Maya's silhouette as she stirs on the mattress on the far left side of their hut. The girl is mumbling in her sleep, making soft, whimpering sounds, and despite herself, Bhima feels her heart soften and dissolve, the way it used to when she breast-fed Maya's mother, Pooja, all those years ago. Propelled by Maya's puppylike sounds, Bhima gets up with a grunt from the mattress and makes her way to where her granddaughter lies asleep. But in the second that it takes to cross the small hut, something shifts in Bhima's heart, so that the milky, maternal feeling from a moment ago is replaced by that hard, merciless feeling of rage that has lived within her since several weeks ago. She stands towering over the sleeping girl, who is now snoring softly, blissfully unaware of the pinpoint anger in her grandmother's eyes as she stares at the slight swell of Maya's belly.

One swift kick, Bhima says to herself, one swift kick to the belly, followed by another and another, and it will all be over. Look at her sleeping there, like a shameless whore, as if she has not a care in the world. As if she has not turned my life upside down. Bhima's right foot twitches with anticipation; the muscles in her calf tense as she lifts her foot a few inches off the ground. It would be so easy. And compared to what some other grandmother might do to Maya—a quick shove down an open well, a kerosene can and a match, a sale to a brothel—this would be so humane. This way, Maya would live, would continue going to college and choose a life different from what Bhima had always known. That was how it was supposed to be, how it had been, until this dumb cow of a girl, this girl with the big heart and, now, a big belly, went and got herself pregnant.

Maya lets out a sudden loud snort, and Bhima's poised foot drops to the floor. She crouches down next to the sleeping girl to shake her by the shoulders and wake her up. When Maya was still going to college, Bhima allowed her to sleep in as late as possible, made gaajar halwa for her every Sunday, gave her the biggest portions of dinner every night. If Serabai ever gave Bhima a treat—a Cadbury's chocolate, say, or that white candy with pistachios that came from Iran—she'd save it to bring it home for Maya, though, truth to tell, Serabai usually gave her a portion for Maya anyway. But ever since Bhima has learned of her granddaughter's shame, she has been waking the girl up early. For the last several Sundays there has been no gaajar halwa, and Maya has not asked for her favorite dessert. Earlier this week, Bhima even ordered the girl to stand in line to fill their two pots at the communal tap. Maya had protested at that, her hand unconsciously rubbing her belly, but Bhima had looked away and said the people in the Basti would soon enough find out about her dishonor anyway, so why hide it?

Maya rolls over in her sleep, so that her face is inches away from where Bhima is squatting. Her young, fat hand finds Bhima's thin, crumpled one, and she nestles against it, holding it between her chin and her chest. A single strand of drool falls on

Bhima's captive hand. The older woman feels herself soften. Maya has been like this from the time she was a baby—needy, affectionate, trusting. Despite all the sorrow she has experienced in her young life, Maya has not lost her softness and innocence. With her other free hand, Bhima strokes the girl's lush, silky hair, so different from her own scanty hair.

The sound of a transistor radio playing faintly invades the room, and Bhima swears under her breath. Usually, by the time Jaiprakash turns his radio on, she is already in line at the water tap. That means she is late this morning. Serabai will be livid. This stupid, lazy girl has delayed her. Bhima pulls her hand brusquely away from Maya, not caring whether the movement wakes her up. But the girl sleeps on. Bhima jumps to her feet, and as she does, her left hip lets out a loud pop. She stands still for a moment, waiting for the wave of pain that follows the pop, but today is a good day. No pain.

Bhima picks up the two copper pots and opens the front door. She bends so that she can exit from the low door and then shuts it behind her. She does not want the lewd young men who live in the slum to leer at her sleeping granddaughter as they pass by. One of them is probably the father of the baby... She shakes her head to clear the dark, snakelike thoughts that invade it.

Everybody's Son

Chapter Eleven

(excerpt)

By Thrity Umrigar

It took Juanita three weeks to make up her mind to relinquish custody. David could scarcely believe the news when he got the phone call from a caseworker at Children's Services. Before hanging up, he broached the subject of a permanent adoption, and the woman at the other end of the phone sounded pleased.

Anton was over at a friend's house, so David broke the news to Delores soon after he got home, careful to leave out the part about adoption.

"I don't understand it," Delores kept repeating. "Something must've happened to that poor woman in jail. I mean, why would a mother willingly give up her child? It doesn't make sense, David."

He grimaced. "That's what addiction does, honey," he said. "It dulls even the maternal instinct. I've seen it happen a thousand times."

"I mean, I don't know how much she knows about how Anton is doing." Delores's voice was incredulous. "What if he was unhappy with us? How could she abandon him like that, without even making an effort to see him?"

"Well, she did it once, didn't she? Abandon him?" He heard the strange, harsh note in his own voice. "You think a few years in the slammer will change that?"

Delores turned to him, shocked. "This news is going to break the little fella's heart. So what do we do?"

David focused his pale blue eyes on a spot beyond his wife's shoulder, afraid to look her in the face. "I don't know," he mumbled.

Delores sighed and reached for his hand. "To tell you the truth, I was looking forward to getting our life back," she said. "Don't get me wrong—I've grown very fond of Anton. I don't regret what we've done to, you know, help him. But it's hard, taking care of someone else's kid. And we are not spring chickens anymore. Know what I mean?"

His heart hammered so furiously that he felt light-headed for a moment. Was Dee going to fight him on this? After all the strings he'd pulled, the hurdles he'd overcome? Somehow he had not stopped to entertain this possibility.

Delores was looking at him, waiting for him to answer. "What would you like to do?" he said, hearing the tightness in his voice. "Have him be shunted from one foster home to another?"

Her head shot up and her eyes flashed with sudden anger. "Don't you dare lay this on me, David. It was your idea to go down this road. And as always, I went along, just to make you happy. In any case—"

"Wait, what? You did it to make me happy?" David felt his face flushing, felt a muscle work in his jaw. "You have some gall, Dee. I did this for you. For us. Because I thought—foolishly, as it turns out—that having a child in the house would—" He cut himself off, frightened by the look on Delores's face.

"Would do what, David?" Dee's voice was low. "Bring James back? Help me forget my only son? Erase the memory of my James in that coffin? What did you think would happen just because you brought a stranger into my house? And now you want me to do what? Kiss your ring in gratitude?"

He stared at her wordlessly. "This is how you feel? After all this time?" he finally whispered. And then, louder, "If this is how you felt, why the hell did you say yes? I never... I would've never done this thing if you'd objected."

She spat out a laugh. "Did I say yes, David? Did you even ask me if this is what I wanted? I mean really ask me? Or did you just assume what was best for us?"

He turned his back on her, afraid that he was going to cry. He picked up the small jewelry box on their dresser and set it back down absently, trying to gather himself. "I'm sorry," he said at last. "I—I had no idea. You must've resented me so much these past two years."

"David." Delores sighed. She patted the edge of the bed. "Come here. Come sit next to me." She rested her hand on his thigh. "Sweetheart. I know you meant well. I know that, okay? It's just that, you're like a hurricane and I... Everything that's in your path just gets swept along."

He shook his head. "I'm sorry," he said again. But he was wondering when he and Dee had drifted this far apart. Should they have gone for therapy, as she had wanted after James's death? He had refused, unable to bear the thought of talking to a stranger about his beloved son. And Dee had fallen so silent in those early months after the funeral. Often he would come home to find her sitting quietly in James's room, looking out the window. Something twisted in his gut then, but when he tried to ask her about her day and whether she'd left the house, she would smile that strange new smile and look away.

But that was years ago, David thought. Slowly, it seemed as if she had found her way back—volunteering again at the Rape Crisis Center, resuming her activities for the League of Women Voters, working alongside him in the yard. And yet it was true—he had lost the laughing, irreverent woman he'd fallen in love with. That Dee was gone, replaced by the woman who was sitting beside him, telling him that she wanted her life back. That he would have to relinquish Anton after all. David's stomach heaved at the thought.

He felt claustrophobic, their large bedroom closing in on him. He took her hand, kissed it lightly, and mumbled, "I need some fresh air. I think I'll go to the track and run a few laps. I shouldn't be long."

"You're not eating?"

"You go ahead," he said, not meeting her eye. "I'll grab something on my way back."

He forced himself not to notice the droop of her shoulders as she turned away from him. "As you wish," she said.

When David got home at nine, Anton and Delores were on the couch watching TV, Delores's arm flung casually around the boy. David shook his head imperceptibly, unable to reconcile Dee's resentful words earlier in the evening with the tableau of domesticity in front of him.

"Hey, David," Anton said, his eyes glued to the television set.

"Hey, buddy. How was your evening?"

"Fine."

Delores, he noticed, had not bothered to so much as acknowledge his presence. He stood around uselessly for another moment and then headed for the shower.

When he walked into their bedroom a half hour later, Delores was gathering her pillows. "What're you doing?" he asked.

"I'm sleeping in the guest room tonight," she said. "I want to watch some TV and don't want to keep you up."

"I don't mind. Tomorrow's Saturday—"

"—and you have the pancake-breakfast fund-raiser," she interrupted. "You have to be at St. Michael's by eight, remember?"

He moved toward her and put his hands on her shoulders, searching her face. "How do you do it, Dee? How—?"

"Do what?"

"Watch out for me even when you're mad at me?" He bowed his head. "I... You're the most important thing in my life, Dee. If you don't know that by now, I don't know what..." He felt the tears roll down his cheeks and brushed them away roughly.

"David. Calm down. It's okay. We'll figure something out. Okay? But please. Just for tonight I need a good night's sleep." She kissed him on the cheek. "I'll wake you in the morning. Now get some rest."

Alone in bed, he thought back on what had just happened, what he'd just said. It was true. Dee was the most important thing in his life. Between her and Anton, it wasn't even close.

But then something churned inside him. Why should he have to choose? Most men didn't have to decide between their children and their wives. But Anton was not his blood. And therein lay the rub.

He took several deep breaths, trying to calm his mind. Control yourself, he scolded himself. Nothing's been decided yet. Maybe Dee will come around. She cares about Anton. You know that. Now try and sleep.

But throughout the night, his hand kept feeling the empty place in the bed where Dee ought to have been.

Delores continued to sleep in the guest bedroom into the following week. Each night they waited until Anton went to his room and then said a perfunctory good night to each other. David knew he was being punished, but some instinct told him not to push Dee, to give her the time she needed to figure out whether she could imagine a permanent future with Anton. And yet, with each passing day, his anxiety and anger grew. Dee was holding not just him hostage but Anton, too.

24

(Reetika Vazirani, 1962—2003)
瑞蒂卡·瓦齐拉尼

作者简介

瑞蒂卡·瓦齐拉尼（Reetika Vazirani, 1962—2003），美国印度裔作家、医生，出生于印度帕蒂亚拉（Patiala），6岁时随家人移居美国。她在韦尔斯利学院（Wellesley College）获得文学学士学位，在弗吉尼亚大学（University of Virginia）获得文学硕士学位。瓦齐拉尼曾是斯威特布莱尔学院（Sweet Briar College）和威廉玛丽学院（College of William and Mary）的驻校作家。

瓦齐拉尼的主要作品包括两部诗集：《白象》（*White Elephants*, 1996）和《世界酒店》（*World Hotel*, 2002）。《白象》获得巴纳德新女性诗人奖（Barnard New Women Poets Prize）。这本诗集中的许多诗都是关于诗人回到印度，以及她在那里寻找自己身份的尝试。《世界酒店》获得2003年的阿尼斯菲尔德－沃尔夫图书奖（Anisfield-Wolf Book Award）。这部诗集分为两个部分：《创造玛雅》（"Inventing Maya"）和《是我，我不在家》（"It's Me. I'm Not Home"）。这本诗集延续了瓦齐拉尼对身份、文化以及转型过程中带来的激动与背叛之间的张力的多面探索。瓦齐拉尼还获得了手推车奖、诗人和作家交流计划奖（Poets and Writers Exchange Program Award）、草原帆船公司（Prairie Schooner）的格伦娜·卢切奖（Glenna Luchei Award）等各类奖项。瓦齐拉尼2003年去世后，她的作品集《拉达说》（*Radha Says*, 2009）由莱斯利·麦格拉思（Leslie McGrath）和拉维·尚卡尔（Ravi Shankar）负责编辑，于2009年由醉船媒体出版社（Drunken Boat Media）出版。

诗歌《年轻的国家》（"It's a Young Country"）和《星期五交谊会》（"Friday Mixer"）均选自诗集《世界酒店》。在《年轻的国家》中，诗人将美国的困境与自己的困境联系在一起，警醒人们要"轻装上路"。《世界酒店》描述了一个印度女孩跳舞时穿的衣服所折射的不同含义。

作品选读

It's a Young Country

By Reetika Vaziirani

It's a young country

and we cannot bear to grow old
James Baldwin Marilyn Monroe
Marvin Gaye you could've sung the anthem
at the next Superbowl
We sing *America You are*
magnificent and we mean
we are heartbroken
What fun we chase after it
Can't hurry go the Supremes
Next that diva soprano
For whom stagehands at the Met
wore the T-shirt I *survived* the battle

We leave for a better job
across the country *wish you were*
here in this hotel two of us one
we are with John Keats on his cot
in the lone dictionary I'm falling again
on dilemma's two horns
If you are seducing another
teach me to share you with humor
Water in my bones and the sound

of a midnight telephone *Hello love*
I am coming I do not know
where you sleep are you alone

We grow old look at this country
its worn dungarees
picking cotton dredging ditches
stealing timber bullets prairies
America's hard work *have mercy*
leaders in order to form a more perfect ten
some step forward some step back
neighbor here's a seat
through orange portals lit tunnels
over Brooklyn Golden Gate
weather be bright wheels turn yes
pack lightly we move so fast

Friday Mixer

By Reetika Vaziirani

The Chapel Hill Rotary invited me twice,
and I wore Aunty's yellow sari. I laugh,
for ten years I lived on a mountain.
I show them Mussoorie.
They say it looks like the Blue Ridge.
They're fascinated by so much silk—six
yards on one girl—but I like dresses and
scarves, red nail polish, and I will
have to learn to dance.

25

(Daniyal Mueenuddin, 1963—)
戴尼亚尔·穆伊努丁

作者简介

戴尼亚尔·穆伊努丁（Daniyal Mueenuddin, 1963—），美国巴基斯坦裔小说家，出生于洛杉矶（Los Angeles）。在巴基斯坦度过童年，13岁时随母亲移民美国。从达特茅斯学院（Dartmouth College）毕业后，他返回巴基斯坦帮父亲料理家族农场。1993年，他返回美国就读于耶鲁法学院（Yale Law School）。穆伊努丁毕业后在国际人权组织短暂工作，后从事律师和企业法律顾问工作。后来，他厌倦律师工作，立志成为作家，于是攻读亚利桑那大学（University of Arizona）创意写作硕士课程，于2004年获得学位。

他的第一部短篇小说集《别人的房间，别样的风景》（*In Other Rooms, Other Wonders*, 2009）斩获多个奖项，包括2010年英联邦作家奖（Commonwealth Writers' Prize），并进入2009年的国家图书奖和普利策奖决选名单。这部小说集被翻译成16种语言。这些短篇小说呈现一个从传统向现代过渡的巴基斯坦，生动展现巴基斯坦的风土人情和社会百态、逐渐瓦解的封建制度与西化的生活方式的碰撞以及巴基斯坦底层社会与权势阶层的生活状况。生动逼真的细节刻画不仅使小说画面感十足、人物形象跃然纸上，而且使读者感慨命运、贫穷对于人生的影响，深入地思考人性。

《电工纳瓦布丁》（"Nawabdin Electrician—The Life of a Wily Pakistani Electrician"）和《我们的巴黎女士》（"Our Lady of Paris"）均选自短篇小说集《别人的房间，别样的风景》。《电工纳瓦布丁》入选2008年美国最佳短篇小说选集（*The Best American Short Stories of 2008*），讲述了电工努力赚钱养家的故事。节选部分描

述电工在一个夜晚骑摩托车回家遭劫匪抢劫未遂后，受伤的两人被赶来的村民送往诊所。《我们的巴黎女士》（"Our Lady of Paris"）讲述一对巴基斯坦父母拆散儿子与美国女友的恋情，节选部分讲述美国女孩海伦（Helen）初次见男友苏海尔（Sohail）父母哈鲁尼（Hayatullah）和拉菲亚（Rafia）的场景。

作品选读

Nawabdin Electrician—The Life of a Wily Pakistani Electrician
(excerpt)
By Daniyal Mueenuddin

It seemed very peaceful. In the distance, the dogs kept barking, and all around the crickets called, so many of them that they made a single gentle blended sound. In a mango orchard across the canal some crows began cawing, and he wondered why they were calling at night. Maybe a snake up in the tree, in the nest. Fresh fish from the spring floods of the Indus had just come onto the market, and he kept remembering that he had wanted to buy some for dinner, perhaps the next night. As the pain grew worse he thought of that, the smell of frying fish.

Two men from the village came running up, panting.

"O ..., they've killed him. Who is it?"

The other man kneeled down next to the body. "It's Nawab, the electrician, from Dunyapur."

"I'm not dead," said Nawab insistently, without raising his head. "The bastard's right there in those reeds."

One of the men had a single-barreled shotgun. Stepping forward, aiming into the center of the clump, he fired, reloaded, and fired again. Nothing moved among the green leafy stalks, which were head-high and surmounted with feathers of seed.

"He's gone," said the one who sat by Nawab, holding his arm.

The man with the shotgun again loaded and walked carefully forward, holding the gun to his shoulder. Something moved, and he fired. The robber fell forward into the open ground. He called, "Mother, help me," and got up on his knees, holding his hands to his waist. The gunman walked up to him, hit him once in the middle of the back with the butt of the gun, and then threw down the gun and dragged him roughly by his collar onto the road. Raising the bloody shirt, he saw that the robber had taken half a dozen buckshot pellets in the stomach—black angry holes seeping blood in the light of the torch. The robber kept spitting, without any force.

The other villager, who had been watching, started the motorcycle by pushing it down the road with the gear engaged, until the engine came to life. Shouting that he would get some transport, he raced off, and Nawab minded that the man in his hurry shifted without using the clutch.

"Do you want a cigarette, Uncle?" the villager said to Nawab, offering the pack.

Nawab rolled his head back and forth. "Fuck, look at me."

The lights of a pickup materialized at the headworks and bounced wildly down the road. The driver and the other two lifted Nawab and the robber into the back and took them to Firoza, to a little private clinic there, run by a mere pharmacist, who nevertheless kept a huge clientele because of his abrupt and sure manner and his success at healing with the same few medicines the prevalent diseases.

The clinic smelled of disinfectant and of bodily fluids, a heavy sweetish odor. Four beds stood in a room, dimly lit by a fluorescent tube. As they carried him in, Nawab, alert to the point of strain, observed the blood on some rumpled sheets, a rusty blot. The pharmacist, who lived above his clinic, had come down wearing a loincloth and undershirt. He seemed perfectly calm and even cross at having been disturbed.

"Put them on those two beds."

"*As-salaam uleikum*, Doctor Sahib," said Nawab, who felt as if he were speaking to someone very far away. The pharmacist seemed an immensely grave and important man, and Nawab spoke to him formally.

"What happened, Nawab?"

"He tried to snatch my motorbike, but I didn't let him."

The pharmacist pulled off Nawab's shalvar, got a rag, and washed away the blood, then poked around quite roughly, while Nawab held the sides of the bed and willed himself not to scream. "You'll live," he said. "You're a lucky man. The bullets all went low."

"Did it hit..."

The pharmacist dabbed with the rag. "Not even that, thank ...."

The robber must have been hit in the lung, for he kept breathing up blood.

"You won't need to bother taking this one to the police," said the pharmacist.

"He's a dead man."

"Please," begged the robber, trying to raise himself up. "Have mercy, save me. I'm a human being also."

The pharmacist went into the office next door and wrote out the names of drugs on a pad, sending the two villagers to a dispenser in the next street.

"Tell him it's Nawabdin the electrician. Tell him I'll make sure he gets the money."

Nawab for the first time looked over at the robber. There was blood on his pillow, and he kept snuffling, as if he needed to blow his nose. His thin and very long neck hung crookedly on his shoulder, as if out of joint. He was older than Nawab had thought before, not a boy, dark-skinned, with sunken eyes and protruding yellow smoker's teeth, which showed whenever he twitched for breath.

"I did you wrong," said the robber weakly. "I know that. You don't know my life, just as I don't know yours. Even I don't know what brought me here. Maybe you're a poor man, but I'm much poorer than you. My mother is old and blind, in the slums outside Multan. Make them fix me, ask them to and they'll do it." He began to cry, not wiping the tears, which drew lines on his dark face.

"Go to hell," said Nawab, turning away. "Men like you are good at confessions. My children would have begged in the streets."

The robber lay heaving, moving his fingers by his sides. The pharmacist seemed to have gone away somewhere, leaving them alone.

"They just said that I'm dying. Forgive me for what I did. I was brought up with kicks and slaps and never enough to eat. I've never had anything of my own, no land, no house, no wife, no money, never, nothing. I slept for years on the railway station platform in Multan. My mother's blessing on you. Give me your blessing, don't let me die unforgiven." He began snuffling and coughing even more, and then started hiccupping.

Now the disinfectant smelled strong and good to Nawab. The floor seemed to shine. The world around him expanded.

"Never. I won't forgive you. You had your life, I had mine. At every step of the road I went the right way and you the wrong. Look at you now, with bubbles of blood stuck in the corner of your mouth. Do you think this isn't a judgment? My wife and children would have begged in the street, and you would have sold my motorbike to pay for six unlucky hands of cards and a few bottles of poison home brew. If you weren't lying here now, you would already be in one of the gambling camps along the river."

The man said, "Please, please, please," more softly each time, and then he stared up at the ceiling. "It's not true," he whispered. After a few minutes he convulsed and died. The pharmacist, who had come in by then and was cleaning Nawab's wounds, did nothing to help him.

Yet Nawab's mind caught at this, looking at the man's words and his death, like a bird hopping around some bright object, meaning to peck at it. And then he didn't. He thought of the motorcycle, saved, and the glory of saving it. He was growing. Six shots, six coins thrown down, six chances, and not one of them killed him, not Nawabdin Electrician.

Our Lady of Paris
(excerpt)
By Daniyal Mueenuddin

At dusk the following day, Sohail sat watching Helen dress for their first dinner with his parents. He wore a sports jacket, a black cashmere turtleneck, and pleated trousers; she rolled black stockings over her legs, which were pink and damp from the shower. Walking to the closet, naked but for the stockings, she removed a black dress, stepped into it, pulling it over the flare of her hips. She turned her back to him, and he zipped it, then stood for a moment holding her close, inhaling the scent of her hair.

They walked past the halfhearted Christmas tree in front of Notre Dame and then along the left bank of the Seine, among the headlights of scooters and cars, the crowds rushing home into the twilight, the tourists everywhere taking pictures, the Parisians with buttoned-down faces. The wet streets glittered. Helen walked beside Sohail, keeping up with him, her heels clicking. She drank in the city around them, moving so quickly, so differently.

A barge passed, going upstream, long and fast, smoking into the night, the lit cabin cozy and cheerful above the cold black water.

"You know," she said thoughtfully, "the Seine doesn't divide Paris, it keeps the city together. It's just the right width, not a little stream but a public place in the heart of the city."

Sohail leaned down and kissed her. "That's a great image, the river *not* dividing Paris."

"It's yours," said Helen. "For your next poem."

His parents were staying in an apartment on the Quai des Grands Augustins, overlooking the Seine. Sohail and Helen went up to the second floor, found the door, and he had just touched the bell when a voice called, "Coming."

"Hello, darling," said his mother, presenting her cheek to kiss, looking past him to Helen. She had a husky, attractive voice and was dressed quite plainly, a long white cotton tunic embroidered in white over slim-fitting pants.

Helen extended her hand, palm flat, and looked Sohail's mother in the eye, directly and ingenuously. "Hello, Mrs. Harouni. I'm Helen."

"And I'm Rafia. Welcome." She had fixed a stiff smile on her face.

Sohail's father stood to one side, a smallish man with a little mustache, precisely dressed in a thick brown tweed suit with a vest and muted tie and brilliantly shined shoes of a distinctive tan color. As he took Helen's coat he said, "Welcome, welcome. Thank you for coming." But his statement appeared to be reflexive, without connection to his mental processes. Putting the coat on a hanger, he looked at her closely, with shrewd eyes. Sohail had thrown his coat on a chair near the door.

"Very nice," said Sohail, looking around at the apartment, which had high ceilings and diminutive fittings. A woman on the stereo sang in French, and his mother had lit candles.

"It belongs to Brigadier Hazari," said his father, sitting down again in front of the fire.

Rafia and Helen had moved into the living room. The mother leaned down and looked at Helen's necklace, an Afghan tribal piece, silver with lapis.

"Isn't that pretty."

"Sohail gave it to me. It's one of my favorite things."

Rafia said to Sohail, turning and smiling at him, "Will you get Helen and yourself whatever you want—it's in the kitchen." Then to Helen, "Come sit here by me."

Sohail brought a drink for Helen and one for himself. His father sat back in the sofa, his drink on his knee, and looked sedately about the room. Rafia began.

"I promised Sohail not to embarrass him, not to say how much I've heard about you." She had little dimples when she smiled. "But it's true, he keeps telling me about you, it's sweet."

"Ma, please. That makes me sound like I'm fifteen," said Sohail.

"It's the simple truth. And why shouldn't I say it, it's nice to see you happy. But please come help me with dinner. Bring your drink."

As mother and son went into the kitchen, Helen heard Rafia whisper to Sohail, "But she's *so* pretty."

Helen was left with Mr. Harouni, who did not seem disposed to conversation. He looked complacently at the fire, his glass sweating. After hesitating to have a drink, Helen had accepted a white wine, reminding herself that she was an adult. Now she took a sip of the wine, trying to relax. She had been sitting up erect, halfway forward in the seat.

Still looking into the fire, Mr. Harouni observed speculatively, "Sohail was very happy at Yale." She waited for more, but the father seemed to be content placing this statement on the table between them, a sufficient offering.

"He really was, Mr. Harouni. He's been happy as long as I've known him." She wanted to be as straight with his parents as possible.

"Please, call me Amjad." The thick tweed of his suit and the smallness of his hands and feet made him appear to Helen like an expensive toy. He spoke very quietly.

She decided to press on, to maintain even this slight momentum of conversation. "His life in Pakistan is so different, at least from what I know. But he has an American side, what I think of as American. He's very gentle—I don't mean Americans are gentle, they're not. But it's easier to be gentle in a place where there's order."

She paused, took a sip of her wine, waited for a moment.

"Go on," said Mr. Harouni.

"He and my mother got along well, even though—she's a secretary in a little Connecticut town, and she has a house with cats and a garden. He liked that. At first I thought he was pretending, but he wasn't."

"It's a wonderful country. There's nothing you people can't do when you put your minds to it. I admire the Americans tremendously." He sipped from his glass, the ice cubes clattering. "So many of our young people want to live in America—I suppose Sohail as well."

"He talks about it," she said cautiously. "But he talks about Pakistan a lot too. When he and I first met he told me stories about Pakistan for hours."

"And what about you? What would you like to do?"

"I want to be a doctor. I just sent out my applications to medical school." She blushed as she said this, the color unevenly creeping up her fine-grained cheekbones.

"On the East Coast?"

"In New York, maybe. When I was little my mother would drive me to the city, to the Museum of Natural History or the Met, or sometimes we would just walk around looking at the stores and the people. I've always wanted to live there." She paused again, conscious that she might sound pathetic. "It feels like the center of everything. And it's not the way it used to be, it's safe and clean, you can walk through the park at midnight."

The father looked at her with an expressionless face. "Perhaps Sohail can set up a branch of our company there."

Sohail had come in and heard this last part of the conversation. He sat down on the arm of Helen's chair, put his hand on her shoulder, and said, "Now you've seen it, Helen. That's as close as my father comes to humor." He leaned forward, took his father's empty glass, and stood up. "I warn you, this man has more factories than your mother has cats. Watch out for him. Stick to name, rank, and serial number."

Mr. Harouni smiled appreciatively.

"We both want the same thing—what's best for you," said Helen in a flirtatious tone quite new to her. "Why would I need to be careful?"

They had dinner at a small table under a spiky modern chandelier painted with gold leaf, Mr. Harouni sitting at the head and filling their bowls with bouillabaisse, saffroned and aromatic. Rafia tasted hers from the tip of her spoon and said, "It's good. It's from Quintessence—that's the new chic place, supposedly." Sohail poured the wine and then turned down the lights, so that the table was illuminated by candles.

A bateau mouche glided by on the Seine, its row of spotlights trained on the historic buildings along the quay, throwing patterned light through the blinds onto the living room wall. For a moment they carefully sipped the hot stew.

Helen felt she should break the silence. Just as she was about to begin, Rafia turned to her.

"Do you know, Sohail was almost born in Paris?" She sipped from her spoon, looking at Helen sideways. "I was in London to have the baby, and I was enormous and felt like an elephant—so I begged Amjad to come over with me and let me pick out some outrageous outfits. I thought I'd have my girlish figure back the day after I delivered."

Sohail beamed across at Helen, his face framed by two wavering candles. "You can tell this is one of my mother's tall tales—by the simple fact that she's never begged my father for anything. If she had said she ordered my father to Paris it might have been true."

"In any case, you were almost born here, in the HÂtel d'Angleterre."

"I wish it had happened," said Sohail. "For a Pakistani being born in London is about as exciting as being born in Lahore. Paris would be glamorous."

Rafia tilted her head toward Helen. "Where would you have liked to be born?"

"I've never thought of that. The first time I met Sohail he asked me where I'd like to be buried."

"In seven years of dating, that line has never once failed." Sohail appeared to be saying the first thing that came into his head, filling up the gaps in the conversation.

"Don't be flip, Sohail. Amjad, where would you like to have been born?"

The father, who had been drinking his stew with the equanimity of a solitary patron in a busy café, looked up from under his brows.

"I suppose in the happiest possible home. And not in India, I think. And not in Europe. Perhaps in America."

This interested Helen, relieving her irritation at the conversation between mother and son, which seemed too practiced, as if they were performing together, and in their display excluding her.

"Why America?" she asked. Her oval face reflected the light of the candles.

Placing his forearms on the table, still holding his spoon, Mr. Harouni looked for a moment over his wife's head at the opposite wall. "You know or you correctly assume that I was born into a comfortably well-off family. All my life I've been lucky, my business succeeded, I've had no tragedies, my wife and I are happy, we have a wonderful son. The one thing I've missed, I sometimes feel, is the sensation of being absolutely free, to do exactly what I like, to go where I like, to act as I like. I suspect that only an American ever feels that. You aren't weighed down by your families, and you aren't weighed down by history. If I ran away to the South Pole some Pakistani businessman would one day crawl into my igloo and ask if I was the cousin of K. K. Harouni."

Rafia touched his arm. "Darling, you're too old to be menopausal. Americans aren't more free than anyone else. Just because an American runs away, to Kansas or Wyoming, doesn't mean that he succeeds in escaping whatever it is he left behind. Like all of us, he carries it with him." She turned to Helen. "Let me ask you. Do you think you're free?"

"I'm not old enough yet to know. I think that at twenty-one many girls think they are."

"Brilliant!" said Sohail. He poured more wine for himself and for his parents;

Helen put her hand over the mouth of her glass.

After a moment Mr. Harouni stood up and began gathering their dishes. He prevented Sohail from rising to help him, saying, "No, no, you sit, let me do this."

"You have to admit, my dad's pretty evolved," said Sohail. "He even likes to cook."

Her mind cooling, prickly from the wine, Helen listened to Sohail and his mother talking about their plans for the next few days, museums and the ballet on Christmas Eve. Rafia had a slight British accent, but softer than that, more rounded—as if the accent had been bred by the personality, as one of her individual characteristics. So this is how Sohail grew up, Helen thought. She wondered what lay beneath the angularities of Rafia's character—a woman so imposing not only in her speech but in her manner, the way in which she moved her hands, the angle at which she held her head. In any case, Helen would manage with Rafia, they would make their peace.

26

(Jhumpa Lahiri, 1967—)
裘帕·拉希莉

作者简介

裘帕·拉希莉（Jhumpa Lahiri, 1967—），美国印度裔小说家，出生于英国伦敦的一个印度移民家庭，幼年随父母迁居美国罗德岛州。拉希莉毕业于伯纳德学院（Bamard College），继而在波士顿大学（Boston University）深造，获得硕士和博士学位。前期使用英语写作，近年来以意大利语写作，同时从事意语文学翻译。任教于普林斯顿大学。

拉希莉的主要作品有短篇小说集《疾病解说者》（*Interpreter of Maladies*, 1999）和《不适之地》（*The Unaccustomed Earth*, 2008），长篇小说《同名人》（*The Namesake*, 2003）和《低地》（*The Lowland*, 2013）。拉希莉的处女作《疾病解说者》获得美国笔会/海明威文学奖年度最佳虚构处女作和2000年普利策小说奖，拉希莉成为普利策小说奖史上最年轻的获奖者（33岁）。《不适之地》出版后，登上《纽约时报》畅销书榜单，又获弗兰克·奥康纳国际短篇小说奖。拉希莉近年来用意大利语写作，出版两本文集：《另行言之》（*In Altre Parole,*（*In Other Words*, 2017））以及《书之衣》（*Il Vestito Dei Libri,*（*The Clothing of Books*, 2017））。2018年，拉希莉的第三部小说也是她的首部意大利语小说《我之所在》（*Dove mi trovo*）正式出版，她以 *Whereabouts* 为题推出了该书的英译本。此外，拉希莉因翻译多米尼科·斯塔诺内（Domenico Starnone）的小说《骗局》（*Trick*）荣获2018年度国家图书奖翻译文学奖（National Book Award for Translated Literature）。

拉希莉的小说有明显的自传色彩，多刻画她所熟悉的美国孟加拉裔移民，叙述他们在异国生活里遭遇的文化冲突，以及作为个体在社会生活里必然经历的悲欢离合、希望和失望、挣扎与困惑。她的语言精致、微妙，又很自然，在从容、冷静的叙述中蕴含着一种内在的力量。

《疾病解说者》("Interpreter of Maladies") 选自短篇小说集《疾病解说者》，该篇获得欧·亨利短篇小说奖、《纽约客》杂志年度最佳处女作并入选《美国最佳短篇小说年鉴》。小说讲述一对美籍印度夫妇携带孩子回印度探亲旅行的故事。作者通过达斯夫妇（Das）一家探讨人与人的隔阂与理解困惑、失落与抗争、移民的移居困境。节选部分讲述达斯夫人向导游倾吐压抑在心底多年的婚外情和私生子的秘密。

小说《低地》讲述印度纳萨尔运动对于兄弟二人的命运影响，小说时间跨度长达半个世纪，地域跨越印度和美国，包含一个家族四代人的人生经历，将个人命运与国家命运融入叙事。选段出自小说第一章，介绍故事主人公尤得彦（Udayan）和妻子格瑞（Gauri）的相识过程。

作品选读

Interpreter of Maladies
(excerpt)
By Jhumpa Lahiri

Mr. Das headed up the defile with the children, the boys at his side, the little girl on his shoulders. Mr. Kapasi watched as they crossed paths with a Japanese man and woman, the only other tourists there, who paused for a final photograph, then stepped into a nearby car and drove away. As the car disappeared out of view some of the monkeys called out, emitting soft whooping sounds, and then walked on their flat black hands and feet up the path. At one point a group of them formed a little ring around Mr. Das and the children. Tina screamed in delight. Ronny ran in circles around his father.

Bobby bent down and picked up a fat stick on the ground. When he extended it, one of the monkeys approached him and snatched it, then briefly beat the ground.

"I'll join them," Mr. Kapasi said, unlocking the door on his side. "There is much to explain about the caves."

"No. Stay a minute," Mrs. Das said. She got out of the back seat and slipped in beside. Mr. Kapasi. "Raj has his dumb book anyway." Together, through the windshield,

Mrs. Das and Mr. Kapasi watched as Bobby and the monkey passed the stick back and forth between them.

"A brave little boy," Mr. Kapasi commented.

"It's not so surprising," Mrs. Das said.

"No?"

"He's not his."

"I beg your pardon?"

"Raj's. He's not Raj's son."

Mr. Kapasi felt a prickle on his skin. He reached into his shirt pocket for the small tin of lotus-oil balm he carried with him at all times, and applied it to three spots on his forehead. He knew that Mrs. Das was watching him, but he did not turn to face her. Instead he watched as the figures of Mr. Das and the children grew smaller, climbing up the steep path, pausing every now and then for a picture, surrounded by a growing number of monkeys.

"Are you surprised?" The way she put it made him choose his words with care.

"It's not the type of thing one assumes," Mr. Kapasi replied slowly. He put the tin of lotus-oil balm back in his pocket.

"No, of course not. And no one knows, of course. No one at all. I've kept it a secret for eight whole years." She looked at Mr. Kapasi, tilting her chin as if to gain a fresh perspective. "But now I've told you."

Mr. Kapasi nodded. He felt suddenly parched, and his forehead was warm and slightly numb from the balm. He considered asking Mrs. Das for a sip of water, then decided against it.

"We met when we were very young," she said. She reached into her straw bag in search of something, then pulled out a packet of puffed rice. "Want some?"

"No, thank you."

She put a fistful in her mouth, sank into the seat a little, and looked away from Mr. Kapasi, out the window on her side of the car. "We married when we were still in college. We were in high school when he proposed. We went to the same college, of course. Back then we couldn't stand the thought of being separated, not for a day, not for a minute. Our parents were best friends who lived in the same town. My entire life I saw him every weekend, either at our house or theirs. We were sent upstairs to play together while our parents joked about our marriage. Imagine! They never caught us at anything, though in a way I think it was all more or less a setup. The things we did those Friday and Saturday nights, while our parents sat downstairs drinking tea... I could tell you stories, Mr. Kapasi."

As a result of spending all her time in college with Raj, she continued, she did not make many close friends. There was no one to confide in about him at the end of a difficult day, or to share a passing thought or a worry. Her parents now lived on the other side of the world, but she had never been very close to them, anyway. After marrying so young she was overwhelmed by it all, having a child so quickly, and nursing, and warming up bottles of milk and testing their temperature against her wrist while Raj was at work, dressed in sweaters and corduroy pants, teaching his students about rocks and dinosaurs. Raj never looked cross or harried, or plump as she had become after the first baby.

Always tired, she declined invitations from her one or two college girlfriends, to have lunch or shop in Manhattan. Eventually the friends stopped calling her, so that she was left at home all day with the baby, surrounded by toys that made her trip when she walked or wince when she sat, always cross and tired. Only occasionally did they go out after Ronny was born, and even more rarely did they entertain. Raj didn't mind; he looked forward to coming home from teaching and watching television and bouncing Ronny on his knee. She had been outraged when Raj told her that a Punjabi friend, someone whom she had once met but did not remember, would be staying with them for a week for some job interviews in the New Brunswick area.

Bobby was conceived in the afternoon, on a sofa littered with rubber teething toys, after the friend learned that a London pharmaceutical company had hired him, while Ronny cried to be freed from his playpen. She made no protest when the friend touched the small of her back as she was about to make a pot of coffee, then pulled her against his crisp navy suit. He made love to her swiftly, in silence, with an expertise she had never known, without the meaningful expressions and smiles Raj always insisted on afterward. The next day Raj drove the friend to JFK. He was married now, to a Punjabi girl, and they lived in London still, and every year they exchanged Christmas cards with Raj and Mina, each couple tucking photos of their families into the envelopes. He did not know that he was Bobby's father. He never would.

"I beg your pardon, Mrs. Das, but why have you told me this information?" Mr. Kapasi asked when she had finally finished speaking, and had turned to face him once again.

"For ...'s sake, stop calling me Mrs. Das. I'm twenty-eight. You probably have children my age."

"Not quite." It disturbed Mr. Kapasi to learn that she thought of him as a parent.

The feeling he had had toward her, that had made him check his reflection in the rearview mirror as they drove, evaporated a little.

"I told you because of your talents." She put the packet of puffed rice back into her bag without folding over the top.

"I don't understand," Mr. Kapasi said.

"Don't you see? For eight years I haven't been able to express this to anybody, not to friends, certainly not to Raj. He doesn't even suspect it. He thinks I'm still in love with him. Well, don't you have anything to say?"

"About what?"

"About what I've just told you. About my secret, and about how terrible it makes me feel. I feel terrible looking at my children, and at Raj, always terrible. I have terrible urges, Mr. Kapasi, to throw things away. One day I had the urge to throw everything I own out the window, the television, the children, everything. Don't you think it's unhealthy?"

He was silent.

"Mr. Kapasi, don't you have anything to say? I thought that was your job."

"My job is to give tours, Mrs. Das."

"Not that. Your other job. As an interpreter."

"But we do not face a language barrier. What need is there for an interpreter?"

"That's not what I mean. I would never have told you otherwise. Don't you realize what it means for me to tell you?"

"What does it mean?"

"It means that I'm tired of feeling so terrible all the time. Eight years, Mr. Kapasi, I've been in pain eight years. I was hoping you could help me feel better, say the right thing. Suggest some kind of remedy."

He looked at her, in her red plaid skirt and strawberry T-shirt, a woman not yet thirty, who loved neither her husband nor her children, who had already fallen out of love with life. Her confession depressed him, depressed him all the more when he thought of Mr. Das at the top of the path, Tina clinging to his shoulders, taking pictures of ancient monastic cells cut into the hills to show his students in America, unsuspecting and unaware that one of his sons was not his own. Mr. Kapasi felt insulted that Mrs. Das should ask him to interpret her common, trivial little secret. She did not resemble the patients in the doctor's office, those who came glassy-eyed and desperate, unable to sleep or breathe or urinate with ease, unable, above all, to give words to their pains.

Still, Mr. Kapasi believed it was his duty to assist Mrs. Das. Perhaps he ought to tell her to confess the truth to Mr. Das. He would explain that honesty was the best policy.

Honesty, surely, would help her feel better, as she'd put it. Perhaps he would offer to preside over the discussion, as a mediator. He decided to begin with the most obvious question, to get to the heart of the matter, and so he asked, "Is it really pain you feel, Mrs. Das, or is it guilt?"

She turned to him and glared, mustard oil thick on her frosty pink lips. She opened her mouth to say something, but as she glared at Mr. Kapasi some certain knowledge seemed to pass before her eyes, and she stopped. It crushed him; he knew at that moment that he was not even important enough to be properly insulted. She opened the car door and began walking up the path, wobbling a little on her square wooden heels, reaching into her straw bag to eat handfuls of puffed rice. It fell through her fingers, leaving a zigzagging trail, causing a monkey to leap down from a tree and devour the little white grains. In search of more, the monkey began to follow Mrs. Das. Others joined him, so that she was soon being followed by about half a dozen of them, their velvety tails dragging behind.

The Lowland

Chapter 1

(excerpt)

By Jhumpa Lahiri

Normally she stayed on the balcony, reading, or kept to an adjacent room as her brother and Udayan studied and smoked and drank cups of tea. Manash had befriended him at Calcutta University, where they were both graduate students in the physics department. Much of the time their books on the behaviors of liquids and gases would sit ignored as they talked about the repercussions of Naxalbari, and commented on the day's events.

The discussions strayed to the insurgencies in Indochina and in Latin American countries. In the case of Cuba it wasn't even a mass movement, Udayan pointed out. Just a small group, attacking the right targets.

All over the world students were gaining momentum, standing up to exploitative systems. It was another example of Newton's second law of motion, he joked. Force equals mass times acceleration.

Manash was skeptical. What could they, urban students, claim to know about peasant life?

Nothing, Udayan said. We need to learn from them.

Through an open doorway she saw him. Tall but slight of build, twenty-three but looking a bit older. His clothing hung on him loosely. He wore kurtas but also European-style shirts, irreverently, the top portion unbuttoned, the bottom untucked, the sleeves rolled back past the elbow.

He sat in the room where they listened to the radio. On the bed that served as a sofa where, at night, Gauri slept. His arms were lean, his fingers too long for the small porcelain cups of tea her family served him, which he drained in just a few gulps. His hair was wavy, the brows thick, the eyes languid and dark.

His hands seemed an extension of his voice, always in motion, embellishing the things he said. Even as he argued he smiled easily. His upper teeth overlapped slightly, as if there were one too many of them. From the beginning, the attraction was there. He never said anything to Gauri if she happened to brush by. Never glancing, never acknowledging that she was Manash's younger sister, until the day the houseboy was out on an errand, and Manash asked Gauri if she minded making them some tea.

She could not find a tray to put the teacups on. She carried them in, nudging open the door to the room with her shoulder.

Looking up at her an instant longer than he needed to, Udayan took his cup from her hands.

The groove between his mouth and nose was deep. Clean-shaven. Still looking at her, he posed his first question.

Where do you study? he asked.

Because she went to Presidency, and Calcutta University was just next door, she searched for him on the quadrangle, and among the bookstalls, at the tables of the Coffee House if she went there with a group of friends. Something told her he did not go to his classes as regularly as she did. She began to watch for him from the generous balcony that wrapped around the two sides of her grandparents' flat, overlooking the intersection where Cornwallis Street began. It became something for her to do.

Then one day she spotted him, amazed that she knew which of the hundreds of dark heads was his. He was standing on the opposite corner, buying a packet of cigarettes. Then he was crossing the street, a cotton book bag over his shoulder, glancing both ways, walking toward their flat.

She crouched below the filigree, under the clothes drying on the line, worried that he would look up and see her. Two minutes later she heard footsteps climbing the stairwell, and then the rattle of the iron knocker on the door of the flat. She heard the door being opened, the houseboy letting him in.

It was an afternoon everyone, including Manash, happened to be out, and she'd been reading, alone. She wondered if he'd turn back, given that Manash wasn't there. Instead, a moment later, he stepped out onto the balcony.

No one else here? he asked.

She shook her head.

Will you talk to me, then?

The laundry was damp, some of her petticoats and blouses were clipped to the line. The material of the blouses was tailored to the shape of her upper torso, her breasts. He unclipped one of the blouses and put it further down the line to make room.

He did this slowly, a mild tremor in his fingers forcing him to focus more than another person might on the task. Standing beside him, she was aware of his height, the slight stoop in his shoulders, the angle at which he held his face. He struck a match against the side of a box and lit a cigarette, cupping his whole hand over his mouth when he drew the cigarette to his lips. The houseboy brought out biscuits and tea.

They overlooked the intersection, from four flights above. They stood beside one another, both of them leaning into the railing. Together they took in the stone buildings, with their decrepit grandeur, that lined the streets. Their tired columns, their crumbling cornices, their sullied shades.

Her face was supported by the discreet barrier of her hand. His arm hung over the edge, the burning cigarette was in his fingers. The sleeves of his Punjabi were rolled up, exposing the veins running from his wrist to the crook of the elbow. They were prominent, the blood in them greenish gray, like a pointed archway below the skin.

There was something elemental about so many human beings in motion at once: walking, sitting in buses and trams, pulling or being pulled along in rickshaws. On the other side of the street were a few gold and silver shops all in a row, with mirrored walls and ceilings. Always crowded with families, endlessly reflected, placing orders for wedding jewels. There was the press where they took clothes to be ironed. The store where Gauri bought her ink, her notebooks. Narrow sweet shops, where trays of confections were studded with flies.

The paanwallah sat cross-legged at one corner, under a bare bulb, spreading white lime paste on stacks of betel leaves. A traffic constable stood at the center, in his helmet, on his little box. Blowing a whistle and waving his arms. The clamor of so many motors, of so many scooters and lorries and busses and cars, filled their ears.

I like this view, he said.

27

(Maya Khosla, 1970—)
玛雅·科斯拉

作者简介

玛雅·科斯拉（Maya Khosla, 1970—），美国印度裔作家、生物学家。她曾在孟加拉国、缅甸、不丹、英国、印度和美国的一些地方生活过，获得索诺玛县荣誉诗人称号（Poet Laureate Emerita of Sonoma County）(2018—2020)。现在在加利福尼亚州担任生物学和毒理学的顾问。

玛雅·科斯拉的作品主要包括诗集《基尔骨》（*Keel Bone*, 2003）、《风与光的所有火焰》（*All the Fires of Wind and Light*, 2019），以及非虚构作品集《水网》（*Web of Water*, 1997）等。《基尔骨》获得了多萝西·布鲁斯曼诗歌奖（Dorothy Brunsman Poetry Prize）。《风与光的所有火焰》荣获 2020 年奥克兰笔会/约瑟芬·迈尔斯奖（PEN Oakland/Josephine Miles Award）。她还获得了路德维希·沃格尔斯坦奖（Ludwig Vogelstein Award），以及海德兰艺术中心（Headlands Center for the Arts）和新德里梵蒂冈基金会（Sanskriti Foundation）的驻留权。

她的诗作发表在《威斯康星评论》（*Wisconsin Review*）、《塞内卡评论》（*Seneca Review*）、《文学评论》（*Literary Review*）等杂志上。她也曾为电影《尘埃之村》（*Village of Dust*）、《水之城》（*City of Water*）和《暗流涌动》（*Shifting Undercurrents*）撰写文章，并拍摄了一部关于在气候变化时期如何防火的电影。

诗歌《播散》（"Dispersal"）、《提供之物》（"Offerings"）选自诗集《基尔骨》。诗人描述了春天的死亡和希望，特殊的石头和天气、河流和家园、生物和人。读者能够在她的诗歌中获得恐惧、喜悦等共鸣。

作品选读

Dispersal

By Maya Khosla

Oak crickets dedicate their shrilling to the stars:
tireless desire pitched into the jeweled universe
with the most power a chorus of cells can muster.

Such surges are rooted at the core, native
to the multimillion nuclei in each being,
To the fledgling dread of a kestrel, preparing
for first fight. To an apple's thump on earth,
kernels of yearning sealed in the double darkness
of sugars and night-rose coat. Each stores formulae

for longing and reaching with genetic perfection.
And after water is filtered, tent pegs fastened, fruit sliced
the valley stilled, I enter that world one mouthful

at a time. Up along its rim, the lapping grasses
are lighter for the absence of prickly seed-heads
quick-released into my socks as I passed.

Offerings

By Maya Khosla

for R. Schwartz

A woman donates one of her kidneys, saves

a life. She awakens at dawn and the world

feels altered. To rise fearless after parting
with the body's inner sense of bilateral symmetry

is to understand anew that dawn's scissors of wind,
which slice first light into ribbons the shape of leaves,

will not annihilate them. She can now watch birds
flickering in the sun and feel the inner magnet of hope

that propels them to snap ties with known terrains,
venture across landscapes never traversed. Migration, too,

is the mind in storm, the mind prepared to shed all
but the vector between given and received,

between an emptied landscape and one rich
with sun and nutrients. Still, there's no denying

the half-emptiness remaining Often her heart
lingers at the edge of what sang

along the slant of branches now swept clean.

28

(Siddhartha Mukherjee, 1970—)
悉达多·穆克吉

作者简介

悉达多·穆克吉（Siddhartha Mukherjee, 1970— ），美国印度裔作家、医生和科学家。他曾在斯坦福大学、牛津大学（University of Oxford）以及哈佛大学医学院（Harvard Medical School）就读，在牛津大学获得致癌病毒研究的博士学位，并在读书期间获得过罗氏奖学金。他已经在《自然》（Nature）、《新英格兰医学期刊》（The New England Journal of Medicine）等期刊，以及《纽约时报》等报纸上发表过文章和评论。他曾担任《2013年美国最佳科学和自然写作》（The Best American Science and Nature Writing 2013）的编辑。

他的作品主要包括《重病之王：癌症传》（The Emperor of All Maladies: A Biography of Cancer, 2010）、《医学的法则》（The Laws of Medicine, 2015）以及《基因：亲密的历史》（The Gene: An Intimate History, 2016）等。《重病之王：癌症传》荣获各类著名文学奖，包括2011年普利策非虚构类文学奖（Pulitzer Prize for General Non-Fiction）和"卫报第一本书奖"（Guardian First Book Award）。该书在2011年被《时代》杂志列入"有史以来100本非虚构书籍"名单。《基因：亲密的历史》在《纽约时报》畅销书（The New York Times Best Seller）排行榜上曾名列第一，并入选《纽约时报》2016年"100本最佳图书"，还入围了惠康信托奖（Wellcome Trust Prize）和皇家学会科学图书奖（Royal Society Prize for Science Books）决赛名单。

《重病之王：癌症传》描述了那些为了生存而在严苛的治疗方案中奋战的人，增加了我们对这种标志性疾病的了解，为那些寻求揭开癌症神秘面纱的人提供了希望。选段部分出自《重病之王：癌症传》第一部分，讲述了玛丽·位达德·拉斯克（Mary Woodard Lasker）通过童年和少女时期的三段有关疾病的回忆，使她认识到疾病对生命的毁灭近在咫尺，随时随地都在威胁人类，这也促使她走进癌症研究的领域。

作品选读

The Emperor of All Maladies: A Biography of Cancer

Part Two: An Impatient War
(excerpt)
By Siddhartha Mukherjee

Mary Woodard was born in Watertown, Wisconsin, in 1900. Her father, Frank Woodard, was a successful small-town banker. Her mother, Sara Johnson, had emigrated from Ireland in the 1880s, worked as a saleswoman at the Carson's department store in Chicago, and ascended briskly through professional ranks to become one of the highest-paid saleswomen at the store. Salesmanship, as Lasker would later write, was "a natural talent" for Johnson. Johnson had later turned from her work at the department store to lobbying for philanthropic ventures and public projects—selling ideas instead of clothes. She was, as Lasker once put it, a woman who "could sell... anything that she wanted to."

Mary Lasker's own instruction in sales began in the early 1920s, when, having graduated from Radcliffe College, she found her first job selling European paintings on commission for a gallery in New York—a cutthroat profession that involved as much social maneuvering as canny business sense. In the mid-1930s, Lasker left the gallery to start an entrepreneurial venture called Hollywood Patterns, which sold simple prefab dress designs to chain stores. Once again, good instincts crisscrossed with good timing. As women joined the workforce in increasing numbers in the 1940s, Lasker's mass-produced professional clothes found a wide market. Lasker emerged from the Depression and the war financially rejuvenated. By the late 1940s, she had grown into an extraordinarily powerful businesswoman, a permanent fixture in the firmament of New York society, a rising social star.

In 1939, Mary Woodard met Albert Lasker, the sixty-year-old president of Lord and Thomas, an advertising firm based in Chicago. Albert Lasker, like Mary Woodard, was considered an intuitive genius in his profession. At Lord and Thomas, he had invented and perfected a new strategy of advertising that he called "salesmanship in print." A successful advertisement, Lasker contended, was not merely a conglomeration of jingles and images designed to seduce consumers into buying an object; rather, it was a masterwork of copywriting that would tell a consumer why to buy a product. Advertising was merely a carrier for information and reason, and for the public to grasp its impact, information had to be distilled into its essential elemental form... Each of Lasker's widely successful ad campaigns—for Sunkist oranges, Pepsodent toothpaste, and Lucky Strike cigarettes among many others—highlighted this strategy. In time, a variant of this idea, of advertising as a lubricant of information and of the need to distill information into elemental iconography would leave a deep and lasting impact on the cancer campaign.

Mary and Albert had a brisk romance and a whirlwind courtship, and they were married just fifteen months after they met—Mary for the second time, Albert for the third. Mary Lasker was now forty years old. Wealthy, gracious, and enterprising, she now launched a search for her own philanthropic cause—retracing her mother's conversion from a businesswoman into a public activist.

For Mary Lasker, this search soon turned inward, into her personal life. Three memories from her childhood and adolescence haunted her. In one, she awakes from a terrifying illness—likely a near-fatal bout of bacterial dysentery or pneumonia—febrile and confused, and overhears a family friend say to her mother that she will likely not survive: "Sara, I don't think that you will ever raise her."

In another, she has accompanied her mother to visit her family's laundress in Watertown, Wisconsin. The woman is recovering from surgery for breast cancer—radical mastectomies performed on both breasts. Lasker enters a dark shack with a low, small cot with seven children running around and she is struck by the desolation and misery of the scene. The notion of breasts being excised to stave cancer—"Cut off?" Lasker asks her mother searchingly—puzzles and grips her. The laundress survives; "cancer," Lasker realizes, "can be cruel but it does not need to be fatal."

In the third, she is a teenager in college, and is confined to an influenza ward during the epidemic of 1918. The lethal Spanish flu rages outside, decimating towns and cities. Lasker survives—but the flu will kill six hundred thousand Americans that year, and take nearly fifty million lives worldwide, becoming the deadliest pandemic in history.

A common thread ran through these memories: the devastation of illness—so proximal and threatening at all times—and the occasional capacity, still unrealized, of medicine to transform lives. Lasker imagined unleashing the power of medical research to combat diseases—a power that, she felt, was still largely untapped. In 1939, the year that she met Albert, her life collided with illness again: in Wisconsin, her mother suffered a heart attack and then a stroke, leaving her paralyzed and incapacitated. Lasker wrote to the head of the American Medical Association to inquire about treatment. She was amazed—and infuriated, again—at the lack of knowledge and the unrealized potential of medicine: "I thought that was ridiculous. Other diseases could be treated... the sulfa drugs had come into existence. Vitamin deficiencies could be corrected, such as scurvy and pellagra. And I thought there was no good reason why you couldn't do something about stroke, because people didn't universally die of stroke... there must be some element that was influential."

In 1940, after a prolonged and unsuccessful convalescence, Lasker's mother died in Watertown. For Lasker, her mother's death brought to a boil the fury and indignation that had been building within her for decades. She had found her mission. "I am opposed to heart attacks and cancer," she would later tell a reporter, "the way one is opposed to sin." Mary Lasker chose to eradicate diseases as some might eradicate sin—through evangelism. If people did not believe in the importance of a national strategy against diseases, she would convert them, using every means at her disposal.

Her first convert was her husband. Grasping Mary's commitment to the idea, Albert Lasker became her partner, her adviser, her strategist, her coconspirator. "There are unlimited funds," he told her. "I will show you how to get them." This idea—of transforming the landscape of American medical research using political lobbying and fund-raising at an unprecedented scale—electrified her. The Laskers were professional socialites, in the same way that one can be a professional scientist or a professional athlete; they were extraordinary networkers, lobbyists, minglers, conversers, persuaders, letter writers, cocktail party-throwers, negotiators, name-droppers, deal makers. Fund-raising—and, more important, friend-raising—was instilled in their blood, and the depth and breadth of their social connections allowed them to reach deeply into the minds—and pockets—of private donors and of the government.

"If a toothpaste... deserved advertising at the rate of two or three or four million dollars a year," Mary Lasker reasoned, "then research against diseases maiming and crippling people in the United States and in the rest of the world deserved hundreds of millions of dollars." Within just a few years, she transformed, as *Business Week* magazine once put it, into "the fairy ... of medical research."

The "fairy ..." blew into the world of cancer research one morning with the force of an unexpected typhoon. In April 1943, Mary Lasker visited the office of Dr. Clarence Cook Little, the director of the American Society for the Control of Cancer in New York. Lasker was interested in finding out what exactly his society was doing to advance cancer research, and how her foundation could help.

The visit left her cold. The society, a professional organization of doctors and a few scientists, was self-contained and moribund, an ossifying Manhattan social club. Of its small annual budget of about $250,000, it spent an even smaller smattering on research programs. Fund-raising was outsourced to an organization called the Women's Field Army, whose volunteers were not represented on the ASCC board. To the Laskers, who were accustomed to massive advertising blitzes and saturated media attention—to "salesmanship in print"—the whole effort seemed haphazard, ineffectual, stodgy, and unprofessional. Lasker was bitingly critical: "Doctors," she wrote, "are not administrators of large amounts of money. They're usually really small businessmen... small professional men"—men who clearly lacked a systematic vision for cancer. She made a $5,000 donation to the ASCC and promised to be back.

Lasker quickly got to work on her own. Her first priority was to make a vast public issue out of cancer. Sidestepping major newspapers and prominent magazines, she began with the one outlet of the media that she knew would reach furthest into the trenches of the American psyche: *Reader's Digest*. In October 1943, Lasker persuaded a friend at the *Digest* to run a series of articles on the screening and detection of cancer. Within weeks, the articles set off a deluge of postcards, telegrams, and handwritten notes to the magazine's office, often accompanied by small amounts of pocket money, personal stories, and photographs. A soldier grieving the death of his mother sent in a small contribution: "My mother died from cancer a few years ago... We are living in foxholes in the Pacific theater of war, but would like to help out." A schoolgirl whose grandfather had died of cancer enclosed a dollar bill. Over the next months, the *Digest* received thousands of letters and $300,000 in donations, exceeding the ASCC's entire annual budget.

29

(Ayad Akhtar, 1970—)
阿亚德·阿赫塔尔

作者简介

阿亚德·阿赫塔尔（Ayad Akhtar, 1970—），美国巴基斯坦裔剧作家、小说家，出生于纽约市，但在威斯康星州密尔沃基市的郊区长大。阿亚德于1988年从中央中学（Central High School）毕业之后，在布朗大学（Brown University）主修戏剧。1997年进入哥伦比亚大学（Columbia University）深造，主修研究生电影课程，获得电影导演艺术硕士学位。2020年他接替小说家珍妮弗·伊根（Jennifer Egan）出任美国笔会主席。2021年，阿赫塔尔被纽约州作家协会（New York State Writers Institute）任命为"纽约州作家"（New York State Author）。阿亚德荣获美国艺术与文学院（American Academy of Arts and Letters）文学奖和伊迪丝·沃顿小说荣誉奖（Edith Wharton Citation of Merit for Fiction）等其他各类奖项。

阿亚德的主要作品有戏剧《耻辱》（Disgraced, 2012）、《隐形的手》（The Invisible Hand, 2012）、《是谁，是什么》（The Who and the What, 2014）、《垃圾品：债务的黄金时代》（Junk: The Golden Age of Debt, 2017）以及小说《美国苦难》（American Dervish, 2012）、《故乡挽歌》（Homeland Elegies, 2020）和电影作品《内战》（The War Within, 2005）和《大而不倒》（Too Big to Fail, 2011）等。其中，《耻辱》荣获2013年普利策戏剧奖（Pulitzer Prize for Drama）和"托尼奖"（Tony Award）提名；《隐形的手》获得奥比奖（Obie Award）、外国批评家协会约翰·加斯纳奖（Outer Critics Circle John Gassner Award）；《垃圾品：债务的黄金时代》获得"肯尼迪美国戏剧奖"（Kennedy Prize for American Drama）、2017年斯坦伯格编剧奖（Steinberg Playwriting Award），并再次获得"托尼奖"（Tony

Award）提名。他的第一部小说《美国苦难》已经被翻译成20多种语言出版，包括英语、意大利语、挪威语、荷兰语、丹麦语、德语和西班牙语等。《故乡挽歌》获得美国图书奖并入围安德鲁·卡内基优秀小说奖（Andrew Carnegie Medal for Excellence in Fiction）决赛名单。

阿亚德的创作涉及各种主题，包括美国穆斯林的经历、宗教和经济、移民和身份等。他通过笔下的人物，探索了伊斯兰教在美国文化中被描绘和代表的各个方面。《耻辱》是2012年首演于芝加哥的一部后"9·11"政治戏剧。该剧讲述了拒绝、掩盖穆斯林身份的巴基斯坦裔律师阿米尔·卡普尔（Amir Kapoor）在表面和谐的家庭晚宴上，终因种族政治问题而与种族背景迥异的家人朋友反目成仇的悲剧故事。选段部分出自《耻辱》第三幕，讲述了阿米尔得知妻子与艾萨克的婚外情之后，面对艾萨克的戏谑和挑衅，怒不可遏地对妻子挥拳暴打。这表明阿米尔以凝视白人女性为突破口向美国主流社会发起攻击。

《故乡挽歌》融合事实与虚构，讲述了在"9·11"事件后，巴基斯坦移民父亲和儿子在美国寻找归属的故事，涉及穆斯林移民在美国的生活、"9·11"恐怖袭击、金钱、政治等话题。选段部分出自小说《故乡挽歌》第六章，是整个故事发展的高潮部分。主人公阿亚德（Ayad）的父亲西坎德（Sikander）在威斯康星州的一个小镇上因渎职而受审。在离开美国去往巴基斯坦躲避债务之前，西坎德将卡洛琳（Caroline）介绍给阿亚德认识。作者借主人公父亲之口抛出终极问题：成为一个美国人究竟需要什么？

作品选读

Disgraced

Scene Three
(excerpt)
By Ayad Akhtar

Isaac You're married to a man who feels a blush when Ahmadinajad talks about wiping Jews into the ocean. Steven is a huge fund-raiser for Netanyahu. I have no idea why Amir would go anywhere near a guy like that Imam.

Emily (*rushed*)　For me. He did it for me.

Oh ....

Pause.

Isaac　He doesn't understand you. He can't understand you.

He puts you on a pedestal.

It's in your painting.

"Study After Velázqucz."

He's looking out at the viewer—that viewer is you. You painted it. He's looking at you.

The expression on that face?

Shame. Anger. Pride.

Yeah. The pride he was talking about.

The slave finally has the master's wife.

Emily　You're disgusting—

Isaac　It's the truth, Em. And you know it. You painted it.

Silence.

If what happened that night in London was a mistake, Em, it's not the last time you're going to make it.

A man like that...

You *will* cheat on him again. Maybe not with me, but you will.

Emily　Isaac.

Isaac　And then one day you'll leave him.

Em. I'm in love with you.

Isaac *leans in to kiss her.*

Emily *doesn't move. In or out.*

Just as the front door opens—

Jory *enters. In a huff. Returning for* **Isaac** *and her things. Ready to leave for the evening—*

Jory　Isaac, we need to get out of here—

—*but stopped in place by the moment of intimacy between her husband and* **Emily**.

Isaac　Honey?

Jory　What the fuck is going on here?

Amir *enters, inflamed.*

Amir　You wait a week to tell me this? And the second I say something you don't like hearing, you walk away from me in mid-fucking-sentence?

Who *are* you?!

Jory *just stares at her husband...*

Amir What? (*Looking around.*) What?

Jory (*to* **Emily**) Are you having an affair with my husband?

Amir Excuse me?

Isaac (to **Jory**) Nobody's having an affair.

Jory I walked in here and they were kissing.

Emily That is not true! Amir, it's not true.

Jory They were kissing. (*Pointing*) There.

Emily That's not what was happening.

Jory I know what I saw.

Emily Isaac told me about them making you partner. I know how much longer Amir has been there than you. I was upset. I was crying.

Isaac I was consoling her.

Jory By kissing her?

Emily (*incredulous*) We weren't kissing! Why do you keep saying that?!

Jory (*to* **Isaac**) Are you having an affair with her? Tell me the truth.

Isaac Honey. I already said. We're not having an affair.

Jory So *what the fuck* were you doing when I walked in here?

Isaac (*going to his wife*) I was hugging her because she was crying.

Jory Get off me!

Emily I was upset they made you partner.
I know how much longer Amir has been there.
I was crying.

Amir *turns to* **Jory**. *Vicious.*

Amir First you steal my job and now you try to destroy my marriage? You're fucking evil. After everything I've done for you?

Jory *goes over to get her purse. As if to leave.*

Jory I know what I saw.

Amir (*exploding*) You have any idea how much of myself I've poured into that place? That closet at the end of the hall? Where they keep the cleaning supplies? That was my first office!
Yours had a view of the fucking park!
Your first three years? Were you ever at work before anyone else in the morning? Were you ever the last one to leave?
'Cause if you were, I didn't see it.

I *still* leave the office after you do!

You think you're the nigger here?

I'm the nigger! Me!

Isaac (*going to his wife*)   You don't need to listen to any more out of this asshole.

Jory (*to* **Isaac**)   Don't touch me.

Amir (*to* **Isaac**)   You're the asshole.

Isaa   You better shut your mouth, buddy!

Amir (*to* **Isaac**)   Or what?!

Isaac   Or I'll knock you on your *fucking* ass!

Amir   Try me!

Jory   (*to* **Isaac**)   GET OFF ME!

Inflamed, **Isaac** *finally releases his wife facing off with Amir.*
When suddenly...

Amir *spits in* **Isaac**'s *face.*

Isaac *wipes the spit from his face.*

Isaac   There's a reason they call you people animals.

He turns to his wife.

Then turns to Emily.

Then walks out.

Amir (*to* **Jory**)   Get out.

Jory (*collecting her things*)   There's something you should know.

(*At the door*) Your dear friend Mort is retiring.

And guess who's taking over his case load? Not you. Me.

I asked him, "Why not Amir?"

He said something about you being duplicitous.

That it's why you're such a good litigator. But that it's impossible to trust you.

(*At the door*) Don't believe me?

Call Mort. Ask him yourself.

Let me guess.

He hasn't been taking your calls?

She walks out.

Pause

Emily   Have you lost your fucking mind?!

Amir *turns away; withdrawing into himself. Pacing The inward spiral deepening*

Emily   Amir!

Amir She's right. He hasn't been taking my calls.
Emily I'm gonna get you that coffee.
She heads for the kitchen...
Leaving **Amir** *on stage by himself for a moment. As he watches the swinging door sway. Back and forth.*
Emily *returns. A mug in hand.*
Amir Em.
Something in **Amir**'s *tone—vulnerable, intense—stops her in place.*
Amir Are you sleeping with him?
Pause.
Emily *puts the mug down on the table.*
Beal. Finally shakes her head.
Emily It was in London. When I was at Frieze.
We were drinking. I's not an excuse...
I's just...
We'd just been to the Victoria and Albert. He was talking about my work.
And...
Seeing how her words are landing on her husband, she makes her way to him.
(*Approaching.*) Amir, I'm so disgusted with myself. If I could lake it back.
All at once **Armir** *hits* **Emily** *in the face. A vicious blow.*
The first blow unleashes a torrent of rage, overtaking him. He hits her twice more. Maybe a third time. In rapid succession. Uncontrolled violence as brutal as it needs to be in order to convey the discharge of a lifetime of discreetly building resentment.
[*In order for the stage violence to seem as real as possible obscuring it from direct view of the audience might be necessary—for it to unfold with* **Emily** *hidden by a couch, for example*]
After the last blow, **Amir** suddenty comes to his senses, realising what he's done.
Amir Oh my ...
Just as...
There's a knocking at the door.
Beat.
And then more knocking.
Finally, the door gently opens. To show **Abe**, *who looks over and sees—as we do—* **Emily** *emerges into full view on the ground, her face bloodied.*

Abe *looks up at* **Amir**.
Lights out.

作品选读

Homeland Elegies

Pox Americana

(excerpt)

By Ayad Akhtar

I don't know how Father scored a reservation at Eleven Madison Park for a 7:00 p.m. dinner on a Thursday night. I'd only been for lunch—appropriately enough, with Riaz—at a table just a few feet from James Murdoch, his wife, and Google's Eric Schmidt; there hadn't been an empty table at that lunch hour, and I recalled Riaz telling me it could be even harder to get in for dinner. Somehow, Father got a table. The choice didn't surprise me. His hankering to mark his status was as innate to him as his Punjabi accent. And in theory, I didn't mind the notion that we were meeting for dinner at Eleven Madison Park, where a meal for two could easily set us back three bills. But why now? Why the needless luxury when he didn't have the money to spend on it anymore? For years, I'd been hearing tales of my friends' parents getting older, the bizarre moods, the night terrors, the disturbing lapses in memory, the peculiar new inclinations, the mottled new colors to their personalities. I assumed at least some of Father's behavior around money was related to his advancing age. As I walked over from the subway, crossing Madison Square Park, I resolved to force the conversation with him that night. I needed to know what was going on.

But he wasn't alone.

He was sitting in a corner at a table for four, and beside him was a woman in red. Across the room, I couldn't tell if her hair was white-blond or white-gray, but even from a distance, her face was striking—round eyes and a long face I recognized at once from her daughter: it was Melissa's mother, Caroline.

I could hear my heart inside my ears.

Father saw me and rose. There was something spry about his escape from the corner, something firm in his embrace that I didn't recognize. I smelled the alcohol on his breath, but he didn't seem drunk. "Ayad, there's someone I want you to meet," he said, holding my arm now, his voice quivering just enough for me to notice that he was nervous.

"Yeah, I think I got that already…"

He turned back to the table, still holding my arm. "Caroline," he said, presenting me, "this is my son." She stood, her small, veined fist closed tightly around her napkin, her striking face softened with a searching half smile. She reached her other hand out toward me. Her grip was warm and wet.

"It's so nice to meet you," she said quietly. As I began to take my place, Father lingered beside me with a vacant look. "Sikander," she said, again softly. "You can sit down now." The way she pronounced his name—with the proper emphasis on the second syllable and its gentle *d*, and all the correct proportions to the vowels, all the more striking for being spoken with an American accent—signaled an intimacy between them I couldn't deny. She encouraged him to sit again, but he didn't move.

"What's going on?" I asked.

"I'll be right back," he said.

Once he'd disappeared beyond the row of tree-tall bouquets dividing the dining room, I realized just how angry I was.

"I'm sorry," she said softly.

"For what?" I asked. I heard myself. I sounded like an asshole.

"I asked him to make sure you knew. I didn't want you to be blindsided. I wanted to be sure you knew. So you had a choice."

"A choice?"

"About whether you were okay meeting me or not." She paused. "You've been part of my life for so many years. I just… I feel like I know you. I know how much he loves you. How much you love him. I just want to…" She stopped, her lips holding in—it seemed—a feeling of sympathy she wasn't sure I would want to feel from her.

"It's fine," I said. "It's not you. It's him. He's been very unpredictable lately."

"I know," she said with finality.

And that was all we said. I sat there in silence and stared down at the table. I could still feel my heart in my ears. I realized I couldn't stay, but I knew I couldn't leave until he returned. And then, all at once, he was back, slipping into the corner place beside her. He still looked nervous, but I couldn't deny what I saw before me: he'd never looked so much himself—which is to say, that face I'd known my whole life seemed more clearly what it was, what I'd always known it to be, as if some intervening, disfiguring filter I'd never understood to comprise so much of his appearance had fallen away, and, for the first time, I was beholding him without it. "So," he began brightly. "The bathrooms are stunning. I highly recommend the trip." Neither of us replied. He pulled his readers from his breast pocket and picked up a menu just as the waiter appeared and asked me what I was drinking.

"Not sure yet."

The waiter nodded and turned to my father, indicating his almost finished drink: "Another vodka gimlet, sir?"

"Please," Father said politely, tossing back the rest and handing him the glass.

"Go ahead and bring the whole bottle," I blurted out to the waiter, who looked understandably startled.

"I'm sorry, sir?"

"I said, just bring him the whole bottle. He's probably gonna go through at least that much by the time he's done."

"Ayad."

"What, Dad?! Hmm?"

He looked up at the waiter. "Just the gimlet will be fine. Thank you."

Caroline was moving along the bench to the table's edge. "I'm just going to freshen up. I'll be right back," she said meekly as she got out and left us.

"Can you be civil, please? Can you stop behaving like a child?" Father glared, then took up the menu.

"Civil?!" I yelped. "I'm the one behaving like a child?! Me?!—"

"I said stop it—"

"I'm the one who needs babysitting through his court case? Drunk in casinos, in jail? I'm the one who's supposed to be civil?!" If I'd been paying attention, I might have noticed the silence growing around us.

"That's enough."

"You're right. It is enough. You mind telling me what's going on with you?"

"With what?"

"What happened to all your money?"

"None of your business."

"Isn't that exactly what it's become now that I'm paying for all this ridiculous stuff—"

"Ridiculous? You think I didn't pay for you? For years?"

"Don't change the subject."

"Just one more month, Daaad. I'll have rent next month, Daaad." His high-pitched, open mockery of my American accent continued to draw the notice of those around us.

"You've been using that one on me now for ten years. I couldn't make it on my own. I needed your help. I know that. I'm sorry! I'm sorry it took me so long! How many times do I have to thank you before you'll leave me alone about it? I couldn't have done any of it without you! You're the only reason any of it happened! Okay!? Does that make you happy!?" I was shouting, and around us, the dining room had gone silent. I thought I felt Father's impulse to strike me—or maybe this was only the consciously admissible form of my own long-buried desire to hit him—and saw the scarlet bloom rushing up his neck. My heart lurched, stuffing my ears with its relentless throbbing. "You're an embarrassment," he said nastily as he lifted the menu again and hid himself from me. I saw the waiter heading for our table with the maître d' in tow. I wasn't about to be chastised in public any further.

"Fuck this," I said, then got up and walked out.

The night was brisker than I recalled. At the corner, whatever was coursing through my veins pushed me into the oncoming traffic. Car horns blared as I wove my way across Madison Avenue back into the park, defiant. The rage felt like a heat that would burn me if I didn't release it. But where? How? On whom? On what? A young couple passed me, arm in arm. I suddenly wondered if my fists could be used to shake the feeling. To ask the question—I knew—was already to avoid it. I wanted to scream; I knew I wouldn't do that, either.

I staggered a little farther into the park and fell onto an empty bench. My eyes burned. I buried them in my palms and rubbed, and kept rubbing. There, inside, I saw him. He was large, and I was small. I remembered watching him from a doorway in our first house, standing by a window, impossibly grand in the daylight, opening and reading mail. I longed for him then, to be lifted in his arms, in that light. It was a yearning I'd felt my whole life. Hadn't he done that? Hadn't he and Mother given all they could? Why hadn't it been enough? Why, despite all they'd given, all they'd done—both of them, their whole lives—why had it still never felt like enough?

The tears were coming up now from a pain in my chest, from a longing fissure in a heart I'd always known was broken.

I felt my phone vibrating in my pocket. I pulled it out to see two missed calls from him. I had to go back inside. I couldn't pretend I didn't want to. I couldn't pretend I didn't need him.

I headed back to the restaurant.

As I emerged from the park, I saw him on the other side of Madison Avenue. He was standing beside a cab and helping her into the back. It looked like he was going to follow her in. "Dad!" I cried out. And again: "Dad!" He heard me and looked up. I saw her long, worried face appear in the window. He leaned in and spoke to her, then shut the door and stepped away from the car, watching it pull off and disappear up the avenue.

I crossed the street and found him leaden, retreated.

"I'm sorry," I said, starting to cry again. I didn't know what I was apologizing for, but I knew I had to apologize.

"No, no," he said, shaking his head slowly. "No," he said again.

"Dad, I'm sorry. I'm so sorry," I said again, grabbing his coat and pulling him toward me. He resisted my embrace.

"No, beta, no."

But I pressed in and drew him closer, pressing myself to him, feeling him as tightly against my body as I could. I held him there until he stopped resisting. It wasn't until he tried to speak that I realized he was also crying now.

"I lost it all," he moaned into my shoulder. "All of it. I lost it all."

I didn't ask for an explanation. I didn't want one. I didn't need one. I was sure I would find it all out soon enough. Only the embrace between us mattered now. If only I could hold him closer, I thought, hold him longer, maybe what was broken in both of us would finally be mended.

30

(Kiran Desai, 1971—)
基兰·德赛

作者简介

基兰·德赛（Kiran Desai, 1971— ），美国印度裔小说家，出生于印度新德里（New Delhi），14岁时和她的母亲——著名作家阿妮塔·德赛（Anita Desai）迁居英国，一年后移民美国。1993年毕业于本宁顿学院（Bennington College），从霍林斯大学（Hollins University）和哥伦比亚大学获得创意写作硕士学位。

德赛的创作主要包括两部小说。第一部小说《番石榴园里的喧闹》（*Hullabaloo in the Guava Orchard*, 1988）一经出版便得到各方权威人士的盛赞，入选美国著名文学杂志《纽约客》的印度小说特刊，获得英国作家协会（British Society of Authors）颁发的贝蒂·崔斯克奖（Betty Trask Award）。德赛以娴熟的方式对人物进行了生动的描写，充满了幽默感，以精湛的手法详细描述了人们的普通生活和信仰。第二部小说《继承失落的人》（*The Inheritance of Loss*, 2006）荣获国家书评人协会小说奖（National Book Critics Circle Fiction Award）以及2006年度布克小说奖，德赛成为2000年以来首位获该奖项的女作家。《继承失落的人》深入探讨了人类思想的影响，强调了20世纪的国家和全球问题，其中一些问题一直持续到现在，如全球化、多民族文化、经济不平等以及恐怖主义的暴力活动等。这部小说表达了被边缘化的印度人进行勇敢的反抗以保存微弱却凛然不可侵的自我。

《番石榴园里的喧闹》以印度最偏远的北部为背景，描述了一个名叫桑帕斯·查瓦拉（Sampath Chawla）的年轻人的故事。第一个选段部分出自《番石榴园里的喧闹》第十章，有关一名间谍认为桑帕斯在撒谎并对他进行测试直至揭开真相的描写。第二个选段部分出自《继承失落的人》，讲述了包括比居（Biju）在内的签证申请者在领取办理签证号码时的场景，生动刻画了印度人不惜一切代价移民美国的决心。

作品节选

Hullabaloo in the Guava Orchard

(excerpt)
By Kiran Desai

Sampath looked down at his charming visitors.

"Why are there so many opinions about the nature of ...?" asked a disguised spy from the Atheist Society (AS) and a member of the Branch to Uncover Fraudulent Holy Men (BUFHM). "Some say he has form. Others say he is formless. Why all this controversy?"

"The city inspector makes a journey to see a river," answered unsuspecting Sampath, "but he goes right at the time of the monsoon. He comes home and says the river is an enormous sheet of water with very high waves. Many months later, his aunty makes the same trip. She comes home and says: 'Sadly my nephew is a bit of an idiot. The river is nothing but a dirty little drain.' At the height of the summer a neighbour makes the same trip and says: 'That whole family is unintelligent. The river is nothing but a dry stretch of mud.'"

"Can anybody comprehend all there is to know about ...?" asked someone else.

"Once you have broken the bottle you can no longer distinguish the air inside from the air outside."

"Baba, can you talk about the problem of religious unrest in our country?"

"Haven't you heard a mother-in-law shouting at her daughter-in-law: 'Is this the way to prepare dal?' Of course she thinks her way is best. But north, south, east and west, everyone eats lentils in some form or another and everybody receives their nutritional benefits."

"I try to interest my children in spiritual matters, but they turn a deaf ear."

"There is no sign of the fruit when you buy the shoot. A watermelon does not exist unless it is the watermelon season. Before you cut it open you should always put your ear to the rind while tapping on the side. In this way you can make sure it will be completely ripe."

The spy made notes in a school notebook and scratched his head dubiously. This was his first important mission since he had joined the society that boasted of such distinguished members as the man who had revealed the mechanism that gave rise to the electric-shock guru, the woman who had uncovered the exploding-toilet scam, the clerk who had hidden himself in a vat of sweetened curd to overhear a conversation that led to the indictment of the BMW guru for everything from money-laundering and tax fraud to murder by poison. In fact, it had been a lucky thing the clerk had not eaten any of that curd.

The spy was determined that he too would thus distinguish himself. He was lonely in Shahkot; his village was far away and he was as yet unmarried. He hated his job as a teacher at the public school, hated the boys who drew unflattering portraits of him in their notebooks and pulled faces behind his back. Often he gave them exercises to do and escaped to the staff room, where he sat staring out of the window and smoking cigarettes. One day he would show the world; he would rise above his poverty-stricken childhood, the hovel he had grown up in with eleven brothers and sisters, his drunken and drugged father, his worn-out mother. One day the world would turn its attention to him at last. Applause. Prizes. Newspaper reporters. He would hold his face out to the light and, in the midst of adulation, discover his poise, discussing fluently and with the seriousness of an intellectual on television his opinion of things. "Well, you know, liberation, as I comprehend it, comes from freeing yourself from the tawdry grasp of superstition. This is not a simple matter, you understand, for it is embroiled in historical issues, in issues of poverty and illiteracy." Yes, his life had been hard. But he would overcome.

"What should I do, sir?" he ventured once more. "I do not know what path I should take. I do not know what questions to ask. In fact, I do not even know what I want."

"A child cries for its mother's milk, doesn't it?"

"I do not understand."

"A baby bird cries for an insect."

"But, sir... milk and insects?"

"A mother knows what its child wants and recognizes her child from the noises it makes. Consequently, you will be quite all right if you stop asking questions and wait for your mother to come to you. Be patient."

"But—" he persisted. "But, sir—"

Sampath's head began to buzz. What on earth was this man being so annoying for? He looked out into the leafy avenues about him and gazed moodily into the distance.

The spy from the Atheist Society looked happier. Clearly Sampath was at a loss for a reply to his clever questioning and was trying hard to avoid him. He went behind a tree and made more top-secret notes in his school notebook. "Avoids questioning by pretending otherworldliness. Unable to discuss deeper matters of philosophy."

Below Sampath the hallowed silence grew until Ammaji became uncomfortable with the quiet so loud and so big. "Oh," she said, "sometimes his mind leaves the earthly plane. Don't be offended."

It had not occurred to anybody to be offended.

"I myself have seen many holy men like this," said Lakshmiji. "Sometimes they sit completely still. Nothing can move them. They are like a bird on her eggs. Sometimes, though, they are frivolous and laugh, leap and dance. Yes, they can be like a child or a madman. Other times, instructing others, they return to the plane of consciousness to share their wisdom.

"Yes, it is the face of a vijnani, no ordinary countenance at all. Look, just look at his face."

Sampath's normal usual face! Pinky listened with astonishment to the things she was hearing.

"Oh," said Ammaji, chiming in delightedly as she rolled a betel leaf, "he was born with spiritual tendencies. Everybody was saying maybe he is a little mad, maybe he is a little simple-minded, but it is just that he could never interest himself in the material world. One time I gave him five rupees to pay the milkman and the next thing I heard was the milkman shouting: 'Oi, ji. Look, ji, what your grandson has done.' There was a strong breeze that day and while the milkman was measuring the milk, he had made a boat out of the bill and floated it into the canister. And hai hai, when it came to school what a terrible time we had. All the time: fail in Hindi, fail in Sanskrit, fail in mathematics, fail in history. Never could he concentrate on his studies."

......

How could he fool all these people? wondered the spy from the Atheist Society peeping out from behind the tree. What hold did he have upon them? What was it about him? He sniffed the air. The scent of cardamom and cloves wreathed up into the leaves from a cooking pot somewhere. Cardamom and cloves and... what else? He sniffed again. The smell entered his nostrils and wormed its way into his brain. Yes... he sniffed. Something else... He made some more notes in his book.

In the mouse-hole-sized room he rented in a house full of lodgers, he drew up a plan for his investigation of the case that included research into Sampath's past and a list of all the basic information he should know about his suspect: when he slept, whom he talked to, what he ate and drank.

Then the spy remembered the mysterious smell in the orchard that day. A whiff of it still clung to his skin and clothes.

Could Sampath be drugged?

What had been cooking in that pot?

No doubt he was smoking ganja—it grew wild all over the hillside. But perhaps he was taking opium as well? And who knew what else?

The spy thought late into the night.

The Inheritance of Loss

Thirty

(excerpt)

By Kiran Desai

His second attempt at America was a simple, straightforward application for a tourist visa.

A man from his village had made fifteen tries and recently, on the sixteenth, he got the visa.

"Never give up," he'd advised the boys in the village, "at some point your lucky day will come."

"Is this the Amriken embassy?" Biju asked a watchman outside the formidable exterior."

"*Amreeka nehi, bephkuph*. This is U.S. embassy!"

He walked on: "Where is the Amriken embassy?"

"It is there." The man pointed back at the same building.

"That is U.S."

"It is the same thing," said the man impatiently. "Better get it straight before you get on the plane, *bhai*."

Outside, a crowd of shabby people had been camping, it appeared, for days on end. Whole families that had traveled from distant villages, eating food packed and brought with them; some individuals with no shoes, some with cracked plastic ones; all smelling already of the ancient sweat of a never-ending journey. Once you got inside, it was air-conditioned and you could wait in rows of orange bucket chairs that shook if anyone along the length began to bop their knees up and down.

First name: Balwinder

Last name: Singh

Other names:————

What would those be??

Pet names, someone said, and trustfully they wrote: "Guddu, Dumpy, Plumpy, Cherry, Ruby, Pinky, Chicky, Micky, Vicky, Dicky, Sunny, Bunny, Honey, Lucky..."

After thinking a bit, Biju wrote "Baba."

"Demand draft? Demand draft?" said the touts going by in the auto rickshaws. "Passport photo *chahiye*? Passport photo? Campa Cola *chahiye*, Campa Cola?"

Sometimes every single paper the applicants brought with them was fake: birth certificates, vaccination records from doctors, offers of monetary support.

There was a lovely place you could go, clerks by the hundreds sitting cross-legged before typewriters, ready to help with stamps and the correct legal language for every conceivable requirement...

"How do you find so much money?" Someone in the line was worried he would be refused for the small size of his bank account.

"*Ooph*, you cannot show so little," laughed another, looking over his shoulder with frank appraisal. "Don't you know how to do it?" How?

"My whole family," he explained, "uncles from all over, Dubai-New Zealand-Singapore, wired money into my cousin's account in Tulsa, the bank printed the statement, my cousin sent a notarized letter of support, and then he sent the money back to where it had come from. How else can you find enough to please them!"

An announcement was made from the invisible loudspeaker: "Will all visa applicants line up at window number seven to collect a number for visa processing."

"What what, what did they say?" Biju, like half the room, didn't understand, but he saw from the ones who did, who were running, pleased to be given a head start, what they should do. Stink and spit and scream and charge; they jumped toward the window, tried to splat themselves against it hard enough that they would just stick and not scrape off; young men mowing through, tossing aside toothless grannies, trampling babies underfoot. This was no place for manners and this is how the line was formed: wolf-faced single men first, men with families second, women on their own and Biju, and last, the decrepit. Biggest pusher, first place; how self-contented and smiling he was; he dusted himself off, presenting himself with the exquisite manners of a cat. I'm civilized, sir, ready for the U.S., I'm civilized, mam. Biju noticed that his eyes, so alive to the foreigners, looked back at his own countrymen and women, immediately glazed over, and went dead.

Some would be chosen, others refused, and there was no question of fair or not. What would make the decision? It was a whim; it was not liking your face, forty-five degrees centigrade outside and impatience with all Indians, therefore; or perhaps merely the fact that you were in line after a yes, so you were likely to be the no. He trembled to think of what might make these people unsympathetic.

Presumably, though, they would start off kind and relaxed, and then, faced with all the fools and annoying people, with their lies and crazy stories, and their desire to stay barely concealed under fervent promises to return, they would respond with an indiscriminate machine-gun-fire of NO!NO!NO!NO!NO!

On the other hand, it occurred to those who now stood in the front, that at the beginning, fresh and alert, they might be more inclined to check their papers more carefully and find gaps in their arguments... Or perversely start out by refusing, as if for practice.

There was no way to fathom the minds and hearts of these great Americans, and Biju watched the windows carefully, trying to uncover a pattern he might learn from. Some officers seemed more amiable than others, some scornful, some thorough, some were certain misfortune, turning everyone away empty-handed.

He would have to approach his fate soon enough. He stood there telling himself, Look unafraid as if you have nothing to hide. Be clear and firm when answering questions and look straight into the eyes of the officer to show you are honest. But when you are on the verge of hysteria, so full of anxiety and pent-up violence, you could only appear honest and calm by being dishonest. So, whether honest or dishonest, dishonestly honest-looking, he would have to stand before the bulletproof glass, still rehearsing answers to the questions he knew were coming up, questions to which he had to have perfectly made-up replies.

"How much money do you have?"

"Can you prove to us you won't stay?"

Biju watched as the words were put forward to others with complete bluntness, with a fixed and unembarrassed eye—odd when asking such rude questions. Standing there, feeling the enormous measure of just how despised he was, he would have to reply in a smart yet humble manner. If he bumbled, tried too hard, seemed too cocky, became confused, if they didn't get what they wanted quickly and easily, he would be out. In this room it was a fact accepted by all that Indians were willing to undergo any kind of humiliation to get into the States. You could heap rubbish on their heads and yet they would be begging to come crawling in...

"And what is the purpose of your visit?"

"What should we say, what should we say?"

They discussed in the line. "We'll say a *hubshi* broke into the shop and killed our sister-in-law and now we have to go to the funeral."

"Don't say that." An engineering student who was already studying at the University of North Carolina, here for the renewal of his visa, knew this would not sound right.

But he was shouted down. He was unpopular.

"Why not?"

"You are going too far. It's a stereotype. They'll suspect."

But they insisted. It was a fact known to all mankind: "It's black men who do all of this."

"Yes, yes," several others in the line agreed. "Yes, yes." Black people, living like monkeys in the trees, not like us, so civilized...

They were, then, shocked to see the African-American lady behind the counter. (..., if the Americans accepted them, surely they would welcome Indians with open arms? Won't they be happy to see us!) But... already some ahead were being turned away. Biju's worry grew as he saw a woman begin to shriek and throw herself about in an epilepsy of grief.

"These people won't let me go, my daughter has just had a baby, these people won't let me go, I can't even look at my own grandchild, these people... I am ready to die... they won't even let me see the face of my grandchild..." And the security guards came rushing forward to drag her away down the sanitized corridor rinsed with germ killers.

The man with the *hubshi* story of murder—he was sent to the window of the *hubshi*. *Hubshi hubshi bandar bandar*, trying to do some quick thinking—oh no, normal Indian prejudice would not work here, distaste and rudeness—story falling to pieces in his head. "Mexican, say Mexican," hissed someone else.

"Mexican?"

He arrived at the window, retreating under threat, to his best behavior. "Good morning, ma'am." (Better not make that hubshi angry, yaar—so much he wished to immigrate to the U.S. of A., he could even be polite to black people.) "Yes ma'am, something like this, Mexican-Texican, I don't know exactly," he said to the woman who pinned him with a lepidopterist's gaze. (Mexican-Texican??) "I don't know, madam," squirming, "something or the other like this my brother was saying, but he is so upset, you know, don't want to ask all the details."

"No, we cannot give you a visa."

"Why ma'am, please ma'am, I already have bought the ticket ma'am..."

And those who waited for visas who had spacious homes, ease-filled lives, jeans, English, driver-driven cars waiting outside to convey them back to shady streets, and cooks missing their naps to wait late with lunch (something light—cheese macaroni...), all this time they had been trying to separate themselves from the vast shabby crowd. By their manner, dress, and accent, they tried to convey to the officials that they were a preselected, numerically restricted, perfect-for-foreign-travel group, skilled in the use of knife and fork, no loud burping, no getting up on the toilet seat to squat as many of the village women were doing at just this moment never having seen the sight of such a toilet before, pouring water from on high to clean their bottoms and flooding the floor with bits of soggy shit.

31

(Akhil Sharma, 1971—)
阿基尔·夏尔马

作者简介

阿基尔·夏尔马（Akhil Sharma,1971—），美国印度裔作家，出生于印度德里，8岁时随家人移民美国，在新泽西州的爱迪生市（Edison Township）长大。夏尔马毕业于普林斯顿大学（Princeton University），在伍德罗·威尔逊公共和国际事务学院（Woodrow Wilson School of Public and International Affairs）获得公共政策学士学位。在斯坦福大学的写作项目中获得了斯特格纳奖学金（Stegner Fellowship），并分别荣获1995年和1997年欧·亨利奖（O. Henry Award）。夏尔马还担任罗格斯大学纽瓦克分校（Rutgers University-Newark）创意写作项目助理教授。

夏尔马很早就开始写作，他的第一部长篇小说《顺从的父亲》（*An Obedient Father*, 2000）分别荣获2000年笔会海明威奖（Hemingway Foundation/PEN Award）以及2001年怀廷作家奖（Whiting Writers Award）。第二部长篇小说《家庭生活》（*Family Life*, 2014）耗时13年，甫一出版，即广受好评。2014年被《纽约时报书评周刊》和《纽约杂志》评为"最佳图书"，2015年获得福里奥文学奖（Folio Prize），2016年6月斩获被称为"奖金最高的国际文学奖之一"的国际都柏林文学奖（International Dublin Literary Award）。

夏尔马曾在《纽约客》、《小说》（*Fiction*）、《美国最佳短篇小说集》（*The Best American Short Stories Collection*）和《欧·亨利奖得主》（*The O' Henry Award Winners*）等选集上发表过作品。他的短篇小说《大都会》（"Metropolis"）被选入《1998年美国最佳短篇小说》（*1998 Best American Short Stories*）作品集，并于2003年被拍成同名电影。

小说《顺从的父亲》以1991年拉吉夫·甘地被暗杀前后的旧德里为背景，记录了低级政治机会主义者及其职能部门的幕后勾当，审视了印度家庭和整个社会中不同程度的腐坏。选段部分出自小说第一章，描述了故事主人公拉姆·卡兰（Ram Karan）在妻子、女婿相继去世后与女儿（Anita）和外孙女（Asha）首次生活在一起的场景。《家庭生活》是一部自传体小说，描写了20世纪70年代末印度少年阿贾伊·米什拉（Ajay Mishra）一家从德里到美国，遭遇家庭悲剧后挣扎求生的经历。这部小说涵括灾难和生存、附属和独立、自我与责任之间的张力。选段讲述了阿贾伊·米什拉一家移居美国后的安稳生活，但是哥哥比尔朱（Birju）突然离世引发了家庭变故。

作品选读

An Obedient Father

One

(excerpt)

By Akhil Sharma

The last twelve months had been long and sorrowful. They began with my wife, Radha, finally dying of cancer. A few months later, I had a heart attack that woke me in the middle of the night screeching, "My heart is breaking," so loudly that my neighbors kicked open the door of the flat to see what was happening. More recently, my son-in-law Rajinder had died when his scooter slipped from beneath him on an oil slick. And then Anita, my daughter, and eight-year-old Asha had come to live with me, bringing with them a sadness so apparent that sometimes I had to look away.

Asha was asleep on my cot with one knee pulled up to her stomach. My room is a windowless narrow rectangle, and the little light from the balcony and kitchen, funneled through the common room behind me, was a handkerchief on her face. Asha sometimes fell asleep on my cot while she waited for me to leave the bathroom. I knelt beside the cot to wake her gently. Her eyelids were trembling.

When Rajinder was alive and Anita used to bring Asha with her on visits, I would ask Asha how school was and offer her round orange-flavored toffees that, despite her laughing denials, I claimed grew on a small tree in a cupboard. Nothing else was expected from me. Since they had moved in two months ago, misery as intense as terror had drained all the fat from Asha's body, making her teeth appear larger than they were and her fingers impossibly long. This made me try to say more, but when I asked her about herself, I felt false and intrusive.

As I kept looking at Asha, I noticed it was possible to see her as pretty. Her face was almost square and her hair chopped short like a boy's, but there was something both strong and vulnerable about her. She had long eyelashes and a mouth that was too large for her face and hinted at an adult personality. I wondered whether I was finding beauty in Asha because her youth was a distraction from my own worries, like turning to a happy memory during distress. I put a hand on Asha's knee. It was the size of an egg and its delicacy made me conscious of her lighter-than-air youth and of my enormous body pressing down on my scarred heart.

In the squatter colony a hand pump creaked and someone made clucking sounds as a horse stomped. I heard Anita's sari sighing as she moved about the kitchen. The municipality gave our neighborhood water in the morning for only three hours. "Wake up," I said. "The water will go soon."

Asha stepped out of the bathroom into the common room.

She wore her school uniform, a blue shirt and a maroon skirt. The common room is nearly empty and has pink walls and a gray concrete floor. In a corner a fridge hums, because the kitchen is too small to hold it. Along a wall crouch a pair of low wooden chairs. On the bathroom's outside wall are a sink and a mirror. Asha looked in the mirror and combed her hair. The prettiness she had had while sleeping was still there. I could take care of Asha, as I had by arranging her admission to Rosary School. The idea of purpose soothed me.

Father Joseph was going to be difficult and disorderly. I had no subsidized land or loan to offer in immediate return for the money I needed to collect. The funds were for the Congress Party's parliamentary campaign, and the favors earned by donating would have to be cashed in later. Also, this was the second time in twelve months that Parliament had been dissolved and elections called. Most of the principals I handled for Mr. Gupta, the supervisor of Delhi municipality's physical education program, were resisting a second donation. Besides, I had to collect enough to impress the Congress Party officials who reviewed Mr. Gupta's efforts, but I could not take so much that Father Joseph would later resist giving when the money was for those of us who worked in the education department.

Asha went onto the balcony and hung her towel beside mine on the ledge. In comparison, hers looked little bigger than a washcloth. When she returned, I asked, "Do you want some yogurt?" The only time Asha ate anything eagerly was when she thought that the food was in some way special. Asha normally got yogurt only with dinner. I ate yogurt twice a day because the doctor had suggested it.

For a moment she looked surprised. Then she said, "Absolutely."

"Get two bowls and spoons and the yogurt."

Asha brought these. I was too fat to fold my legs and so usually sat with them open in a V. She knelt before me and, placing the bowls between my legs, began spooning yogurt into them. I was wearing just an undershirt and undershorts, as I normally do around the flat. But that morning, because I had seen Asha as pretty for the first time, I felt shy and tried pulling in my legs. I couldn't, and a bright blossom of humiliation opened in my chest.

Anita stepped to the kitchen door. "What are you doing?" she asked. Anita was wearing a widow's white sari. For a moment I thought she was asking me.

"Nanaji said I could have some yogurt," Asha answered.

Anita considered us. Her forehead furrowed into lines as straight as sentences in a book. She was short, with an oval face and curly hair that reached her shoulder blades. Anita turned back into the kitchen. I believed she felt her presence was a burden on me. When I offered to pay for Asha's schoolbooks, Anita refused, even though Rajinder had not left her much. She also gave me detailed accounts of what she bought with my money.

Anita came out of the kitchen with our breakfasts. She and Asha sat across from me. We all had a glass of milk and a salty paratha. Asha ate her yogurt first and quickly. When she could no longer gather anything from the inside of the bowl with the spoon, she licked it.

"We should buy more milk so you can make more yogurt for her," I told Anita. I was carefully scraping my bowl to get the last drops. I held the bowl at chest level and dipped my mouth down to suck on the spoon, because bringing my hand up to my neck caused it to tremble. The yogurt's sourness made my shoulder muscles loosen and made even this indignity bearable.

"She wouldn't eat it."

"I would," Asha said.

"She'd eat it two days, Pitaji, and then stop."

Asha stared into her lap.

After a moment Anita contemptuously added, "Milk is going up every day. I ask why and the milkman says, 'Tell America not to fight Iraq.'"

"His cows drive cars?" My voice came out loud and Anita's face froze. "Let's try it for two days, then," I added softly, feeling sorry that Anita thought I could turn on her.

Anita gathered our plates and stood. She went into the kitchen and squatted beneath the stone counter that runs around the kitchen at waist level. She turned on a tap. It gave a hiss, but only a few drops fell out. Anita sat down and looked at the plates for a moment. Beneath the counter were several tin buckets full of water.

"Thank ... we had water this long," I said.

Anita turned to me, and she appeared so intent I thought she might be angry. "We should thank ... for so little?" She did not wait for me to answer. Anita began washing the dishes with ashes and cupfuls of water from a bucket.

Often I felt Anita was acting. She wore only white and always kept her head covered as if she were a widow in a movie. These details, like many others about her, appeared so exactly right, they felt planned.

"We should buy a water tank," I said. "Ever since I became Mr. Gupta's man, I make so much money I don't even know how to hide it." Anita did not respond. My guilt thickened. The kitchen is tiny, yet Anita spent most of her days there, even reading the paper while crouched on the floor. I think Anita did this because she filled the kitchen completely and this comforted her.

I asked Asha to get me a glass of water from one of the clay pots in the corner of the room. When she brought it, I held up the pills I must take every morning and asked, "Do you know what these are?"

"Medicine, Nanaji."

"Yes, but they are of three different kinds. This one is a diuretic," I said, lifting the orange one with my thumb and forefinger. "It makes me get rid of a lot of water so that my heart doesn't have so much to move. This one"—I pointed to the aspirin—"thins my blood, and that also means my heart works less. And this one," I said, referring to the blue one with a cross etched on it, "is called a beta blocker." I said beta blocker twice because it sounded dramatic. "This keeps my heart from getting excited."

I had not meant to start the explanation, but the quick self-pity and anger it evoked made me realize guilt was irritating me. I continued talking and the feelings eased. I was glad I had found an opportunity to reveal some part of my life, because it would make my asking Asha questions feel more natural. I held the pills out for a moment and then swept them into my mouth.

Family Life
(excerpt)
By Akhil Sharma

We began being invited to people's houses for lunch, for dinner, for tea. This was so Birju could be introduced to these people's children. Back then, because immigrants tended to be young and the Indian immigration to America had only recently begun, there were few Indians who could serve as role models.

We took the subway all over Queens, the Bronx. We even went into Manhattan. We traveled almost every weekend. My mother would sit quietly in people's living rooms and look on proudly as Birju talked.

Once, as we were getting ready to leave our apartment to go on one of these visits, Birju said, "Why do we have to go?"

My mother answered, "They have a girl they want you to marry." She said this and laughed.

"For me," my father said, "there is one thing only." He rubbed his thumb and forefinger together. "Dowry."

"Leave me alone," Birju said.

My father grabbed Birju and kissed his cheek. "Give me one egg, chicken. One egg only."

"Don't say that," my mother said. "We're vegetarian. Say, 'Give me some milk, goat, clean, pretty goat.'"

The pride of getting into his school changed Birju. He sauntered. Entering a room, he appeared to be leaning back. When we spoke, he would look at me as if he were looking at someone bafflingly stupid. One time when he looked at me this way, I blurted, "You have bad breath." I felt foolish for having pitied him when he was studying.

My mother acted as if everything Birju said was smart. One afternoon, as he sat leaning back in a chair at the kitchen table, only two of the chair's legs on the floor and one skinny arm reaching behind him and touching the wall so that he would not fall, he told our mother, "You should be a tollbooth collector."

"Why?" she asked from the stove, where she was boiling frozen corn.

"In a tollbooth, people will only see your top."

My mother had been talking about trying to get a government job. She didn't want to wear uniforms, though, because her hips embarrassed her.

She laughed and turned to me. "Your brother is a genius."

I wished I had thought of what Birju had said.

I wondered sometimes if my parents loved my brother more than they loved me. I didn't think so. They bothered him and corrected him so much more than they corrected me that I assumed they secretly preferred me to him.

Birju got a girlfriend. The girl was Korean. She had creamy white skin and a mole on her left cheek. She would visit while our parents were at work. I didn't like Birju having a girlfriend. A part of me thought that to be with a different race was unnatural, disgusting. Also, when she came over and they went into our parents' room and closed the door, I could see that Birju would one day be leaving our family, that one day he would have a life that had nothing to do with us. And since he would be going to the Bronx High School of Science and was the most valuable person in the family, this made me angry.

When Nancy was visiting, I would sometimes get upset. I would go knock on my parents' door and when Birju opened it, I would say he needed to give me milk.

After Nancy left, Birju used to hum, move around the apartment excitedly, periodically bursting into song. I once asked him what he and Nancy did behind the closed door. He said, "Babies like you don't need to know such things."

We went to Arlington again in the summer. By now, after almost two years in America, I had grown chubby. I could grip my stomach and squeeze it. Birju was tall and thin. He was five feet six and taller than our parents. He had a little mustache and tendrils of hair on the sides of his cheeks.

Once more I lay on my aunt's sofa and watched TV. Once more the TV shows in the afternoon were different from the ones in Queens, and they made me feel that I was living far from home. Once more I saw the lawns outside the houses of Arlington, and it seemed to me that the people who lived in these houses must be richer, happier, and more like those on TV than my family or our neighbors in Queens.

Most days, Birju went to a swimming pool at a nearby apartment building. One afternoon in August, I was stretched out on my aunt's sofa watching Gilligan's Island when the telephone rang. The shades were drawn, making the room dim. After she hung up, my aunt came to the doorway. "Birju had an accident," she said. I didn't understand what she meant. "Get up." She motioned with a hand for me to rise. I didn't want to.

Gilligan's Island was half over and by the time we got back from the pool where Birju was swimming, the show would be finished.

Outside, it was bright and hot. We walked along a sidewalk as cars whizzed by. There was a hot breeze. I kept my head down against the glare, but the light dazzled me.

The apartment building that had the pool was tall, brown, with its front covered in stucco and carved to resemble brick. The pool was to the side, surrounded by a chain-link fence. The building towered over it, like it felt disdain for the pool. There was a small parking lot next to the pool and an ambulance was parked there with a crowd of white people gathered by its rear.

We came up to the crowd. Being near so many whites made me nervous. Perhaps they would be angry with us for causing trouble. Birju should not have done whatever he had done.

My aunt said, "You wait," and moved forward. She had arthritis in one hip, and she pushed into the crowd with a lurching gait.

I remained at the edge of the crowd. Alone, I felt even more embarrassed. I couldn't see what was occurring. A minute passed and then two.

My aunt came back through the crowd. She was hobbling quickly.

"Go home," she said, her face strained. "I have to go to the hospital."

I started on my way back. I walked head down along the sidewalk. I was irritated. Birju had gotten into the Bronx High School of Science, and now he was going to get to be in a hospital. I was certain our mother would feel bad for him and give him a gift.

As I walked, I wondered whether Birju had stepped on a nail. I wondered if he was dead. This last was thrilling. If he was dead, I would get to be the only son.

The sun pressed heavily on me. Considering that Birju was going to a hospital, I decided I should probably cry.

I pictured myself alone in the house. I imagined Birju getting to be in the hospital while I had just another ordinary day. I imagined how next year Birju was going to get to be at the Bronx High School of Science and I would have to go to my regular school. Finally the tears came.

32

(Sharbari Zohra Ahmed, 1971—)
沙巴里·佐赫拉·艾哈迈德

作者简介

沙巴里·佐赫拉·艾哈迈德（Sharbari Zohra Ahmed,1971—），美国孟加拉裔小说家、剧作家，出生于孟加拉的达卡（Dhaka），在康涅狄格州和埃塞俄比亚长大，曾在北京学习过中文。1994 年毕业于纽约州玛丽蒙学院（Marymount College）。1997 年在纽约大学获得创意写作硕士学位。她曾在曼哈顿维尔学院（Manhattanville College）教授创意写作，在圣心大学（Sacred Heart University）教授电影和电视制作。同时，她也是美国广播公司（ABC）制作的电视剧《匡蒂科》（Quantico）第一季的写作团队成员。艾哈迈德目前在康涅狄格州诺沃克市的诺沃克社区学院（Norwalk Community College）教授英语写作，正在创作一部名为《雅斯敏》（Yasmine）的小说。

艾哈迈德的创作主要包括短篇小说集《永井夫人的海洋》（The Ocean of Mrs. Nagai, 2013）、小说《她脚下的尘埃》（Dust under Her Feet, 2019）、戏剧《葡萄干而非处女》（Raisins Not Virgins, 2003）及各类散文、故事等。她的短篇小说和散文发表在《葛底斯堡评论》（Gettysburg Review）、《亚太裔美国人杂志》（Asian Pacific American Journal）等文学期刊上，包括《悬挂》（"Hanging It", 1998）、《选择去月球的男孩》（"A Boy Chooses to Go to the Moon", 2000）、《百事可乐》（"Pepsi", 2003）、《通缉》（"Wanted", 2003）和《永井夫人的海洋》（"The Ocean of Mrs. Nagai", 2005）等。艾哈迈德的作品经常描写跨文化相遇的更个人化的方面，正如在《葡萄干而非处女》中，艾哈迈德采用了嵌入式的历史和喜剧手段来揭示文化概念的复杂性，并试图消解沟通中存在的潜在差距和误解的危险。

《葡萄干而非处女》是她最受欢迎的一部作品,收录在短篇小说集《永井夫人的海洋》中,讲述了一个充满活力的年轻美国伊斯兰教女性努力寻找自我的故事。这个故事最初是由艾哈迈德在 2003 年写成的剧本,她自己制作并主演。后来被改编为电影剧本,入选 2008 年翠贝卡电影节(Tribeca Film Festival),并在纽约戏剧工作室"隔壁 2020"(New York Theater Workshop's Next Door 2020)演出季再次上演。节选部分讲述了来自曼哈顿的年轻孟加拉裔美国人萨哈·萨拉姆(Sahar Salam)与具有类似文化背景的律师里兹万(Rizwan)的相遇过程。

作品选读

Raisins Not Virgins
(excerpt)
By Sharbari Zohra Ahmed

When the day arrived to meet Rizwan, Sahar, to her private mortification, took pains with her appearance. She had been going back and forth on the subject of her dress since the day before. Since the fateful day she had sought her mother's counsel on the subject of marriage, Sahar resorted to sophomoric subterfuge. The several times Rizwan had attempted to contact her directly she had conveniently been out of town, or her answering machine had accidentally erased his messages. Her mother, as usual, was undeterred and, unbeknownst to Sahar, encouraged Rizwan to take the same attitude. She wore Sahar down slowly, passively, like water would do to a rock, but in much less time. Rizwan's voice on the answering machine, disconcertingly deep as it was, revealed nothing to help Sahar's imagination along.

Two days later in a restaurant, Sahar glanced in an accent mirror next to the maitre'd's station before walking to the table where Rizwan sat waiting for her. She had worn a snug wrap around top that accentuated her cleavage, and painted her lips MAC vixen maroon with nails to match. She had gotten auburn highlights the day before, blazing, the faggy hairdresser had called it, a new technique, very bold.

The last bit of sabotage. She could have gone either way. She could have scared him off by appearing dreadfully homely or she could play a vampiress and let the chips fall where they may. She was too vain (and paradoxically hopeful) to attempt the former.

He looked anxious and impatient, tapping the tip of his fork against the edge of the table and taking small quick sips of water from a tumbler. He was dressed casually and stylishly and had a thick head of hair that waved back from his face. His lanky legs jutted out from beneath the tablecloth. He was indeed fair skinned as promised, fairer than her actually, she noticed to her dismay and then became more dismayed that she was thinking about such things. If a person she had never met threw her into such confusion, then this couldn't be good.

"This is ridiculous," Sahar said under her breath and turned to leave. She would make up some excuse to her mother, who would then have to face Rizwan. "It is not my problem," Sahar thought, not at all sure it wasn't.

The maitre'd, who had been silently observing Sahar observing Rizwan asked if she was ready to be led to her table. She shook her head and walked out of the restaurant. Once outside, she felt suddenly free and took a deep breath. She began walking east towards the park. She was going to sit on a bench and watch ratty New York pigeons fight over bread and scantily clad roller bladders glide by. That was her new plan for Saturday night. And when she was done doing that for however many hours she deemed fit, she was going to go back to her tiny apartment in Chelsea and finish off the bottle of Grey Goose her friend Wanda had left when she was by last week. Her answering machine would be turned off, her shades pulled down, her body cozily encased in pima cotton drawstring pants and tank top with shaggy slippers to match, her blazed hair pulled back into a jaunty pony tail, and her anti-blemish, anti-aging crème would be smeared into place.

"Sounds like a plan," Sahar thought. But she just couldn't face the emptiness of the apartment yet, so she was going to sit in the park and take some air.

Sahar found an unoccupied bench underneath a thick oak tree and plopped down. She closed her eyes and listened for a while to the soft rustling of the leaves. The sun threw long shadows on the asphalt at her feet. It gradually grew darker and Sahar opened her eyes, straining to read the hands on her watch. Seven o'clock and the sun hadn't completely set. Summer was fast approaching. Summer, minus the heat that released the stench of old urine from winter hibernation in the subway and wilted her hair and the flowers at Chelsea market, was her favorite season. It was happy-go-lucky carnality and inevitably led to string-free sexual liaisons. Twenty-eight was too young to relinquish all that, Sahar decided sitting on the bench. A couple frolicked in the dying light with their Jack Russell Terrier and a glow in the dark Frisbee. Sahar watched the ghostly green disk fly through the air and land at the foot of one of the men and he flicked it to his partner, who snatched it out of the air and then ran to embrace him. The dog jumped excitedly between their knees as they folded into a prolonged hug. When they finally let go of one another, the dog was panting and Sahar was crying. She didn't realize it at first. She felt something wet roll down her cheeks, but she didn't immediately register it as tears.

She sniffed and stood to leave, glancing back at the couple who were laughing at their dog's antics. She could tell they all loved each other. They were a family; a pair of queens and their stunted dog and she, a pretty, smart, funny, passable cook, couldn't make a family of her own. She had to resort to standing up unknown men chosen by her mother in chic eateries.

When Sahar emerged from the 23rd street station, it was raining, a sudden spring deluge that threatened to drown everything. She ran the seven blocks to her apartment, holding her clutch over her head as an inadequate shield. Since it was made of cloth most of the contents of her bag were soaked, including the piece of paper that had Rizwan's cell, home, and work numbers printed on it. The ink had bled, making the numbers illegible.

"Just as well," Sahar thought. It occurred to her that she could use this as a viable excuse. Something had come up, so she couldn't make the date, and the sudden violent rain shower had destroyed his contact numbers. Allah's will.

Her hands were slippery. She struggled with the key to get the door open and even when she had unlocked the door the wood had swollen around it so that she had to push to make it budge. She leaned on the recalcitrant door with her shoulder and it finally gave way, with more force than she had applied to it. She looked behind her to see Rizwan, soaked and smiling sheepishly down at her. He said, "You're a fast runner. Are you still crying or is that the rain?"

Sahar felt the heat rise to her face as she attempted to gather her thoughts.

"It's rude to stalk people," she said finally, after trying hard to find some witty retort.

"Well, that's an understatement if I ever heard one," Rizwan replied. "I wasn't stalking you. The waiter at the restaurant came to get me when you ran out and I ran after you, but I had to cancel the order first because I had ordered a drink. I couldn't catch up to you immediately and when I found you, you were asleep on a park bench."

"I wasn't asleep," Sahar said.

"I didn't want to disturb you, so I waited for you to open your eyes," he continued as if he hadn't heard her. "Then, when you did, you started staring at the gay couple with the dog and the next thing I knew, you were bawling."

Sahar scowled. "I wasn't bawling," she said. This guy likes to sum things up, she thought. He is summing me up. I don't like to be summed up. I can't be summed up. I defy definition, dammit!

"Are you alright?" Rizwan said. "Your face is all scrunched up."

"I am perfectly alright, and I don't bawl," she said. "Well, whatever it was. Do you mind if I come in?" He ran his fingers through his thick hair, which was dripping, and smiled at her. "I need to dry off and then I'll be out of your hair. I wanted to see if you were okay."

Sahar walked in first and held the door open for him. With his height and broad shoulders, he all but swallowed up the narrow foyer.

She pointed up the stairs. "Third floor, apt G," she said.

"Lead the way," he said and smiled at her again. His eyes, against all odds, were blue. Her mother had failed to mention that small detail. Sahar squinted to see if they were fake. Fake eyes would end the entire matter right then and there. Rizwan playfully squinted back.

"Let me guess, you didn't wear your glasses," he said.

Sahar, taken aback by his audacity, said, "You have balls, I'll give you that."

"You didn't expect that from a nice Muslim boy, huh?" He looked at her and frowned, mock serious. "I guess you didn't want to get your veil all wet?" When Sahar stared at him slack jawed, he said, "You do normally wear hijab, don't you?"

"Eh?" Sahar swallowed and brushed away a strand of wet hair. Rizwan smiled pleasantly back at her even though her gaze was now decidedly hostile. She wanted to flee until she remembered that it was her foyer that he was clogging up.

Finally, she said, "Oh yeah, I've got a ton of them upstairs, all colors and patterns. But I decided to go bare today."

"Good. I wouldn't want anything to distract from your cleavage," he said, his grin widening.

For once, Sahar's apartment was tidy. She had cleaned up in anticipation of just what was happening, Rizwan dropping in. Everything was in its proper place; books on shelves (and neatly stacked on never used stove), green chenille throw draped with careless elegance behind recently vacuumed, only slightly stained couch. There was bottled water in the fridge and a fruit platter—her mother had dropped it by that morning, much to Sahar's irritation. She'd even borrowed a plant from her neighbor, who had a green thumb. Sahar was known to kill even cacti if they were left in her care but believed that a thriving plant indicated somehow her ability to raise a child to adulthood. She was in advertising after all. It was all about perception.

33

(Vandana Khanna, 1972—)
凡达娜·卡娜

作者简介

凡达娜·卡娜（Vandana Khanna, 1972— ），美国印度裔诗人，出生在印度新德里。卡娜获得弗吉尼亚大学文学学士学位、印第安纳大学（Indiana University）艺术硕士学位，曾任《洛杉矶评论》（*Los Angeles Review*）的诗歌编辑。

她的第一部诗集《去阿格拉的火车》（*Train to Agra*, 2000）获得了2000年"蟹园评论第一图书奖"（Crab Orchard Review First Book Prize）。《下午的马萨拉》（*Afternoon Masala*, 2014）获得了米勒·威廉姆斯·阿肯色州诗歌奖（Miller Williams Arkansas Poetry Prize）。卡娜的作品还获得耶伦诗歌奖学金（Yellen Fellowship）和手推车奖提名。她的诗歌还被收录在《美国亚裔诗歌：下一代》（*Asian American Poetry: The Next Generation*）和《不可分割：当代美国南亚裔诗歌选集》（*Indivisible: An Anthology of Contemporary South Asian American Poetry*）等文学选集中。

诗歌《去阿格拉的火车》（"Train to Agra"）选自同名诗集《去阿格拉的火车》，表达了作者对两种不同文化融合的呼吁，以及思考流离失所经验和流民身份对一个年轻的印第安美国女性身份建构的影响。诗歌《新娘准则》（"Mantra for a New Bride"）选自诗集《下午的马萨拉》，诗人将女性气质和种族特征同时通过复杂交织的新娘形象展现出来。

作品选读

Train to Agra

By Vandana Khanna

I want to reach you—
in that city where the snow

only shimmers silver
for a few hours. It has taken

seventeen years. This trip,
these characters patterned

in black ink, curves catching
on the page like hinges,

this weave of letters fraying
like the lines on my palm,

all broken paths. Outside,
no snow. Just the slow pull

of brown on the hills, umber
dulling to a bruise until the city

is just a memory of stained teeth,
the burn of white marble

to dusk, cows standing
on the edges like a dust

cloud gaining weight
after days of no rain. Asleep

in the hot berth, my parents
sway in a dance, the silence

broken by scrape of tin, hiss

of tea, and underneath,

the constant clatter of wheels
beating steel tracks over and over:

to the city of white marble,
to the city of goats, tobacco

fields, city of dead hands,
a mantra of my grandmother's—

her teeth eaten away
by betel leaves—the story

of how Shah Jahan had cut off
all the workers' hands

after they built the Taj, so they
could never build again. I dreamt

of those hands for weeks before
the trip, weeks even before I

stepped off the plane, thousands
of useless dead flowers drying

to sienna, silent in their fall.
Every night, days before, I dreamt

those hands climbing over the iron
gate of my grandparents' house, over

grate and spikes, some caught
in the groove between its sharpened

teeth, others biting where
they pinched my skin.

Mantra for a New Bride

By Vandana Khanna

Forget the painted flowers
rusting on your hands.

Forget you lined the part
in your hair red, the color

of brides. Forget your
mother-in-law wanted

someone fairer. Forget
you were never a ....

Forget they tried to light
you on fire. Forget

you never learned
how to drive. Forget

you had a baby
at fifteen. Forget

the supple want
of your skin. Forget

the rasp and resin
of your prayers rinsed

in the steam
of the garden. Forget

to cover your face
when you hear
the numb hymn
of your name rising

salted and sullen
from their lips.

34

(Kamila Shamsie, 1973—)
卡米拉·夏姆斯

作者简介

卡米拉·夏姆斯（Kamila Shamsie, 1973—），美国巴基斯坦裔小说家，出生于巴基斯坦卡拉奇（Karachi），曾就读于卡拉奇语法学校（Karachi Grammar School）。卡米拉从汉密尔顿学院（Hamilton College）获得了学士学位，随后在马萨诸塞州的阿默斯特学院（Amherst College, Massachusetts）获得了创意写作硕士学位。她经常往返于卡拉奇、伦敦和纽约，并在汉密尔顿学院教授创意写作。

卡米拉·夏姆斯的主要作品包括小说《在沿海的城市中》（*In the City by the Sea*, 1998）、《贵与贫》（*Salt and Saffron*, 2000）、《制图学》（*Kartography*, 2002）、《神秘的信件》（*Broken Verses*, 2005）、《烈日灼痕》（*Burnt Shadows*, 2009）、《烈火国土》（*Home Fire*, 2017）等。《在沿海的城市中》曾入围英国约翰·卢威连·莱斯奖（John Llewellyn Rhys Prize），并获得1999年度总理文学奖（Prime Minister's Award for Literature）。《制图学》和《神秘的信件》均获得了巴基斯坦文学奖（Award for Literature in Pakistan）。《烈日灼痕》入围橘子奖（Orange Prize for Fiction）。卡米拉的书已被翻译成20种文字，畅销各国。她还荣获巴基斯坦帕特拉斯·博卡里奖（Patras Bokhari Award）、英国文化委员会70周年文化关系奖（British Council's 70th Anniversary Cultural Relations Award），被评选为21世纪"橘子奖"（Orange）作家。

第一个选段出自小说《在沿海的城市中》第十一章，讲述了哈桑（Hasan）十分喜欢的政治家叔叔萨尔曼（Salman）因叛国罪被捕后给他的家庭和生活带来的影响。第二个选段出自夏姆斯的最新小说《烈火国土》第一章，讲述了伊思姆

（Isam）初到美国，在最喜欢的一家咖啡馆竟然遇见了跟她们兄弟姐妹从小一起长大的埃蒙（Eamonn）。

作品选读

In the City by the Sea

Chapter Eleven

By Kamila Shamsie

Hasan dragged his throbbing legs into his room. Ami's voice called to him but he yelled back, "Can't come now. Nature calls!" and shut the door behind him. He leaned against the door and allowed his body to slide to the ground, his hair squeaking and bristling in its descent along the whitewashed wood. Now what? He wondered, hugging his knees to his chest. He looked around. Something was different. His bed. The blue summer coverlet had made its appearance. Hasan crawled across the room, pulled himself on the bed and ran his hands in circles along his coverlet in greeting. Ami must have removed his duvet last night or this morning. The thought was cheering. If Salman Mamoo's situation really were desperate Ami would not have concerned herself with bedspreads.

It seemed that for once, though, Ami had entered his room without rearranging his bookshelf. Hasan ran a proprietary eye along the books across the room from him. Both Ami and Zehra had reacted strongly when Hasan arranged his books alphabetically. "It looks so ragged," Ami had complained. And Zehra had just rolled her eyes and said, "First, books are alphabetized by author, not title. Second, it's not like you've got an entire rainforest worth of books. Tall to short, favourite to least favourite. Those are the only acceptable categories. No need to get democratic about books, okay?" This was the day after the military coup, and seemed unfair. So Hasan did not tell Zehra about the comfort of order, or the reassurance of knowing that every new book would have a place already awaiting it, or the thrill of finding alliterations by stringing together the first words (articles aside) of titles: Hagar Hamlet Haroun Harry Higher Hookey Hockey Horse.

Hasan closed his eyes. A is for ACE, he thought. A is for the day Salman Mamoo first mentioned the name Anti-Corruption Enterprise, the day after he resigned his portfolio and addressed the crowds who met him at the City's airport, his voice lowering just when everyone expected it to rise, lowering to an intimacy as he said, "Give your imaginations a little freedom again. There are few realities that can withstand collective belief. Let me tell you something I've often imagined of late... a political party called the Anti-Corruption Enterprise."

B is for Beach. Salman Mamoo's favourite haunt, the one place that beat anything the North had to offer. It was Salman Mamoo who taught Hasan how to hypnotize himself by rocking back and forth on his heels on the wet sand, watching his toe imprints fill with water and disappear. And it was Salman Mamoo also who agreed it would be a travesty to squeeze into shoes for the car ride home just when one's toes had spread so wide apart they could cover the length of a two-week old turtle's shell.

C is for Cricket...

Hasan had made his way through the English alphabet and had progressed to *zal* in Urdu when a foot kicked open his door, and Zehra walked in bearing a plate of chicken tikkas in one hand, and a plate of *na'an* in the other. Ogle bounded in after her, and darted forward to grab Hasan's socks in his mouth. As these were still on Hasan's feet there was a momentary scuffle, from which both emerged triumphant. Ogle, with one sock dangling from his mouth; Hasan with one sock on his right foot. Zehra, sitting cross-legged at the foot of the bed, rolled her eyes. Og! Drop!' she commanded. The Labrador spat out the sock and lunged for Hasan's right foot. Hasan jumped backwards and hit his head against the wall.

"Ow!" he growled, glaring at Ogle.

The dog retreated to a corner, and contented himself with chewing on a slipper.

"I don't know what's got into him today," Zehra said. "He's never this frisky in the afternoon."

"Remember why you named him?"

"Hmm... his connection to the Prez."

"Yeah," Hasan said, taking a lemon-slice between his fingers and squeezing it with a vigour that far exceeded the lemon's capacity to provide juice.

"Well, I bet he's frisky today."

Zehra didn't say anything, but handed Hasan the hottest *na'an*, the one at the bottom of the stack. Hasan smiled. He had made the same gesture of consolation and sympathy towards Zehra when her mother died, years ago. Or so Zehra had once told him. For her that moment marked the beginning of their friendship, though Hasan couldn't remember the gesture any more than he could remember a time when he and Zehra weren't friends. Hasan shook his head. Zehra's mother's death had nothing to do with Salman Mamoo's situation. Nothing.

Hasan bounced the na'an from palm to palm, not allowing it to settle in one spot long enough to burn him. When it had cooled just a fraction, he ripped off a piece and bit into it, savouring, with closed eyes, its mixture of lightness, chewiness, and warmth.

"You know, all the clichés about love are also true for food," Zehra observed, her pinched fingers holding a piece of *na'an* over the fleshiest part of the chicken breast. With a flick of her wrist she tore a piece of meat off the bone, and popped *na'an* and chicken into her mouth. Food is blind? Hasan considered this for a moment and decided—yes, true enough. All conversation stopped while Hasan and Zehra chewed on the chicken's mix of charred exterior and succulent interior, bound together by Imran's "mystical spices." When they had devoured the meat, the room filled with the sound of paperthin ribs cracking between Hasan's teeth, interspersed with the ring of tongue-smacking as Zehra sucked the spices off her fingers.

"So, what have you heard?" Hasan asked.

Zehra squeezed lemon juice on her fingers to cut the grease and shrugged. "Not a lot. Just that Uncle Salman's trial is on the nineteenth of next month. You didn't know that?" Hasan shook his head. "I guess that's what Ami wanted to tell me," he said. "Good. So he should be free before the summer holidays start." He avoided Zehra's eye. There was silence again.

"Why doesn't Uncle Shehryar disconnect the phone?" Zehra asked finally. "It keeps ringing every five minutes."

"I don't know. I guess in case someone calls with news about how to help Salman Mamoo. I mean, Aba must know someone who can help."

Zehra toyed with her wishbone for a few seconds before blurting out, "Look, grown-ups can't always fix things. I know. I mean, I didn't always know and so I was angry with my father. And even now, sometimes, I want to yell at him because if it had been her liver or her kidneys that would have been one thing, but it just seems he should have known if something was wrong with her heart."

"It's not the same thing," Hasan said. "Look, I should go and sit with my parents. I'll come over later."

Hasan followed Zehra and Ogle out of the room, then turned towards his parents' room with some reluctance. The phone rang the moment he entered the room. "My turn," Ami said. "Hello... oh, Farah Apa... No, just that the trial is next month. On the nineteenth."

Hasan turned to Aba. "So, any calls about Salman Mamoo?"

Aba managed his lop-sided smile. "About fifty! But all just questions. Oh, except for one a few minutes ago. I answered, and this man on the other end identified himself as a party worker. I said, 'I'm really not in a festive mood. Try calling the President,' and, 'of course, it turned out he meant...'"

"Political party."

"Hmmm. You probably should have answered the phone."

"Oh, Aba! Was he offended?"

"I believe so." He said, "I mean POTPAF." I said, "POTPAF yourself." So he said, "Party Of The Present And Future. That is the Anti-Corruption Enterprise's new name."

"ACE has become POTPAF!"

"I presume this was done without Salman's approval. Anyway, once we had established that the caller wasn't a waiter or a bartender he said he was calling all Salman's supporters who weren't DICOOC..."

"What?"

"Dead, In Coma, or Out Of Country. So, the party..."

"POTPAF!" Hasan laughed louder than he would have at any other time.

At least Aba was trying to be normal.

"Yes. POTPAF is arranging a protest rally this evening."

Hasan stopped laughing instantly. "Where?"

"We're not going."

"Why not?"

"Listen, Huss. These are dangerous days. Now more so than before. So for all our sakes you mustn't talk to anyone about Salman or the President. Understood?"

"I know that already, Aba. I never say anything, except to Zehra. But why can't we go?"

"I have a feeling this rally will be an opportunity for people in the party to stir up trouble, and we'll only get hurt if we're a part of it. ... knows I admire the struggle, but there are certain prices I cannot pay to assist it." Hasan's mouth tightened, and Aba added, "I would rather live under a dictator and have Salman safe at home, than achieve democracy through his imprisonment." Hasan had been looking above Aba's head at Ami's newest painting, watching for the moment when the strokes of greens and browns would transform themselves into suggestions of shapes, but now he snapped his attention back to Aba's face; had it been his imagination or had Aba paused, almost fumbled, before the word "imprisonment"?

Aba held up his hand. "I know. You think it's cowardice, and it's true that I'm placing my needs above the greater good, but if it is cowardice it's based not on fear, but on love. Is any of this getting through to you?"

"Yes," Hasan said shortly. "You wish Salman Mamoo would agree to give up politics and make a statement supporting military rule."

"Well, I don't know about that. He would hate himself, you know. Besides, it's people like your Salman Mamoo who change the world. And son, it needs changing."

Hasan turned his attention to the newspaper's comic strips. Aba had always laughed at people who offered up morals and capsule philosophies; he said it revealed the quantity of bad television that people watched. "Roll credits," Hasan muttered, making sure Aba couldn't decipher his words.

Home Fire

Chapter One

(excerpt)

By Kamila Shamsie

When Hira Shah had brought her to see this studio apartment, the morning after her arrival in America, the landlord had drawn attention to the skylight as a selling point to offset the dank built-in cupboard, and promised her comets and lunar eclipses. With the memory of the Heathrow interrogation still jangling her nerves, she had been able to think only of surveillance satellites wheeling through the sky, and had rejected the studio. But by the end of the day's viewings it had become clear that she wouldn't be able to afford anything nicer without the encumbrance of a roommate. Now, some ten weeks later, she could stretch out in the bed, knowing herself to be seeing but unseen. How slowly the parachutists seemed to move, trailing golds and reds. In almost all human history, figures descending from the sky would have been angels or ... or demons—or Icarus hurtling down, his father, Daedalus, following too slowly to catch the vainglorious boy. What must it have felt like to inhabit a commonality of human experience—all eyes to the sky, watching for something mythic to land? She took a picture of the parachutists and sent it to Aneeka with the caption Try this someday? and then stepped out of bed, wondering if spring had arrived early or if this was merely a lull.

......

That had been the only time she had truly, purely missed her brother without adjectives such as "ungrateful" and "selfish" slicing through the feeling of loss. Now she looked at his name on the screen, her mouth forming prayers to keep Aneeka from logging on, the adjectives thick in her mind. Aneeka must learn to think of him as lost forever. It was possible to do this with someone you loved, Isma had learned that early on. But you could learn it only if there was a complete vacuum where the other person had been.

His name vanished from the screen. She touched her shoulder, muscles knotted beneath the skin. Pressed down, and knew what it was to be without family; no one's hands but your own to minister to your suffering. We'll be in touch all the time, she and Aneeka had said to each other in the weeks before she had left. But "touch" was the one thing modern technology didn't allow, and without it she and her sister had lost something vital to their way of being together. Touch was where it had started with them—as an infant, Aneeka was bathed and changed and fed and rocked to sleep by her grandmother and nine-year-old sister while Parvaiz, the weaker, sicklier twin, was the one who suckled at their mother's breast (she produced only enough milk for one) and cried unless she was the one to tend to him. When the twins grew older and formed their own self-enclosed universe, there was less and less Aneeka needed from Isma, but even so, there remained a physical closeness—Parvaiz was the person Aneeka talked to about all her griefs and worries, but it was Isma she came to for an embrace, or a hand to rub her back, or a body to curl up against on the sofa. And when the burden of the universe seemed too great for Isma to bear—particularly in those early days after their grandmother and mother had died within the space of a year, leaving Isma to parent and provide for two grief-struck twelve-year-olds—it was Aneeka who would place her hands on her sister's shoulders and massage away the ache.

Clicking her tongue against her teeth in remonstration of her self-pity, Isma pulled up the essay she was writing and returned to the refuge of work.

By mid afternoon the temperature had passed the 50 degree Fahrenheit mark, which sounded, and felt, far warmer than 11 degrees Celsius, and a bout of spring madness had largely emptied the café basement. Isma tilted her post-lunch mug of coffee toward herself, touched the tip of her finger to the liquid, considered how much of a faux pas it might be to ask to have it microwaved. She had just decided she would risk the opprobrium when the door opened and the scent of cigarettes curled in from the smoking area outside, followed by a young man of startling looks.

His looks weren't startling because they were exceptional—thick dark hair, milky-tea skin, well-proportioned features, good height, nice shoulders. Stand on any street corner in Wembley long enough and you'd see a version of this, though rarely attached to such an air of privilege. No, what was startling was the stomach-turning familiarity of the man's features.

In her uncle's house—not an uncle by blood or even affection, merely by the habitual nature of his presence in her family's life—there was a photograph from the 1970s of a neighborhood cricket team posing with a trophy; it was a photograph Isma had sometimes stopped to look at as a child, wondering at the contrast between the glorious, swaggering boys and the unprepossessing middle-aged men they'd grown into. It was really only the ones she knew as middle-aged men she paid much attention to, and so she'd never given particular thought to the unsmiling one in the badly fitting clothes until the day her grandmother stood in front of the picture and said, "Shameless!" poking her finger at the young man.

"Oh yes, the new MP," the uncle said, coming to see what had drawn out a pronouncement of such uncharacteristic venom. "On the day of the final we were a player short and this one, Mr. Serious, was visiting his cousin, our wicketkeeper, so we said, Okay, you play for us, and gave him our injured batsman's uniform. Did nothing all match except drop a catch, and then ended up holding the trophy in this official photograph, which went into the local newspaper. We were just being polite to offer it to him, since he was an outsider, and only because we were sure he'd have enough manners to say thanks but the captain—that was me—should be the one to hold it. We should have known then he would grow up to be a politician. Twenty pounds says he has it framed on his wall and tells everyone he was man-of-the-match."

Later that day, Isma overheard her grandmother talking to her best friend and neighbor, Aunty Naseem, and learned the real reason for that "Shameless!" It was not the unsmiling one's choice of career but a cruelty he'd recently shown to their family when it would have been easy for him to act otherwise. In the years after that, she'd paid close attention to him—the only one in the picture to grow up slim and sharp, bigger and brighter trophies forever in his sights. And now here he was, walking across the café floor—not the hated-admired figure he'd grown into but a slightly older version of the boy posing with the team, except his hair floppier and his expression more open. This must be, had to be, the son. She'd seen a photo that included him as well, but he'd ducked his head so that the floppy hair obscured his features—she'd wondered then whether that was by design. Eamonn, that was his name. How they'd laughed in Wembley when the newspaper article accompanying the family picture revealed this detail. An Irish spelling to disguise a Muslim name—"Ayman" become "Eamonn" so that people would know the father had integrated. (His Irish-American wife was seen as another indicator of this integrationist posing rather than an explanation for the son's name.)

The son was standing at the counter, in blue jeans and a quilted olive-green jacket, waiting.

She stood up, mug in hand, and walked over to him. "They only open up this counter when it's busy."

"Thanks. Kind of you to say. Where is—?" His vowels unashamedly posh where she had expected the more class-obscuring London accent of his father.

"Upstairs. I'll show you. I mean, I'm sure you understand 'upstairs.' I should have said, I'm going there myself. Coffee's cold." Why so many words?

He took the mug from her hand with unexpected familiarity. "Allow me. As thanks for rescuing me from being the Englishman Who Stood at the Counter for All Eternity. Who you could be forgiven for confusing with the Englishman Who Gets Lost Going Upstairs."

"I just want it heated up."

"Right you are." He sniffed the contents of the mug, another overfamiliar gesture. "Smells amazing. What is it? I wouldn't know an Ethiopian from a Colombian if..." He stopped. "That sentence doesn't know where to go from there."

"Probably just as well. It's the house brew."

She stood where she was a moment, watching him walk up the stairs, which were bracketed on one side by potted ferns and on the other by a wall with ferns painted on it. When he glanced down toward her, mouthing "Not lost yet," she pretended she had simply been preoccupied by her thoughts and returned to the little table in the alcove, angling her body so that her own shadow kept the sunlight from her computer screen. Slid her fingers over the wooden tabletop, its knots, its burns. Guess who, she started to type into her phone, then stopped and deleted it. She could too easily imagine the tone of Aneeka's response: Ugh! she'd say, or Why did you even talk to him?

He didn't return. She imagined him seeing a short line at the counter and placing her mug down with a shrug before walking out the upstairs exit; it left her both vindicated and disappointed. She went up to buy herself another coffee and found that the machine had broken down, so had to settle for hot water and a tea bag that leaked color into it. Returning downstairs, she saw a mug of fresh coffee at her table and a man folded into the chair next to it, legs thrown over the arm, reading a book in the shape of the gap in the bookshelf above his head.

"What is it?" he said, looking at the cup of tea she set down on an empty table. He examined the tag at the end of the tea bag. "Ruby Red. Not even pretending it's a flavor."

She held up the mug in thanks. The coffee wasn't as hot as it could have been, but he must have had to carry it down the street. "How much do I owe you?"

"Five minutes of conversation. That's what I spent standing in the queue. But after you're finished with whatever you're doing."

"That could be a while."

"Good. Gives me time to catch up on essential reading about..." He shut the book, looked at its cover. "*The Holy Book of Women's Mysteries. Complete in One Volume. Feminist Witchcraft, ... Rituals, Spellcasting, and Other Womanly Arts...*"

One of the undergraduates looked up, glared.

Isma slung the laptop into her backpack, downed her coffee. "You can walk to the supermarket with me."

35

(Aimee Nezhukumatathil, 1974—)
艾梅·内茨库马塔尔

作者简介

艾梅·内茨库马塔尔（Aimee Nezhukumatathil, 1974— ），美国印度裔诗人，出生于芝加哥（Chicago），父亲是印度裔，母亲是菲律宾裔。内茨库马塔尔获俄亥俄州立大学（Ohio State University）学士和创意写作硕士学位。她目前在密西西比大学（University of Mississippi）任教，同时也是杂志《俄里翁》（Orion）的诗歌编辑。

内茨库马塔尔的创作主要有诗集和散文集。诗集包括《神奇水果》（Miracle Fruit, 2003）、《在驶入火山》（At the Drive-In Volcano, 2007）、《好运鱼》（Lucky Fish, 2011）和《海洋》（Oceanic, 2018）以及与罗斯·盖伊（Rose Gay）合编书信体自然诗集《花边和黄铁矿》（Lace and Pyrite, 2014）。自然散文集《美妙世界》（World of Wonder, 2018）和畅销故事书《鱼骨》（Fishbone, 2000）。其中，《奇迹水果》获得全球菲律宾文学奖（Global Filipino Literary Award），《在驶入火山》获得2007年巴尔克内丝诗歌奖（Balcones Poetry Prize），《好运鱼》斩获埃里克·霍弗尔图书奖（Eric Hoffer Award）。

内茨库马塔尔荣获多个奖项，包括手推车奖、安戈夫奖（Angoff Award）、博特莱特奖（Boatwright Prize）、理查德·雨果奖（the Richard Hugo Prize）和美国国家艺术基金会的资助。多族裔的文化背景给她的诗歌创作提供了独特的视角和丰富的内容。她的诗歌自然流畅、语言生动、意象鲜明、颇有意趣。

诗歌《咬一口》（"One Bite"）选自诗集《神奇水果》，诗歌以儿童的语气描绘吃到新鲜水果的惊喜之情。《一个地球仪只是一个星号，每个家庭应该有一个星号》("A Globe Is Just an Asterick and Every Home Should Have an Asterick")选自诗集《好运鱼》，诗歌以新奇的意象开篇，普通的地球仪也变得不平常，情感和历史感蕴含其中。

作品选读

One Bite

By Aimee Nezhukumatathil

Miracle fruit changes the tongue. One bite,
and for hours all you eat is sweet. Placed
alone on a saucer, it quivers like it's cold
from the ceramic, even in this Florida heat.

Small as a coffee bean, red as jam—
I can't believe. The man who sold
it to my father on Interstate 542 had one
tooth, one sandal, and called me

"Duttah, Duttah." I wanted to ask what
is that, but the red buds teased me
into our car and away from his fruit stand.
One bite. And if you eat it whole, it softens

and swells your teeth like a mouthful
of mallow. So how long before you lose
a sandal and still walk? How long
before you lose the sweetness?

A Globe Is Just an Asterick and Every Home Should Have an Asterick

By Aimee Nezhukumatathil

Before a globe is pressed into a sphere,
the shape of the paper is an asterisk.
This planet is holding our place in line:
look out for metallic chips of meteor
hurtling through the universe. On my drive
to work, I saw my neighbor's lawn boiling
over with birds. Like the yard was a giant lasagna
and the birds were the perfectly bubbled cheese,
not yet crisped and brown. And I was hungry
to keep driving, driving all the way down
to central Florida, to my parents' house
and into their garage, and up the pull-down stairs
in their attic to find my old globe from 1983.
I used to sit in the living room with Kenny Rogers
playing on mom's record player. I spun and spun
that globe and traced my fingers along
the nubby Himalayas, the Andes—measured
with the span of my thumb and forefinger
and the bar scale that showed how many miles
per inch. I tried to pinch the widest part
of the Pacific Ocean, the distance between me
and India, me and the Philippines. The space
between the shorelines was too wide. My hand
was always empty when it came to land, to knowing
where is home. I dip my hands in the sea. I net nothing.
Only seaweed, a single hapless smelt.

36

(H. M. Naqvi, 1974—)
纳克维

作者简介

纳克维（H. M. Naqvi, 1974— ），美国巴基斯坦裔作家，出生在伦敦（London），在巴基斯坦的伊斯兰堡（Islamabad）和阿尔及利亚的阿尔及尔（Algiers）度过童年。纳克维曾在金融服务行业工作，在波士顿大学（Boston University）和拉合尔管理科学大学（Lahore University of Management Sciences）教授创意写作，是艾奥瓦大学国际写作项目的荣誉研究员（International Writing Program at the University of Iowa）。

纳克维荣获各类奖项，包括DSC南亚文学奖（DSC Prize for South Asian Literature）、佩勒姆诗歌奖（Pelham Prize for Poetry），并代表巴基斯坦参加了1995年在密歇根州安阿伯举行的全国诗歌大满贯比赛（National Poetry Slam）。纳克维曾为《大篷车》（*Caravan*）、《环球邮报》（*Global Post*）和《福布斯》撰稿。

纳克维在美国文坛的初次亮相就引发了广泛关注。他的处女作《同乡密友》（*Home Boy*, 2009）受到评论界的普遍好评，并获得2011年DSC南亚文学奖。纳克维立足自己的"伊斯兰－西方"双重身份，用文学的方式生动地再现了美国伊斯兰群体在"9·11"事件后的尴尬处境。他的第二部小说《哥萨克人阿卜杜拉的作品选集》（*The Selected Works of Abdullah the Cossack*, 2019）向读者展现了一个既迷人又熟悉的卡拉奇。

纳克维在小说《同乡密友》中描述了"9·11"事件前后三个巴基斯坦裔青年人在美国的遭遇。选段部分出自小说第十一章，描述了恰克在经历了大都会拘禁中心连续48小时的审讯、折磨、恐吓和莫须有的指控后在米妮阿姨家参加聚会，并与母亲通话的场景。这一经历使原本怀着"美国梦"的恰克身心俱疲，不得不重新审视自己的身份。

纳克维的第二部小说《哥萨克人阿卜杜拉的作品选集》是一部关于地方、家庭和忠诚的凄美传奇。阿卜杜拉（Abdullah）曾经是他父亲的奥林匹斯酒店（Hotel Olympus）的经理，但在大多数亲戚眼中，他是个挥霍无度、不负责任的人。选段部分出自小说《哥萨克人阿卜杜拉的作品选集》第二卷，描述了阿卜杜拉被一位名叫朱格努（Jugnu）的神秘女士从街头暴徒手中解救的过程。

作品选读

Home Boy

Chapter 11
(excerpt)
By H. M. Naqvi

As I slunk downstairs, I heard somebody saying, "We've suffered a singular calamity. Thousands of innocents have died in the most cruel and most spectacular way. Now, we need to take the fight to them. We have to secure our borders and our way of life…" Cupping the cigarette behind my back, I followed the voice back to the dining room. It belonged to one of the floppy-eared brothers. "We need to seek the terrorists in our midst, and if they happen to be Muslims, Arabs, or South Asian, so be it! Security is our inviolable right!"

The audience processed the discourse without protest, but I felt compelled to speak up. I felt hot and bothered. "Every state has the right to security," I averred. All heads turned to me: Mini Auntie, Busty, Tubby, Haq, Niggo, the Federal Minister, the American couple, as well as the Young People's Table. "The point is how do you go about it? In the name of national security, states commit crimes—"

"What crimes?"

"You threw a hundred thousand Japanese into camps, whole families—women, children, old people—because they posed a security threat. That's not right. That's wrong. And now it's us. It's me." Fueled by adrenaline, I continued, "I've been in jail for the last forty-eight hours. I was humiliated, starved, physically and mentally abused. Mini Auntie's brother, Ali, is still inside. We're not model citizens—I'm not a citizen at all—but I can tell you this much: we've done nothing wrong. This is no way to treat human beings, and this is no way to achieve security!"

There was pin-drop silence for a few moments. Then Mini Auntie rose. "Why didn't you tell me, child?" she asked, embracing me in a bear hug.

"I, um, tried—"

"I'm sorry—"

"No, I'm sorry." I should have said, I'm an idiot, but didn't.

We repaired to the kitchen where, among open pots, greased pans, and dirty china and cutlery, she asked me to relate the events that had led to our incarceration, "slowly and clearly," as if she were enjoining an alarmed patient. As I narrated the story—minus the cab, the kidnapping, and the porn watching—Mini Auntie listened, arms folded, interrupting once or twice to clarify this or that detail, and when I finished, she hung her head in thought.

I braced for a tongue lashing: Who told you to go to Connecticut? Who do you think you are? Saviors? Adventurers? The Three Musketeers? This is not cops and robbers! This is real life! Instead she opened the fridge, scooped a generous helping of homemade mango mousse, and served it to me in a bowl. "Eat, child, eat." Swallowing a mouthful, I tasted the sharp tang of guilt. While I was footloose and fancy-free, savoring mousse and meatballs, AC was being treated to interrogations and a meager dollop of prison gruel.

"Go upstairs," Mini Auntie instructed. "Call your mother. I'm sure she'll be delighted."

"What are you going to do?"

"I'm going to go to this Metropolitan Detention Center."

"Then I'm coming with you."

"No, you're not, child."

"Yes, I am," I protested.

Raising a reproving eyebrow, she persisted in her famous no-bullshit tone. "You're going to finish your dessert, and then you're going straight home. To bed. Doctor's orders." She added, "If you like, we can call your mother together."

The threat worked. I licked the bowl clean, put it in the dishwasher, and wiped my face with a paper towel. Outside, a hush fell over the dining room when I appeared. Blushing, I escaped upstairs.

It was already tomorrow in Karachi, already morning and, at nine, probably already hot. The monsoon having passed, the Indian summer would be in full sweaty swing. Not that the weather ever slowed Ma any: she would have said her prayers by now, oiled her hair, lapped the roof in shalwar and sneakers, and bathed, humming, as she was wont, tunes from the Golden Age. She might have been sipping a cup of tea in the veranda or picking at lightly salted pomegranate seeds with the Dawnspread out before her. I imagined she would be in her contagiously sunny morning mood. Clearing my throat, I picked up the receiver and dialed. The phone rang once. "Hello?" I called.

"Shehzad beta," Ma replied flatly, an acknowledgment of fact. I couldn't tell whether she was groggy or it was a bad line. I waited for her to ask how I was, where I'd been, why I hadn't called, but she said nothing.

"I'm sorry I haven't called, Ma," I began, hoping that she would interrupt me. "But... well... things have been hectic." It was a sorry excuse articulated particularly unconvincingly. I listening closely for some softly uttered word, a muted bromide, a sigh even, but Ma steadfastly maintained radio silence. "Are you there?"

"Haan, beta."

"Ma, I'm very, very sorry."

"Shehzad," she finally said. "It's been exactly ten days since I heard from you. You have not told me about what is happening over there, so I will tell you what is happening over here. It has rained for weeks. There has been some flooding. The other day I slipped on the stairs outside—"

"Ma!"

"Don't worry, beta. I'm all right. I'm not dying, I'm not ill. It's just a sprain. I wouldn't have even mentioned it, but I do now because... well... as I was sitting with my foot in ice water, I thought, surely my son could find the time to ring for one minute, just one minute, just to say a quick hello-how-are-you, for no other reason except that he knows it would make his mother happy. So I sat by the phone, waiting and waiting, hoping you would ring, but you did not. So I did. I rang many, many times, and when I didn't hear back, I began to get worried. I thought, maybe something's happened to him. These days, with all these terrorists running around in America, you don't know. So I rang your work number. I know, I know, I'm not supposed to—you've told me never to call you there—but I had to hear your voice. Instead, a recorded voice told me over and over, Please check the number and dial again. I began ringing here and there; I must have spoken to ten, fifteen people. Then somebody told me that your number was disconnected because the building you worked in had collapsed several weeks ago."

Closing my eyes, I held my forehead and was suddenly the little boy who had broken the expensive crystal vase, hoping, wishing that when he opened his eyes, things would be different, like they used to be. The vase, of course, had been replaced; life had continued as before. When I opened my eyes, however, perched on the edge of Mini Auntie's four-poster, the room remained the same, still and oppressive, and Ma was saying, "I told myself, be calm, there must be an explanation for this. I called Mini, and she told me she hadn't heard from you or Ali. I didn't want to frighten her so I acted casual, but I was very frightened, I've been very frightened. I haven't slept for two nights."

The line crackled, prompting me for an explanation. The moment of reckoning was finally upon me, and it wasn't as if it was unexpected; it had been a long time coming. I wanted to say that I wished I were with her, pressing her feet, applying Tiger Balm, that I had never wanted to leave in the first place, but the moment demanded truth, not sentimentality.

Just as I began to explain, however, Mini Auntie marched in to change into her sneakers and collect her large black Mary Poppins tote and slim cell phone, which was fixed to a socket beside me. "Still on the phone, child?" she asked, crouching, unplugging the device. "Tell Bano everything's going to be all right."

"Everything's all right, Ma."

"Is that Mini?" Ma asked.

"Um, yes, yes it is," I replied, uncoiling the receiver.

"Can I talk to her?"

There was no defensible reason why Ma could not chat with her old friend, except, of course, that her old friend would tell her exactly what had transpired. With Mini Auntie in earshot, I chose my words carefully: "I'm actually over for dinner, Ma."

"Oh. Acha. Mini must be busy. Well, give her my love."

"Can I call you from home?"

There was a pause, a second or two of deliberation, before Ma said, "Yes, that's okay, that's fine."

"I love you, Ma—"

"Beta?"

"Yes, Ma."

"I don't want to be a bother, but you know... I need to bother you once in a while... I need to hear your voice. I need to know you're taking your vitamins—"

"I know, I know—"

"I need to know that your office has not collapsed in some terrorist attack."

"I'm fine, Ma. Don't worry about me."

"And beta?"

"Yes, Ma."

"Please say your prayers. You need to thank ... that you're alive and happy."

"Yes, Ma."

After bidding her khuda-hafiz, I returned downstairs. The guests had dispersed apace, save a gangly, unassuming "uncle" whom I had met once chez Mini Auntie and once outside Chirping Chicken. One of the most sought-after corporate lawyers in the city, Mr. Azam was accompanying Mini to the Metropolitan Detention Center, presumably for moral support and legal firepower. "Chalo," Mini Auntie said, flicking the hall lights and wrapping herself in a beige pashmina. "Cha-lain," chimed Azam.

As we walked to the corner to flag a cab, I repeated my plea to tag along, arguing that I was "in a way indispensable" because I knew the "ins and outs of the place," which was, of course, one hundred percent baloney; I didn't know how I got in or how I got out.

Kissing me on the forehead before climbing into the cab, Mini Auntie said, "Get some sleep, child." Then she waved, and I waved back. I watched the cab careen down East End as if watching a departing locomotive train leaving behind clouds of nostalgic smoke. Lighting the depleted, lipstick-stained cigarette, I then ambled up East 86th like a free man.

The Selected Works of Abdullah the Cossack

Volume II

(excerpt)

By H. M. Naqvi

One afternoon during the Holy Month, I experience that indistinct but unmistakable sensation of being followed. It occurs in the broad vicinity of Empress Market, environs I know like the inside of my pocked, pallid thigh; once upon a time, I would accompany Papa to the landmark to purchase meat & vegetables for the kitchens at the Olympus, clutching an extended finger, cloth bag slung over my shoulder. The structure's sturdy walls and imposing tower reminded me of a storybook castle. Indeed, some of my fondest childhood memories reside in the stalls and alleys of this sprawling compound—a musty, indeed magical realm, inhabited by that spirited, mercurial species: the butcher, Heir of Original Man. If you do not know what you want, he jeers at you like a harlequin, but if you do, and Papa did, he is an obliging djinn: a sleight of hand would yield a cut of clod or silverside. At the time, of course, I could not distinguish tongue from tripe, but I have since developed the sense and sensibility that allows me to appreciate the modalities, indeed, the majesty of meat.

But I am not in the market for protein or produce; Barbarossa procures the meat for the household—I suspect he serves up blinded cockerels on occasion—and my roots, tended lately by one Bosco, are famous across Garden. I have been lecturing the lad on Topics in the Horticultural Sciences since he has been in my stewardship (what has it been? a fortnight? two?) addressing matters that include the Requisite Water for the Healthy Development of Vegetation in Sandy Loam and Coastal Subtropical Conditions. Brow furrowed, legs crossed, he takes notes. There are, however, secrets about various processes—the Modulation of pH Levels in Soil with the Use of Milk, for instance—that I cannot, or rather, will not disclose. You have to learn some things by doing, by living. And Bosco is doing.

No, I am on my way to pick up reference books required to tackle the only enterprise of any consequence in my life, The Mythopoetic Legacy of Abdullah Shah Ghazi (RA) (and, if Lady Luck smiles, several dog-eared copies of a local digest that features Lesbian trysts). The fact of the matter is that I need to get out of the Lodge, and my head. Although not temperamentally paranoid—anxious, yes, but not paranoid—I sense a sulfuric conspiracy. There have been intimations even prior to the Major's visit.

The other week, for instance, I woke to an unfamiliar mechanical clamour, deriving from the general vicinity of the vegetable garden. To my shock and weak-kneed horror, a large diesel generator, veritably as alien as a UFO, materialized by the boundary wall, belching smoke. My calculations suggested that the device occupied 17 percent of my patch, ravaging the zucchinis and cherry tomatoes that garnish my cold pasta salads. When I protested to Babu that evening, I was told in a tenor reserved for recalcitrant children that the "loadshedding situation" had compelled him to acquire a secondhand, Korean-manufactured 6 kVa generator.

"I'm not concerned about the capability of the dashed contraption! I'm concerned about its placement, partner, and the smoke—look at that smoke!"

"We had no choice." We who? I would have liked to ask. "You see," he gestured, "the line from the street enters here from the grid." The fact had the force and function of a full stop.

But it's not just a matter of generators: if I were to construct a treehouse for the Childoos in the old banyan in the backyard (a project I have been mulling for years, even if I do not possess the stamina or knowhow), there would be strident demurrals, drama. And a treehouse is a major infrastructural undertaking; I even have to inform the authorities if I solicit the services of a plumber when the commode gets backed up. A plumber for ...'s sake! One cannot even relieve oneself without negotiating the dashed administration!

I feel somewhat unstable, somewhat unhinged. I am in good company: everyone turns lunatic in the Holy Month, or worse—small, testy, sanctimonious. In fact, the only time one feels the presence of ... during this disconsolate period is when one happens to be on the streets at the break of fast: the city seems uninhabited then, and in the resonant silence, there are Intimations of Providence. But the streets remain raucous till then, teeming with the faithful, hurried, harried, haggling over the price of fritters.

Consequently, I find myself walking in circles. But I am not a famous walker: my gait is laboured due to the girth of my thighs and recurring gout in my knee, not to mention the cotton sack slung over my shoulder, weighed down by a thermos of water, a box of cardamom biscuits, a spare pair of knickers, and a volume of Müller's Sacred Books of the East. And my size, complexion, the drama of my parasol presumably attract gawkers, street children, the attention of pye-dogs—try as I might, I cannot avoid notice. But I have attracted something odd, ineffable, today, like the shadowy fireflies that flit across the field of vision in the sun. Perhaps it's the heat; perhaps, Ateed or Raqeeb—it is, after all, the Holy Month.

By the time I arrive at the narrow environs of Afghan Alley, populated by merchants lounging on rolls of fabric, swatting flies, I am parched and panting. Just as I raise the rim of my thermos to my maw, a hoarse admonition rings out: "Kya karti hay?" or What are you doing?

Turning, I find a lupine lad sporting a fanned beard. "Kya lagta hay kya kar rahi hoon?" I reply, or What does it look like I'm doing?

"Tum musalman ho?" he persists, or You a Musalman?

I am asked to elucidate my relationship with ... in the bright light of day—a parlous query at the best of times. What to say? What to do? When I was young, of course, I would have run. The boys chased me in the playground at Jufelhurst—the Brothers Ud-Din I recall, neighbours, nemeses—chanting, Fatty Boy, Fatty Boy, turn around; Fatty Boy, Fatty Boy, touch the ground. Although I was chubby if not quite corpulent, and the jibes were not particularly clever—sticks, stones, and that whole thing—there were occasions when I was tripped or biffed as well. Returning home, I would shove my head in Mummy's ample bosom, red-eyed, and lie, complaining of headaches. Since she suspected migraines, she took me to a hakim, an autistic chap who lived on a farm amongst goats and a broken Jeep and prescribed proprietary medieval remedies packaged in satchels tied with string. The foul concoction wrought of reddish powdered leaves turned glutinous and slimy when mixed with milk. I suffered it daily even though it made me retch, suffered it for Mummy's sake.

And later, much later, I attracted violence for different reasons: when I would brush against some young hothead at the Shadow Lounge, I would be mistaken for the Goliath to his David. As a result, I learnt to avert my gaze, slouch, shrink into myself.

But not anymore; I am too old, too large. Breaking wind, I holler. "This is Currachee! This my city! I could be Catholic, Protestant, Pentecostal, Hindoo, Amil, Parsee. I could be Shia, Sunni, Ismaili, Bohra, Barelvi, Sufi, Chishty, Naqshbandy, Suhrawardy, Wajoodi, Malamati, Dehria, anything, everything. If you want to ask such questions then go back to Kabul!"

As the commotion attracts attention, I find myself surrounded by five or six chaps, intent on mischief if not a riot. "O you who believe," the boy persists, flies swarming around his head, "fasting is prescribed for you as it was for those before you, that you may become pious!"

"The Prophet (PBUH) said, 'What is better than charity and fasting and prayer?

Keeping peace and good relations between people!'"

And for the next five, ten, fifteen minutes, a dashed eternity, we are locked in an excitable roadside doctrinal debate that features piecemeal quotation of scripture, anecdotal evidence, tenuous analogies, madcap allusions, CP4. After a chorus of alhumdulillahs, the learnt perspectives of grandfathers, uncles, the neighbourhood maulvi, a veritable Renaissance Man, are invoked. I want to say, "Bhaar main jaye tumhara chacha!"—viz., The hell with your uncle!—but instead attempt to communicate that there are manifold realities, and they have no claim on mine.

"My piety," I proclaim, "is between ... and me. How dare you intervene!" They can do what they want to do—shave their moustaches whilst letting their pubic beards run amok—only if I can do what I want to do: drink water in the middle of the street in the middle of the Holy Month. I am a diabetic for ...'s sake! My ... allows it if theirs does not. "If you're sensible, then your ... is sensible," I proclaim, "but if you're a dolt, your ...'s a dolt!"

My antagonist swats my flask to the ground. The horde smells blood. Fatty Boy, Fatty Boy, turn around; Fatty Boy, Fatty Boy, touch the ground. I am ready. I have been ready since my birthday. It will be a good death, a noble death. But before I am knocked down, kicked in the ribs, beaten to watermelon pulp, and interred at the end of the urine-stained alley, I perceive movement from the corner of my eye.

Turning, I behold a looker in the fray, an equine-faced, flinty-eyed dame in a low-cut canary kameez and tangerine pyjama. "Oye!" she cries like a traffic warden. Leaving me to my own devices, the horde turns on her, jeering & jostling, shoving & shouting, "Scamp!" "Hussy!" "We will break your legs!"

Although it's an opportune moment to flee, I am not a bad man, a dishonourable man; I stand before my ...sent saviour like a boulder and declare, "You pray five times a day, keep your fasts, but this is the way you treat another human being? A lady? Shame on you! Shame on you all! If this is your creed, I am a Kaffir!"

There is a pause, a moment pregnant with peril—the smell of sweat is thick in the air like spoiled meat—then one of the lads picks up my flask and hands it to me. I guzzle a quart before my audience in one glorious swig—verily, water tastes like wine when one's thirsty—then beckon to the dame with a wave of the hand. Hopping over a crate like a lady, she grabs my hand like a man, and we dash like Bonnie and Clyde, leaving the faithful to contemplate exercises in eschatology, epistemology & logos.

"I am very grateful to you," I say, hailing a taxi.

"You should be," she replies matter-of-factly.

I ask her name. I hear Jugnu. I ask where I should take her. "I am with you," she announces. I look into her fantastic, indeed obsidian eyes. I am certain I know her from somewhere else.

37

(Amit Majmudar, 1979—)
阿米特·马吉穆达尔

作者简介

阿米特·马吉穆达尔（Amit Majmudar, 1979—），美国印度裔诗人、小说家、医生，在克利夫兰地区长大。他在阿克伦大学（University of Akron）获得了理学学士学位，在东北俄亥俄州医科大学（Northeast Ohio Medical University）获得了医学博士学位。

马吉穆达尔的作品主要包括诗集和小说。诗集主要有《0°, 0°》（*0°, 0°*, 2009）、《天地》（*Heaven and Earth*, 2011）、《吉祥痣》（*Dothead*, 2016）、《他在孤独中做了什么》（*What He Did in Solitary*, 2020）。《0°, 0°》入围美国诗歌协会诺玛·费伯第一图书奖（Poetry Society of America's Norma Faber First Book Award）的决赛，《天地》荣获唐纳德·贾斯蒂斯诗歌奖（Donald Justice Poetry Prize）。长篇小说包括《分裂》（*Partitions*, 2011）、《富足》（*The Abundance*, 2013）及《锡塔亚那》（*Sitayana*, 2019）。《分裂》入围 HWA/戈尔兹伯勒皇冠历史小说奖（HWA/Goldsboro Crown Prize for Historical Fiction），并被柯尔库斯评论（*Kirkus Reviews*）评为 2011 年最佳处女作小说（Best Debut Fiction）。此外，还有一部中篇小说《阿扎齐尔》（"Azazil"）。马吉穆达尔凭借短篇小说《被拘留者的秘密生活》（"Secret Lives of the Detainees"）获得 2017 年欧·亨利奖。

马吉穆达尔的诗歌被收录在很多选集中，包括《1988—2012 年美国最佳诗歌》（*Best of the Best American Poetry* 1988—2012, 2013）和《诺顿文学导论》（*The Norton Introduction to Literature*, 2012）。马吉穆达尔也曾荣获安妮·哈雷奖（Anne Halley Prize）和手推车奖，是俄亥俄州的第一位桂冠诗人（2015）。马吉穆达尔

的诗歌探索了身份、历史、精神信仰和死亡的主题。

《分裂》的故事背景是1947年印度暴力分裂时期，讲述了人们被迫远离家乡、四处漂泊，寻求安全之旅的故事。选段部分出自小说第二部分，讲述了锡姆兰·考尔（Simran Kaur）作为锡克教女性总是在家族男性强加的暴力下生活，被剥夺了选择生存机会的权利。诗歌《吉祥痣》("Dothead")收录在同名诗集《吉祥痣》中。诗人根据自己的经历，描述了一名有印第安血统的美国高中生和他的"白人"同学之间的对话。这首诗刻画了来自不同种族的美国人所面临的文化挑战，尤其是在青少年时期，因为大多数人缺乏多元文化的意识和对差异的不信任。

作品选读

Partitions

Departure

(excerpt)

By Amit Majmudar

She is in that room, with the others. She maintains the reserve befitting the eldest daughter. She is barely fifteen. Simran. How solemn she looks, as if she senses everything to come. Her little brother, Jasbir, tires of his mother's dupatta and rests his head in her lap. Simran rubs his velvety ear between her thumb and forefinger, the way he likes. I watch her fingers, rhythmic, gentle, and strangely delicate for one who does so much washing, milking, husking. Her movements remind me of the regular, meditative way a mala circulates through holy fingers. One of her younger sisters sneaks over to the door to try to listen. Simran glances at her mother, who clicks her tongue and gestures the girl back. Her mother is just as curious, and so is Simran, about what the men are saying, but still she calls her back. It's not that she wants her children to stay calm, or to let her children stay children this half hour longer. Rather fear, almost superstitious, makes her keep her children close to her. Not hearing their taya's stories, she feels, will protect them. To hear the horror will bring it into being.

The men whisper too softly to be heard anyway, even in that small house. Their women, they are saying, without tears, without guilt, are safe. A pistol lies in one of the grown son's palms. It is wrapped in bright purple cloth. He drops the ends of the cloth and holds the gun flat on his palm. The women have been smuggled to a place where they cannot be touched. Two nights ago, every door in the village had started shaking, as though a train were coming through at full speed. There hadn't been much time. There is not much time now. Does he have morphine in the house? Not to keep them quiet, his women are strong, just as theirs were, and they would not try to run away.

Simran's father puts his hands over his eyes and shakes his head. I do not know what he does not want to see: the sight of his brother telling him what must be done, or the vision of him doing it. Or the vision of what will happen to his wife and children if he doesn't. Of the three, this last is the one he cannot bear.

The Mussulmaans, says his brother, came with scythes the shape of the crescent on their new flag, shovels stolen off farms on the way in, butcher knives until then used only for halal killing. Clubs with nails sticking out of them, shovels edged with dried blood. Lathis of varying lengths and woods. Hammers, both the curved end and the flat. One even swung an Englishman's walking stick.

"And Jasbir?"

"He'll slow us down."

"You never know when we'll have to run, Chacha. What will you do? Carry him?"

"There are Mussulmaans who would love to have a boy. Save him."

"How can I do this?"

"How we did it. Harpreet will help."

"He did the work back home."

"After this, I am joining up. We have our own armies, across the border. I will go to Amritsar, pray there for strength, and join."

"What do we do first?"

"Do you have any morphine?"

"Some. For her tooth, last year." Simran's father has never, except after making love, said his wife's name, not directly, not in reference to her. "There's not much left of it."

"Is it a powder?"

"No." He raises thumb and forefinger. "A bottle. A little bottle."

"That's better."

"Will it be enough?"

Harpreet nods. "They are small girls."

Harpreet's younger brother, who has been holding the pistol, sets it before his knees and brings the folds across it reverently, as though covering the Granth. More whispers.

I go back to Simran, still rubbing her brother's ear. It makes him drowsy. So I am with her when the latch grates across. It chills her to discover that the door was secured from without. The door opens. Her father stands in the doorway, gazing at this group huddled at the other end of the room. His brother, he realizes, is right. It must be done; it is the only way to protect them. If annihilation were all, they might as well risk flight. But the women and the boy risked something worse. To live in their shacks: his girls their wives, daily servitude, nightly violence, in a few years not even remembering their true nature. Coming to smell as they smell, eat as they eat. Bearing Muslim sons who would grow up never knowing their grandfather was a Sikh steely as his kangan and proud. Conversion. To bow to their holy city, kiss their book, recite their prayers. Die now, and they would die Sikhs, intact, pure in the eyes of the ten Gurus. Dying a Sikh, for being a Sikh—this must be the women's glory. For the men, there would be valor in the streets yet and blood on the kirpan. But neither he nor his, he decides, will live as anything else. Better annihilation than long life giving some slum Mussulmaan pleasure and service and sons. So when her mother whispers, "What did they say?," his voice is calm.

"Heat us up some milk."

Her mother visibly relaxes, this domestic request somehow proof that the threat either has passed or never was. "What do you want in it?"

"Cardamom. And make enough for all of us."

"Should we come out?"

"Not yet."

"Is it true? Are the mobs close?"

Her father looks first over his shoulder, then back at his daughters. The swell of pride and defiance, just moments earlier, has petered out. His hands go over his chest and start kneading each other. "The milk," he says.

Jasbir sits up. "Let them come. They'll see what we Sikh boys can do."

Her mother says, "Simran, go."

Simran rises and hurries past her father. Her taya and her cousin do not look at her. One looks at the ground, the other at a small dark-blue bottle in his hand. Harpreet doesn't look at her, either, but his eyes are closed. He is sitting cross-legged on the floor, something wrapped in purple cloth in front of him, not a book. His lips move in a prayer to which he gives no voice.

Thirty-six miles east of the railway station, the train my boys have jumped off will hiss to a stop. Ravine to one side, empty farm to the other. A solitary boy, not more than fourteen, fuzz across his top lip, green-eyed, is going to lower the colorful flag he has been waving. It is a stick with a girl's choli nailed to it. Little sewn-in hexagons of mirror, bright pink and orange paisley, the kind of thing young village girls wear. He will step off the tracks, drop the stick with the choli, and pick up an ax. The train will be a half hour from any station, east or west. Twenty minutes from the border.

This signal and this spot were arranged at the station in Pakistan, while Sonia and my boys were still in the crowd. Six bearded men had boarded into the front car. They had no weapons. They had come to talk.

The driver, a Hindu named Chandan Singh, will see the signal and will pray. He will tug his earlobes and crank the lever to scrape this train to a halt. In his defense, he had refused to do it for money, or at least for the money they offered. They had to say his address to him and tell him how many children he had and how old. After that, they refused him any money at all. As if by requiring the threat, he had lost the privilege of being bought fairly. Right now, as his train rushes toward the far convergence of the rails, and Keshav is shouting the word Maover six hundred heads, Chandan regrets that he did not agree right away. At least there would have been money. The lost opportunity makes him flush under his beard. That will change, of course, when he is actually faced with the killing. Or rather with the sound of the killing—he will look forward the whole time, his hands still on the levers, focused on the track ahead. He will not see the men stride out of the ravine bearing axes and farm tools like it inerant workers. Or how unhurried they are. Well after dark, a stick will rap the side of his car, the way bus passengers tap the side of the bus to say they have gotten off. Chandan will shift the levers, this one forward, this one back, and he will coast his cargo across the border, never speeding beyond the lightest, softest rock and click.

It will be midnight by the time the train makes it into the station, every compartment closed and locked, door and window. At Amritsar, the platform will sense something wrong about the train well before it stops. People will start pressing back from the tracks while the train is still a dot of light no bigger than a star. The platform will stay quiet as the train inches into place. The absence of anyone on the roof, maybe, or the emptiness of the windows. The stationmaster will part the crowd and throw wide a compartment door. The first gush will reach his feet. He will skip back, and leave his sandals in place, soaked, the bottom step still dripping.

A clamor of pots pulls my attention back in time to the present. Simran has been clumsy, and she is never clumsy. Her father walks over to check. Kerosene odor, milk placid in the pot, the flame adjusted to a blue corona. The cups have been drying on a rack. Still wet. One end of her dupatta lies on her palm, the other covers her small fist. She turns each cup twice around her fist and sets it down. Most of the drops are on the outside. Her father circles back.

"Six," he says, intervening before she dries any for the men. Each cup is a death, in his mind, and he does not want any more prepared.

She lines up five cups beside the stove.

"One more."

She looks up. "I'm not thirsty."

"You'll drink."

This is enough, the words, and the agitation that has overtaken his hands and feet: her father paces, he makes and unmakes a fist with his left hand, checking the flame and the milk. The right hand he holds in a fist over his heart, as if taking a vow to protect something. Simran wonders at that. She doesn't know that the hand has the vial in it. Her younger cousin had gone out and now comes back through the door. He stops when he sees her. Harpreet breaks his meditation. The men drift to the door and get the news. Simran's father breaks away abruptly and points at Simran.

"Pour it out and go back in the room." She doesn't move quickly enough. "Pour it out!"

The lukewarm milk splashes over the sides of the cups. His jitter is close to panic now and contagious. Two of the cups, silver, have tiny letters engraved just under the rims. They are name day cups, given to honor a new child, full name and birth date. Once-bright cups, saved in a chest for some years, they have finally, for want of money to buy new ones, fallen into daily circulation. The letters are uneven, done by an untrained silversmith's hand that used the point like a pen. Simran sees her own cup. She has seen it so often, in the after-dinner pile and in her siblings' hands, she has ceased to think of it as hers. By the time it came out of the chest, she had been too old to claim it or demand it. But now, for the first time in years, she notices her name, and she thinks, just for a moment, of her birth. Of herself as a newborn in this very house, her father's beard black and her mother just two years older than Simran is now.

"Leave them there."

She rises off her knees, her legs seemingly unaware of her weight, a movement whole and graceful. She stands as tall as her father. Then she is back in the room, her mother and sisters and brother sitting. She keeps standing after the door closes and the latch grates into place again.

"Milk? This early in the morning?" Her mother searches Simran's profile. "And a morning like this?"

"It's for us."

Her mother says nothing more. Simran steps back until she touches the wall and slides to the ground.

Dothead

By Amit Majmudar

Well yes, I said, my mother wears a dot.
I know they said "third eye" in class, but it's not
an eye eye, not like that. It's not some freak
third eye that opens on your forehead like
on some Chernobyl baby. What it means
is, what it's showing is, there's this unseen
eye, on the inside. And she's marking it.
It's how the X that says where treasure's at
is not the treasure, but as good as treasure.—
All right. What I said wasn't half so measured.
In fact, I didn't say a thing. Their laughter
had made my mouth go dry. Lunch was after
World History; that week was India—myths,
caste system, suttee, all the Greatest Hits.
The white kids I was sitting with were friends,
at least as I defined a friend back then.
So wait, said Nick, does your mom wear a dot?
I nodded, and I caught a smirk on Todd—
She wear it to the shower? And to bed?—

while Jesse sucked his chocolate milk and Brad
was getting ready for another stab.
I said, Hand me that ketchup packet there.
And Nick said, What? I snatched it, twitched the tear,
and squeezed a dollop on my thumb and worked
circles till the red planet entered the house of war
and on my forehead for the world to see
my third eye burned those schoolboys in their seats,
their flesh in little puddles underneath,
pale pools where Nataraja cooled his feet.

38

(V. V. Ganeshananthan, 1980—)
V. V. 加内桑坦

作者简介

V. V. **加内桑坦**（V. V. Ganeshananthan, 1980—），美国斯里兰卡裔小说家、记者，在马里兰州（Maryland）长大。加内桑坦于2002年在哈佛学院（Harvard College）获得学士学位，2005年在艾奥瓦作家工作室获得硕士学位。2007年，她又获得了哥伦比亚大学新闻学研究生院（Columbia University Graduate School of Journalism）的硕士学位，在那里她是以布林格研究员（Bollinger Fellow）身份专攻艺术和文化新闻学。她还曾在密歇根大学的海伦·泽尔作家项目（Helen Zell Writers' Program）、拉德克里夫学院（Radcliffe Institute）任教，2015年以后在明尼苏达大学（University of Minnesota）教授创意写作课程。除此之外，她曾任南亚记者协会副主席（South Asian Journalists Association），美国亚裔作家工作室（Asian American Writers' Workshop）理事会成员以及美国斯里兰卡研究所的理事会成员（American Institute for Sri Lankan Studies）。

加内桑坦的作品出现在许多主要的报纸和期刊上，包括《格兰塔》（Granta）、《大西洋月刊》（The Atlantic Monthly）和《华盛顿邮报》等。2008年，她的处女作《爱情婚姻》（Love Marriage, 2008）入围橘子奖，并被《华盛顿邮报》评为2008年世界最佳图书之一。她将于2023年1月出版她的第二部小说《无兄弟的夜晚》（Brotherless Night）。

《爱情婚姻》这部小说以斯里兰卡和北美一些散居社区为背景，讲述了1983年斯里兰卡爆发内战之后，一个斯里兰卡家庭如何应对流离失所、传统割裂和信仰动摇的故事。选段部分出自小说第九部分，讲述了主人公雅利尼（Yalini）在表妹的婚礼上第一次真正地看到了印度教的婚姻仪式，而这与她在美国所看的结婚仪式是不一样的。通过雅利尼的叙述，我们看到了被压抑的记忆的痕迹，以及她在融合饱受战争蹂躏的斯里兰卡与和平的美国的现实对比时遇到的困难。

作品节选

Love Marriage
(excerpt)

By V. V. Ganeshananthan

I have dinner with my family together the night before Janani's wedding, which I have come to think of in the same way as a funeral. I thought that after this, we would never see one another. We would not miss one another, either. But we were family. And we owed one another this: one last night together in the house where her father had died and loved us both, so differently.

What is left of a family: Murali, Vani, Janani, Yalini. We invite Lucky and Rajie, because they have acted like our relatives, and because their presence honors my late uncle, whom we buried not so long ago. We sit around the table, eating a vegetarian meal, because that is the auspicious thing to do. None of us, even and perhaps especially Janani, knows Suthan any better than we did the first day we met him. What does he stand for? Who is she marrying?

I think at her: You don't have to do this. But I do not say it.

And I am not wrong. As my mother is serving out the rice, a Tamil man whose interests in Toronto rival Suthan's is walking up to the locked doors of the Tamil community center with bolt cutters. He is a tall man, about Suthan's age and height; he has a darker face, and a full beard, but he is skinny, and he wears similar black clothing. He has waited for darkness. Four other men flank him.

......

It is at my cousin Janani's kalyānam, her wedding, that I first truly see and learn the Hindu rites of marriage. It is the first wedding in my generation of the family. I watch what transpires, wondering all the while if I will ever stand where Janani stands today, in an Arranged Marriage or a Love Marriage: wearing Wedding-Red. I am younger than she in more ways than one, although in true time, she has fewer years than I.

Because neither my mother nor I trusts my sense of Sri Lankan dress and propriety, she drapes my sari for me, as she did in the fittings. I have lost weight since she sewed the blouse, and my arms hang loosely in the sleeves, which according to fashion should be tight. I wear my grandmother Tharshi's earrings. My mother pronounces me dressed only after she dips her little finger in black *pottu* and anoints me with this paste, which is used to mark the foreheads of UnMarried Women. In Sri Lanka, this is done every day. My mother continues this custom, wearing the Wedding-Red mark of Married Women every morning. I only wear *pottu* for Weddings.

All my life, my mother has been my teacher. This is also true in the temple. My mother has taught me that a Hindu temple is very clean. As in most Hindu households, you must remove your shoes before entering and wash your feet. She reminds me that when I sit on the ground I must keep my legs crossed and make sure that I do not disrespect the ... by pointing my feet toward them. Do you have your period? Remember, if you have your menses the priests will not allow you inside the temple.

Now, as my cousin Janani is getting Married, is only my third or fourth time inside a real temple. The temple near our house was just being built when I was growing up. Hindus traveled far away to be married, and we worshipped the ... in a house on the temple site, which we treated as a real temple nonetheless. The priests came from India and wore only white cloths knotted around their waists. They tied threads of saffron around their hands and ankles for luck. They washed the ... and dressed them in silk. They offered them milk, honey, and yogurt. They marked them in bright colors: red, but also the holy ash called *viphuti*, which smells sweet, and saffron that had been turned into a paste. When they were done anointing the ..., we also wore these colors of worship. Most of the priests did not speak English, and so I did not talk to them. When I did not understand what was happening, I asked my mother. When we prayed I knelt beside or behind her and imitated her. I stood when she stood, clasped my hands together when she did, blessed myself with the holy fire that the priest held when she did.

I remember that during one special ceremony, my mother and I walked with a group of women behind the men, who carried an elaborate gold litter with one of the ... in it. I asked my mother why we could not carry the litter. She shook her head, her eyes still on the litter moving on the men's shoulders. There are no women priests, she said. Women have never carried the gods.

The house held all the gods for the temple, including the nine planets. My mother taught me that in prayer, we circle these nine deities. We each have a *nat'sattiram*, which is the star of birth. She taught me that at a certain point, in a certain prayer, the priest asks what my star is. I am *swāthi*. If I am ever Married, I will have to remember this. If my parents are superstitious, they will ask an astrologer to see if my star aligns with the star of my intended.

The most sacred place in a wedding ceremony is called the *mānavarai*. It is the altar. It is adorned with flowers, and it faces East, where the sun rises. In America the ceremony is strange enough to us that at weddings, guides explaining its different stages are passed out. The wedding guide takes us through the wedding ritual from beginning to end.

The priest recites the names of the forefathers of both bride and groom and asks for their blessings. My father had said that in Sri Lanka, a person did not bear his ancestors all his life. This is almost true. They appear only at the beginning and the end.

As you come out of the island, and as you return to it. And as you are Married.

When Janani told me that she actually wanted to get Married, at first I did not believe her or understand. It was March, right before her father died. We were sitting out in the cold, gray yard. He had stopped taking walks there mostly. My father gave him pain medication four or five times a day.

"I want to get married here," she said. It will make part of what is going on there, forever.

"You are a part of it anyway," I said.

She did not believe me.

Her father died in April, just as blades of green were beginning to rise out of the gray garden behind that strange house. The house did not belong to us, and yet we had done so many personal things there. It had begun to feel like a home. We had sat vigil together at his bedside and cooked him meals in that kitchen. We had slept in those beds, and he had died there. That, of course, was the most personal thing. I know that some people do not want to be in houses where people they have loved have died, but I did not want to leave that house. It was the only place where I had known him. I thought that if I walked out the door and into Canadian spring sunshine it would feel like a world in which he had never existed.

But it was worse for her. It had to have been worse for her, because he was her father. I am guessing when I say this; she did not talk to me. And I was born lucky: I still have my father, and he is an exceptional man. I knew that she grieved not only for her father's passing, but for where and how it had taken place. This was still not her country, and yet he had moved into it so easily and died here. He had shown an ability to adapt that should have surprised no one and instead surprised everyone. I knew that she had sometimes listened at the door as my uncle talked to me, telling me about his life, and I wondered if she already knew what he was telling me, or if she just resented it. She too had been educated as a radical, but her education had been different from his, because she had grown up inside the movement and possibly still believed in it. And her father was not just telling me about politics. He was telling me about Meenakshi, whom she had never known, and Justine, who was from another world, that she did not know. She had never seen a white person before leaving Sri Lanka.

The variety of her father's loves dismayed her, I think, whether she already knew of them or not. She wanted him to love the few things that she already knew: she resented his frankness with me, perhaps because she did not know why he felt he owed me anything. She had never had to share him.

Janani is very angry with me, he said to me on one of his last days. It was true that although she had gone into his room and spent more time there as the months wore on, she did not seem to speak. Even if it was only the two of them in there and I passed by outside, I heard nothing. Little conversation. Occasionally, a little bit of Tamil: Appa, do you need some water? Sometimes my father went in to check on him. He would carry in a small mug of water and a few pills, and my uncle would swallow them with great effort. Often he had a headache and would ask me to draw the curtains to block out the dull light off the snow. But he almost never stopped talking.

My daughter hates me because I have decided what I think, he said. But you don't hate me, even though I've sacrificed your independence by being here.

You're only here for a short while, I said to him. I'm hardly giving up my independence.

His eyes widened in alarm. Oh, no, he said. You don't understand. They told me when I came here that they were permitting this because of the family's loyalty. I gave them a promise. You know that the Tigers have supporters here. It was a trade—I came here, and you and your mother and your father are expected to toe the line. You don't have to do anything dramatic. But you can't really speak against them. Not here.

I didn't promise them anything, I said.

Sometimes promises can be made for you, he said. Sometimes in life things don't work out as smoothly as we'd like. It doesn't matter what you say when you're walking around. Say what you have to say to be safe. You can still decide what you believe and say that to yourself.

If someone had said that to you back when you were joining the Tigers you would have disagreed with them, I said. Of course it matters what you do. I can't think something and act in another way.

Not even to save yourself or your parents from a certain degree of pain?

In my memory, he is still saying this, and I am still shaking my head, unable to agree with him. Although I know that the reason Janani's face is blank and cold is because she has not yet accustomed herself to the idea of a future.

中国人民大学出版社外语出版分社读者信息反馈表

尊敬的读者：

  感谢您购买和使用中国人民大学出版社外语出版分社的 _____ 一书，我们希望通过这张小小的反馈卡来获得您更多的建议和意见，以改进我们的工作，加强我们双方的沟通和联系。我们期待着能为更多的读者提供更多的好书。

  请您填妥下表后，寄回或传真回复我们，对您的支持我们不胜感激！

1. 您是从何种途径得知本书的：
   □书店　　　□网上　　　□报纸杂志　　　□朋友推荐
2. 您为什么决定购买本书：
   □工作需要　□学习参考　□对本书主题感兴趣　□随便翻翻
3. 您对本书内容的评价是：
   □很好　　　□好　　　□一般　　　□差　　　□很差
4. 您在阅读本书的过程中有没有发现明显的专业及编校错误，如果有，它们是：
   _____
   _____
   _____

5. 您对哪些专业的图书信息比较感兴趣：
   _____
   _____
   _____

6. 如果方便，请提供您的个人信息，以便于我们和您联系（您的个人资料我们将严格保密）：
   您供职的单位：_____
   您教授的课程（教师填写）：_____
   您的通信地址：_____
   您的电子邮箱：_____

请联系我们：黄婷　程子殊　吴振良　王琼　鞠方安
电话：010-62512737，62513265，62515538，62515573，62515576
传真：010-62514961
E-mail：huangt@crup.com.cn　　　chengzsh@crup.com.cn　　　wuzl@crup.com.cn
　　　　crup_wy@163.com　　　jufa@crup.com.cn
通信地址：北京市海淀区中关村大街甲59号文化大厦15层　　邮编：100872
中国人民大学出版社外语出版分社